I0637724

Copyright © 2023 by Kenneth Edwin Sloan

First Published in the United States in 2023 by Stream of Experience Productions, Pagosa Springs, Colorado

Portions of this book were published in 2010 by Stream of Experience Productions under the title "The Moor Express." Those contents have been revised and substantially extended in this book.

All rights reserved. No part of this publication may be reproduced, stored in a retrieval system, or transmitted, in any form or by any means without the prior written permission of the publisher, nor be otherwise circulated in any form of binding or cover or format other than that which it is published and without a similar condition being imposed on the subsequent purchaser.

All characters in this publication are fictitious and any resemblance to real persons, living or dead, is purely coincidental.

ISBN: 979-8-9891390-0-2 (paperback)
ISBN: 979-8-9891390-2-6 (hardcover)
ISBN: 979-8-9891390-1-9 (ebook Kindle)
ISBN: 979-8-9891390-3-3 (ebook ePub)
ISBN: 979-8-9891390-4-0 (Audio book)

Notes, references and resources for this book:
www.rafop.com

Stream of Experience Productions:
www.stream-of-experience.com

Picture Credits:
The picture of the so-called "Venus of Malta" is licensed from the National Museum of Archaeology, Malta. *Their Disclaimer: "This book includes an image made available by Heritage Malta. The views expressed herein are those of the author and can therefore in no way be taken to reflect the official opinion of Heritage Malta."*
The cover background picture of the sun over the Mediterranean sea shining through thin clouds is by Kenneth Edwin Sloan
The picture of Daphne Anne Caruana Galizia in the dedication is open source from her Wikipedia page.
The blue butterfly on the back cover is licensed from iStock.

The Rise and Fall of Patriarchy: Herstory

A Historical Novel about Gender Reconciliation

Journey of Lives Book 1

by Kenneth Edwin Sloan

Dedication

This book is dedicated to Daphne Anne Caruana Galizia née Vella (1964–2017) the courageous Maltese investigative journalist, political blogger and anti-corruption activist who was killed by a car bomb on 16 October 2017 in retaliation for her continued reporting even after repeated death threats as well as physical attacks on her home and even household pets. Thank you Daphne for your fearless example.

And heart-felt dedication also to the sisters and brothers around the world – in the past, in the present and in the future – who work, sometimes alone and unnoticed, for equity and justice. You know who you are.

Gaienhofen am Bodensee, Germany

2:14 PM, April 22, 2015 C.E.

Martyna's Dream

She was lying on her back with her arms at her sides. The pressure on her body – coming from every direction – was immense and overwhelming. But worse was the inability to breathe, to take breath in, to breathe it out, or to make a sound of any kind. Her body was absolutely contained and embedded. And then the inner pain began in her chest and spread into her left arm.

What is this place? she asked herself in panic. Why am I here? Is there a way out?

Her eyes were sealed closed but still she sensed her surroundings: above her, below her, left and right, only packed dry earth and white stone. All cold and confining and utterly lifeless.

I must call for help, she thought to herself, and struggled with all her might against the seeming impossibility of making a sound in this rigid body.

Then something did happen. There was a sound welling up in her but not through her lungs or throat. A muffled struggling scream of a sound came out of her belly. A shaking began like an earthquake within her. Everything broke apart.

...

Martyna awakened and opened her eyes. She took a conscious in-breath then let it out slowly. Yes, she could breathe now.

She became aware of the room around her: the silver coffee service on the small table to her left, the vase of purple spring flowers also on that table, her dark blue dress over her lap and her bare arms resting on the supports of the wheelchair. And there was more: the figure kneeling on the floor by her, the glass of the enclosed terrace in front of her, beyond that the expanse of space, patches of light blue sky between high thin clouds, the gray lake below where the fields and orchards ended. And even more: the dark green curve of the hills on the other side of the lake, the afternoon sunlight slanting down here and there.

Martyna relaxed. This was indeed her world. She inhaled the familiar smells: the room and its many plants, the scent of spring greenness from the fields outside, the dusty perfume of the rain that had been this morning.

It was all still here. She was still here.

Agnes, her face anxious and concerned, was kneeling at Martyna's right side holding her hand. "It was that dream again, wasn't it?"

Martyna nodded. She closed her eyes, looking inward, trying to understand, to catch some glimpse of what the dream was about, where it was pointing her, what it meant for her. Her sense of being buried in stony earth, of being unable to breathe or make any sound, was receding now. What persisted was the pain in her left shoulder and upper left arm.

"What do you need?" asked Agnes still holding her hand.

"Coffee, fresh coffee and strong," Martyna managed to say, croaking it out as best she could, flexing her left arm to see if that relieved the sharp pain there. It did not. Ah well, after almost 90 years of life and many ups and downs pain was not so important to her. It came and went. One needed only patience. Or at least that had always worked before. And this time? She was not so sure.

Agnes released the hand she had been holding, stood up from where she had been kneeling on the floor, picked up the tray with the coffee service on it and hurried off to the kitchen to make fresh coffee.

Martyna gave up trying to understand the dream. She let it go, back to wherever it had come from, as it had several times before in the last months. Instead of thinking about the dream she directed her mind to the present moment, to the here and now.

That had become her habitual response regardless of what happened to her or around her: to be simply present and to let arise whatever came into her awareness without holding on to what had been or imagining what might follow. Relaxing into the present moment she discovered again how happy she was to have Agnes as her companion. It had all worked out well. In 1995 both Martyna's husband and her beloved brother had died within a short time. She quickly discovered that she no longer wanted to live in the family house in Lodz where she had been since the war. Her daughter and most of her other relatives lived nearby but that had become a burden as well. There always seemed to be one thing or another that people quarreled about. And Martyna did not like that.

Her work as a midwife that she had loved so much for so long was also coming to an end just at that time – she was too old to keep up with the demands of it.

And finally she was tired of being the matriarch of the family with everyone asking her about her opinion in situations where they should be deciding on their own. It was time for her daughter to take over the job, if the job needed doing at all. So what to do with herself?

Martyna had decided to return to Germany. Not back to Leipzig where she had lived as a young woman but to the village Gaienhofen

4

on the north shore of the lake the Germans called the Bodensee. She had visited here twice for long summer holidays and both times had felt wonderfully at home. So she had sold the family house in Lodz – that had belonged mostly to her at that point – and used her part of the money to buy this small stone house on a hillside surrounded by hay fields and apple orchards with a broad view of the lake. The house had required considerable renovation, especially the plumbing and the addition of the glass-enclosed terrace on the southeast side as an extension to the small living room. But she had had enough money left over even after the renovations and moving expenses to organize herself a modest income for whatever years she might have left.

To her surprise her granddaughter Agnes had expressed immediate interest in accompanying her on her relocation. Though only twenty-five Agnes was already convinced that Lodz was not where she wanted to live – "too stuffy and traditional" is how she had expressed it. So Martyna's plan was for Agnes a welcome opportunity. And that Agnes would be accompanying Martyna made it much easier for the rest of the family to accept the move. Agnes and Martyna had found a good life for themselves caring for the house and garden and living simply day by day. After some initial difficulties they had also gotten along well with the other residents in the small village. Their twenty years together in Gaienhofen had gone by quickly.

Martyna had noticed that at the beginning Agnes was not particularly happy and had trouble finding friends. That had gradually improved. And then Agnes had discovered that men – who had always disappointed her – were not the only possible partners and had found herself a steady girlfriend in the village. Agnes was happy now.

How pleasant it would be after Martyna's death for Agnes to discover that the house and everything else of Martyna's had been left to her. Then perhaps her friend Adele, who had a flower shop in the village, could move into the house with her. They would certainly decorate it new. They would have a good life together. Martyna smiled to herself again. That is what life is about: finding happiness with others.

Thinking of such pleasant things helped but the pain was still there, even stronger now and pulsing in an unusual way. She did her best to relax into it and to let it have its way with her.

As she did, memories of her life began to come into her mind like the air bubbles one saw in the lake rising to the surface from somewhere in the depths before they were released and disappeared. Some pleasant memories but also painful ones: the unexpected deaths of her husband and her brother. They were too young to die, much too young. And it had been lonely without them.

In the midst of her memories she could not ignore that the pain in her arm was getting even deeper and sharper, knife-like and twisting. And her breathing was becoming more difficult, more labored. Again she did her best to relax into it, to let it flow over her like a passing ocean wave. But it did not flow over her; it only grew stronger. She tried to call out to Agnes who was still in the kitchen but no sound came out of her straining mouth. Her eyes wide open, her entire visual field changed suddenly to a bright mustard yellow. How interesting, she thought to herself, and lost consciousness.

Lela's Guide to After Death Experiences

"Martyna?"

Martyna heard her name being called. She opened her eyes and tried to locate who had spoken. Her vision was not normal: everything in the room appeared luminous.

"Martyna?" The call came again. It seemed to be coming from behind her.

She turned her head to the right and was startled to see a person she did not recognize sitting on the sofa looking at her. It was a woman – not old and not young – with a dark brown complexion, dark eyes and shoulder-length straight black hair. The woman wore a knee-length pleated skirt of some thick material that was beige but with traces of red and held with a belt. She was bare above her waist. Her mature breasts shone in the light as if they had been oiled. There was a green stone nestled between them which was suspended from a cord around her neck.

The whole effect was quite exotic. This woman was definitely not some neighbor from the village. And barefoot! Agnes should have given the woman some house shoes, Martyna thought to herself. The stone floor was always so cold.

"Who are you?" asked Martyna.

Instead of answering the woman pointed to a place next to her on her right then patted that place on the sofa. She looked at Martyna and tilted her head, eyebrows raised, in question.

Martyna was confused. It had been years since she had been able to walk or even move her wheelchair herself without assistance. The woman persisted by nodding an encouraging "yes, you can do it."

And then, surprising herself, Martyna did just that: she stood up and walked over to the sofa. It was easy, effortless really. She stood there for a moment by the sofa just enjoying the simple pleasure of standing on her own without support. The mysterious woman stretched out her arm and pointed to where Martyna had been sitting before. After some hesitation Martyna's gaze followed the outstretched arm and looked back at where she had been.

Her mind spun in confusion – someone had put a life-sized doll, dressed in Martyna's clothes, into her wheelchair! Now the doll was flopped over in disarray, the head sagging down on the chest, eyeglasses dangling from one ear, the sparse white hair, the thin mottled arms at awkward angles, very still. And then Martyna suddenly understood – it was not a doll, it was her body. Her shriveled old body. She had finally died. Really died. This was no dream, of that she was certain. She sat down on the sofa.

A torrent of thoughts and feelings, of memories, hopes and fears washed over her. An ocean of life lived, suddenly there all at once. She struggled to find some ground.

"My name is Lela," said the woman and Martyna was back on the sofa looking into that open face and for the moment she grew calm.

"Do I know you?" Martyna asked.

"In some ways no and in some ways yes," said the woman.

"I am dead, right? I mean, that is my body over there," she pointed with her outstretched arm. "But I am somehow sitting here with you."

"Yes, that is the situation" the woman answered. "It is good that you understand it so quickly."

A crash interrupted their conversation. Agnes, returning from the kitchen with the coffee tray, had seen Martyna's body, dropped the tray, then thrown herself onto Martyna's lap crying out loud powerful sobs. The white porcelain vase of flowers that had been on the table lay now shattered on the floor with the purple flowers in disarray among the wet shards. It was clear that Agnes could not see them and had no idea or sense that they were sitting there such a short distance from her.

Martyna, watching all this, noticed how calm about it all she was – the leaving her body, the silver coffee service on the floor with fresh coffee flowing now onto the rug that she had brought with her from Poland, the broken vase that had belonged to her mother, Agnes's crying. It was all just as it was. There was nothing to judge or react to.

Martyna turned to face this mysterious woman, this Lela.

"So ...Lela... what happens now?"

Lela smiled at the directness of the question. "That depends on you. There are choices. But maybe we should go somewhere else as things may be distracting here."

Suddenly Martyna was sitting with Lela on an iron and oak wood bench next to a large willow tree along the gravel footpath that followed the lake shore. It had been Martyna's favorite place to sit while taking a break on her strolls along the lake in the years when she had still been able to walk. Martyna surveyed the lake up close: the tall water grass at the edge, the ducks here and there, a pair of swans gliding along, two sailboats in the distance.

"Can't I just stay like this, seeing everything, hearing everything, but without the burden of a body?" Martyna said, enjoying the quick change of scene and the absence of pain. She smiled broadly at the thought of it. Then she quickly grew thoughtful.

"But how is it that I have died, that I left my body back there in the house and yet can be sitting here talking with you and seeing all of this?" Martyna asked, indicating the lake vista with a sweep of her arm. "How can I be seeing when I have no eyes!"

"Your question is a good one but finding an answer that you will understand is not easy," responded Lela. "So let me first ask you a question: do you ever see things in your dreams?"

"Of course I see things in my dreams! Doesn't everyone? That's normal."

"But when you are asleep and dreaming your physical eyes are closed. That means you are seeing things but not by using your normal eyes. Am I right?"

"Well, yes. I never thought about that before. You are right: I am seeing things and hearing things and touching things – all of it, in my dreams. So are you saying this is a dream, that we are sitting here in a dream?"

"No, I am not saying this is a dream. I want you to consider that behind your physical senses you have always had other related senses that were not dependent on your physical body. And now that you have no physical body those other senses are more available. Can you imagine that could be true?"

"I am trying," responded Martyna. "So the senses I am using now were always there but I did not use them except in my dreams?"

"You can think about it that way if it helps. The main thing is that once your life energy – that is, Martyna – has left the body these are the senses that you still have. And if they are developed enough and you are clear enough in your mind you can experience and navigate the world that they show you."

"What do you mean 'clear enough in my mind'? I thought my mind was in my brain. So how can I still have a mind?"

Lela paused, searching for a way to answer. "Who are you?" she asked.

"Well, I am Martyna of course!"

"And how do you know you are Martyna?"

"I just know; it is right there when the question comes 'who are you'."

"Exactly: this sense of being who you are, of knowing who you are, is what organizes your perceptions and thoughts and feelings and memories. And this is all a function of what we can call 'mind'. But it is not a 'thing.' It is a process. And this process can use the physical brain but is not dependent on it. Does that help?"

"Actually no, that does not help. I am more confused now."

"I can understand that you feel that way – it is a confusing subject. But for right now – for what is happening between us – can you just accept that you have no physical body but still have a sense of being yourself and can perceive and respond to what you perceive? Even when you do not understand how that can be."

"Okay, I have no body so no eyes and no brain, but can somehow be here with you," said Martyna with some sense of frustrated resignation. "I don't understand it, but it is nicer than how things were in my broken old body. So, can I just stay like this?"

"Yes, you could try that. But I do not recommend it. Some people take that route. Mostly those are people who refuse to accept the fact of their death or those who cling to an old injustice or something that for them was incomplete in their life. So they do not move forward. But it is not 'real life.' And over time the subtle body that you now have will grow weaker and weaker. It will fade away but you will still be there. And you will become hungry to experience something more substantial. Having made the choice once, however, choosing something else later will become more and more difficult."

"That does not sound like much fun," responded Martyna. "What about heaven? Our priests talked about that a lot and some of them seemed to actually believe it. Is that an option for me?"

"Of course it is an option – there are innumerable heavens, visualized then realized by various groups as somehow better than life in a body. You were not particularly devout but if you really want it I am sure we can find a place for you in one heaven or another. You always did your very best and you loved well. Those are the two things that count. But knowing you as I do I think you might find any of the heavens somewhat boring."

"What do you mean 'visualized then realized'? asked Martyna. "Either there is a heaven somewhere or there is not, right? There always seemed to be a lot of disagreement about whether heaven existed or not and if it did exist what it was like and who would get in and who not. With so much confusion about it I had decided even as a child that it was just a story cooked up by the church to keep us in line."

Lela was again thoughtful. "Have you ever visited the cathedral of the Virgin Mary in Konstanz?"

"Well, yes, I have. We did a tour of the city there during holidays before I moved here. That cathedral was the best part of the tour for sure. We were able to go onto the observation platform very high up. It was wonderful to look out at the world and the lake. I think that is when I decided I wanted to move here. But what does that have to do with heaven?"

"Do you think the cathedral has always been there?"

"No, of course not. People built it."

"Yes, people built it. Someone had a vision, then that vision was shared, then the intention to build something special was set. And collecting resources and the building work continued in steps and stages over 1500 years to the present day. Am I right?"

"I don't know how old it is but something like that has for sure happened. But why are you telling me this?" asked Martyna.

"Can you imagine that something very similar to the building of that cathedral has happened but not in this material world? Can you imagine that someone or some group had a vision of what could be or of what was needed then worked together over a long period of time to plan and construct what you could call a heaven? And over time more people joined them. And that there have been many different visions and many different resulting projects like that over the history of humanity? Therefore we have so many different ideas of what kinds of places there are for people after they leave the body. And these don't have to be exclusive places just for the 'good ones.' Most tribal people developed communities of ancestors who continued to exist in a non-material world but were able to communicate with those still in the material world."

"This is a really new idea for me. I have to think about it. But it would explain why there are so many contradicting descriptions. And I must admit the idea of a heaven somewhere some day for me never had much appeal. Even if it existed, it always sounded like a kind of escape. So you are right, that does not sound like what I want even if heavens do exist." Martyna grew thoughtful.

"Then what about hell? If I don't go to some heaven does that mean that hell is my only other possible choice?"

"Hell is something that *happens* to someone who has left the body or even before they have left the body and not something the person consciously chooses. They are like a piece of wood in a river: because of how they have lived their life and the conditions of their death they are carried forward by powerful forces. And that can end up in very painful experiences that you could call hell."

"So people planned and created a hell? That is even harder to believe than what you said about where heavens come from!"

"You are right," replied Lela. "Planning a hell is unusual. What happens instead is that each time someone has the intention to harm or exploit someone else a pattern of harm and exploitation is strengthened – in that person and in the world. Then others often feel attacked by that person's actions and instead of reacting skill-fully they in their turn begin harming or exploiting others. From there it can cycle into larger and larger patterns of suffering."

"And then that goes on forever?" asked Martyna.

"No, eventually the pattern reaches a peak of intensity and self-destructs. And even before that point those involved can always no-tice the pattern and choose something else. When the pattern col-lapses those caught in it have again the chance to understand that they are the sources of their own suffering, directly or indirectly. They may realize that there is another way to live free of the inten-tion to harm or exploit. And then go forward from there. But often they simply repeat the old patterns. Once a strong pattern has begun and many are participating it is very challenging to leave the pat-tern. Luckily the universe is patient with us and knows that in the end we will all learn our lessons."

"So that's it: a fading ghost, a heaven or a hell?" Martyna paused to reflect. "Actually none of that sounds very appealing to me. I re-ally liked being alive! The juiciness and unpredictability of it!" She smiled and paused again thinking about her life. "But those three are my only options?"

"Not at all," responded Lela. "The most common next step after leaving a body is to incarnate again in some other time and place and in some other body. And then to continue one's education, one's development, one's creative expression, or to meet up with others and so on. That is what happens to most beings. And not just people. Animals too and in a way all living things."

"Wow, so that means that I have lived before?"

"In a way no and in a way yes. You as Martyna are unique. Mar-tyna is a one time event. But there is something in you that makes Martyna who she is that has lived before and will probably live again. Something that carries your story forward and connects across lives."

"Is that my soul?"

"Soul is like all kinds of similar words – it tries to put something that is unique and indescribable in a very small box. Then people at-tach many different ideas and judgments to that box. In the end probably more harmful than helpful. But if you need a word then call it your soul."

"So somehow some part of me has lived before and was alive in me as Martyna and can live again?"

"Yes, you could understand it in that way."

Martyna looked up into the light blue sky with its scattered high thin clouds. She looked down at her hands together in her lap on the dark blue dress. Her arthritis was gone; the gnarled joints were back to normal and the skin was clearer than it had been in a long time. It was a lot to take in. This was new territory for her. But somehow it made sense. There were questions in her mind though.

"So everyone gets to choose what happens to them next after they die?"

"No, choosing is not usual. For the majority of people it is a natural unconscious process. You can think of it like going to sleep in the evening, dreaming awhile then waking up in a new life with only vague memories of what has been before.

"And the new life that you experience – the circumstances of a next life – is a result of how you have lived before, of what you did and did not do. So everyone is deciding every day – based on how they live – not just how future days will be for them in a life but how a future life that they may experience will be if they reincarnate instead of taking some other path."

"But if something in me – my soul – has lived before then why do I not remember those lives?"

"Some people do remember but it is usually more of a burden than a help. One life at a time is enough for most of us."

"How do *you* know that I have lived before?"

Lela paused for a moment then answered. "Because I was there with you."

"Who are you then? Are you my 'guardian angel'?"

"Believe me, I am no angel!" replied Lela with a grimace. "I am just a friend who cares what happens to you. But a person just like you."

"And so does everyone have someone like you who meets them after they die to help them decide what they want to happen next like you are here for me?"

"No. Most people are so unprepared that when they leave the body their immediate experience – if they consciously experience anything at all – is like a dream made up of the parts of their life they have not previously seen or accepted or that they struggle to release. Even if someone tries to meet and support them such people are not able to connect or to understand what is being offered. So for them there is no choosing."

"Who is it that comes to meet them and tries to support them?"

"It is quite open. People can be met and helped by a relative, a friend, a trusted teacher, or just someone who has taken an interest in them. The helper can be a person who has themselves died or someone who is still alive but has the ability to communicate with those who have died. The call for help from someone leaving the body may also be answered by other kinds of beings who live in non-material worlds but have some connection to human life. And all of those who are assisting the person who has left the body will have their own ideas about what the process means and what choices there are. Or if there are choices at all." Lela paused for a moment. "Just as I do.

"The most important thing," Lela continued, "is that a person who is leaving the body asks for help. Then the second most important thing is that they are ready to accept help in whatever form it appears even if it is not in the form they expected or wanted. You in your case did both things – you called out for help and you have accepted the form in which it has come to you. And therefore here we are."

"You mean that is what my dream was about? Was it about dying, about my dying?" asked Martyna.

"That is part of what the dream was about. But it was also about memories that you carry from other lives and premonitions of future lives and challenges you will face."

"Are there always challenges, then?" Martyna asked.

Lela paused before she answered. She seemed to be deciding something. Then Lela spoke looking at Martyna intently.

"When you incarnate, yes, there are always challenges: being born, finding out who you are and what there is for you to do, learning to face suffering, learning to understand and support others, knowing when to protect that which needs protecting and in the end learning to meet death. That is what incarnation is about. That is what it is for. And through encountering these challenges and finding our way forward we become new and larger selves regardless of how often we think we have failed and regardless of how often we must choose again which road to follow or which new road must be created. That is what we are doing. That is what you are doing."

Lela leaned back on the bench and looked out at the lake. Martyna did the same.

A mother Mallard duck paddled along the water's edge followed by a straggling line of six ducklings each doing its best to keep up and not get distracted by all the tantalizing things around them. Martyna had always liked ducks and swans and birds of all kinds. It had been one of the reasons she had chosen this place to move to, so that she could see them every day. It had not been easy to find a suitable place as lots of people wanted to live in the area. But the old farmer's house was in such bad condition that no one else had wanted it enough to deal with the trouble of it. So...

"Martyna?"

"Yes?"

"You need to stay focused if you can. Our time is limited. Your moment of choice is now. You have not noticed it perhaps but it has been a week since you left your body. This process is like birth and is closely linked to birth. So once it starts it has its own rhythm and it is best to follow that rhythm."

"But it has only been a few minutes!" protested Martyna.

"That is how it seems to you but all sense of time for you now is deceptive. Do you remember what we were talking about?"

Martyna searched her mind. She knew they had been talking about something important but she could not remember what. "No, I don't," she answered simply.

"You need now to visualize what kind of next existence you want for those parts of you that will continue. I can help you formulate that based on what I know about you. But the visioning process, the releasing of your attachments to this last life and the incarnation process it leads to – if you choose to incarnate – are yours alone."

"And then what I envision is what my soul's next life will become?"

"Perhaps. But almost always there are other factors that affect the outcome: like lessons that have to be learned, debts that must be acknowledged, what other people want or the love that needs to be expressed. "

"And then someone decides for me?"

"No, there is no one who decides. It is like raindrops forming in clouds then falling to the earth. It is like water flowing downhill to the ocean then rising again into the sky. It just happens by itself."

Martyna grew thoughtful. She noticed a growing dissatisfaction in herself over what she was hearing from Lela.

"You seem to know so much about me, even about my past lives," she said after a while. "But I know nothing about them! I know only Martyna. And that is not fair. How can I decide what I want to happen next if I don't know what has come before? I have had so many questions in my life about why things happened as they did. It was all so hard to understand and now before I understand my last life you tell me I need to visualize some next life? I won't do it! I strike! Unless I can know what has gone before I refuse to go forward. And I mean it!"

Lela sat quietly looking into Martyna's defiant gaze.

"Is that really what you want: to remember past lives so you can make a better choice for the next life?" Lela's voice was soft and measured. "It is possible for me to organize that with you. But you need to be really sure. It will be very painful for you. But if you can work through the pain of remembering I am sure it will help you understand more about this last life. And probably help you decide your intention for the next life."

Martyna thought about it for a few moments. Looking out at the lake she saw that it had become darker now. The sun was setting in the west. A gentle breeze was bending the sea grass and rippling the water's surface. She looked back to Lela.

"Yes, I really want to remember," she said.

"Alright, it shall be as you wish. And since your intention for this remembering is so clear what will be shown to you are the key decisions that have been made in the journey of lives that brought you to where you are now," said Lela. "Do you understand that?"

"No, I don't understand," said Martyna. "What do you mean with 'key decisions' and 'journey of lives'? You said that I am unique, Martyna, with my life and the decisions that I have made. I understand that much. But now you make it sound like there have been decisions made in some other lives by some other me or someone else that have affected me in this life. I can understand how some decisions, like the ones my parents made, have affected me directly. But how can it be that something someone chose long ago in another place affects me? How is that possible?"

"You are right," replied Lela. "It is a mystery that is not easy to understand. Simplest for you perhaps is to think of the journey of lives as a book with many chapters. The chapters are each unique. But what happens in one chapter affects conditions and choices that need to be made in the chapters that follow, even if the chapters are about different people in very different places and times – they all carry the story regardless."

Martyna was still confused. "So I am going to experience all of the stuff in all the lives since the beginning of time that have affected my life? That sounds like way way too much!"

"Yes, it would be too much. What you will experience is determined by your intention. Since your intention is to find answers to questions you have about your last life and to become clearer about what you want for the next life that is what you will experience. You will only remember the lives and events that directly affected your circumstances and your choices in this last life. Does that explanation help?"

"Yes, it does," replied Martyna. She hesitated for some moments. "But now I am afraid. I am really afraid!"

"It is quite alright to be afraid," said Lela. "But if you want I promise I will try to be there with you."

"Thank you," responded Martyna. "Yes, please help me when I need it. That would be very good!" She struggled not to cry. She laughed a small embarrassed laugh.

"It is time" said Lela. "Give me your hand."

Martyna reached out her left hand to take Lela's offered right. Martyna noticed that her own hand and arm had grown semi-transparent – looking at them she could see the dark brown of the bench wood behind them. She closed her eyes.

Lela closed her own eyes and bent her head forward.

"Your name was Alya."

Hagar Qim Temple on Malta
2636 B.C.E.

Alya and Karu

Alya stepped out of the shade of the temple entrance and into the sunlight. After a restless and troubled night full of difficult dreams she had overslept.

It was another cloudless day with light streaming from the sun rising in the east behind her. In front of her the land sloped away in white limestone outcroppings and small brown leafless bushes curving downward until the cliff edge. Then beyond that boundary was the broad still ocean glittering in the sun, stretching to the horizon. Above it all was the brilliant light blue sky filled with the soft murmur of the waves washing against the base of the cliff far below, the screech of a passing seagull and the smell of the sea.

The small island she called Little Sister rose up like a breaching whale in the near distance. "Good morning Little Sister," she said out loud.

"And good morning back to you too Big Sister!" came her brother's response from behind her mimicking a female voice. He gave a nervous laugh.

When she had gotten up a few minutes before her twin brother Karu had been asleep or at least appeared to be asleep. And she had hoped he would stay that way. But now he was up and awake and making his kind of irritating joke. He looked at her expectantly. Could she avoid talking with him? Maybe she could put it off a little longer.

He stood now with his hands on his hips, a fading smile still on his clean-shaven face. His shoulder-length black hair was in disarray, uncombed after his night's sleep. His skirt, worn and needing to be washed, was low on his hips, the red belt leather tied in a casual knot. He stood barefoot on the smooth forecourt stones. His brown skin was red on his heavily muscled shoulders and arms from too much sun.

"I have to take care of my plants now," she said after considering her options.

"Of course, do what you want," he responded with a resigned tone in his voice and went back into the temple.

Alya took the leather water bucket from its place by the temple door and headed down the path to her right, curving around the north side of the temple, descending into a small ravine where water flowed when there was rain.

Long ago, people had built a growing area on the side of the ravine framed on the downhill side by a stone border and filled with soil collected from other growing plots that had been abandoned. Someone had planted a row of fig trees that were now almost as tall as Alya. The growing patch had been carefully built: when it rained the first water would flood the encircled area then overflow and descend to a stone catch basin. Then Alya would empty the catch basin as it filled and carry the water up the hill to the cistern. Later in the year when the trees and other plants needed water she reversed the process.

The fig trees were thriving. They regularly sprouted shiny green leaves with their special pattern, even with the little water they got and the intense heat in the summers. They had had no fruit yet but Alya expected it to come by next year at the latest. She brought them water from the cistern when she felt they absolutely needed it. Today she simply squatted at the base of one of the trees and peed.

Crossing the ravine she continued up the side of the hill to the cistern, a retainer carved into the limestone bedrock. This particular cistern was large – three times as deep as she was tall with a round opening half her height wide. She moved the stones holding the woven mat that covered the opening in place and pulled the mat aside. She fastened the water bucket to the woven leather rope and dropped the water bucket into the cistern, let it sink for a moment then pulled it up. Every year of her time here at the temple the water level each spring had been lower than the year before. How much longer would there be water here at all? Such a depressing thought; she pushed it away.

She took a careful sip of water from the bucket for herself, tied it closed, put it onto her shoulder and went downhill to the growing patch in the direction of the Men's temple. The growing patch had been there for many generations but it had not been planted or cared for in a long time. Normally it would have been taken care of by the caretaker for the Men's temple. But there was no caretaker for the Men's temple and had not been the whole time she had been at Hagar Qim. Why was that? she had wondered at first. But now she knew. The young boys had other things they wanted to do instead of caring for an old temple alone and far from the more exciting life in the city.

The growing patch was further downhill so it had the chance to catch more water and save it in the earth. Alya had taken thorn bush branches and built a fence around it – replacing the one that had been there but had fallen apart – to protect it from animals. These plants she had started herself a month before: forty precious lentil seeds. She brought the plants water whenever they needed it. She watched for plant-eating insects and removed them when she found them.

Yet somehow all of that did not help. Almost all the seeds had sprouted as she had hoped. But there had been no real progress. Instead of growing and stretching green shoot leaves the new sprouts were still small and weak as if paralyzed. Pale and tenuous. What was happening? Who could understand it, and most of all what could be done? She had asked Lela at the very beginning – What is wrong with the plants here? Why do they not grow? Lela's answer had been a shock: it had been getting harder and harder to get plants to grow over the last generations, she said, even when they had enough water and sun. Not just here but everywhere on the island. No one knew why. It hadn't to do with something Alya was doing or not doing. Lela told her to just do her best and harvest what she could. Which is what she had done.

It was unusual to water plants in the morning when the hot sun of the day might take most of the moisture. But she felt like she had to do something so she untied the water bucket then used a shell that she kept there to dip out water and place some at the base of each sprout.

Then that was done. She took the water bucket, closed the gate to the fence behind her and began the uphill walk back to the temple where she knew Karu would be waiting for her.

Since he had arrived the previous evening she had the sense he wanted to talk with her about something. He had said nothing directly but she could feel it. So far she had avoided that possibility by changing the subject or inventing some excuse. It had been years since they had had a serious conversation that had ended in anything but a bitter argument regardless of the topic. And she did not want that to happen again. It was always so painful.

When they had been small they had gotten along together. But when they were ten their mother died of a coughing-fever that she had gotten from traders who had visited the island. Others had gotten sick as well but their mother Falila was the only one who had died. People said that the birth of the twins years before had been very difficult for her. Looking back at her memories as a young child Alya thought that probably her mother had never fully recovered her strength. And there had been other difficulties.

Some people believed that a boy and a girl growing in the same mother was a bad omen. Perhaps the children had already broken the Agreement about male and female lying together only when blessed by the Council? So there had been a cloud over all three of them from the beginning. Some children were hesitant to play or work with Alya and Karu. Then when their mother died, nodding wise heads: "I told you so! An unlucky family." Alya still bristled at the memory of overhearing that terrible judgment. So Alya had grown up not only without a mother but had never had real friends.

Alya did not know who her father was. When she was small and first learned that babies came after men planted their seed in a woman she had been curious and had asked her mother directly, "Who is my father?"

Falila told Alya that it was not good to talk about such things. Alya had not understood why knowing who your father was could be a bad thing and so she repeated her question insisting on an answer. "That is not for you to know. It is not good for you to know. Stop now and do not ask me again!" Her mother had grown stern.

So in the end Alya had given up and accepted that she would never know. She gradually understood that no one knew or if they knew would not admit knowing. Sometimes she had seen men looking at her in a kind way or helping her with something and so she would think to herself, "Perhaps this is my father." But since mothers and fathers were always selected from groups living far from one another – not knowing each other before and forbidden from maintaining contact after their time of pairing – the chances were low that she had ever been right.

If it had not been for Lela being chosen by the Council to look after Karu and Alya after their mother's death, who knows what would have happened to her, Alya thought to herself. Lela was not like a mother telling you what you needed to do and not do. She was more like a friend that Alya could go to when she had problems. It was Lela who had organized this temple keeper work for Alya and thereby given her a way of life that suited her.

Karu had never gotten along with Lela. He openly resented her concern and care for them. So it was. Alya couldn't understand why he resented someone who was trying to help them. Men were often difficult and hard to understand.

Instead of withdrawing like Alya had done Karu became more social and wild after their mother's death, provoking and being provoked in competition with other boys. The profession that had been chosen for him – stone cutter in Tarxien – had suited him fine as it had the image of being strong and important. Tarxien was the only stone quarry on the island that was still in operation, cutting stone for the extensions to the large temple complex there. So at least Karu had had something to do these last few years. And he had become very strong, which he enjoyed. Stonecutters also got extra food rations because of the demands of their work. Unlike most others he did not struggle to have enough to eat.

Alya had been surprised the summer before when she had visited Tarxien at how much she disliked the temple extension project that Karu was so enthusiastic about. It consisted of bigger than life-sized carved stone figures of council members with their identifying red pleated wool skirts sitting or – in one enormous case – standing. What is the purpose of these statues? she had asked herself. By The Agreements we are all of equal worth, only with different responsibilities. Something she did not like had crept into her world.

She had asked Lela directly what Lela thought about the new large statues of specific people. Lela had changed the subject. Alya was clear that for Alya herself the small statues made from fired clay were much more beautiful than any giant stone carving could ever be. Like the small statue that she cared for here at Hagar Qim in "her" temple.

Karu was sitting on the stone bench in the forecourt when she got back to the temple. She hung up the water bucket at its place by the temple entrance. What was she going to do about Karu? she asked herself. Maybe she should try a different approach.

"I have to sing the morning prayers now before the sun gets much higher. Why don't you join me? It has been so long for you. Probably you have forgotten the words. But maybe not. Or you could do the drum. How about it?"

"Aren't you hungry?" He asked instead of answering. "I really do need to eat something."

"We have the things that you brought for me from the temple supplies: dried figs, goat cheese and dried goat meat. Does any of that sound like what you want?" she asked.

"What I want is something entirely different," he said with a smile.

What is that about? Alya asked herself. More riddles. She did not ask what he really wanted.

"You know where the food is, so help yourself to whatever you want. I am not hungry," she said and started to walk into the temple.

"Sit down for a moment, can't you? I have brought you something special from Tarxien. I hope you like it." He reached into his travel bag that was on the ground next to where he sat and took out a small package wrapped in a palm leaf and tied with a wool cord. He placed it in front of him on the stone and indicated a place opposite him for her to sit.

Alya was intrigued in spite of her distrust. She did not remember Karu ever bringing her a present. What could it be? She sat down straddling the stone as he was.

Without saying anything more Karu slowly untied the cord and unwrapped the palm leaf. There inside it was a gray rectangular block of something. Alya did not know what it was.

"What is it?" she asked.

"It is something good to eat!" he answered enthusiastically. He picked it up, took a bite of it, chewed a few times and then offered it to her. "Here, try it. It's wonderful."

Alya took it in her hand. She looked at it more closely but still did not know what it was. She took a small bite and began to chew it.

"That is a piece of fish!" she exclaimed angrily. She spit out what she had in her mouth and threw the piece in her hand back at him. He let it fall to the ground.

"Wonderful you say? Are you crazy? It is forbidden!" she said loudly.

"If there is anything crazy going on it is that perfectly good food like this fish is forbidden to our people, our people who are starving!" he answered angrily and folded his arms together on his chest.

"Where did you get it?" she asked accusingly.

"From the traders who are at the harbor. I helped them move their boat and so they gave me some fish they had caught and dried themselves. It is the main thing they live on since they are on the ocean so much. For them it is impossible to believe that for us it is forbidden."

"But you could explain it to them, right? How in our grand-mother's time it was determined that the problem with so little rain was because we had angered Mother Ocean by eating her children. So it was decided to stop eating her children otherwise the situation would get worse and worse. Did you explain all that? Explain how important it is?"

"I tried but they only laughed. They said that if all that had been true there should be more rain now, but there is not, not for anyone around here. They said that maybe Mother Ocean has gone into re-tirement! Maybe she has made way for new gods that are more con-cerned with what happens to those who follow them."

"Are these the same traders that were here two moons ago? I heard bad things about them. How can they still be here? The limit for traders is one moon."

"They are the same traders. They say they like it here and plan to stay. They say we need their help as our leaders have not yet under-stood how things work now. The Council Speaker ordered them to leave but they just ignored her. For them all of our rules are point-less and old-fashioned. They do what they want, not what they are told."

"And you are listening to all this dangerous evil?"

"Alya, a lot of it makes sense. They say that men are more power-ful and should be making new rules. And that we need to get rid of the old-fashioned women's rules."

"Like what kind of new rules?"

"That is why I came here to see you, why it is so important that I talk to you. Not everyone knows it yet but soon the men will let ev-eryone know that men are the new leaders. The Council will be abol-ished. And most important: men will give the orders, not women. That is what I wanted to talk to you about."

"But our people will never agree to all of that! We will refuse this craziness!"

Karu had an answer. "Some will refuse of course but many will accept it. Almost all the men I have talked to think it would be good to try it, at least for a while, and see how it is. Our people are desper-ate for a new way, a new path. You are so isolated out here at the edge of the island in your temple with everything provided for you from the temple supplies. You don't understand how it has been these last years."

Alya was almost passing out from shock – these trader men were taking over and the island's men were supporting them, were on their side if Karu was a representative.

"So is that what you wanted to talk to me about? It sounds like we will all find out about it soon enough."

"Actually, I wanted to talk about a part of it: about you and me and where we will be in this new organization of things."

"Well, I know where I will be, right here taking care of my tem-ple!"

"Sorry, but no, that will not be possible. All the temples will be closed, forbidden, so you will not be able to stay here. The old out-dated ways must be left behind to make space for the new way of things. So you must find some other place and some other way to live."

Alya was being hit with a series of heavy blows – the temples closed? How could that be? And could the Council defend them against all of this? Not possible – they had never developed any weapons nor skills in fighting. But the traders always had weapons with them and from the look of their scars were experienced in us-ing them.

Long ago their people's defense had been the threat that if traders did not follow the rules of the Council Mother Ocean would send storms to destroy their ships and drown them all. There were stories of this really happening. And that had been enough to protect them. But now? The traders were no longer afraid. So what could her people do? What could Alya do? she asked herself.

"If that really happens and the temples are closed then I will just live somewhere with some goats as far as possible from people."

"That will also not be possible. Every woman must belong to some man, must be under his control – that will be the new rule. It will be announced very soon. No women will be allowed to just run wild. The traders say that is what has gotten us all into this mess: women running wild, telling men how to live."

Alya tried to calm her confusion. She breathed in and out as slowly as she could. She summoned all her training as a temple keeper to try to find a way to answer him.

Lela had hinted that something like this might be coming. "Difficult times are ahead," she had said. "We must all be prepared to do our parts." And now here it was: difficult times indeed.

Alya looked again at Karu sitting opposite her on the stone, his arms still folded on his chest, his face determined. There is something he has not yet told me she thought to herself. She was sure of it.

"Why are you really here?" she asked quietly, leaning forward. "If all that you describe is really happening, is really going to happen, I would have found it all out soon enough. Why aren't you back in Tarxien celebrating with your new friends?"

"That's what I wanted to talk to you about," he said. His face relaxed and his arms opened.

"When I found out about all these changes happening, especially the part about every woman having to belong to some man, I immediately thought about you. You may not believe it, and I know it has never been easy between us, but I really do care about you. So I became worried about what would happen to you in this new time."

"You worried about *me*?" she asked, incredulous. "About *me*?" she laughed a bitter laugh. "You are joining up with these foreign savages who are set to destroy everything that our people value, all that we have learned over so many generations about how to live with one another and you are worried about *me*?" She shook her head in disbelief.

"Yes, I am worried about you. But then I realized that these changes could be the fulfillment of your deepest wish, your heart's desire! There is a way for you, for us, I am sure of it."

"What deepest desire of mine? What way for us?"

"You want a child, right? Maybe you thought I didn't know, but I do know. Your deepest desire is to have a child, to become a mother. Am I right?"

Alya was stunned. He did understand something about her after all. She could not answer, just sat in shock, his question reverberating in her head.

Then she nodded. Yes, he was right.

Just before she became 15 and eligible to be chosen to have a baby the Council had decided that until the harvests improved no new children would be planted. The possibility that new children would be brought into the world but then starve was unbearable for everyone. So Alya's dream of having a child, of achieving the status of Mother and of having that child be her focus for her life was postponed. That is what she had told herself then when she first heard about the decision. But recently – after five years with harvests continuing to dwindle – she had begun to accept the bitter probability that she would never have a child of her own or have even children of others to care for. Nor would anyone else. That is how it was. There was nothing to be done about it.

Karu filled the painful silence:

"In this new way of doing things each man can plant his seed in a woman as often as he wants as long as the woman belongs to him and he is able to provide for the babies that come from it. So men can have their children, their sons and daughters, and help them grow up strong. It isn't just the mothers who can have children and call them their own like it is now."

It was a lot to take in at once. "Let me understand this: in this new way of doing things I will *belong* to some man? I will be his *property*? And he can plant babies in me whenever he wants?"

"That sounds so negative – you will be his *responsibility*, to care for you and your children and make sure you have what you need."

"And what if I don't want to belong to some man? What if I don't want to have someone else be responsible for me?"

"How that will work is not yet clear. There are possibilities being discussed."

"And who is involved in these discussions? Are there women involved?"

"I don't think so. All the women get so crazy when the subject is even mentioned."

"And what if I don't want to grow the seed that some man plants in me?" asked Alya.

"That will not be for you to decide – the new rule is that the planted seed and the child that comes from it belong to the man who planted it. So refusing to carry it is to steal from that man, to take what is his and so must be punished. This has already been discussed and decided."

Alya stood up facing him.

"Karu, get out of here, leave! All this that you have told me has made me so angry that I am afraid of what I might do to you. So go, now!"

"But Alya, you have not yet heard the most important part: you don't have to worry that you will be owned by one of these trader men – that would be terrible, they smell so, they let their beards grow and are so rough with everything. And the men from our people are all weak and afraid right now and I am not sure one of them would be able to take care of you."

A terrible thought occurred to Alya. She suddenly realized where this was headed.

"So what man, exactly, do you think I should belong to?" she asked sarcastically.

Karu stood up, facing her.

"You can belong to me of course! I am strong and smart. The trader men like me. I am sure I will do well in the new way of things. By the old rules for a brother and sister to be together to plant babies was forbidden. But I asked Landran about it – he is the most important person among the traders – about you becoming my woman even though you are my sister and he just laughed and said 'Of course, why not?'"

Karu smiled, pleased with himself. He had actually done it: had told her how he felt about her and had explained to her that there was a way forward for them.

So that was it, Alya thought to herself. That is what is behind all of this. He is not worried about me. He just wants what he wants and will say and do anything to get it. It made her even more angry to think about it now that she understood his whole plan.

"Like I said: get out!" she shouted. Waving her arms at him, turning away, beginning to cry and not wanting him to see it.

Instead of leaving he came to her and put his arms around her.

"Just give it a chance; just give *us* a chance!" he pleaded.

Enraged, Alya freed her arms and attacked his face, scratching his cheeks left and right with her fingernails."

"Oww!" he let go of her immediately. He stepped back, examining the blood on his hands as he felt his wounds.

Karu glared at her for a moment then picked up his travel bag and walked away without looking back, shaking his head and muttering to himself.

Alya did not watch him as he walked away. She fled into the temple, into the innermost chamber in front of the altar. Prostrated herself on the red wool rug in front of the altar. Wept quietly.

Lela had known something like this was coming, had always known, Alya realized.

Lela had prepared her for it. But Alya had not really believed that the day would come when their way of life would end. But here it was, unmistakable.

Alya sat up and looked at the altar. The small Mother figure was there in front of her as it always was: upright in the sand, the large breasts, the bent left arm. The emblem of all that was good and nourishing in the world, in a small figure.

Alya wept now at the beauty of it, at the simple honesty of it. Not trying to be anything different from exactly what it was: the source of life. No goal or purpose but to nourish the world.

The warning about great difficulties was not all that Lela had told her.

"When the time comes, and you will know when that time is, you must take the Mother from the altar and hide her somewhere in the temple in a place that you have prepared where she cannot be found except by someone who knows where she is."

"So then I will tell you where she is, so you can find her," Alya had replied.

"No, do not tell me, do not tell anyone."

"But then how will she be found?"

"She will be found when you are ready for her to be found since you are the only one who will know where she is. Do not worry about it. When the time comes for her to be found you will know that it is time and you will make it possible for her to be found," Lela clarified.

"But why hide her, then, if I will just find her again?"

"We do not know how long it will be before it is time for her to be found. It may be a long time, a very long time."

"But then I will no longer be here to find her!"

"Yes, I know it is hard to understand. But you need to trust me and do as I ask. Can you promise that you will do it, that you will prepare a place and then hide her there when the time comes?"

"Yes, I promise."

And that is how the conversation had been two years before. Thinking about it now gave her hope. If Lela saw this terrible disaster coming and made plans for it – like Alya hiding the Mother – then there was hope.

"There is hope." She said it out loud. She was no longer crying. "And each of us must do our part, as we have promised."

Alya stood up and walked back into the first chamber of the temple. There she moved the dirt and sand from around the side edge of one of the large central paving stones. Then lifted up the smaller side paving stone next to it and put that stone aside. Here was her hiding place. Under the large paving stone she had carved out a small chamber in the white stone, big enough for the statue. The large paving stone was supported on three sides by bedrock; it would not fall and crush the Mother even in the most powerful earthquake. A red wool cloth and red ocher powder in a small leather pouch were already waiting in the hiding place.

Alya went back into the innermost temple room. She took the Mother from the altar and carried her back to where her hiding place had been prepared. She sprinkled the red ocher onto the statue then took the cloth and wrapped the statue carefully. She put the Mother into the hiding place then filled the space around it with earth and small stones and packed it all so that it was firm. Even if someone removed the covering stone on the side they would only see earth and stones and not more. She replaced the side covering stone. She cleaned the area around it of dirt and sand to hide the traces of the hiding place.

Looking at it, she was satisfied. No one would ever guess that a treasure was hidden there. Even if the entire temple collapsed the paving stones would hold and would protect the Mother. Of that she was sure.

So now what should she do?

She stood up. She took and released a few deep breaths. She went into the first storage room, took her traveling bag and put all the food that she had plus a gourd of water into it. She hung the bag on her shoulder. Everything else she left where it was. She would come back for it. Or she would not. Simple.

When she was back outside she turned and looked at the temple building itself: an enormous structure of giant white stones, most of them taller than twice her height, curving walls making a series of rounded nested chambers with painted walls and lintelled doorways between the chambers, one leading to the next.

From the beginning of her time at the temple she had wondered what it was all really for. People she had asked had said that the temples had been built to "give the sacred a home." But that had never made sense to her – the sacred was everywhere, in everything. It needed no home.

But now, today, she finally understood. She was certain. The temples had been built over so many generations, with so much effort, in order to make a safe place for hiding the wisdom of her people. All of which might otherwise be lost in the dark times that were coming. That had come.

She looked out to sea. "Goodbye Little Sister" she said and started on the long walk to Tarxien. She wanted to see first hand what was going on there. Maybe Karu had exaggerated. But she doubted it.

As she walked she struggled to understand why Karu and apparently many others were not resisting the dictates of the traders. The thought came to her that perhaps the rules of the Council had been too hard on the men.

She remembered a bitter argument that she had had with Karu the previous year when she had visited him in Tarxien. Karu like everyone else understood that men planting their seed in women of child-bearing age had to be controlled in order to keep from having more people than they could feed on their small island. So there had to be a way to keep men from planting their seed when it had not been approved by the Council. Karu even agreed to that much. But he did not agree to the rule the Council had established to enforce this.

The rule among them was that a man who – without Council approval – lay with a woman who had not passed beyond her child-bearing years would, after a hearing before the Council, be castrated in a public ceremony.

Castration was what was normally done with male animals that were difficult to control or that were not selected for breeding. For Alya this seemed like a reasonable way to deal with the very important challenge of keeping their population size under control. But Karu was violently opposed to this practice even though the penalty was rarely carried out. At the same time he had no alternative approach to offer. The fact that men could play all the sex games they wanted with one another or with women who were beyond the age of child-bearing – and no one would complain or even comment – did not seem to appease him.

Was there another way to control how many new babies there would be? Alya asked herself the question but did not herself have any answer. What was clear was that Karu and the other men had had complaints about how they were treated. And so were ready for a change.

33

Tarxien

"What do you want?" said her mother's sister Bandra when Alya showed up at the door to the house where Bandra lived. The tone was not welcoming. Bandra had always disliked Alya and had never made a secret of it. But now it was the only place Alya could think of that she could stay since she could not stay with Karu.

"I need a place to stay here in Tarxien for a few days while I take care of some things."

"I thought you were at the Hagar Qim temple taking care of that."

"I was, but not right now. The temple is okay and it will just be for a few days. Can I stay with you?"

Bandra clearly did not want Alya in the house.

Alya reached forward her traveling bag, opening it wide to show what was inside. "I have food and water for your house – I will not be a burden."

Bandra peered into the bag and reconsidered. "Alright then, but only for a few days. Follow me."

So Alya now had a corner on the roof for herself under a palm leaf structure that would protect her from the sun and a place at the table when those living in the house had their daily meal.

As she had expected, what Karu had told her was actually happening. People that she came into contact with in Tarxien – people she knew and ones she overheard talking – were still wondering what would really happen. There were rumors that the temples and even underground sacred places would be closed or dedicated to new gods "because the Mother goddesses have failed us" was the way it was expressed by some. But this was more than most people could imagine and so was not taken seriously by many such as Bandra and the others in her household.

"So, they are going to take the Mother Sun out of the sky and dry up Mother Ocean? I don't believe it. It is all just foolish mentalk," was what Bandra said. "Just wait. It will all blow away like a winter storm."

No one seemed to have understood the part about each woman needing to belong to some man. But Alya could see how all the parts fit together in this new way of things. She was convinced the traders were bringing in a system that had been developed somewhere else, that had been worked out before.

Watching them from a distance move around in the town, watching them with one another, she was convinced they could not have thought it through themselves. A friend had pointed out Landran, the one that Karu had mentioned. He was tall with long wild hair and a full beard. He looked very strong. Most of all Alya noticed his eyes that seemed to be seeing everything at once. But no, this man had not thought up all of this. Like the fever they had brought that had killed her mother this new way of things was something they had gotten somewhere else.

"Have you seen Lela? Do you know where she is?" Alya had asked Bandra on the second day she was there.

"No, I haven't seen her in a while – maybe a week – and I have no idea where she is now," Bandra answered. "Come to think of it, it is strange – she had been around here every day before that, listening to people, making suggestions, very much involved. And now, nothing!"

No one else she had asked could remember seeing Lela recently.

Alya sat on the roof alone and gazed into the northern sky. She reached out with her mind to find Lela. In the past she had sometimes been able to connect in this way. But now she could not find any trace no matter where in the sky or in her mind she searched.

On the morning of her third day in Tarxien she was awakened by one of Bandra's daughters coming up to the roof.

"Alya, there is someone at the door that wants to talk with you."

Alya stood up and followed her down the ladder. At the door was a young boy that Alya did not know.

"What do you want?" she asked.

"Karu sent me. He says it is important that he talks with you. He says he has some news that he thinks will please you. I can take you to him. We need to hurry." The boy stood waiting for her answer.

Alya looked at the boy. About ten years old she guessed. He was clearly nervous. She considered her options. Karu knew where she was but she had already assumed that. And maybe it was something important. Maybe it was something she needed to do.

"Okay," she said and stepped out of the doorway and into the street. The boy turned and hurried off. Alya followed him.

After a few minutes it was clear to Alya where they were headed: toward the main temple complex.

Three blasts of a trumpet sounded, echoed from the distance ahead. It was the signal for people to gather at the temple, normally for ceremonies or announcements. It had been so for many generations. What would it mean now?

The boy did not lead her to the temple forecourt but instead to a building on a side street where people could trade for things to eat and drink. Karu was standing there. He smiled when he saw her.

"I am so glad you have come! I was afraid..." he began.

"What do you want?" Alya interrupted him.

He indicated that they should move into the building, away from people standing around. She followed him.

"I am so sorry about the other day, about our argument," he said.

Alya stood listening with her arms folded on her chest and her face stern. There was no one near them now. It was private between them.

"Later I thought about it," he continued, "about what you said, and I thought about how I would feel if I were in your place. What I mean is that I understand about your wanting to be able to say no when asked to be owned by a man," he paused, collecting himself. "Even if that man is me."

Alya just stood there saying nothing. So far there was nothing for her to say, to answer or to ask.

"So I talked to Landran and the others about it. I told them that I think that it is a good idea to allow women to refuse when they are asked by a man. Otherwise there may be a lot of problems."

"And they agreed?" she asked, surprised.

"Well yes, they did agree after a while. But they said that the woman would have to have some reason, some good reason, to refuse."

Alya was thoughtful. "Okay, but that does not explain why you want me to be here with you now. Why did you send the boy to get me and tell him we should hurry? What do you need me for?"

"In a few minutes Landran and the others will make the announcement about the new rule of each woman belonging to a man. You heard the call to assemble. Just to make it more understandable for everyone, he wanted there to be a demonstration as to how it will work. The main part is that – in front of everyone – he will ask Theria to be his woman.."

"Theria! The Theria that is on the Council?" asked Alya in shock, interrupting him.

"Yes, that Theria," answered Karu.

"But she would never agree!"

"There you are wrong. As I tried to tell you the other day there are different ways to see this change. And the truth is that Theria has already agreed. Being the woman of an important man like Landran she will be able to do a lot of good – she can influence decisions, she can make things better for our people – of that I am sure."

"And be important herself," added Alya.

"Yes, that too," agreed Karu.

"But that still does not explain why I am here," she repeated. "What do you need me for?"

"Well, I told Landran that I had asked you to be my woman – he had asked me about it when he saw the scratches on my face – and so I had to tell him that I had asked you but that you had refused. Then that started the discussion again about if women could refuse. And then it was agreed that a woman could refuse if she had a good reason."

"Okay, but one more time: why am I here?"

"After Landran has explained the new rule to everyone and he and Theria together announce that she will be his woman, Landran thought it would be good for you and I to be there as an example for everyone of how it works for a woman to refuse – of how it can work."

Alya did not like the sound of this at all. She shook her head in disbelief and just wanted to get away, to escape. She looked for the best way past him out of the shop and thought about where she could run to after that. And wondered if he would try to stop her or if he would chase after her.

"I don't want to do that. I don't want to be any part of this. I don't trust it," she said.

Two trumpet blasts, very close, filled the air. It was almost time to begin.

"There is nothing to be worried about, Alya. I asked Landran if something would happen to you, some kind of punishment, and he said no, not at all. And don't you see, this is what you wanted – for women to have a choice. I thought you would be grateful for this chance."

He is really deep into this madness, isn't he, thought Alya to herself. She weighed her options, gathered her courage.

"Okay, I will do it," she said.

Karu smiled, took her arm and led her out of the shop in the direction of the temple forecourt.

The Announcement

Many people were already assembled on the temple forecourt. Karu pushed his way forward, elbowing through them, with Alya's right arm still in his grip. Then they were through and standing in the first row of the half-circled assembly.

Landran was standing in the center with two of his men beside him – left and right – and the other traders in the background. Behind him on the square stone was not the flower or food offering that usually stood there when there was a ceremony. Instead there was the lower trunk and root, dark and polished, from a small tree. Looking at it, Alya realized it was like a penis standing erect on the root ball.

Landran had taken some care in his personal preparations. His wild hair was tied back in a bun and his beard had been trimmed. His vest and skirt were of foreign material with gold-colored patterns. It looked strange to Alya but was clearly meant to signal that he was someone important.

Landran gave a sign with his arm and the trumpet now sounded once.

He looked around at the people gathered, nodding to himself, bestowing approval.

"Thank you all for coming here today," he said, surprisingly. He opened his arms wide, raised them.

"Today is a very important day for you all, the people of this beautiful island, because today marks the end of the painful darkness that has held you in its grip for much too long. The end of starvation when there was plenty to eat all around you. The end of mindless submission to old beliefs and rules that have no place in the new world that is arising now. And most importantly, the end of the incompetent leaders that have misled you and have been responsible for your suffering."

Landran looked around at the audience. These were not new words, thought Alya to herself. Based on what she had heard he had been saying the same things for some time but in smaller circles. Now it was being made official. She looked around at the crowd herself: women and men, old and young. No one turned and left. No one shouted out a challenge. What she saw on many faces, men and women alike, was a mixture of fear and hope.

"What we have shared with you before is that my men and I are the representatives of an important god that has been neglected in your prayers and neglected in your offerings. I am of course speaking of Father Ocean, he who rules the mighty ocean, whose kingdom is all around you. Too long you have neglected his rules, ignored his commands. Instead you have followed Mother Ocean and enthroned her in your temples. But as you have seen yourselves, Mother Ocean has turned her back on you – there is no more rain, no more fertility in your crops – to the point where you have even stopped having babies. But after so long wandering in darkness I am telling you that there is another better way." He looked around at the audience.

"Continue following the path your old leaders have found for you and you will all simply die, your people will die, and be forgotten. Is that what you want?"

There were shaking heads and sounds of No, that is not what we want. Landran nodded again.

"So listen and you will yourselves understand the path you must take to prosperity and freedom."

Landran motioned to someone in the crowd. Theria came forward and stood at his side. She did not look happy but she was composed and ready with a dignified posture and perfectly trimmed and combed hair.

"As I said, today is a very important day in the progress of the community here. Today we throw off the old worn ways of the past in which the mother, the woman, was the leader in everything and men were her unwilling servants.

"Did this ever make any sense? Men are stronger, are better able to provide for the people and are better able to defend them than women. So what have you been doing all these many generations? I will tell you: it was a senseless clinging to the world of children who are dependent on their mothers when they are young. Nothing more than that.

"So as of today, each woman must be under the responsibility of a man who will care for her, provide for her and their children, and protect them from whatever dangers arise. This is Father Ocean's command, which he has given to us so that we can share it with you.

"This is a big change, we know. And it will take some time. But it begins today. Theria, who was on your Council, has come forward to help me demonstrate how it will work. Please pay attention."

He turned to face Theria. "Theria, you are a beautiful and talented woman. I am impressed by how you have carried your responsibilities in the past. But it is clear now that those responsibilities have been too much for you and the people have lost their way.

"I offer you my support and protection, for you and all your children, as well as the children we will have together.

"Do you accept my request that you be my woman?"

Theria paused, then answered simply, "Yes."

Landran put his right arm around her, pulled her closer to him and helped her turn to face the crowd.

"So, you all see how simple it is to embrace the future and to begin to build our new better life together one person at a time.

"And one among us, Leotes, has learned in a foreign land to magically record important things on tablets of clay so that they are not forgotten. So whenever a man chooses a woman Leotes will be told the name of the woman and what man has chosen her so he can write it onto a tablet. Leotes, show the people the magic tablets."

Leotes, one of the traders, came from the rear and held up a clay tablet still glistening from moisture. He looked at it and then said very loudly, "Theria has been chosen by Landran as his woman." Then stepped back out of the way. Landran nodded vigorously.

"We had planned for that to be the end of our announcements for today, but yesterday Karu came to me and told me that he had asked Alya to be his woman – he already knew what our new approach would be. For those of you who know Karu, you know what a strong, intelligent man he is with extraordinary skills in working with stone. Clearly a man with a future among us. Come here, please, can you Karu?"

Karu walked to the center. Theria used the chance to disappear into the crowd. Karu was nervous but also not disliking the attention. Landran placed him at his right with a hand on his shoulder.

"And after talking with Karu it was clear that for the new system to work smoothly in all cases a woman must have the possibility of refusing to belong to a man. I think we can all understand that, that a man might be unsuitable for her for various reasons. So, we have decided that a woman can refuse a man who has chosen her as his woman. But she must tell him her reason to refuse him – so that he can improve himself, for example.

"So to let you all know how that can work we have asked the woman that Karu asked and who refused him to be here with us today. Alya, can you come here as well?"

Alya reluctantly made her way to the center. Stood to Karu's right. Faced the crowd.

"Let's show everyone how it works. Karu, go ahead and ask her."

"Alya, will you be my woman, that I may care for you and protect you and our children?"

"Good, good," said Landran. "And now Alya you must answer."

Alya hesitated. Drew in a breath, then answered, "No, I will not be your woman."

The tension in the crowd was palpable. No one breathed.

"Now, Karu, you need to ask her her reason and she must answer."

"Why will you not be my woman?"

Alya hesitated, struggling to answer. She had not thought this part through. She realized there was nothing that she could criticize or refuse about Karu himself. Should she tell the truth? Karu had promised there would be no punishment. And someone needed to tell the truth.

"I will not be his woman because I think it is wrong for one person, whether man or woman, to own another person, whether man or woman." There, it was said.

"Oh my, my my!" said Landran in a relaxed way. "It does seem like we have a problem here. We can understand – and accept! – that a woman would not want to be owned by a man because there is some weakness or fault in him. But it is something else entirely for a woman to refuse to be owned by a man because she refuses to accept the new way of things, the new order of society, that every woman should be owned by a man. That is a serious attack on our principles, on the foundation of the new society that we are constructing, that Father Ocean has commanded us to build.

"For such a serious attack on our new way of life, I am afraid there must be serious consequences, very serious consequences." He shook his head sadly then looked at Alya in a penetrating way.

He motioned for Alya to stand facing him. She did so.

"Alya, I understand that all of this is very new for you and you probably did not realize what a deep offense your words were for Father Ocean, to refuse him, to refuse his support and protection in the form of his representative on earth, a man. Am I right?"

Alya panicked: it was a trap, after all. She had to choose now, whether to tell the truth or to try to stay alive. She made her choice.

"You are right, I did not understand how serious it was."

"And do you understand now?"

"Yes, I understand now."

"Good, very good," said Landran. He surveyed the audience then looked back to Alya.

"And do you promise to never say such things again?"

Alya nodded.

"What?"

"I will never say such things again," Alya said quietly.

"Louder, please!"

"I will never say such things again," repeated Alya.

"I am relieved. I am truly relieved.

"But perhaps we need to make sure you keep your promise. Close your eyes."

Alya was shaking with fear. She closed her eyes.

Landran reached behind him with his right hand for the phallic tree and root. In one swift motion he brought it up and across as a club and smashed it into Alya's left jaw crushing the bones and knocking her to the ground.

"Stop!" called out Karu, "you promised she would not be punished!"

"That was before we realized how serious her crime was," answered Landran laconically.

He raised the club to strike again. Karu moved forward and grabbed Landran's right arm. Landran struggled for a moment but Karu's two arms were stronger than Landran's right.

With his left hand Landran pulled a stone knife from his belt and slid it deep into Karu's solar plexus. Karu struggled then fell.

Landran used the club to deliver a second savage blow to Alya's head, crushing the skull.

Landran looked around at the horrified audience. He placed the phallic club back on the stone block. He wiped the knife blade on his skirt and placed the knife back into his belt. He looked again at the audience, surveyed them from left to right, peering into each face.

"So, we have learned more lessons today than were planned. Most important is that Father Ocean does not allow challenges to his rules or to his representatives to go unpunished.

"And so I can announce today one more thing we had planned for later. You men," he pointed to four of the trader men. "Take the bodies of these two to the ocean. Cut them into pieces and throw the pieces to the fish for food. "

The men moved to take the bodies away.

"And that is another new commandment: whoever defies Father Ocean's rules or his representatives will be killed, their bodies cut up and the pieces thrown to the fishes.

"No longer will the bones of these disbelievers be laid in a holy place under the earth for their souls to be received by the ancestors. For those who defy Father Ocean's laws, who defy his representatives, their bodies will be sacrificed to feed Father Ocean's children. Only then, when his children are fed by the fresh blood of sacrifice, will Father Ocean send the rains again. And because they support this sacrifice, those in the community who are faithful to him will be welcomed to eat as much as they need of the fruits of the sea. For that is the rule of life: sacrifice brings bounty, without first giving there can be no taking."

Landran walked quickly away.

The crowd stood for some moments buzzing with exclamations and mutterings then dispersed leaving the forecourt in huddled groups that hurried down the side streets.

Aftermath

Martyna and Lela stood looking at the two spirit forms, Alya and Karu, lying where their bodies had been on the blood-smeared stones. Eyes closed, slowly writhing in pain.

"What can we do?" asked Martyna after a while.

Lela sighed. "They are caught in the trauma of it all. And unlike you at the moment of your death they were unprepared."

Lela knelt by the side of Alya's struggling spirit.

"Alya?" she whispered gently. "Alya?"

She turned to Karu. "Karu? Karu?"

There was no indication that either of them had heard.

Time passed. Lela and Martyna waited. The surrounding temple forecourt scene faded, grew indistinct and disappeared.

And then there was movement. Karu's spirit, still lying, became aware of Alya's spirit near him. He moved slowly toward her, reaching out to her. His hand found her hand. Her hand took his. Their bodies pulled together. They were lying arm in arm, pressed against each other, still struggling in their nightmare. But together.

Lela knelt and put a hand on the heads of each one of the two. She closed her eyes and bent her head forward.

After a while Lela stood up.

"Their journey forward now is clear and beyond their control or our influence. Their entanglement is so deep that nothing now can stop it or impede it. It must all play out."

Martyna looked at Lela. "Alya tried to find you when she came to Tarxien but could not. Where were you? Why weren't you here to stop this from happening?"

Lela sighed. "Do you really want to know?"

"Yes."

"Some days ago three of Landran's men followed me at night. They caught me, killed me and cut up the body. Then threw the pieces into the ocean there at the end of the island as the tide was going out. The next day they pretended to be looking for me by asking people where I was. And when I could not be found they spread the rumor that I had run away because I was afraid of them."

Martyna nodded understanding. "But you were still here in spirit, as you are now. Alya reached out for you in her prayers yesterday. But you did not come to her, did not give her a sign. You did not intervene. Why not?"

"Sometimes it is best to leave people on their own even when they ask for help. It may be a way for them to find out who they really are. I can assist in some cases but the choices are for each one to make for themselves."

"I see. Maybe I can even understand that a little.

"But what happens now?" asked Martyna. "It all seems so hopeless. So dark. For them and for their people. For this world."

Lela did not answer. She waited. She looked at the spirits of Alya and Karu which were now more peaceful as they lay together. Their apparent bodies became more and more translucent.

She looked at Martyna. "So, have you seen enough now of your past lives? Are you ready to choose your own way forward?"

"No, I want to know what happens to them next. I want to know how they go forward. Is that possible?"

"It will again be painful for you but if you really want to accompany them you can."

"I really want to. It is their story but it is my story as well."

Lela nodded. "Then kneel by them and place your hands on them. Join with them. Pray for them. Pray for the selves you have been."

Martyna knelt. She placed her hands on their heads. She prayed. She stood up.

Lela waited as the two spirit bodies on the ground slowly faded and then disappeared. She turned to Martyna. "Come now, we have done what we could do. Take my hand."

West of Mount Kilamanjaro in Africa
640 C.E.

Waking Up

Niwana opened her eyes. Above her was only darkness but when she turned her head to the right she could see the first gray traces of morning light around the edges of the cloth that hung over the door to the hut. She was exactly in time!

Her twin brother Timo was lying next to her with his head nuzzled against her left shoulder and his left arm loose across her belly, still deep asleep. She hesitated before she woke him, paying attention to how it felt to wake up next to him in the early morning. Soon there would be no more of this. As soon as her woman's blood started it would be the absolute end of her living here with her parents. The other girls that were as old as she was, twelve, had all already moved into the single women's house even when their blood had not started. They liked it there. They could not understand why Niwana clung to staying at home as long as she did, like a child. And Niwana did not tell them.

She and Timo could not wait too long to get up this morning – if their father came in from having stood the night watch before they had made their escape their day would be ruined. Niwana had worked out their plan the day before. Since Timo was almost a man their mother Mira could no longer tell him what he could or could not do. Timo could just leave and go out into the hills for whatever reason he wanted as long as only their mother was around. Mira feared what might happen to Timo alone in the hills. But Mira had a lot of faith in Niwana. So if Timo went then her mother would allow Niwana to go with him; she might even insist that she go.

If their father Farah were here when they tried to leave it would be a very different story: Timo would be sent off to study with the other boys his age who were already living in the single men's house and he would have to stay with them the whole day. Niwana would have no choice but to spend the morning dying cloth with the other girls her age with her grandmother as her teacher. Her mother had reminded her about it the day before. In itself that would not be so bad: Niwana loved the textures, colors and patterns, especially when she could make them look like animals in the finished cloth. But to go into the hills today with Timo would be much more exciting.

Niwana found Timo's cheek with her right hand and brushed it lightly with a fingertip. Timo did not react so she tried it again. Finally he roused himself enough to bring his free hand up to his face. Instead of finding the fly that he expected he found his sister's hand

and without waking took her hand in his. Niwana moved her hand from his and then gently squeezed his nose closed between her fingers.

"Hey!" He woke quickly, gasping for air. "Stop that!"

Niwana did not answer. She rolled over to the right supporting herself on her elbows.

The next voice was that of their mother from the mat near them in the hut.

"Niwana, you leave your brother alone! It's not right for a girl to treat a boy like you do, even if he is your brother."

Niwana did not answer. How she treated her brother was an old complaint in the family. But she did not care what anybody said or thought. It was something between them.

"Mama, can you fix us something to eat now? We are really hungry," said Timo, fully awake now, in an exaggerated way.

Then he broke out laughing uncontrollably as if it was some kind of joke. Niwana also began to laugh. They both laughed and laughed for some moments as if being hungry was the funniest thing in the world.

"Okay," said Mira, slowly and a little suspicious. "I had thought we would wait to eat until your father gets back from standing watch. But he has been in such a bad mood lately maybe it would be more fun if we ate now, just us."

The twins sat up and clapped their hands together in glee – the plan was working.

Mira laughed with them, got up, and prepared their breakfast. Their good mood was infectious even though she did not understand it. She was spoiling them terribly these days. The hut would soon feel very empty with just her and Farah.

She had always hoped for more children. Niwana and Timo had been her first. It had been very difficult for all three of them – a first birth with twins and Mira so young still, only a girl really. Luckily Farah's mother Mitwa who was the midwife for the village was there to help. Otherwise it could have been much worse. They all three survived the birth but something had broken in her and she was never again pregnant. For years she had expected Farah to take another wife. It was an embarrassment for an important man like him to have only two children. She would have not minded; helping care for the new children that would come with the new wife – who would probably be young and not know much – sounded like fun to her. Maybe now that their children were leaving their hut Farah would finally do it. The thought pleased her. It gave her something to look forward to and offset her sadness that her children were leaving.

Fear

Farah stood at the crest of the earth mound at the center of the village stockade. From here he was higher than the stockade walls and had a view of the surrounding countryside in all directions. Right now there was not much to see on the ground as it was still dark. Overhead the dome of brilliant patterned stars still dominated the sky. They were especially bright on a moonless night like tonight had been.

He closed his eyes and breathed the damp early morning air into his chest slowly through his nose. The smells of the village and its surroundings came to him: the cattle now stirring in the compound, the greenness of the bushes that grew near their water source, the dark moistness of the source itself, the smoke of the first early dung fires, the dusky smell of the people of his village, and the dry hills of earth and stone in all directions. There was nothing unusual or dangerous to be found.

Farah opened his eyes and stretched his neck. He scanned the eastern horizon where a line of orange light now emerged from the darkness along the southern edge of the mountain.

He heard someone approaching and turned to see Ajuba coming up the south side of the small hill, walking slowly, his white grizzled hair shining in the predawn light.

Farah shifted the watch spear from his right hand to his left hand.

Ajuba came to stand before Farah. He paused for a moment then with a slight bow held out his right hand. Farah shifted the watch spear to Ajuba's hand and made his own slight bow. His watch was now over and the morning watch had begun.

"How was the night?" Ajuba asked.

Farah was surprised at Ajuba's question and at first did not know how to answer. What could he say about the night? He felt his jaw tighten as the truth of the night rose from his belly and forced itself through his throat and into his mouth.

"I was afraid," he heard himself say. He looked down at the ground between them.

Stooping over and looking up the shorter Ajuba peered into Farah's face, trying to see in the dim light what might be written there. Farah had been in the first group of boys that Ajuba had led through their manhood initiation many years before. Farah had grown into a good man who carried his responsibilities well. He took excellent care of his cattle, was faithful to his family and was generous to those in need. And now Farah was afraid.

What terrible times we live in, Ajuba thought to himself.

"I know," was what he said to Farah.

And he did know. He had felt the fear come into the village in the night just as he had in the other nights since the last full moon began to die. But he did not know what he was afraid of.

Ajuba put his left hand on Farah's shoulder and smiled. "Interesting times, huh?" he said, cocking his head to the side.

Farah did not respond, still looking down at the ground between them, struggling with the shame of having been afraid.

"The world is a surprising place; if you think you understand it you are stupid!" Ajuba quipped with an old adage.

He squeezed Farah's shoulder and gave him a friendly push. "Go now and see what your woman has waiting for you!" he said.

Farah looked up now, thankful for the graceful way that Ajuba had helped him save face.

A large red and black cock came out of a roosting hut as Farah came down the hill. The cock scratched and pecked in the dust for a moment then ruffled its feathers. It turned to face the east, raised its beak to the dark sky, drew in its breath decisively, and crowed long and loudly. Paused, crowed again. It cocked its head sideways at Farah as he passed. Farah nodded his respects.

Farah did not return directly to his own hut. Mira and the children are probably still asleep, he thought to himself. No reason to wake them yet. He had another destination in mind: the hut of his mother, Mitwa. Since his father had been killed two years before in a lion hunt everyone had expected Mitwa to leave the hut they had shared and join the other widows in the single women's house since her husband had had no brother to take her in. But she had not done that, saying she still had too much to do and the other women only wanted to gossip. Farah found her hut flap already tied open at this early hour with a fire going inside and his mother busily pounding some kind of plant in a stone bowl by the firelight.

"Greetings, honored Mother," he said in a respectful way as he came to the door of the hut. "May I come in?"

It was after all his mother's hut and no longer his home. She was a woman with many moods; it paid to approach her carefully if you wanted something from her.

"Oh, hello Farah! Good to see you. Of course you can come in. Is it alright if I work while we talk? I have to get these dyes ready for the young girls to use this morning. Which reminds me, when will Niwana be moving into the single women's house? It isn't right for her to wait so long, even if she doesn't have her blood yet. And running around with Timo all the time instead of being with the other girls, that's also not right! People are talking you know. Mira told me she agreed with me but you held back for some reason. My father certainly wouldn't have let me hang around the family hut when I was her age, I will tell you that!"

Mitwa pounded the plant fibers savagely several times as if to make her point with so much effort going into it that she had to stop speaking. Nothing in her bearing indicated she wanted or expected an answer from Farah. That was just how she was.

Farah had spent the early years of his life wondering how she did it – how did she know anything when she spent all of her time talking? But she did know some things; that was why he was here. One had to wait until she noticed you were there and waiting, which required patience. So he sat silently. It did not take as long as he had expected.

Mitwa actually stopped her pounding. She put the stone down on the edge of the bowl and rotated her large body to face Farah.

"Son, what is it?" she asked. "You've come here for something serious I know and not just to watch me pound red dye root, right? So what is it?"

Farah realized this was going to be harder than he had thought. He searched for words. To his surprise his mother simply waited without saying anything. Maybe he had misjudged her. Then he knew what he had to say.

"Mother, I am worried about Timo. If father were here I could talk to him about it but he isn't here so I talk to you. To put it simply I am afraid that Timo will have difficulty to become a man. He is always with Niwana and pays no attention to the other boys except to Sura. And I am afraid that Sura is only Timo's friend because Sura is hot for Niwana. When Niwana goes into the single women's house I am not sure of what will happen. I am afraid Timo will break in some way. If we do the normal thing and send Timo into the single men's house I fear they will treat him as a weakling and refuse to honor him. Do you have any ideas of what I can do? Or what someone else can do? I have not talked to anyone about this. For a father to doubt that his son can become a man is terrible. If Timo found out I felt this way it would shame him beyond measure. Have you anything to tell me or advise me?"

Mitwa paused for a moment considering her answer.

"Farah, I have no idea what your father would have said if you had asked him this. He saw the world through a man's eyes and I see it through a woman's heart. I can't answer in his place – that would be wrong. This is a man thing you are asking about. I think you can trust Ajuba about it. Why don't you ask him?"

It was a good answer, Farah knew, but for today it wasn't enough.

"I know, Mother," he answered. "But I can't bring myself to ask Ajuba, I just can't. I've tried, believe me, but it would be somehow like letting him down, like letting everybody down."

"I'm sorry, Son, but then it looks like this is one problem you will have to work out for yourself," responded Mitwa quietly after another pause.

She waited when he said nothing in response and then continued with more force in her voice.

"And if I may say so it seems to me that *you* are the one with the real problem, not Timo, and not – above all – Niwana. Figure out what is troubling you and maybe Timo will be okay. I can tell you that much, from a woman's point of view, without crossing the line into men's things."

Farah was stunned by her words. He had come to ask for help with Timo, her grandson, and she attacked him personally instead of giving him a useful answer. There was nothing for him here. He had been wrong in coming to talk to her, wrong to tell her of his concern for Timo, wrong again as he had always been wrong in her eyes. Rising quickly he stood and left her hut without another word. He felt the fear again that he had felt in the night, mixed now with shame, making him feel weak and vulnerable and sick in his belly. It was a terrible feeling, the worst he had ever known.

Dancing

Niwana always got a special surge of excitement when she moved out of sight of the high stake walls of the compound. Their plan had worked and they were free for the day just to be together.

"Come, let's race," she said to Timo who was walking beside her. She broke into a fast run before he had a chance to answer. Her bare feet found just the right landing places in all this jumble of rock, thorny brush and dry sandy soil even though she did not seem to look down. Her legs were longer than his, as she was somewhat taller than he was. But that did not explain how she did what she did. He was always amazed by it, this ability to run that she had. Other boys their age could probably run faster or longer, he thought. There had never been a contest between the other boys and her to find out – that would be unthinkable. But he had never seen anyone run with such ease.

Timo looked around before he decided what to do. If she wanted to race, he would race. But he did not want anyone to see what he knew would be the natural outcome: she was faster than he was and had always been. He started running in a halfhearted way. She was already far ahead of him flying over the rough brushy ground. In his reverie, watching her run, his left foot touched a thorn bush and he got a painful thorn in the side of his foot. He paused to pull it out while it was still fresh. She raced on ahead. It was not so important if he lost sight of her – he knew where she was going. When he had the thorn out he walked onward rather than running. She had won again. That's just how it was.

"You are so slow!" she teased when he finally arrived at their secret place.

It was a dry hollow depression near the top of a small hill, about 10 paces across at the bottom. When you were down inside it no one could see you unless they climbed up the small hill. There were thick bushes all around, two dried out acacia trees on the south side and a ring of dried elephant grass. In the middle was only sand. Maybe once there had been water here, explaining the ring of bushes and grass plants, but there was no trace of water now and all but the largest bushes were dried up. They had discovered it a year before and came here from time to time when they could get away from the village.

She stood up from the flattened grassy area under the larger of the two trees where she had been resting. Niwana had her hands on her hips and was smiling at him. She had always been thin but her body had been filling out the last year; she had breasts now and under the band of decorated cloth she had wrapped around her waist her hips were widening. Timo looked at her as she stood there and had to swallow hard. She was the most beautiful thing he had ever seen.

"Are you ready? Can we start now?" she asked.

"No, I'm tired. I have to rest. And we need to talk," he said and lay down on his back on the flattened grass next to where she had been.

He had been so happy about their plan to be together for the day and then surprised when it had worked – Niwana was so smart! But now that they were here the old difficulties became very present for him.

"What is there to talk about?" she asked and lay down by him on her side looking at him.

"You know what," he declared angrily. "These things that I've been teaching you from what I learn in the boy's lessons – I shouldn't be doing it. It's wrong!" He rolled away from her onto his side.

"And why is it wrong?" she asked in a patient voice.

"You know I can't tell you that – it's just wrong, that's all. It's the way the world works, the way our people have always done things. If we don't follow the rules terrible things will happen!"

"Are you sure?" she asked quietly.

"Yes, I am sure," he answered.

"Then why have you been teaching me the things you have been teaching me this last year?"

"Because I can't say no to you; I have never been able to. I don't know why." He tried hard not to cry. She put her hand on his shoulder and waited for him to work through it. They had had similar conversations several times.

After a while Niwana got up, walked over to the densest dried bushes and pulled two wooden spears from their hiding place.

"The spears are still here," she said.

She crouched down sitting on her heels holding one spear upright in each hand, the blunt ends resting on the sand, waiting for him.

The spears were short – only about as long as the children were tall – but from strong dense wood sharpened then hardened with fire and tree sap on one end. Timo had "borrowed" them from the weapons shed next to the single men's hut. Sometimes these training spears were used for throwing exercises, even though they were not weighted like real throwing spears, so it was possible that some would get lost, he had told himself. His silence when Ajuba had asked the boys where the two missing spears could be had been a terrible pain for him. He had not expected that Ajuba kept such a close watch on boy's training spears, so it had been a shock when the question came. He was sure that Ajuba sensed that he was not telling all he knew but for some reason the old man accepted that Timo knew something about the spears but would not tell him. For Timo it had been just one more mark of shame in his growing accumulation.

After a while Timo slowly rose and stood facing Niwana. She stood up and held out the spear in her left hand to him. As if in a dream he stepped toward her and took the spear then stepped back. As always he could not believe he was doing it, but here he was, as if practicing the two-person spear dance with a girl was the most natural thing in the world.

He went into the opening crouching position, his right hand under the middle balancing point of the spear, raising it so it was parallel with the ground, pointing toward Niwana's chest. His left hand hung free but away from his body, a counter-balance. In the real dance they would have shields to carry but in the early training phases you did the dance without shields, so that was okay as he had explained to her. Niwana mirrored his movements going into the crouch, balancing her spear in her right hand, pointing it at his chest, her left hand free as a counterweight. She smiled at him; the pleasure of this forbidden play was sweet to her.

And Timo smiled back. The moment he was in position he also felt the power and mystery of the dance flow into his body. Having a girl across from him instead of Sura or one of the other boys that was usually there when they practiced would have been impossible with any girl except Niwana. But with her it felt exactly right.

They had no drummer so Timo had to sound out the rhythm with his voice. It was also the way the boys practiced sometimes, so it was not so unusual. Niwana had wanted everything to be just the way it was when the boys did it.

"Tam, tam, ta-ta-tam; tam, tam, ta-ta-tam; tam, tam, ta-ta-tam; Tam TAM" he began the rhythm sequence, then repeated it over and over as they worked their way deeper and deeper into trance.

For the first three measures they circled left, moving their feet and bodies to the rhythm, keeping the spears held high and pointed at each other. On the last loud TAM of the fourth measure they both thrust hard with their spears at the chest of their partner, simultaneously springing to their right in the circle. The rules were that you thrust hard at where your partner had been standing at the moment of the second loud TAM and took no advantage of the fact that you knew which way he was going to jump to avoid your spear. That it was symmetric gave it a special beauty. The reality of the spears and their sharpened points made for plenty of excitement and helped one concentrate.

The dance was a distilled expression of the tall warrior's creed: consummate skill in hand-to-hand fighting, fearlessness in the face of danger, and absolute trust in your fellow warrior.

It is a dance about following the rules, thought Timo to himself, with the small part of his mind that was not involved in the dance. And here I am dancing it but breaking all the rules.

The dance was performed as a public contest on festival days by the warriors of their village, with real drumming of course. A jury of old men decided which pair of warriors won. Points were given for the symmetry and smoothness of the dancing and for the ferociousness of the spear jabs. The best pairs of warriors had added synchronized high-jumps, yells, and reverse-circling to make it more exciting for themselves and the audience.

Niwana had been seeing the dance regularly her whole life. It represented everything for her that was beautiful and dangerous and grown-up and controlled by men. So it had been the natural first thing for her to pressure Timo into teaching her. Why had he agreed to it, in the end? Why did he continue with it? Niwana herself did not know, though she had from time to time asked herself this question. And perhaps today would be the last time they would do this together. She had solemnly promised Timo that as soon as she got her woman's blood, and became a woman, she would give up the dance and everything he had taught her for good. It had been just a child's game, then, and not real. This was how she could explain it to herself and to him.

She noticed that she was losing her concentration and so focused more on the dance. Her mind emptied and there was nothing in her whole world except Timo's chanting voice and the circling and lunging movements of their bodies. It was wonderful.

Farah and Mira

The door flap on Farah's hut was tied open when Farah arrived there. Mira was busy preparing barley bread to cook on the fire for him to eat and singing softly to herself. The bed blankets were already folded and put away. This surprised him – usually the twins would have still been here and the family would have eaten together.

"Where are the twins?" he asked.

Mira broke off her singing, turned from her work, and looked at him. "What is wrong?" she asked.

"I just asked where the twins are," he answered, an edge in his voice, staring at her.

"They got up early and have already gone out to play," she answered, then lowered her eyes from his steady gaze. It made no sense to try to talk to him about the problems with Niwana when he was in this state. And it would only worry him more if he knew they had gone out into the hills.

"Are you hungry?" she asked instead.

"No," he answered and sat down on the sitting mat abruptly without looking at her.

She came over and sat down behind him, her arms around him, her head on his shoulder, the food she had been preparing for him forgotten.

"You must be tired," she said, then sat back and began to massage his shoulders and neck.

He closed his eyes, his head falling forward, feeling now just how tight his neck and shoulders had become through the long night.

He raised his head, again looking into space as if for answers.

"I was..., it is..." he tried to tell her how the night had been, how the fear felt in his body. He was desperate to talk to someone. But the words would not come.

She moved around to sit opposite him, looking into his face, looking into his eyes. She put a finger on his lips and shook her head slightly side to side.

"You don't need to tell me," she said softly. She brought her hands back to her sides. He looked into the fire, not meeting her gaze.

She got up, walked to the hut opening and pulled loose the knot that held the door covering open. It slid closed. She walked over and unfolded their sleeping blanket and spread it out on the ground. She took his simple loin cloth off him and set it aside. Then she unwrapped and set aside the cloth she wore around her waist. She lay down in front of him and pulled him down to her on the sleeping blanket.

Sura

A cow waiting in the corral for its turn in the morning water distribution mooed plaintively, impatience in its voice. The other cows stood silent but expectant, clustered facing the corral gate.

Sura had watering duty this morning. He took the greased leather watering bucket from the hook by the corral and carried it to the source at the far edge of the stockade where the two hills came together. He used the long cantilevered hoist there to bring the water up from deep in the earth. Then he poured the water carefully into the watering bucket until it reached the mark that had been decided. It was not as much as the cows would want but it would keep them alive. As he returned to the corral with the bucket the cows crowded around, each trying to get ahead of the others. He unhooked the corral gate, squeezed in, and latched the gate closed behind him. He picked a cow and put the bucket down in front of her, fending off the others with his free hand. Once it was clear that a cow had been selected the others waited patiently, confident from long habit that they would get their turn. He had to hold the bucket steady while the cow drank or she would knock it over. He understood her eagerness: it would be all the water she would get this day.

The watering was routine for Sura; his thoughts wandered. The subject that occupied his thoughts these days was Timo's sister Niwana. Although she still lived in the hut with her parents and Timo she was almost a woman now. Sura had first noticed her years before when they were both small children. She fascinated him though he did not know why. The way she laughed drove him crazy and he could never get enough of it. She was not like the other girls who were always running away from the boys and acting shy. She even played games with the boys sometimes, tagging along with Timo though it always got her into trouble with the adults. And so what would happen when the time came for choosing partners? Did he have a real chance with her? What reaction would he get from his parents when they found out he wanted Niwana? They had already warned him of his friendship with Timo, implying that there was something not right in Timo's family, telling him to have other friends too.

Sura lost control of the bucket as he daydreamed and the cow buffeted it trying to get the water at the bottom. The bucket fell over. He quickly caught it so that only some drops were lost. Luckily it had been almost empty. He looked up to see if anyone had seen his negligence. No one had seen. Water was so precious! The same cow that had mooed before mooed again, this time even more plaintively. He spoke to her.

"There is enough water for all of you, Keecha; no need to bellow!"

Reckoning

The sun had moved higher in the cloudless sky when Farah and Mira were awakened from their sleep. Sura was at the door flap speaking in an excited voice.

"Farah, Ajuba says for you to come to the front gate and bring your shield and spear. We have a visitor!"

"I am on my way," answered Farah through the flap.

Sura had volunteered to fetch Farah for Ajuba because it seemed a chance to meet up with Timo and maybe Niwana. Timo had not been with them at the boy's lessons that morning and so he had assumed they were for some reason still in their hut. But the sound of Farah's answer indicated that they were not there so he headed back to the main gate of the compound with the others who were gathering.

Farah stood up and wrapped and tied his loin cloth around himself. He took his spear and shield from their resting place on the wall beside the door flap then turned to face Mira who was still lying half-wrapped in their sleeping blanket, propped up on one elbow watching him. Their eyes met for a moment and he was gone out the door.

Mira got up and dressed herself quickly. As a woman she was not allowed to use or even touch men's weapons. But she selected a long blunt club used for softening leather hides from the women's tools in a basket at the back of the hut. She hefted the tool and gave it a test swing. Yes, it would do. Maybe she would find some leather that needed softening. She was full of worry for the twins – she should have told Farah that they were out of the compound somewhere in the hills. But she had not told him and she felt an instinctive panic about the situation. She decided to look by the water source; sometimes they played there. It was out of the question to go out into the hills to look for them. It would not be allowed, she sensed, and then she had no idea where they might have gone. From the feel of things this was no normal visitor since the men had to go to meet him armed. Farah had known something about some danger they were in these last few days. He had given her signals but had not told her anything specific. Men! They were always the same. So she had not known of the danger and had let the twins go into the hills! The more she thought about it the more upset Mira became.

When Farah joined them the men of the tribe were already outside the gate of the stockade standing in a line facing west, holding their spears and shields at the ready in a show of strength. He took his place to the left of Ajuba who was in the center of the long line. They were an imposing sight – forty trained warriors ready for whatever might come.

A short man without weapons stood across from them at a distance of a child's stone's throw. There were no other people in sight. The man's face was calm and showed no expression. His body and the carriage of his head were straight and dignified. Over his shoulders he wore a short cape of leopard skin with beaded tassels. On his head was a beaded leather cap. His skin was darker than that of Farah's people, his face rounder, and his body more muscular. In his arms he held the limp body of a small antelope. Over his right shoulder was a strap from which hung a large water gourd. By the way it hung it was clear that it was empty.

It was not the first time that Farah had seen this man: it was Rasta, the chief of the short people in this area. For him to come here alone without his attendants was very unusual. Farah understood now why Ajuba had summoned them all to meet him.

Rasta waited for some moments as if to make sure they had all arrived then began to speak in the trading language that all the tribes in this region used.

"I have come again as my people have come before to ask you to trade with us for water from your source. I offer this antelope in return. For many generations you have shared your water with us when times were difficult and our sources went dry. Our Ancestors tell us we should ask again that you share with us even though you have refused us before. We do not have much but we are ready to trade whatever we have for the water. Without the water we will die. Our children are already dying and our women are weeping. Please help us."

Rasta took several steps forward, bowed low, and placed the antelope on the ground and then the water gourd next to it. He stepped back and stood waiting for an answer.

Farah's outer expression was unwavering. But inside he was in turmoil. He knew the answer that Ajuba would now give. All the men of his village had discussed it together many times in the last moon cycles. The drought was so long and so severe that it seemed to them that if they shared the water from their source with the short tribes around them they themselves would run out of water and themselves die. Their only chance was to hold their water for themselves alone. If the Ancestors of the short people could not organize water for them then it was certainly not up to Farah's people to do it. Why should Farah's people risk their own lives and the lives of their women, children, and cattle to help strangers? It made no sense. But still Farah struggled with his feelings. He could sense the desperation in this proud man who had come to them in complete humility alone and begging. What courage there was in such an act! And he spoke of children dying. Farah thought of his children and of how desperate he would be if they were dying. But a decision had been taken and the Ancestors had agreed to it. There was nothing to be done.

Ajuba stepped forward. He bowed his upper body in respect.

"Rasta, we are honored by your presence here today. We thank you for your offer of trading for water. It is a fine antelope that you have brought, with a beautiful skin. But we ourselves are now running out of water and must use what little we have left to keep ourselves and our cattle alive. I am sorry that our answer must again be no. We cannot trade with you for water. May your Ancestors help you in your time of difficulty. May your people survive this test. We have spoken."

With this Ajuba bowed again and stepped backward to take his place in the line.

Rasta stood for a moment. He looked along the line of men opposite him, meeting their eyes. Then he turned and walked away quickly leaving the antelope and empty water gourd on the ground where he had placed them.

The line of men stood without moving or speaking until Rasta had disappeared over the edge of a hill. Then, at Ajuba's command, they began to file in two lines back into the stockade.

Within moments there was a shout of alarm from the last man entering the stockade. All now turned to look back out through the gate. Rasta had wasted no time. He was coming back over the crest of the hill where he had disappeared. He was not alone. Behind him and spreading out on both sides were many other warriors of the short people, all armed for battle, all moving silently toward the village stockade at a steady determined pace.

Farah felt a shock of awe at the audacity of the attack: Rasta had abandoned all advantage of surprise by coming first to ask to trade for water. With the warriors of Farah's village ready and alerted Rasta's warriors would have no chance. But as seconds passed Farah and the others began to realize that something unprecedented was happening. The number of warriors coming over the hill behind Rasta was clearly many more than from Rasta's own tribe or even of all the short people from the nearby tribes. There were short people warriors that had come long distances to fight here today behind Rasta. This was something that had never happened before.

"All of you inside. Close the stockade. Take your positions," ordered Ajuba.

Mira was the first to discover the cunning behind Rasta's plan. As she came to the area of the water source trying to find the twins she climbed the stockade to a watch perch to see if they were on the other side. She was startled to see instead a group of short black warriors, painted for fighting, carrying weapons as well as primitive ladders – trees with some limbs left on the sides – busy setting them up against the outside of the stockade wall. The stockade was two men's lengths high – no one had ever used ladders against it before in an attack. She let out an alarm cry. Village warriors who had been distracted by the attack on the gate came running and climbed up to their defensive positions on perches along the inside of the stockade. But even more quickly the short warriors began to climb their makeshift ladders and jump down over the top of the stockade into the compound.

Mira had still not found the twins. She headed for the front gate to look for Farah. It was slow going as she had to detour around the fighting that was now going on everywhere. She finally reached the line of huts facing the front gate.

It was chaotic there. The village warriors near the gate to the stockade were deep in hand-to-hand defense. The short people had brought up a battering ram made of the lower trunk of a single large tree with side branches left on as handles. They had come at a run and smashed through the stockade gate on the first try. Now the short warriors were pouring through the shattered gate. Many were being wounded or killed by the defenders but there were so many of them that their casualties made no difference.

Farah's people had the advantages of height, superior weapons, and a reputation as famous warriors that had always before enabled them to prevail in skirmishes or ritual combat. The stockade was their impregnable last defense. But now these advantages were not sufficient. They were outnumbered ten to one and had been outsmarted by Rasta's cunning tactics and superior numbers. They lost their confidence. The short warriors sensed this and shifted into a fighting frenzy that Farah's people could not match. Warrior after warrior of Farah's people fell, swarmed over and clubbed by short warriors.

By the time Mira found Farah he had abandoned his shield and was fighting with his jabbing spear in his right hand and a long club with a sharp stone lashed to its end in his left hand that he had taken from a fallen short warrior. He had his back to the stockade posts and was surrounded by a low wall of dead or wounded short warriors. His face was wild with the energy of the fighting.

"Farah!" shouted Mira when she saw him.

She was immediately grabbed by two short warriors who held her arms fast and wrested the blunt club from her hand. Farah, hearing her voice, looked for her and immediately saw her there. His concentration on the battle was broken. The short warriors in the half circle around him saw this change but stepped back instead of pressing the advantage.

The pause gave Farah a chance to look around. So far as he could see he was the last of his village's warriors standing. Every other village warrior in view was dead or dying. Those lying on the ground but only wounded were being methodically killed by blows to the head. The lifeless body of Ajuba lay not far from him. Short warriors no longer involved in the fighting were already rounding up women and children, tying their hands, and making them lie on the ground in rows. The sounds of the crying of the women and children had replaced the sounds of fighting. But between Farah and the short warriors there was a tense standoff.

Rasta came into view walking from the direction of the source. He approached the semicircle of men surrounding Farah. The men stepped back to open a path between Rasta and Farah. Some of the men helped wounded short warriors to move away from Farah.

"What is your name?" Rasta asked Farah.

Farah did not answer but simply glared back at him with his weapons at the ready. The men holding Mira tried to push her down to the ground so they could tie her but she resisted and again cried out. Farah could not help himself. He turned from eye contact with Rasta to see what was happening to her. Seeing this the men stopped trying to push her down and simply stood holding her. Farah saw an expression of fear and somehow expectation in Mira's face as she looked at him.

What does she expect from me? he asked himself, confused. Clearly their destiny now was to die.

Rasta noticed the exchanged looks. He turned and looked at Mira for a moment then back at Farah and spoke again.

"You may not believe me but I am in truth sorry for what has happened here today. We only wanted to live. We wanted our women and children to live. We wanted nothing more. You left us no choice but this painful stupidity."

He paused as if waiting for Farah to say something but Farah was only more confused. What could this talking be about? It must be a trick to get him to drop his guard like the other tricks that Rasta had used today.

"And now we have a new problem it seems," Rasta continued. "In their eagerness to get water for themselves too many of our warriors crowded around your source. Some fell in. The source walls of earth and stone all collapsed covering the men and filling it. There is no water for us now as well. We do not know the secret of making or keeping such a deep source. We have tried many times but have always failed. We will try to repair your source but my Ancestor's tell me that if we try it without help we will fail."

Rasta paused again as if waiting for Farah to say something. Farah was baffled. What was there that he could say to Rasta?

"You are clearly a great warrior whatever your name is," continued Rasta. "And you have a beautiful and powerful woman as well," he said pausing for an appreciative look at Mira. She tightened her face and spat on the ground in defiance.

Rasta looked back at Farah. He spoke loudly so that all those around could hear as well.

"We both need something – my people need water and you need to live. If you did not want to live you would not have fought so hard. I will make you a deal. If you will help us rebuild your source and teach us to care for it I will in exchange grant you and your family not only life but the freedom to do what you want, to go where you want, to stay here in this place or to leave. This is my solemn promise in the presence of all these people and my Ancestors. Consider carefully."

Mira's eyes grew wide and her mouth fell open as she grasped what Rasta was offering. Not just life but freedom for them as a family. Her body began to shake and she began to cry with thankfulness. There was a way out! Farah needed now only to accept it.

Farah was in a state of confusion. His heart was pounding more now from powerful emotions coming up in him then it had in the heat of combat. He was being asked to betray his solemn blood vow to never reveal the secrets of the source to anyone – to never betray the source of his people's wealth and power – to the very enemies who had just killed them! All of his conditioning over the years rose up in rage at the impossibility of this request. The outrage of his Ancestors at the insult of this choice shrieked in his ears. It was his duty to fight to the death to defend his people and his heritage and not to betray them!

Farah's body began to shake. His arms rose in jerks toward the sky still holding the spear and club. The momentum of generations of warriors surged through him obliterating any alternatives but duty and revenge.

"I will kill you all!" he screamed and charged at Rasta in full fury. The short warriors who leaped to protect Rasta were not quick enough or strong enough. Farah burst past them sending them flying with a wide sweep of the club in his left hand. He struck hard with the spear in his right. But Rasta had moved aside. Farah's spear found Rasta's left arm raised in defense and not his chest. Farah was immediately overwhelmed on all sides, stuck with spears and beaten with clubs until his body lay still.

Rasta climbed to his feet from where he had fallen. Staunching the bleeding from the wound in his left upper arm with his right hand he looked around the scene before him, at the piles of fallen warriors, and then shook his head.

"Today we take no slaves," said Rasta. "Let it be as the tall people's warrior said: kill them all. Kill the women and children too. They are a crazy and dangerous people. We may all die but they will die with us and the world will be free of them."

With that Rasta turned and walked past the piles of bodies through the shattered gate and out of the stockade. The sounds of killing and dying filled the air.

Return

Timo was tired from the dancing. He knew he had to stop soon or lose his concentration which could be dangerous. He called out the ending 'Tam! Tam! Tam!' after a particularly good pair of thrusts and jumps. He and Niwana dropped the spears on the ground and collapsed onto the flattened grassy area. It was in the shade now as the sun had moved further south. They lay side by side on the grass, chests still heaving with deep breaths from the exertion of the dance.

"You are really good," said Timo after awhile. "You are better than Sura for sure." She is good thought Timo. And maybe that is what she needs: to see herself as better than the boys.

"I have a good teacher," she answered simply and smiled at him.

Timo flushed with a mixture of pride and discomfort.

"This was the absolute last time," he said quietly and as seriously as he could.

She said nothing. Fear rose in him that she had tricked him and would not keep her word.

"You promised! And now is the time for you to keep your promise. I heard Mira tell Mitwa that you would be going into the single women's house – even if you don't have your blood yet – as soon as father agrees to it."

This was new information for her – that her father was the one they were all waiting on to decide what she had expected for a long time. What did that mean? she asked herself. But in the current moment she felt a wave of gratitude towards Timo. He had done a lot for her. Maybe it was his turn now to get what he wanted.

"Okay, it was the last time."

"Do you really mean it?" he asked, raising himself on his elbow and turning to her.

"Yes, I really mean it," she answered.

Timo lay back on the grass. His body relaxed and he smiled. He noticed he was thirsty. He was hungry as well.

"Shall we go back now?" he asked.

"Okay," she answered. "What shall we do with the spears?"

"We can take them back," he answered happily. "I can tell Ajuba and the others that we found them in the bushes where the boys had been practicing throwing before they were lost. Ajuba will not believe it – he is too smart for that. But the main thing is that the spears will be back where they belong."

71

Niwana gathered a heap of the dried grass they had been lying on by pulling it out of the ground with the roots from the sandy soil. She tied it in a bundle using some of the longer and stronger stalks. There was no reason not to. If someone asked what they had been doing the whole morning she could at least answer that she had been gathering grass for the cows. She hoisted the large bundle high on her back wrapping supporting strands of the strong grass in each hand to hold it there. She stood waiting for Timo to decide the moment when they would leave. This was a new thing for her – to let Timo decide something. But maybe he needed it.

Timo noticed her waiting and set out in the lead carrying the two spears held together on his right shoulder. Niwana followed him with the bundle of dried grass riding easily along behind her head. She was surprised at how natural it felt to follow Timo. Maybe being a woman would not be so bad after all.

Choice

Rasta sat on the ground outside the compound. The healer from his tribe knelt next to him and applied some herbs to stop the bleeding in Rasta's arm wound. When the healer was sure that the bleeding was slowed he took a piece of cloth and wrapped it around the arm adjusting it so that it was tight enough to protect the wound and control the bleeding but not so tight as to stop the blood flow to the arm.

"That should be enough for now," said the healer expecting Rasta to stand up and continue whatever he had been doing. But Rasta simply sat looking off into the distance. "I am going now to see to the others," he continued then hurried back into the compound with no sign from Rasta that he had heard.

The healer understood Rasta's distracted mood. Everyone knew it by now – they had won the battle but lost the water. They were now even worse off than before with many killed and wounded. At least they could take the cows and anything else they could find in the compound for their own. There would probably be even some water there in storage. But without more water from the source on a continuing basis the cows would be dead in a short time anyway – just a mountain of rotting meat. And after the water they would find in storage containers today there would be no more. This was definitely not how the short people had hoped it would turn out.

Rasta was disappointed with himself. In his shock at seeing the collapsed source – stones and earth and bodies all entangled – he had lost his balance. Everything about the attack had been planned so carefully but he had never considered that the source might close itself to them. Looking back it made sense. Clearly there was strong magic involved in the source to keep it open and functioning. It would not give itself up so easily to those who did not know its secrets. So his first mistake had been his arrogance to think that the source was there for the taking. But his second mistake had been just as serious. In his irritation after he had been wounded by the tall warrior he had given the order that they all be killed. This was against his nature as he was normally a mild and considerate man. He realized now that probably he had been prompted by the Ancestors of the tall people. He was sure that the tall people Ancestors would rather have all the tall people dead than for some other tribe to possess the secrets of their source. It made no sense but that was the way Ancestors were: the lives of the living were nothing to them compared to their own pride. Yes, that was probably it. He had been off balance and they had influenced him in committing his second stupidity by killing all the men who might know the secrets of the source. He shook his head and smiled to himself in amazement – life is always a surprise. He had prepared himself – all of his people had prepared themselves – to die bravely today instead of dying slowly of thirst. But to die slowly of thirst while so clearly reminded of one's arrogance and stupidity was even harder.

Was there another way to find out how the source worked? He could not think of one. All the other villages of the tall warrior tribe in this region had been abandoned in his grandfather's time. The people had driven their cattle southwards looking for better pasture and more secure sources of water. One needed both if one was going to have cows. Rasta's people had been here for as long as they could remember and had felt no need to move. They kept no cattle and therefore did not need so much water. They lived by hunting wild animals and gathering what grew by itself. But the point was that there was no tall warrior village he could go to and ask if they could come and help him restore the source. His grandfather had always said that the people of this village were so secretive that even the other villages of the same tribe were not allowed to know how it was done. So it would not have worked even if there had been another tall warrior village around. Rasta had never been able to believe that. It made no sense. Why wouldn't they have shared such powerful magic with their own people? But after the events of today he was reconsidering. As in so many things his grandfather had probably been right about that as well.

Rasta stood up to go back into the compound to make sure the distribution of the spoils of the battle was fair. He put more vigor into his step than he really felt and firmed up the commitment in his face; it would not do to let the men see how discouraged he was.

He was almost to the gate when one of his men who had been outside with him standing nearby in attendance came up and got his attention.

"Honorable Rasta, look! Some people are coming," said the man and pointed south to where two figures had appeared on the horizon.

Rasta shaded his eyes with his right hand and peered hard to better make out the figures. It was a couple: a man carrying a spear on his shoulder, but no shield, so he was not expecting battle, and a woman walking behind him with a large bundle on her shoulders, probably grass. It was all very ordinary. They were walking in a relaxed way as if they expected nothing was wrong here. Perhaps they were simply returning to their village. The only strange thing was that they seemed quite small even at this distance. Hard to see how it could be a tall warrior couple.

Rasta's discouraged mood was gone in an instant; perhaps there was a second chance for him and his people. If the couple was from this village then the man might know the secrets of the source. Rasta looked around now to see how the scene would look to the new arrivals. Actually nothing was too much out of the ordinary. All the bodies of the dead were inside the compound. He had personally given orders that nothing be set on fire in order to be able to salvage what they could. As a minimum they had planned to have a group of people live here to look after and defend the source. The tree they had used as a battering ram was well inside the stockade. The cows had even stopped bellowing now that the fighting was over.

He turned to the man still standing next to him.

"Fetch me a water gourd with water in it from the compound – there must be some water somewhere in a hut," he said. "And tell all the other men to stay inside the stockade and make no sounds until I tell them to come out."

He himself began to walk slowly along the wide path southwards in the direction of the approaching couple. After two hundred paces he came to a large flat-topped sandstone boulder by a thorn-leaf tree at the side of the path. He sat down in the partial shade and waited.

Within a few minutes the man returned running to Rasta with the water gourd. To the man's surprise Rasta did not drink from it but set it on the ground by the stone.

"The men will do as you say, Honorable Rasta," said the man.

"Then go back with them yourself, Mohan, and say some prayers to our Ancestors for their assistance. Perhaps the day has not been lost after all."

The man returned to the compound. The couple was still approaching but it was clear they had noticed something was not right. Their walking rhythm was disturbed and they were staying closer together. Rasta sat in a relaxed way on the stone saying his own prayers.

Timo spoke first. "There is something strange back at the village. It is mid-day but there is no one outside doing anything."

"Yes, there is someone," corrected Niwana, coming up to stand next to him where he had stopped. "He is sitting on the stone by the resting place on the road. It feels like he is looking at us. From this distance I can't see who it is. And there was another man who has gone back inside the village."

There was nothing to do but continue walking so they did but more slowly.

"He is not one of us!" said Timo. Niwana knew what he meant. She had been thinking it too. But it was so strange to think of some-one not from the village just sitting there by the road with no one else around that she had not said anything out loud.

Timo felt panic rising in him. What should they do? Why was no one from his village outside the compound? But the man sitting by the trail had no apparent weapons, was not threatening them in any way, and the path back to the safety of their village lay past where he sat. They had been seen – he had watched them approaching the whole time – so it would be shameful to run away. There was noth-ing to do but just keep walking. From where they were now Timo could see that the stockade gate was open. If they needed to they could just run for it at the last minute. From the looks of him the man was probably not very fast. Timo said nothing to Niwana but sensed that she was at this point following his lead. So they walked on down the wide path as if everything was as ordinary as could be.

As they came up to where he was the man spoke to them: "Greet-ings! How are you doing today?"

It was an unusual thing to say. Even though it was clear to Rasta that they were children he had decided to try his plan as originally conceived. Two mistakes for one day were enough. As they were children he would have normally ignored them but that would not be useful to him at this point.

Timo stopped in his tracks. Niwana stopped behind Timo almost bumping into him. The man spoke with a strange accent but Timo had understood what he had said. The stranger had addressed Timo as if he were a man and a married man at that. Timo struggled with how to respond. The stranger was well-dressed, almost like a chief or something and clearly one of the short people. He must have no-ticed that they were children. How could he mistake them for adults? Perhaps because he is so short himself, thought Timo. He de-cided to play along.

"I do well," he answered, "and how are you doing today?"

It was the first time he had ever said the phrase with these end-ings out loud grown man to grown man except in play with the other boys. It gave him an unusual not altogether unpleasant sensation. Now perhaps they could go on their way into the stockade.

"I am having a very bad day," replied the man, however, so it was not going to be that easy. "As you can see, I have injured my arm."

He raised his left arm and turned it slightly so they could see that the cloth wrapped around it was not decorative but was stained with dark blood.

"And I have another problem as well."

The man paused, peering into Timo's face as if searching for something.

"You look like a wise young man. Perhaps you could advise me. We could sit here for a moment together and talk." The man indicated a place on the ground next to the stone.

Timo hesitated. He cut his eyes in the direction of the stockade. He could not imagine that they had anything to talk about.

Rasta noticed the boy's hesitation. He saw the clear distrust in the girl's face.

"You are probably thirsty from your work in the hills. I have some water here. Take as much as you need. For your woman too."

He bent over and picked up the water gourd from the other side of the stone and reached it out to Timo.

He is offering us water, thought Timo. He must be a good person.

Timo looked at Niwana. They nodded slightly to each other in agreement. Timo put the spears down within easy reach and Niwana leaned the bundle of grass against the base of the thorn tree. They sat on the ground in front of the stone.

Timo took the water gourd from the man, opened it and drank, then passed the gourd to Niwana. Rasta sat on the stone watching them drink. Niwana had noticed a surprised look on Timo's face as he drank but did not understand it. Niwana drank from the gourd, first a small sip, and then more. She had been expecting the normal surface water that one found in the hills before the drought had taken all the water away – sandy and brackish. But this water was not like that at all. This was the clean sweet water of their source and nothing else. She finished drinking, securely replaced the wooden peg that filled the drinking hole and handed the gourd back to the man who took it and placed it on the ground.

It was not clear what would happen next.

"That's our water," declared Niwana flatly after a few moments as if it were an accusation. Timo was shocked at her audacity. He had been thinking something similar but that was not how you did things. You couldn't just say what you thought out loud even man to man much less a woman speaking to a man. Probably there was some explanation as to why the man had the water.

Rasta seemed to have taken no offense at Niwana's having spoken.

"You mean that this water came from the source inside the compound over there?" he answered mildly. He indicated the direction of the compound with his right arm.

"You know exactly what I mean," answered Niwana continuing in the same accusatory tone.

Timo shuddered and gulped. They were in real trouble now. If the man told Farah how Niwana had been talking to him she would get a beating for sure and Timo too just because he had been here and not stopped her. That was assuming of course that the man did not just kill her on the spot.

"What are your names?" asked the man instead of being angry.

They hesitated and looked at one another.

"My name is Rasta," he said as if to make things equal between them.

"Timo," answered Timo hesitantly.

"Niwana," said Niwana.

"Thank you," said Rasta. "Now that we know one another I feel like I can talk to you about my problem. First, however, I have some very sad news for you Timo and Niwana: There was a battle here this morning and all of the people in your village were killed. They are all dead. If I am right you are the only ones left alive."

Timo jumped up immediately.

"It's a lie!" he shouted. "It's a trick! Come, Niwana! Run!"

He set off running as fast as he could. He looked back and saw that Niwana was not behind him but he continued running anyway until he had disappeared into the gate of the stockade.

Niwana remained sitting. Her face was in her hands and she began crying.

"I'm so sorry," said Rasta. "I can imagine how hard this is for you."

"No you can't!" said Niwana in loud protest, raising her face from her hands for a moment to speak.

"It's all my fault! I didn't honor the rules so now everybody is dead!"

She crumpled over on the ground, rolled onto her right side and curled her body tight all the while crying loudly.

Rasta was confused. Women were not his specialty; he never understood them. It was the boy he needed. Let the girl think what she wanted about why things happened. Who really knew after all?

Rasta was tired from the day. His wound hurt him more than it had before. He reached down and picked up the water gourd from the ground. He held it in his lap for a moment and looked at it. The gourd was not only large and strong it was beautiful. Geometric designs incised in the yellow wood swirled in a spiral around the form.

It had a strap of woven leather dyed in blue and red. He opened the wooden stopper, raised the gourd to his lips and brought a small amount into his mouth, first just to taste. It was wonderful! He had forgotten how good it tasted. He drank more until he was no longer thirsty. He closed the gourd and set it back on the ground. The girl was still lying in the same position crying.

After a while Mohan came out of the stockade leading Timo by a short rope connected to a noose around his neck that tightened when there was tension on it. Timo had his hands tied behind his back. Mohan led the boy along the path to Rasta. Timo's body was tense and he looked down at the ground instead of at Rasta or Niwana.

"Honorable Rasta, we were not sure about your instructions, as to whether it was right for us to bring the boy back to you instead of staying in the compound. The boy came in, found the body of a tall warrior he says was his father and then proceeded to attack us. Although he fought very well," Mohan looked back at Timo for a moment, "we were able to subdue him. Luckily none of our men were hurt. Do you want to speak with him or should we do something else with him?"

Rasta realized he had not been very clear in his orders. At the same time he appreciated the fact that Mohan had understood the direction of his plan even without his having said anything.

"Thank you, Mohan," said Rasta, "you have done well. Leave the boy with me and go back into the compound with the others and wait."

Mohan was not happy with this course of action as the boy could be dangerous and Rasta carried no weapon. But it did not occur to him to question it. He handed Rasta the end of the rope and went back into the compound.

"You see," Rasta began, speaking to Timo, "I was telling you the truth about your people. It is sad, but it is true. They are all dead."

"And you killed them!" shouted Timo defiantly looking up at Rasta for the first time and straining at the ropes holding his hands.

"Yes, I did – or at least my men did – and so now you want to kill us. But what good would that do? Would it bring back your parents? Your friends?"

"Timo, don't you see – it all happened because of us, because of what we did!"

Rasta and Timo turned to look at Niwana who was sitting upright. Her face was streaked with tears but she was no longer crying.

"Will you run away if I take this rope from your neck?"

Rasta's question caught Timo off guard. It was not what he had expected.

"No, I won't run away," he answered.

"Good," said Rasta. He stood up and loosened then removed the noose around Timo's neck. It was not easy for him with his wounded left arm. Rasta coiled the noose and short length of rope carefully and laid it on the ground by the gourd. Timo's hands were still tied.

"Can we continue now as we were?" asked Rasta, indicating with his right hand the place on the ground where Timo had been sitting before.

Timo hesitated then sat down with his legs crossed in front of him. Rasta sat back down on the stone.

Niwana was lying on her side again curled up and crying. She noticed that Timo had sat down near her. She inched her body towards him, reached him, and put her head on his left knee holding his leg in her hands. Her crying became louder. Moments passed.

"Why don't you just go ahead and kill us too," said Timo. "We are not afraid to die."

Rasta nodded at the comment. He could see that the boy was telling the truth. These tall warriors were really something. He would have to play this very carefully.

"You are right, I could do that," he said, then waited for their reactions.

To his surprise the girl stopped crying and sat up next to the boy. Seeing them in this way, sitting side by side, he saw now they looked very much alike. They were twins or at least brother and sister. And they both looked back at him now calmer and with more resolve than they had shown at any point so far.

"We are ready," said the girl. The boy swallowed hard but nodded. The two looked at each other for a moment then back at Rasta.

Now it was Rasta's turn to be caught off guard. He had planned to offer them life and freedom in return for the boy sharing his knowledge of the source and how it functioned, as he had the warrior in the battle, thinking that with a child it might work, and that perhaps the boy knew something about how the source functioned. But if they had no fear of death he had no bargaining power in offering them life. He would have to find another way.

"I have a family too," he began, "I have a son and a daughter."

He paused to judge their reactions. They were listening. That was a start.

"They are older than you two. They have their own families and their own babies now. And guess what?"

He paused and looked at the two children in front of him as if he expected them to guess. They did not so he continued.

"They are all dying; all my people are slowly dying. The babies are dying first. Then the older ones."

He could see that this touched Timo and Niwana as they both reacted in their faces but in very different ways: Timo seemed angered; Niwana seemed shocked.

"Do you know why my people are dying?" asked Rasta, with the emphasis on the why.

This time the question was not rhetorical. He really wanted to know if the children knew why his people were dying. He waited.

After some moments Timo spoke.

"Because you have no water!" he said as if it were obvious and Rasta had been stupid to ask.

"Yes," responded Rasta slowly and carefully. "We are dying because we have no water."

His attention at this moment was on the girl. She was looking at the boy with disbelief on her face.

"Is it true?" asked Niwana, rising up from her sitting position next to Timo, standing and facing him, her hands on her hips.

"Yes, of course it is true," answered Timo. But he did not look up at her. He looked down at the ground in front of him.

"But we have water! Why can't we share it with them?" she asked. Her tone of outrage continued.

"Because if we shared our water with them then we would have no more for ourselves and then we would all die!"

Timo stood up awkwardly without the use of his hands and faced her.

Rasta was intrigued. What an unexpected development. He leaned back to give them room to continue.

"But I knew nothing of this!" protested Niwana.

"Of course not," answered Timo. "You are a child and a woman on top of that. The water is a man's thing. Ajuba told us boys about the decision moons ago so that we would all know and understand when we saw the short people dying or when they came to beg for water. The rule was not to give them any."

"The rule? The Rule? *THE RULE?*" repeated Niwana, her voice rising with disgust. "So: babies are dying and you can do something to help but you don't because you have decided some damn rule?

"I was completely wrong!" she continued addressing the sky instead of the boy or the man. "I thought our village died because you and I broke the rules and the truth is that the village died because it kept its own crazy rules!"

She turned to face Rasta.

"What do you want?" she asked in an unexpectedly calm tone.

Rasta leaned forward toward her. There was emotion in his face now almost desperation.

"I want to know how your source works: how it is built and how you keep the walls from falling in when it is so deep and how you get the water up from so far and why it never goes dry."

Rasta said it all in a rush then straightened and paused to see how she would react. Perhaps he had said too much or too soon but he was tired.

"Don't tell him!" shrieked Timo startled to see that Niwana seemed about to speak.

"Why not tell him?" asked Niwana looking back at him.

"Because then we will have no more water for..." Timo's voice faltered and broke as he realized mid-sentence that his reason for withholding the water from the short people no longer applied. He sat down suddenly. His face went blank and his eyes lost their focus.

"Well, the most important part is the spiral ring of stones around the walls that holds the earth back," began Niwana. "You have to start the stones in a circle at the top then bring it down carefully row by row in a spiral as you dig out the earth, so it is always stable, adding the stones carefully one by one as it goes deeper, pushing them into the earth on the sides even after the water comes in."

"How big are the stones?" asked Rasta, trying to keep up with her and at the same time trying to judge how much she really knew.

"As wide as a man's spread hand, as long as two hands spread touching, and as thick as a thumb is long, with flat sides" recited Niwana. "They are not really stones but clay cooked in the fire."

It was clear to Rasta that she was remembering something and not making it up. Plus it made sense: having the stones flat and the same size would mean that the structure was more stable and could be constructed and maintained under the difficult conditions deep in a hole in sandy earth.

Timo had recovered from his shock and noticed what Niwana was saying.

"Don't believe her; she has it all wrong!" he protested to Rasta.

"Then why did you tell her 'not to tell' when I first brought up the subject?" asked Rasta.

Timo had no answer and once again went into a shocked silence.

Rasta turned to Niwana.

"Niwana, I want to tell you how grateful I am that you are willing to share this information about the source with us. There are others of my people who also need to hear this, as they are the ones who will restore it to operation and maintain it. If it is alright with you I would like to bring them here so we can continue."

Niwana took a breath and nodded. She seemed to want to say something so Rasta waited.

"There is something that I want you to promise before I tell you more," said Niwana finally.

"Of course," answered Rasta, "that would only be fair. What would you like?"

"That you let Timo live; that you don't kill him; that he go free and not be a slave."

Rasta looked from the girl to where Timo sat now on the ground. Timo's eyes were far away. His mouth was moving slightly but no words were coming out.

"It will be as you say: Timo will be allowed to live; he will be free to come and go as he wants; he will not be a slave."

Rasta paused. Niwana did not say more.

"And for yourself?" he prompted.

"Right now I don't know," she said. "It is all so new. I am still confused. Can I think about it and tell you in a few days?"

"Of course," answered Rasta. The more he got to know this girl the more he liked her. He stood up.

"I will go now into the compound to bring the others who need to hear about the source and to let my men know that we have found a solution. Or would you like to come with me?"

"No, I will stay here with Timo," she answered.

Rasta nodded and walked back toward the compound.

Niwana sat down next to Timo and put her right arm over his shoulders. After some moments of resistance he moved his head around and pushed it against her breast. He began to cry, softly at first, and then more loudly. Niwana brought her left arm around now to cradle his head. Timo stopped crying after a while. He raised his head. He sat up.

"You will really do it, won't you, you will tell them everything I told you about the source and how it works." He still could not believe it.

"Yes, I will tell them. Why not tell them?" she answered.

"Because...because..." he knew there was a good reason why not but his mind went blank when he tried to think of it.

"Because you just can't!" he finally blurted out.

"Did you hear that Rasta says you can go free, that they will not kill you, that you will not be a slave?" she asked him trying to cheer him up.

"It's just a lie!" responded Timo.

"They'll promise anything to find out about the source and then kill us both in the end," he said with a vengeance.

"Well, I believe him," said Niwana. "And I really don't see we have any other choice."

"If I can go free then untie me right now! Then I'll believe it," countered Timo.

Niwana thought about it for some moments. Rasta had promised that Timo would be free. There had been no discussion of earlier or later.

"Can I trust you not to do something stupid?" asked Niwana.

"Yes, you can trust me," said Timo. "After all, I am your brother."

Freeing the rope binding Timo's hands was much more difficult than she had expected but in the end she accomplished it just as Rasta and a group of other men returned to join them. The twins were still sitting on the ground next to one another. Timo's hands were in front of him now instead of behind him and he was rubbing his wrists to get the blood flowing again. Niwana stood as the men approached.

Rasta was uneasy when he saw that Timo had his hands free now. But it was very delicate: if he constrained Timo again Niwana would lose faith in Rasta's promises and maybe the whole deal would go bad. He would just try to play it as carefully as he could.

"Niwana," he began, "here are some people that I would like for you to meet."

He indicated the man that had been the one to bring Timo out standing next to him to his right.

"This is Mohan my second in command. If you ever have any questions about anything ask him first," he said.

Niwana took some steps forward to stand in front of Mohan. She looked into his face. Mohan looked back. His face was pleasant for her to look at. He appeared sad in some ways but wise also. She decided she liked him.

Suddenly Mohan's face changed from thoughtful to surprised as his gaze shifted from her to behind her.

"Look out!" he shouted and lunged to his left in the direction of Rasta.

Niwana spun around to see Timo coming at a fast run directly toward Rasta with one of the throwing spears held low in both his hands driving toward Rasta's chest.

"No!" she shouted.

She jumped to her left to intercept him before he reached Rasta. Her jump was so fast that Timo had no time to react – the point of the spear caught her just below the solar plexus and went deep into her body. Timo let go of the spear. Niwana and the spear slumped sideways to the ground. A man noticed the other wooden spear lying on the ground and retrieved it.

Rasta and the men stood in a semi-circle around Niwana's body. Timo knelt beside her, calling out to her to stand up, embracing her, attempting to revive her. But it was no use. It became clear to even him that she was dying and then after some minutes that she was dead.

He stood up finding his rage again.

"I will kill you all!" he shouted, and ran toward Rasta with his bare hands.

Mohan stepped forward and intercepted him, turning Timo's charging body easily and throwing him to the ground. By chance Timo's head struck the sitting stone that was near them and his body slumped unconscious. Blood began to seep from a deep wound on his forehead. Mohan bent over him to feel for a pulse. He checked for breath.

"Honorable Rasta, I regret to inform you that the boy is dead," said Mohan.

"It is just as well," said Rasta. "I am sure that he would have been of no use to us or to himself for that matter."

The men stood looking at the dead children.

Rasta went to the thorn-leaf tree and picked up the bundle of dried grass that Niwana had left there in his right hand. Despite the pain from his arm he used his left hand to break it open and spread the grass on the ground. Mohan bent down and arranged the grass in a rectangle. After exchanging a nod with Rasta, Mohan went over to the body of Niwana. He pulled the spear from her and laid it aside. He reached under her, picked her up in his arms and carried her to the grass. He laid her down there, straightened her legs, folded her hands together over the wound then reached up and closed her eyes. Then he went and picked up Timo and laid him next to his sis-ter with Timo's arms folded in the same way. Timo's eyes were al-ready closed.

As Mohan stood up Rasta spoke.

"I was wrong. They were a great people and worthy of respect. We should always remember them in honor."

Rasta turned and began to walk back toward the compound with Mohan and the others following. Rasta spoke as he walked.

"The girl told me some interesting things about how the source is constructed. It is not much but it is more than we knew before. We should start now to dig it out carefully noticing everything. Maybe we do have a chance. Perhaps the spirit of the girl will help us. Who knows?"

Moving Forward

Mitwa's spirit walked through the village to see what she could do to help. Everywhere the struggling spirits of those who had died were stumbling in circles or writhing on the ground. Confused, angry and afraid. Lost in nightmares.

Ancestors from both the short people and the tall warriors had come and were supporting those for whom support was possible. Unexpected death had arrived with a speed and a savagery for which few had been prepared.

Mitwa had found her son Farah's spirit standing where he had been killed. His body had been taken away by the short people warriors and would be burned with the others as soon as they could organize it. Farah's spirit was standing unsteadily, supported on each side by a tall warrior ancestor. His eyes were open but were blank and unseeing. The ancestors at either side of him were whispering into his ears: "You did well. You fought bravely without hesitation or fear. The honor of the tribe is maintained. You are welcome as a hero among the ancestors." But he did not seem to hear them. There was no change in his expression. His face remained twisted in sadness and fear.

Mitwa stood directly in front of him. But he could not see her. She called to him by name. Called again. She waited but there was no change. "As in life, so in death," she muttered out loud to herself and walked away.

Ajuba's spirit also walked among the spirits of the dead offering support to help them awaken from that which held them captive. Mitwa spoke to him as they passed.

"Have you seen Niwana and Timo's spirits?"

"They both died outside the village at the sitting stone by the trail south. Their bodies lie there. Perhaps their spirits are still there somewhere."

Mitwa concentrated her thoughts. Yes, she realized, they were there. And so she was there too. She stood at the stone looking down at the bodies of the two children lying next to each other. Poor children, she said to herself. They were caught up as we all were in the terrible stupidity of it all.

So much had been lost. Yet as always it had been predictable. All these tribes struggling for survival by taking care of themselves and ignoring or abusing all those who were "not us." There had to be a better way for people to live together. But when would it come? How would it come?

She looked around then saw Niwana's spirit some distance away along the trail south.

Niwana's spirit was looking down at Timo's spirit. Timo was on hands and knees on the trail making angry noises, shaking his head back and forth and crawling very slowly southwards with his eyes tightly closed. As Timo moved Niwana also moved to stay up with him.

Mitwa watched them waiting to see what might be possible. Niwana was in a trance focused completely on Timo's struggling spirit and did not see her.

"Niwana?" offered Mitwa after some time had passed and she felt the moment was right.

Niwana awakened from her trance and looked at Mitwa.

"Oh Grandmother!" she said. "What has happened?" She moved closer and embraced Mitwa.

Mitwa sat down on the ground with Niwana sobbing in her lap. Niwana's spirit body began to shake violently. Her crying grew louder and wilder, peaked and then gradually became quieter. Mitwa simply waited. Time passed.

Mitwa noticed that Timo's spirit had moved further down the trail south. It did not appear to make any difference to it whether Niwana was watching or not.

Niwana sat up and looked around. Back in the direction of the village she saw three vultures busy by the thorn tree with something they had found there. She swallowed hard, nodded her head and pressed her lips together. So it is, she said to herself. She looked into Mitwa's face. Again embraced her. Sat up by herself. Looked up to the clear blue sky. Turned back to Mitwa.

"Thank you for being here," said Niwana. "I don't know what would have happened to me if you had not been here for me. It was terrible. It was a nightmare."

"Of course," answered Mitwa, "it is my honor to be with you here."

"An honor? What do you mean?"

"I mean that it is an honor to accompany such a brave young woman who sees so clearly how things are and is ready to do what it takes to make things better for everyone. Regardless of the price she must pay."

"I don't understand why everyone can't see how wrong things are with how we live," said Niwana.

"Yes, I know. It is also hard for me to understand. But it is so. I had no luck even with my own son. And the road forward to a better way of living is hard to find because everyone is so caught in the old ways."

It was quiet between them for a while.

"So what happens now?" asked Niwana.

"That depends on you. Most of those who have died will join our ancestors in the spirit world. How does that sound to you?"

"That is not what I want at all. It is the ancestors who gave us all the rules and judgments that led to this today. Even I can see that. No, I will not go to the ancestors. Will you go to the ancestors?" she asked.

Mitwa thought for a moment.

"No, I also will not go to the ancestors," she answered.

"Then what will you do?" asked Niwana.

"For now I will help all those I can who are caught in the grip of this terrible tragedy. That will take some time. Then I will go forward."

"What do you mean, 'go forward'?"

"I will start another life as someone else in another time and place. And continue my work."

"What is your work? You were a wonderful grandmother and we girls were always so happy when we could learn things from you. Is that your work?"

"Yes, that is a part of my work at least. But I am supposed to be accompanying you," Mitwa said and smiled. "What do *you* want to do? What is *your* work?"

Niwana thought about it a few moments. "I don't know. I thought up until now that my work was to become strong and powerful like the men so that I could stand against them and teach them how to live without so much fear. But now I am not so sure."

"Are there things you are sure about? Usually it is best to start with those things."

"Well, yes, there are things I do want. I want to live where there is plenty of good water so that people will not have to fight about water. And I want to be in the mountains. My whole life I saw the great mountain in the east every day and wanted to be there but it was never possible. I want to be around animals and trees and birds! They are my favorite things. Is that enough?"

"Well, it is a very good start. Can I ask you a question about what you want?"

"Sure."

"How about people. Do you want to live with a lot of people or with only a few people somewhere on your own?"

"Oh, please, with just a few people somewhere far away from lots of people!"

"Okay, that is very helpful," responded Mitwa. "And do you know what your work – what your offering to the world – will be?"

Niwana shook her head. "I have no idea. Do I have to be clear about that?"

"No. You can just let that develop later. And I think with all you have said you are ready to move forward into whatever comes next. Are you ready?"

Niwana was thoughtful. She looked southward and could see Timo's spirit still crawling down the path. "What about Timo?" she asked. "What will happen to him?"

Mitwa sighed. "He is caught in the shame and rage of having 'failed.' I am afraid there is nothing to be done. He also will not go to the ancestors. They judge him because he did not succeed in killing the enemy of the people nor in dying honorably."

"So then what will happen to him?" Niwana was concerned.

Mitwa hesitated to answer. Considered what she would say. Finally spoke. "You see it there in what his spirit is doing: crawling away from people, blind to everything around him, filled with rage and shame. He is becoming an animal. A wild dog perhaps. Something like that. So he can spend a life fully in his dream of shame and rage and hunger for what he does not have. It is very sad. But there is nothing to be done. The power of his choices in the last hours and moments of life is too strong."

"But that is terrible! There must be something we can do."

"No, there is nothing to be done. You will just have to accept it. He has chosen and now it all moves forward by itself."

"No, I will not accept it at all," replied Niwana decisively. She stood up and walked southward along the trail. Mitwa stood and followed her.

When Niwana reached Timo she sat down on the ground directly in his path. And so in a short time he came to her. His eyes were still tightly closed so he felt her first with his hands as he struggled forward. He tried to push her aside but she could not be moved. He roared loudly lifting up on his knees. But she did not move. He began to beat her with flailing arms and hands. But she did not move.

He raised his body upward from his knees with both arms held high together preparing to smash the obstacle in front of him.

In this moment Niwana moved forward, put her arms around him, embraced him and held her body close to his with her head tight on his right shoulder.

He screamed out a terrible sound from the pain of her embrace. He clawed at her with his hands. But her grip was strong and he could not free himself.

He stood up but Niwana stood up with him. He twisted and turned trying to free himself but he could not.

They fell together to the ground rolling back and forth from his attempts to free himself.

Time passed. He grew quiet, relaxed his body and fell asleep. Niwana freed her arms from under him and stood up looking down at his sleeping spirit body.

She looked to Mitwa who was standing nearby. "Well, to me it looks like something has changed."

"Yes," replied Mitwa, "there has been a change. So now perhaps he has a chance for something better than he was headed for. But you need to take care for yourself. Are you ready to move forward?"

"Yes, I am ready to move forward. But I have one more thing that I want."

"And what is that?"

"I want Timo to be with me so that I can learn – so that we can learn – to live together in a good way. If we two cannot manage to do that then what hope is there for the world?"

Mitwa nodded as she understood. "If that is what you really want then it can be as you say."

Mitwa sat on the ground next to Timo's sleeping form. Niwana sat next to her. Mitwa put her left hand on Timo's head. She reached out her right hand to Niwana, who took it. Niwana placed her other hand on Timo's chest.

"Close your eyes," said Mitwa. Niwana closed her eyes.

"Now focus on the vision of the place you described earlier: in the mountains with good water, far from people, surrounded by trees and animals, with you and Timo. Can you see all of that?"

"Yes, I can see it," replied Niwana.

"Now just stay with that vision holding it gently as long as you can."

After a while Niwana's form slumped softly to the side and slid to the ground. Her eyes were still closed. Her spirit body's chest lifted and fell with her relaxed breathing. Mitwa got up and moved Niwana's form to lie next to Timo's. She placed their hands first on their chests. Then she sat for some minutes with her own eyes closed, her head bent forward and a hand on each head.

The sunlight became intense then dispersed into crystal clear starry night.

Paradox

"Mitwa saw you, am I right?" asked Martyna, turning to look at Lela. The two of them had been sitting on the large flat rock by the thorn tree watching what was happening when Mitwa had come there looking for Niwana. Mitwa had looked directly at Lela, had given her a small nod of greeting and Lela had returned the nod. Martyna was sure of it. Now the scene had changed and there were just Lela and Martyna sitting on the stone by the thorn tree in the late evening dark with a starry moonless sky above them.

"Yes, she saw me. Why do you ask?" responded Lela.

"Did she see me?"

"I don't know. You could ask her if it is important for you to know."

Martyna was thoughtful.

"No, I don't need to know if she saw me. But it was a shock for me when she saw you! If I understand it, she and all of these people have been dead for many hundreds of years. So when I see them it is for me like watching a film, like reading an earlier chapter in a book like you talked about. But how is it that Mitwa can see us – or at least you? We are from a different chapter, a later chapter, but because we are here now things change here, are different perhaps in small or big ways. Even though they are far in the past. Is that right? Is that possible?"

"You do ask very good questions. But for this one I am afraid I have no answer that will satisfy you. It is a paradox and a mystery. Sometimes it seems like the past is fixed and cannot be changed but can be seen or understood in a new and helpful way. And at other times there does seem to be the possibility for a shift in what has happened before. But in my experience that is rare and trying to make it happen is not useful and often leads to suffering. And finally in some moments it seems as if everything is happening all at once – each decision affecting all others – and all of it is perfect even though one can see many possibilities for improvement. Does that help?"

"Nope, does not help." Martyna shook her head in frustration.

Lela sighed. "Well, have you seen enough? Are you ready now to set your intention for what happens next to your story?"

"No, not at all. But I am ready to see what comes next in this story of lives that you are showing me. Right now I am very confused but I really want to know what happens next."

"Okay, then," said Lela. "Take my hand."

Horben im Breisgau, Germany

October 14, 1604 C.E.

The Priest and the Blacksmith

"How much farther is it?" asked the priest as he struggled up the steep embankment.

There had been stones here earlier set to make steps, one could see that. But they had eroded away and the jumble of rocks was now just a hindrance. The path since they had left the road wound through a stand of beech trees and shorter willows along the narrow stream, following the terrain, leading uphill. The men had not seen any houses, huts or other signs of human habitation for an hour. The fall trees were yellow, gold and brown. The ground was covered with the slippery wet leaves making climbing the slope difficult. The priest used his hands to hold his black robes higher trying to keep them from getting soiled and struggled to keep his balance. His thin face was wet with perspiration.

"Not far," answered the shorter man standing higher up with his hands on his hips looking back with barely concealed amusement at the priest's difficulties. He wore brown leather pants and a leather vest dyed green over a linen shirt that had once been white. His bushy brown hair and graying beard framed his laughing blue eyes, his pale cheeks, his red-veined nose.

"It was years ago, as an apprentice, that I helped my master do the metalwork for the house and climbed this trail for the first time. But I never forget a path through the forest. Learned forest ways as a boy."

"And why in heaven's name did they build a house up here in the wild, so far from the village? What with bears and robbers and all? I never understood that."

"It was the woman's idea, I think. She seemed to decide every-thing in the family, like where the house should be built. The man went along with whatever she wanted. And they were from the city, from Freiburg, so I think they had no idea what they were in for up here," answered the shorter man. "There had been an old hunter's hut there by a spring that was abandoned long ago. They bought it from the community then built a house on it as if they were in a vil-lage and not out in the woods on a mountainside." The man laughed at the craziness of it.

They walked on in silence. The way became less steep. The path leveled and turned sharply right against a rising incline. A faint path went to the left. The shorter man followed the path to the left with-out hesitation. The trees thinned as they traveled along the ridge giving a better view of the higher ridges and hills in the distance. The air was cool, the sky almost clear but for the high thin clouds left over from the rain the night before.

They passed a cultivated area: a garden where the trees had been cleared away. Five large red-orange pumpkins poked up from among the weeds. A line of vertical poles with withered bean plants leaned as if they might fall.

"It's just ahead," called out the man in the lead.

And then there it was, the house. The priest could see now what had attracted the woman to this place: it had a charm to it. There was a steep rocky outcropping with a small limestone cliff on the right. The two story house was built against it; the back wall of the house was provided by the cliff face itself. The space in front of the house was flat for about twenty paces then fell away steeply in the direction of the village. The view to the west was magnificent with the Vosges mountains in the far distance and the Rhine Valley – here with a course from south to north – discernible by its broad swath through the lower hills between their position and the distant horizon.

The ground floor house walls were made of stacked cream-colored stones, laid and joined at the corners of the house, the spaces between them filled with mortar and reinforced here and there with wooden beams. The ground floor had no windows but a large wooden door that stood open, wooden posts at its sides and a straight wooden lintel across it at the top. It was dark inside where the sun did not reach. The floor from what they could see was raw earth and straw: a place for animals.

The upper story was constructed of a combination of wooden beams, the same cream-colored stones and the same mortar work between the stones. There were three windows with frames and clear glass and the kind of shutters you would see in a fine house in town but two of the shutters were hanging at angles from their hinges. A framed door at the left end of the house had stone steps that led up to it. The steeply sloping roof was of tied bundles of reeds laid over each other.

A flight of swallows raced past the men at ground level, circled high, then disappeared in a flurry into holes in the end of the house just below the line of the roof covering.

A short distance left of the house was an irregularly shaped basin cut from the stone, open at its top, built into the face of the cliff, its top rim lined with moss, full to the brim. Water flowed out of it and followed a small channel carved in the rock that led to a larger pool of water, also against the cliff face, ringed with stones, but lower down.

There were several goats sitting on the bare ground by the larger pool looking at the two men. A black and brown ram showed particular interest. The ram got up and walked toward them. He bleated a challenge. Another goat stood up and walked toward the two men. It bleated as well.

"What is it?" called a female voice from the house.

A young girl walked out and stood on the top step. She had apparently been talking to the goats as she was clearly surprised to see the men. She was slender with nut-brown curly hair cascading down around her head and was dressed in a faded brown wool dress that needed mending. Her feet were bare. Her face, legs, and arms were deeply tanned. Her features were tight and pulled together.

"Hey Patrick, we have visitors," she called out loudly without shifting her gaze.

She walked down the steps and across the open area between the house and the path. As she walked she whistled a falling pitch and rotated her right arm in a circle; the two goats went back to the others, folded their legs and sat down on the ground, still watching the men.

"You are Christina, are you not?" asked the priest. The girl did not immediately answer but studied the two men.

"What do you want?" she asked after some moments.

"I am Father Gruber, the priest in the village, and this is Ulrich the blacksmith. He helped your parents build the house and was kind enough to lead me here since I did not know the way," said the priest.

Ulrich smiled broadly at Christina. Christina ignored him and continued to focus her attention on the priest.

"I know who you are," said Christina. "I asked you what you want."

She was much more confrontational than the priest had expected. He was certain she and her twin brother were only 14, but looking at her it was hard not to believe that she was older. He began to have serious doubts that he could accomplish his mission this day. But at least he would try.

"Is there somewhere we could sit so we can talk about that, about why we are here?" he asked. He was winded and tired from the climb through the forest and up the ridge; it was more than just a strategy to get her at ease.

"Okay," she said after a pause. "Wait here."

She went back into the upper story of the house then one by one brought out four chairs and put them in the form of a square on a place in the sun by the spring where there were flat stones on the ground. The chairs were carved wood and of fine quality with woven reeds making the seats, worn but in good order.

"Please sit down," said Christina.

The men sat down. She turned and walked to the house and through the large door at the ground floor. She came out carrying a small square wooden table at an angle on her left hip, held by her left hand. The table was roughly made in comparison to the chairs. Using her right hand she freed the end of one table leg from a clump of goat dung as she carried it, wiping her hand then on the side of her dress. She set the table down carefully.

"What would you like to drink? We have water, goat's milk or apple cider," she said, counting them off on the fingers of her left hand. She stood waiting for their answers.

"Cider," said Ulrich decisively.

"Water," said the priest.

"Are you sure neither of you wants to try the goat's milk?" she asked. "It's fresh from this morning." They both shook their heads.

Christina went into the upper level of the house and came back carrying four ceramic mugs in one hand by their handles, an empty ceramic pitcher braced under that arm and a ceramic jug with a leather carrying strap in the other hand. She put the four mugs on the table in front of the four chairs and set the jug down in the center. She took the pitcher over to the spring, filled it, brought it back and set it on the table.

She poured water for the priest. Then cider for Ulrich who was sitting to the priest's right and also cider into the mug in front of the empty chair to her right.

She picked up her mug, walked back into the lower part of the house then returned to the table and sat her mug half full of milk down on the table. She sat down herself.

The three of them looked at their mugs. No one had yet taken a drink.

Christina sighed then turned toward the house. "Patrick!" she yelled at the top of her voice. "We have visitors!" There was a muffled noise from inside the house.

Christina turned back to the men, obviously relieved at signs of life from Patrick.

"Okay, what do you want?" she asked the priest sitting opposite her.

"Perhaps we should wait for your brother?" inquired the priest.

"Fine with me," she said. "Drink up!" She took a large gulp of goat's milk from her mug.

The two men raised their glasses, nodded in her direction, and drank.

"Very good water," said the priest, taking a second sip.

"Mama always said we had the best water in the whole valley," said Christina proudly.

"The cider is also very good," said Ulrich. "Good and sharp!"

"Patrick makes it. Papa taught him how. That's about all Patrick does this time of year: make cider and drink cider," she said.

"Hello?" came a voice from the direction of the house. A young boy was standing on the top step looking down at them, squinting in the glare of the sun. He was wearing pants but no shirt. His hair was the same color and texture as Christina's but his face, chest and arms were pale.

"Patrick, put a shirt on – the priest from the village is here!" she called to him.

He went back into the house.

"You have to just accept him; that's the way he is. I've tried to teach him better but in the end it all comes to nothing."

They sat not saying anything more taking occasional sips from their drinks.

The smith held his mug out for more cider. Christina filled it.

Patrick came out of the house with a shirt now and different pants. Like Christina he was barefoot. Without saying anything he came to the table, sat down and took a long drink out of his mug. He tilted his chair back and his head forward without turning loose of his mug. His curly hair hung over his face.

"Well, now that we are all here, may we begin?" asked the priest.

"Sure," said Christina. Patrick did not react to the question.

"It has been a month now since your mother's death," began the priest, "and we have not seen any sign of your father since the funeral. So some of us in the village are concerned for your welfare."

"Concerned for our what?" asked Christina, not understanding the word.

"Welfare, how things are for you, if you have enough to eat and drink, are safe in this forest, if you have proper...clothes," he said, not able to avoid looking down at her tattered dress.

"We are fine," said Christina. "Right, Patrick?" she asked, without taking her eyes off the priest.

"Yes, we are fine," responded Patrick.

"But you have no parents here now. You are alone here!" protested the priest.

"Papa is just away on business. He will be back soon. We are not alone," said Patrick defensively.

"And we have each other, and the goats. Not alone at all," continued Christina.

"I had just thought perhaps now that things are ... like they are ... you would want to move into the village," said the priest. There, it was said.

"And what pray tell would we do in the village?" asked Christina sarcastically. "Where would we live, for example?"

The priest tightened his shoulders. "Well, perhaps we could find some family in the village that would take you in, assuming of course you would do your share of the work," he ventured.

Both of the children laughed out loud. "Can you imagine that, Patrick? Somebody is going to 'take us in.'"

"How about you, Ulrich?" Christina turned in her chair to face the smith sitting to her left. She leaned toward him, her eyes wide. "Would Isabel share her bed with me again, like she did when we were both just five? Or would you put Patrick and me in the barn with your horses? At least there is lots of hay there; you wouldn't have to pick me up and carry me there to jump on me the way you tried the last two times I was in the village."

Ulrich's cheeks above his beard turned bright red.

"Yes, that's it!" laughed Christina. "We can live in Ulrich's barn like his other animals. What do you say, Patrick? Shall we make our X? You don't get an offer like that every day!"

Both Patrick and Christina laughed without restraint.

The smith stood up. He tightened both hands into fists, breathing hard. The children continued to laugh, showing no fear at all. Then the smith noticed the priest looking at him in horror.

"I'll wait for you down the path, Father. I can't stand to listen to these ... these ... lies about me!" His chair fell over as he turned to leave. He stormed off down the path until he was out of sight.

Christina got up, picked up the fallen chair, placed it again at the table then sat back down at her seat.

She leaned forward across the table toward the priest, both her hands on the table. She was no longer laughing. Her eyes were no longer wide.

Patrick leaned forward so his chair was once more fully on the ground. He poured himself another mug of cider without looking at either one of them and took a long drink from it.

"Is that what you really came here for today, to convince us to move to the village?" she asked, incredulous.

The priest shook his head back and forth. "Actually, I did not have much hope for that when I decided to come up here. I have asked around in the village and there was no one outside of Ulrich with the slightest interest in taking you in. You seem to have a ... reputation. And I see now that perhaps Ulrich's interest was not primarily Christian charity."

Christina did not say anything. She continued to look into his face, waiting.

"The truth is, I am worried about you two up here in the forest by yourselves. I am after all the village priest. I christened you after you were born and my job is to care for the people in my parish, for their welfare and for their ... souls. Including you two, whether you have ever set foot inside the church or not." Now it was his turn to wait to see what she would say.

Christina leaned back in her chair, balancing herself by holding the edge of the table with her hands. "Well, our souls are fine and our 'welfare' as well, so you can just go back to your village and your parish and let us be. Right, Patrick?"

"Right," echoed Patrick with conviction.

"If you change your minds, or need anything anytime, think of me. I will be there in the village. Just come by and see me anytime."

"Okay," said Christina. She looked up at the angle of the sun. She stood up, moving her chair back. "I need to start making goat cheese now. The milk has sat long enough. I want to have some of it ready for the market day coming up." She looked at Father Gruber. "Are we done?"

"Yes, I think we are done," said Father Gruber. He stood up.

"Goodbye Christina," he said. "Goodbye, Patrick. May God be with you." He turned and walked off down the path.

When he was gone Patrick peered up at his sister. She was still standing looking at the place where the priest had been last visible.

"What was this all about?" he asked, sweeping his arm around at the table and chairs and drinks.

"I knew what he wanted as soon as I saw who it was and he wouldn't say straight out why he was here. I have been expecting this since Mama died and Papa went away. If we are not careful they will come and take us and put us in a prison or something. Mama said we should never trust the people in the village here. Thank God none of them have any interest in this piece of land we have or they would have had us out long ago."

"Whatever you say," said Patrick. He got up and walked into the house carrying his mug and the jug of cider.

Christina carried the other things from the table and the chairs one by one into the house. She took the table back into the lower level of the house then started making cheese from the goat milk she had, sitting outside in the sunlight on a stool, churning it first to separate the parts.

She looked down at her dress. At least that part of what the priest had said was right: she needed some new clothes.

Journey

Christina woke up and opened her eyes. It was still completely dark. Why was she awake?

Then it was clear: Patrick was in bed with her again, under the warm feather comforter and the wool blanket that lay on top of that. It had happened several times since their mother had died. He would get drunk, find his way into her bed and sleep there beside her. It was lonely in the house with just the two of them. No harm in it. It was kind of nice in a way.

She took her left arm and slid it under his head, with her left hand on his left arm, so his head was on her shoulder, leaning against her left breast.

He responded by turning more toward her and reaching his left arm up to her chest. His hand found her right breast and circled it. Closed on it.

Is he really asleep? she asked herself.

Then he moved his left leg up and lay closer to her, his body against hers. The form of his erection pressed unmistakably against her hip.

"What the hell is this?" she exploded, throwing off the bed covers and pushing him out so that he hit the floor with a thud.

"What?" he answered faintly, but did not get up.

Christina climbed off the bed on the other side and went into the kitchen. The embers of the evening's fire were still glowing. She took the candle from the table and in a few moments had it lit from the embers, then carried it back into her bedroom and set it on the table by her bed. Her clothes were there on the floor where she had left them. She took off her night shirt and dressed methodically, tying the goatskin skirt around her waist, putting on her linen shirt, then her goatskin vest over it. Patrick continued to make occasional noises from the floor on the other side of the bed.

She went to the kitchen carrying the wool blanket from the bed and the candle. She took her leather carrying skin from a hook by the door and laid it open on the table. It was a large piece of tanned and treated deerskin with narrower strips that came out from it at the four corners that you folded over and then tied around whatever you wanted to carry and to make a shoulder strap. Her eyes scanned the contents of the shelves. She took four winter apples left over from the fall but still good, a bag of shelled walnuts, two candles, flint, steel, wood shavings. A goatskin water bag that was half full hanging on a hook. Her eyes found the little wooden box on the top shelf, painted blue with tiny red and yellow flowers. She took the box down and opened it, bringing it to the candle. Inside was a small leather pouch, tied closed with yarn. She took the pouch out and put it with all the other things and the blanket into her bag, then tied the bag closed. She put the box back on the shelf where it had been. She put on her boots by the door, checked that her knife was in its place in her right boot, put on her winter coat with the hood and the bear fur collar and turned back to the table. She hoisted the bag on her shoulder.

"Where are you going?" asked Patrick quietly. He was standing in his night dress in the doorway to the kitchen.

"Anywhere away from you will be good," she said bluntly.

"Will you come back?" he asked, after a pause.

"I don't know," she said.

She stood looking at him. "Will you take care of the goats?"

"Sure," he answered.

"Promise?"

"I promise," he said.

Christina turned and walked out the door.

The north wind was waiting for her as she stepped out of the house. It was not strong but it was very cold. There was a thin layer of snow on the ground that squeaked when she stepped on it. More was falling in tiny crystals; she could feel them on her face until she turned away from the north to follow the path south. No moon, no stars. She closed her eyes and tried to walk from instinct. She had been born in this house, upstairs in the room, in the very bed, where she slept each night. She had never known any other home.

And now I need to find my way out of this place, she said to herself.

Then she stopped. Find my way to where?

She really did not know where she could go.

She thought a moment about going into the lower floor of the house and spending the night with her goats. Tomorrow would be time enough to decide what to do. But that would be wrong, somehow.

And why was *she* going away? Patrick should be the one who left, so much of it was his fault. But that would never work; he was too weak.

She could go to Elisabeth, she realized suddenly. Elisabeth had been their mother's only friend here. She had helped her mother when the twins were born even though to do such a thing was forbidden by the church. She was called a "woods woman" by the people in the village, since she lived mostly by gathering and trading plants she found in the forest. Her hut was on the other side of the ridge. Could Christina make it there in the dark?

Well, she could try. And if she didn't make it, maybe that was okay. Maybe that would just be better for everybody.

She started off along the path, or at least where she thought the path was. She stumbled against a tree root, found her balance, stumbled again, and fell. She lay on the cold ground for awhile then got up and started walking again, feeling her way more carefully now with her feet through the soft soles of her deerskin boots. The path had a smoother texture, she noticed. Thank God the snow was not deep. Step by step she worked her way forward. She opened her eyes; even though it was so dark, with her eyes open she could sense where the cliff face was on her left. The direction of the wind on her face helped her too; if it blew into her face she had turned the wrong way. She had to keep it at her back until she got to the place where she would go downhill to the road.

After awhile she noticed that her hands were stiff from the cold: she had no gloves and there were no pockets in her coat. When she was younger it had worked to put her hands up the sleeves, left hand in right sleeve, right hand in left. But she had grown. The sleeves were too short now and too narrow.

She opened the ties of her coat, vest, and shirt. She moved her right hand into the opening, finding the way through to her bare belly. She pushed the hand against herself. It was like ice against her skin. She walked on, stopping from time to time to change the hand that she held in her belly. It seemed to work; the fingers on her right hand were more flexible now. Time passed.

How far have I come? she wondered. She had fallen into a trance even though she had not stopped moving.

Christina noticed the steep upward slope of the ground where she stood. She had missed the trail down to the road! That was also the route to the village and to Elisabeth's place. She was on the ridge trail that led south higher into the mountains, and away from Elisabeth and the village and had been for some time.

She turned to head back to find the turnoff that she had passed. The wind pushed against her body; it had grown stronger now. The ice crystals stung her face.

"I won't make it that way," she said to herself and turned around to stand with her back to the wind.

There were no people in this direction, only mountains and forests and animals. Maybe that is where I belong, she thought to herself. She began again her careful shuffle through the cold dark, headed up into the higher mountains.

More time passed. She found herself thinking of her mother, remembering little things about how her mother had been, how she talked, how she looked when she was sad.

Christina stumbled over a stone and fell forward. But instead of falling to the ground she fell hard against another larger rounded stone that was there, directly in the middle of the path.

But I know this place! she said to herself. The trail here makes a half-circle around the stones, and at the top is a flat place with earth and a hole in the cliff from where the stones fell away. I found this place when I was a child and was trying to run away from home.

She began climbing up the pile of stone rubble in the dark carrying her bag on her shoulder. After some minutes she reached the top. She crawled across the flat area to the place where the shallow cave should be. She was right, it was here. It was smaller than she had remembered: instead of a real cave it was merely a hole in the cliff where a large stone had been. She crawled into it, sitting with her back to the cliff. She was out of the wind here and there was no snow on the hard earth.

She sat for awhile with both of her hands inside her coat against her belly. With her goatskin clothes and coat it was really not so bad. She thought of the blanket she had brought and opened the carrying bag. She took out the blanket and spread it over her legs and lap, tucking the sides under her to insulate her from the frozen ground. She found an apple, took it out, and ate it slowly, noticing each bite.

What else did she have? Her hand felt around inside the bag and found the small leather pouch. She took it out and held it in her two hands pushed against her face. Even in the cold she could smell its special smell.

"What is this?" she had asked her mother, noticing the bag on the table one day.

"That's not for you" her mother had said, picking it up and putting it in the painted box then putting the box on the top shelf in the kitchen.

"Why not?" she had asked.

"You are too young," her mother had said. She had been eight, Christina thought.

"When will I be old enough?" she asked.

"When you are a grownup," her mother had said.

And when would that be? Christina asked herself now. Would that ever be? If not now, then when?

She untied the yarn that held the bag closed then reached in with a finger to feel what was there: something crumbly like old cake. She put her head back, turned the bag up and shook all the contents into her mouth. It tasted terrible. She worked to swallow as much of it as she could then found and ate another apple to get rid of the bitter taste. She took a sip of the icy water from her water bag.

Christina curled up under the blanket against the cliff face and waited to see what would happen.

Time passed. Her mind wandered. She shivered under her blanket, pressed her back against the mountain.

Perhaps it has lost its power, she thought to herself, and sighed. She had waited too long.

But just when she had given up hope her body began buzzing, gently vibrating. She smiled and relaxed; something was going to happen.

The buzzing grew stronger, spreading out into her arms and legs. It was like bees in a summer hive, singing to themselves about their world, dancing in her belly, in her chest. It felt good. She snuggled deeper into the blanket, wrapping herself in it, bringing her arms up even closer to her chest and her knees up to her arms. The buzz of the bees inside her grew stronger, reached a peak, then faded slowly away. It was very quiet now, she noticed after awhile.

She became more aware of the things around her: the mountain cliff against her back was like another being, like herself, but different. She could feel the mountain looking at her, feeling happy it had protected her from the wind, wishing her well.

"Hello, Christina," it seemed to say.

"Hello, Mountain," she replied.

There had been a tree growing there at the left of the opening to the little cave. An oak if she remembered right from when she had been here as a little girl. She reached out her right hand to where it should be. Her hand found a root coming out of a space between stones, growing up toward a tree trunk. She stretched to follow the swelling root as it joined the trunk. She felt it higher up. It was an oak tree! She could tell by the bark.

"Hello, Oak Tree," she said.

"Hello, Christina," said the Oak Tree.

She felt alone. She began to cry.

"Don't cry, Christina; I am here with you," said the Oak Tree.

She kept her hand now on the root. It was like holding hands. And then it was not the oak tree, it was her mother sitting there holding her hand. Christina wriggled across the ground, staying under the blanket, to put her head in her mother's lap.

"Oh, Mother, why did you have to go?" she asked.

But her mother did not answer. In fact her mother was not there anymore. Christina did not look at first but she knew whose hand she held now, she knew in whose lap her head lay: it was Death. Her crying stopped.

Death wore a hood – you could not see anything under it, there was no face, no eyes, no mouth. She looked into that emptiness.

"Hello, Christina," said Death.

"Hello, Death," said Christina and relaxed.

Death's lap was not so uncomfortable. Though his hand where she was holding it was very cold indeed.

So this is it, she thought to herself.

A part of her mind remembered her anger at Patrick, her flight into the night, the path, the climbing, the powder from the little bag. That was all far away now and not important.

It is all about meeting Death, she said to herself.

"Good, Christina, very good," said Death. "But it is not just about meeting Death; it is also about meeting Dying."

Death was gone now.

Christina lay on the ground under the blanket, her arms drawn up to her chest. She felt fear in her belly and in her throat.

The sound of the wind became louder. It became a wailing, lonesome wind like sad singing. She was not alone. There were others. All of them lying on the ground like she was, listening to the sad singing wind.

The singing changed; it became a baby crying, crying desperately. She called out to it, she looked for it, and then here it was in her arms – it was her baby. She looked down at it. It had been hurt – the head was cut and bleeding. She tried to stop the bleeding with her hand as she cradled the baby in her arms. "There, there, it will be okay." The baby cried out one more time and then was still. She clutched it to her breast. But it was no use, it was dead. She laid it down on the ground. She cried over it.

Then she heard another baby crying. She turned and it was there in her arms. It was not hurt but it was painfully thin, just skin and bones. It too cried and then stopped. She held it to her breast. She laid it on the ground. She cried over it.

She sat up now very still and straight. She could hear a thousand babies crying, all at once. A thousand babies dying, all at once. A thousand mothers crying over them.

"Stop!" she shouted as loudly as she could, covering her head with her arms. She slumped over and curled up and cried.

It did not stop.

Then she was one of the babies.
She cried out the pain of her broken body.
She cried out the pain of her starved belly.
Then it was her turn, and she died.

* * *

And finally she fell asleep.

Hours later she awoke, sat up slowly and looked around. It was all so different in the daylight. The sunlight was climbing down the line of mountains across the valley in the southwest. The sky was bright blue and the air was cold but there was no wind.

She gathered her things up into the bag, tied it closed, climbed down the steep pile of boulders then walked down the trail back in the direction of her house with the bag slung over her shoulder, eating an apple. But she was not going to her house; she was going to see Elisabeth. That much was clear.

Beret

"If I don't get some meat to eat I am going to die!" exclaimed Patrick.

It was spring and they were sitting out on their terrace having lunch. Nothing from the garden was ready to eat yet. Christina had done her best: on the table were dark bread, goat cheese, a jar of honey and some strawberry marmalade from one of the jars she had put away the previous summer. Patrick had not taken a bite from any of it.

"I think the woods are just full of bored rabbits hoping you will come and try to catch them. Why don't you do something for yourself for a change and for the rabbits of the world?" Christina asked.

"Is that what you really want me to do? Catch rabbits?" asked Patrick.

"No, not really," answered Christina. She knew it was possible to kill the forest animals and not lose their respect, to stay friends. The older men who hunted the deer knew how to do this. She could feel it in the deer skins she got from them, trading for goat cheese. Twice deer had run right past her as they were being hunted by men with spears and dogs. It was serious for the deer but she could see that it was part of their life – in a way they enjoyed it. There were no hard feelings. It was just the way it was.

But Patrick did not know how. He was not that far along. It would be wrong for him to kill the animals even if it was for food. She did not know either, where wild animals were concerned. But she did know how to kill goats.

"Okay, you win," she said. "The truth is I need some meat as well."

"Thanks," said Patrick. He took a piece of bread, smeared marmalade on it and ate it in large bites.

After putting away what they had used for lunch Christina got what she needed ready and went out to where the goats were nibbling on the new grass by the spring. She put the large bowl down on the ground and called the goats to her with a rising whistle.

Soon they were all gathered around her, interested to see what she wanted.

She got down on her knees in front of them.

"Friends, we need some meat for us to eat and to trade in the village." She looked around at the faces of the goats. They seemed to understand.

"So can one of you let me know if it is alright for you, that you are ready?"

She waited. After a few moments most of the goats seemed to lose interest. They wandered back to nibbling grass. There were just two left. Then one walked away and there was only one, a four year old she-goat. Christina had named it Serena from a story that her mother had told her when she was small. Serena had had only one lamb, the previous year, that had died at birth. This year she had not gotten pregnant.

Christina reached out with her left arm and circled it around Serena's head, holding it steady and close to her body. She took the knife out of the bowl with her right hand and brought it up to Serena's neck. In a moment it was done: Serena shivered, then was still. The other goats continued to nibble grass.

Christina held the body up, letting the blood run down into the bowl.

After awhile she took the body up to the kitchen to skin and dress it on the work table they had there. She sat the blood aside in the kitchen, covered with a board, to make sausages with later.

She finished skinning the goat and separated the meat into sections. There was a metal box above the hearth where the heat and smoke from the fire went up. Christina opened it and hung pieces of meat on the hooks there, then closed the black iron door. She started a fire then fed it using small pieces of oak wood that were in a pile against the wall by the fireplace.

"Patrick, come here," she called out the open door.

Patrick had been cleaning out the dung the goats had left during the night, shoveling it into a wooden box. He stopped what he was doing and came from the lower part of the house to where his sister waited for him in the kitchen.

"I am going into the village now to trade some of the meat for flour – we are almost out," she said. "Can you keep the fire going today to cure the meat? The whole day and into the evening if it takes me that long? I have already put the meat in the box and gotten the fire started."

"Sure," he answered and went out of the room, outside, and back into the lower level.

She took the two rear leg sections she had saved and wrapped them in two oiled cloths. She laid her carrying bag out on the table and put the wrapped meat in it then looked around for what else she could take.

Her goat cheese supply was low, so she decided not to take any of that. There was nothing else they had that she could trade.

She took her hat off its place in the wall and put it on her head, adjusting it so it was secure on her head, then tying it under her chin. She had made the hat during late winter from some brown sheep's wool she had traded for on a market day. Her mother had taught her how to make felt from sheep's wool. The hat was the most challenging thing she had ever made. It had a wide flexible brim shorter in the front and a crown that fit her head and hair. She had worked a leather cord into the ring around the brim to make it stronger there. The ends of the cord hung down on the sides so she could tie them.

The hat was for market days to hide herself from the stares of strangers. It was also good in the rain as it still had the oils from the sheep in it.

She put on her boots. Although she preferred to go barefoot in nice weather like this she had noticed that the people in the village treated her better when she wore boots.

She tied her bag closed, hoisted it on her shoulder, left the house and moved down the trail.

Christina did not exactly run but she was fast, flying down the steepest parts of the trail, putting her feet down as seldom as she could, right at the edge of crashing into trees or worse. It was a game she and the mountain played together. Then she came to the road and turned north.

She slowed as she neared the village making herself smaller and looking down so that the hat brim hid her face. She passed some houses then came to the village center with the tavern, coach house, blacksmith and butcher. There were not many people around: some children playing, a beggar going from house to house, some women walking together.

An older man stood outside of the tavern talking to a younger man.

He noticed Christina, raised his arm and called out to her.

"Christina! I need to talk to you."

Christina had no interest in talking to Mr. Bachtal, the owner of the tavern. But he had seen her and there was nothing for it. Christina stopped where she was.

"It's about Patrick and his debts," said Bachtal as he came up to her. Christina did not say anything in response. He continued.

"As you know, for awhile it was just debts to me and sometimes he paid something back. But in the last year, since your mother died, it reached an absolute limit. Your father was a good customer of mine and that is why I let it go on so far. So first there was the issue of the money he owed the tavern."

He paused and took a breath. Christina still said nothing.

"Then Patrick started borrowing money from anyone he could get it from. It was crazy really; he would get money somewhere then come to the tavern and buy everyone drinks, like he was trying to prove something to us all."

"But what is that to me? I don't drink in your tavern," said Christina.

"I know Christina. And if that was all this were about I would not even be talking to you. But there is more. About three months ago a man moved to our village who lends money as a business. Last month he noticed that Patrick was not getting any more credit from me in the tavern and had other debts. He asked around and found out about that piece of land and the house Patrick has from your parents."

"You mean the piece of land that WE have from our parents," corrected Christina.

"Yes, of course," continued Bachtal. "In any case, the man was new here and did not understand what was involved – where your land is, and so on."

"Where are you going with this?" prompted Christina.

"Anyway, one night when your brother was drunk the man put a piece of paper in front of him that promised your piece of land in exchange for what to Patrick must have seemed like a large sum of money. The man told him that it was the only way for Patrick to 'restore his honor.'"

"A piece of paper?" asked Christina. "But Patrick cannot read!"

"I know, but the man read it to him and got others to say what it said. In the end Patrick was convinced and made his X. The man gave him money and kept the paper. Then Patrick paid off the money he owed to me and to all the others."

"And was there money left?"

"Yes, but then Patrick spent it all that night on free drinks for the whole house."

Christina tried to sort through what she had heard.

"So why hasn't the man come and thrown us out of our place?"

"Oh, that is not what he wants at all – what he wants is his money back from Patrick. He says that Patrick tricked him, that the house and land are worthless. He is sour about it, I can tell you."

"Patrick didn't tell me anything about this," said Christina, looking up for the first time into Bachtal's face.

"I am not surprised. It is a pretty sad affair, all in all," said Bachtal. It looked like he was finished talking.

"Thanks for telling me," said Christina and looked around her at the village with new eyes; what other things were going on here that affected her but she did not know about?

Only now did she see Father Gruber and a tall severe looking man dressed in black with a black three-corner hat talking to each other outside the small church further along the street. They were looking at her, had been looking at her, were talking about her – she was sure of it.

Better to just put it all away in my mind for later and get on with my business, she thought to herself.

She went directly to the butcher's shop diagonally across from the tavern.

Butcher Weissmann was not in the shop; he was probably in the back killing or cutting up some animal. Or in the tavern. But his wife Margit was asleep in a chair, leaning back against the wall, snoring. Christina was glad to see Margit. Christina liked her.

Christina sat her bag down on the floor and opened it. She took the two wrapped pieces of goat meat out and laid them on the long board that separated the public side of the shop from where the butcher and his family and apprentices worked.

"Margit, I have something for you," called out Christina loudly. Margit was almost deaf.

Margit woke up and looked around. "Hello, Christina, how nice to see you!" she said.

"Come see what I have for you today," said Christina. Margit got up and came over to the board standing opposite Christina.

Christina opened the wrappings on the meat slowly and carefully, as if she were revealing something precious.

"Aren't they beautiful?" she asked Margit.

"Yes, they are beautiful," replied Margit. "What do you want for them?"

"As much flour as you can give me, different kinds if you have them."

"This is your lucky day!" said Margit and smiled broadly. She looked around behind her toward the back part of the shop. She leaned forward. "The Chief doesn't even know we got it in early this morning, in trade for some week-old deer meat from a trader from Freiburg that didn't know any better."

Margit took the goat meat and hung each piece on a hook among many hooks that lined the back wall of the room without even weighing them. She went to a corner shelf and brought back two cloth bags, one large and the other medium-sized, both tied at the tops, and set them on the board.

"This large one is wheat and the small one is rye. The quality is good," she said. "Just take them and go."

Christina took the two sacks, placed them in her carrying bag with the oiled cloths she had used for the meat, folded it closed, tied it, and hoisted it on her shoulder.

"Thanks," she said to Margit.

Margit leaned forward across the board again and spoke softly: "Elisabeth tells me you are helping her now. That is wonderful, really wonderful. But be careful, Christina, be really careful!"

Christina nodded, then turned and went out the door in a hurry.

Someone she had not seen was coming into the shop at the same time; they crashed together and both fell down, each dropping what they had been carrying. They both stood back up. Christina bent down and picked up her bag. Across from her stood a young woman about Christina's age but better dressed in a dark green fitted traveling outfit with a proper traveling hat. A fancy embroidered traveling bag lay on the floor beside her.

"Sorry," said Christina, "I should have looked where I was going."

"It's okay. I was not looking as well."

"What do you want?" called Margit loudly, still standing at the board.

"I need a place to stay the night; I am traveling ... by myself," said the woman.

"What?" called out Margit loudly.

"I need a place to stay!" shouted the girl.

"The tavern is across the street," Margit shouted back, pointing.

"I went there first but did not have a good feeling about it," answered the woman in a normal tone of voice, speaking now to Christina.

"You have got that right!" said Christina. "The only bed a woman traveling by herself will find there has a man in it with her or maybe several."

"Then where should I stay?" asked the woman.

"What kind of shoes do you have?" asked Christina after a thoughtful pause. With the woman's skirts you really couldn't see.

The woman smiled at the question. She lifted up the front of her skirts with both hands then stuck out her right foot turning it to the side to show off the sturdy traveling boot. It had a separate heel, the kind you wore to ride horses, but you could walk in it as well, since it went only halfway up the calf. She turned her foot to show the other side.

"Will these do?" she asked.

"Oh, yes, they will do very well. Do you have all your things?"

The woman hoisted her bag. "I do now."

"What is your name?" asked Christina.

"Beret," said the woman.

"I am Christina. Pleased to meet you. But now we really do need to get going," said Christina, and went out the door, head down and moving fast. The woman followed behind her, struggling to keep up with Christina's pace.

Margit watched them go, then went back to her chair by the wall and sat down.

    * * *

Beret and Christina were sitting outside at the small table. The remains of the fresh bread, goat's cheese, smoked goat meat and marmalade they had had for a late breakfast were still on the table. The spring day was calm and sunny.

"And what exactly is the place you are going to?" Christina asked. They had talked about many things since she had met Beret the day before but mostly about where Beret came from – the big city of Basel in the south – and the things that had happened to her there. At the very beginning Beret had told Christina where she was going, but just the name, as if that would explain everything. Christina was embarrassed that she had never heard of the place; it had taken some time for her to get back to the subject.

"I'm going to Rupertsberg, to the nunnery founded by Saint Hildegard," she said. She saw Christina's puzzled look.

"Why would you go to a nunnery?" asked Christina. "It sounds like you have a good life with your family in Basel. And some of the things you hear about the nunneries are not very nice."

"I have three reasons," responded Beret, counting them off on the thumb and fingers of her left hand. "First, I have two older brothers who are already fighting over who will get the inheritance when my father dies, which will probably be soon. It is clear there will be nothing at all for me. Second, my father and my brothers have been pressuring me to marry any one of several 'good choices' of men from other families that they have selected for me in order to con-nect the families and – not least – be rid of me. I have met these men and each of them is worse than the one before. And third, I am about convinced that I do not want to belong to any man, no matter who he is. I have seen too much of where that leads. My unhappy mother died last year and I think it was because she was done with that kind of life and simply did not want to live any more. No thank you! I want a different life."

"But in a nunnery there will be the priests who control every-thing. That is how it is I know in the nunnery down the valley from here." responded Christina. "So even in a nunnery there will be some man who controls it all."

"Yes, you are right! And men not just controlling the nuns. I have heard stories of nuns having babies – and not from the holy spirit! – and then terrible things happening to the babies after they were born!"

Christina's breathing became faster. She felt dizzy. She worked to calm herself. She held onto the edge of the table. "Please do not talk about such things!" she said.

"Oh, I am sorry," said Beret. "I didn't mean to upset you."

"It is okay. I am just too sensitive. But since you know all that, why are you still going to join a nunnery, this 'Rupertsberg'?"

"Don't you know about it?" she asked. "It's really famous!"

"No, I actually don't know anything about it," responded Christina. "Tell me."

Beret was happy to oblige.

"It is a nunnery of course, a place for women to dedicate them-selves to God. But it is very different from the normal nunnery; as you say those are run by men priests. Even when there seems to be some Mother Superior in charge she has no real power to decide things. Saint Hildegard was inspired by God to found a new order for women, run by women and independent of men. She even got the church to accept it! Their main nunnery is at Rupertsberg on the Rhine north of here. That is where I am going. The women there run everything themselves, make their own decisions even. They sing a lot, make up new songs, write stories, paint pictures and live with-out men."

Beret bent forward and dropped her voice. "And the main thing is that for the women in Hildegard's order the earth, the sun, the plants, the animals, the body – all of it is sacred and holy. Not like that stuffy old Father God nonsense from the church that is so afraid of anything that is alive."

"And this place really exists and it is just up the Rhine from here?" asked Christina, not believing it was possible.

"Oh yes, it has been there hundreds of years."

Christina was thoughtful.

"How do you get into this place?" she asked.

"It's like a nunnery – you bring your marriage dowry with you and donate it to the community instead of giving it to some man. Then you are in. Great, huh?" answered Beret.

"But I have no dowry," answered Christina softly. "I have no money at all; nothing of any value."

"Best to get a dowry together somehow," Beret continued. "I don't think you can show up like a beggar and be taken in. And it's good too if you know how to do something – I can make up songs and sing, for example."

"Here is my latest song. I wrote it just last week. I can sing it for you.

> Morning comes and I am ready,
> Sunlight shines upon my face.
> Morning comes and I am ready,
> God's grace blooms in my heart.
> Morning comes and I am ready,
> Sowing seeds in springtime's earth."

"Of course it should be in Latin, but my Latin isn't very good yet. I just started learning last year when I decided to apply to be accepted at Rupertsberg."

"That's very nice," said Christina. But her mind was already working on how to get together what she needed to join Hildegard's community.

Beret left the next day. Christina accompanied her back to the village where she was picked up by a coach. She had had to stay the two days in the village because of some confusion about transportation arrangements that her father had made for her.

After saying goodbye to Beret at the coach house Christina went directly to see Elisabeth.

Elisabeth was sitting on the ground weeding the herb garden that was at the edge of the woods near her hut. Christina walked up to her and crossed her arms across her chest. Elisabeth glanced at her then went back to her weeding.

"Do you know about Rupertsberg?" Christina asked.

Elisabeth nodded without looking up.

"Why didn't you tell me?" Christina demanded to know.

Elisabeth got up slowly and walked to the corner of her hut. She washed her hands in an open oak barrel there full of rain water collected from a wooden trough that hung along one side of the roof then dried her hands on a cloth hanging from a wooden peg set in the wall. Elisabeth walked to the birch tree that stood to one side of her house. She pointed to a place on the ground. "Sit down, Christina," she said.

They both sat down, Elisabeth with her back to the tree trunk. Elisabeth looked around searching for the right words to say.

"What do you know about that place?" she asked at last.

"A girl named Beret stayed with me the last two days. She is on her way there to join the community, to be a nun. She says it is run by women and that they live together and honor nature and living things and not just the men's Father God. The women sing and paint and work with plants and heal people and ... all of it."

Christina paused. "Why didn't you tell me?" she asked again.

"And how is Beret going to get into this place, to be accepted into the community?" asked Elisabeth, again ignoring Christina's question.

"Her family is giving Beret's dowry to the nunnery. I think they have money, maybe a lot of it. And Beret can do things: she can read and write and sing and is even learning Latin."

"Aha," said Elisabeth. "That is my answer to you, as to why I did not tell you."

"What do you mean?" asked Christina.

"Rupertsberg and the other places they have started are fine as far as they go but they are for rich women, for educated city girls and the daughters of noble families. Not people like us. I am sorry Christina. I wish it were otherwise. That is why I did not tell you; it would be better for you I thought not even to know that such a place existed than to know it is there but with no way to get in."

Christina tried to understand. "If it is only the rich women who get in, the educated women, then what is all this talk about nature and animals and plants and honoring that? What do these rich girls with their Latin know about that? People like us know about those things!"

"I have asked myself that question," replied Elisabeth. "But in the end it does not matter. It is simply not possible for people like us to get in, or so I understand it. But who knows? Maybe I am wrong, maybe things change."

Elisabeth sighed. There seemed to be nothing more to say. She looked up to the sky, to the thin clouds. The trees were whispering to the wind. A blackbird began singing. She looked back to Christina, who seemed to be feeling much better and was smiling broadly with her eyes closed, her face tilted up.

"What are you thinking?" asked Elisabeth.

Christina opened her eyes and sat up straight. She took a deep breath. Let it out slowly. She smiled again, almost a laugh.

"Well, someone has got to be the first woods woman to join the Hildegard community, right? It might as well be me!" And then she did laugh.

"Good luck to you, Christina," said Elisabeth seriously. "I know that if anyone can do it you can."

Preparation

"What are you looking for?" asked Patrick. He had noticed Christina walking around the outside of the house inspecting the walls. It had been a week since the girl Beret had stayed with them.

He was standing next to her, looking in the direction she was looking, trying to see what she was trying to see.

"I need to find a wall to paint," she said.

"But our walls are stone – they don't need paint," he protested.

"I mean paint pictures of things, like on the walls inside the church."

Patrick looked at her, his face wrinkled in astonishment. "You are even crazier than I thought you were!" he said. "Wait until I tell my friends; they won't believe it!" He laughed and turned to walk away.

Christina stepped over to him and seized his hair from behind with her left hand, pulling his head back. With her right hand she reached down and grabbed him between the legs squeezing until he cried out.

"If you so much as whisper anything about this to any one of your crummy friends I solemnly promise I will cut your balls off," she said slowly with conviction, her mouth next to his ear. Then she squeezed again harder for him to get the point.

"Okay, okay!" he agreed quickly, backing away as she released him. "I was only joking of course – you never understand it when I joke with you. Why is that? Paint the whole damn mountain! I don't care what you do." He walked back into the house.

Christina had noticed his question but could not answer it – the truth was that she had always treated him with contempt. At the same time he was her brother and she had taken care of him since even before their mother had died. It was a strange combination.

With Patrick gone she turned again to look at the house. The large wooden door on the ground level stood open; it seemed to be inviting her. She went inside. The wall at the back was just the lime-stone cliff face, rough and rocky. That would not do. The wall on the right was hard to get to – there were wooden stalls built there to separate the goats from one another when one of them was sick or giving birth. But the wall on the left?

She looked it over carefully. The wall was long, the full depth of the house at this point, about six paces. There were a few hooks in it for things they kept there but it was otherwise not used. The cream-colored stones and mortar in-between were uneven, but that could be fixed.

"What do you think, Wall," she asked. "Shall I paint you?"

She cocked her head to the side and smiled as she waited for an answer. It was definitely "yes."

"Thank you," she said.

She made a small bow to the wall then walked out of the room into the sunlight. She saw her goats looking at her. She ran to them, jumped in the air next to them, then jumped again, shouting sounds, waving her arms. Two of the goats jumped with her.

Patrick stood at the door to the kitchen watching her. He shook his head and walked back into the house.

The next morning Christina was up early. She had found the unused clay, silt and sand left in their storeroom from an earlier unfinished project that she had worked on with her father and carried it down into the animal room.

"Good morning, Wall," she said with enthusiasm.

She began to mix the ingredients, adding water as she went along, trying to remember what her father had taught her. After some experimentation she had a wet paste in a shallow wooden box that looked about right.

She applied the mix to a section of the wall using an iron garden tool she had found, then smoothed it out with a piece of wood. She left it to dry and went on with her work for the day.

The next morning when she came in to look she found that part of what she had applied to the wall had broken off and fallen to the floor. There were cracks in the parts that had not fallen.

She changed her mixture to make it moister with less sand and tried again on another part of the wall.

The next morning exactly the same thing had happened to the new section.

Over the following days she tried everything she could think of but nothing helped. She could mix the ingredients, apply it to the wall and smooth it out, and it would look fine, but parts of it always fell off by the next day.

After two weeks of trying she knew she needed help.

She and Patrick had not been on good terms lately. Patrick often asked her for money to go to the tavern. She had not confronted him about his having sold the house and land. That would be too painful for him, Christina thought. It would shame him. And not help anything.

Sometimes she did give him money for the tavern. She could not stand it when he pleaded with her. Maybe now he could do something for her.

"Patrick, I need help with the wall," she said to him. "Do you have any ideas?"

Patrick looked up at her across their evening meal in the kitchen.

"Actually, no. I've watched what you are doing, and what happens, and I have no idea how to make it work," he said. Then his face brightened. He had a surprise for her.

"But Christoph, my friend from the tavern, is a real expert at making walls. Everyone says he is the best, in walls and everything it takes to build a house."

Christina knew this Christoph. It was true – you could tell by looking at him, at how he walked and held his body – he knew how to do things. It was a big step to ask for help but she was desperate.

"So, can you talk to Christoph about coming up here and looking at the wall, to see if he has any advice?"

"Sure, I would be happy to," said Patrick, without sarcasm.

"But not one word to Christoph or anyone else about the painting idea, right? This is just about getting a wall finished and flat. Agreed?"

"Right; it is just about the wall," he answered.

Two days later Christoph was there, standing next to Patrick, who had shown him the way up from the village.

"I understand you need some help finishing a wall," he said first, making it easier for her. They stood outside in the early summer sun. She had just finished milking her goats and had put the milk bucket down and waited in front of the house when she had seen them coming up the path.

Patrick stood to one side watching them like it was some kind of entertainment. Christina stared at him until he ducked his head, murmured an apology and went into the house.

"Yes," she answered after Patrick was inside the house. "I have tried to do it myself but I can't make it work. I understand you know about these things."

"Can I see the wall?" he asked.

Christina liked that he was clear and direct in a situation he could have used to his advantage. She turned and walked the few steps into the animal room. It was empty now as she had let the goats back outside to forage. She pointed to the wall she wanted to finish.

"This one," she said. She folded her arms and waited for his judgment.

He went to the wall and examined it, touching it with his fingers and scratching at the mortar and stones. He rubbed the residue that came away between his thumb and index finger. He paid special attention to the places where she had tried but failed. Twice he put his face close to the wall and smelled it. Christina had no idea how he could smell the wall with all the years of goat aroma layer on layer on top of each other. But it pleased her to see him do it.

He was finished with his inspection. He turned to her.

"Your problem is that the stones and mortar are so uneven. When you put the mix on it has different thicknesses at different places that do not dry at the same rate so it cracks and breaks off. To make it work you have to put the mix on in layers of the same thickness, then let each layer dry before you put on the next."

So that was it, she thought to herself. There was a trick that you had to know. She looked down at the ground and walked out of the room into the light. He followed behind her. She stood outside for a moment looking around as if she had lost something. Then she looked back at him.

"I also had trouble getting the proportions of the mixture right and getting it smoothed out when I put it on." There was no reason not to tell him everything.

"Those are things that take a long time to learn," he said. "Mostly beginners don't mix it long enough."

She struggled with herself. She had asked him her questions and he had given answers. But what she really needed was his help to do the work.

"Do you think you could help me finish the wall? I want it done soon and I am afraid there may be other things I don't know."

She had expected him to smile or laugh. Instead he looked quite serious. He seemed to be thinking it over.

"I can't pay you money," she said thinking that perhaps that was the ground for his hesitation. "But you can have all the goat cheese you want."

He smiled awkwardly and waved his hands to ward off such a suggestion.

"Oh no," he said. "Patrick and I are friends. I will be happy to do it out of friendship."

"But you are doing this for me and not for Patrick," she said. "I insist that you take some payment for your work."

"Okay," he said. "If you insist."

"Is it a deal then?" She put out her right hand in the way she had seen men do in the market when they made an agreement.

He looked at her outstretched hand for a moment as if he did not understand what she wanted. Then he reached out his hand, tentatively. Their palms touched.

Since he seemed a little handicapped in the moment Christina took his hand in hers, grasped it firmly and moved it up and down. After the first motion he understood what she was doing. He tightened his grip on her hand and moved his hand up and down with hers.

The sensation of his hand in hers as he tightened his grip and moved with her was a shock to Christina's whole body. A torrent of unusual sensations flooded through her. She withdrew her hand, hid it in her other hand and struggled to overcome the feelings in her body. She felt dizzy and had some trouble breathing.

"When can we start?" she asked to cover her confusion. Again he looked at her with a questioning expression, pondering his response.

"I can come next Monday," he said after some moments. "I have some work in the village that I need to finish but after that we should be able to move ahead quickly. There will be time off to let things dry but with good weather the wall should be finished in three weeks."

"Thank you; that would be very good. Until Monday then," she said. Without another word or look she picked up the bucket of goat milk, turned her back and walked up the steps and into the house.

Christoph came as promised the next Monday morning. He walked up the trail leading a middle-sized black horse loaded with two large leather buckets balanced across a carrying saddle. Assorted tools were tied on as well. Christina had seen fine horses like this one before but she had never been up close to one. Her parents had never had a horse although it would have made a lot of sense given the difficulties of bringing things up from the village and her father's trading business. Without saying anything to Christoph Christina went up to the horse and put out her hand open palm upward for the horse to smell. The horse nuzzled her hand for a moment then raised its head and looked at her. The horse had a splash of white hair in the center of its forehead.

"Her name is Estrella. That means 'star' in the language of the country she comes from. My uncle and I got her for work we did on a rich man's house in Freiburg last winter. She was worth more than the work we did but I think the man felt guilty keeping her in the city. He was sick and couldn't ride her any more. He made us promise we would take good care of her and not treat her in a bad way."

For the first time since he had arrived Christina looked from the horse to Christoph. He looked unhappy. How could he be unhappy when he had such a horse? She could not understand it.

"Do we have everything we need?" she asked.

"Yes, at least I think so," he said. "We will need water of course."

"I can get that," she said. She turned and walked into the house.

Christoph unloaded the horse, then bound it at a small tree that stood by the spring on a long line he had brought with him.

"Why are you tying up the horse?" asked Christina as she carried a wooden bucket out of the house and set it on the ground by the spring basin.

"So she won't run away," answered Christoph.

"Why would she do that?"

"I don't know. I just always do it this way," answered Christoph, seeming to actually think about the question.

Christina walked over to the horse. It raised its head and looked at her. She reached up, untied the rope from the bridle the horse was wearing and dropped the rope on the ground. The horse stood there for a moment, looking at her, then put its head down and continued nibbling the grass.

"See? She doesn't run away," said Christina. She walked back to the spring and began to fill the wooden bucket with water using a ladle that lay there.

Christoph stood watching her for a moment then began to carry the materials into the lower level of the house.

* * *

Three weeks later Christoph and Christina stood looking at the finished wall.

It was a beautiful wall; much better than any of the other walls in the house. The color was a light yellow that Christina had selected after Christoph had shown her the possibilities given the materials they had to hand.

Christina went to the wall and put her hands on it, moved her hands over it, enjoying the feel of it. She stepped back from the wall, turned, then walked outside. He followed her.

"Wait here," she said to him.

She went into the house and returned with a large goatskin carrying bag.

"Here," she said handing it to Christoph. "It is the goat cheese I promised, ripened to a good quality. The bag I made myself. You can keep it."

"Thank you," answered Christoph.

He slung the bag over his left shoulder, picked up and put his already packed tool bag over his right shoulder, turned and walked down the trail. After a half dozen paces he stopped and looked back.

She was still looking in his direction.

"Good luck to you, Christina," he said after a moment.

"Good luck to you too, Christoph," she answered.

He turned and walked down the path.

After waiting another week for the wall to dry completely she went down to the room one night with the various dyes and pigments she hoped to use for colors, expecting to paint. She had a candle with her for light. But it did not go as she had expected. The candle light was not right somehow and their supply of candles was too limited if she was going to do much of this. Most of all, however, she had no idea how to begin. She sat there until the candle burned completely down. The wall remained blank.

After a few nights of this she hit on an alternative for lighting. She remembered then located a ceramic lamp bowl with a cloth wick that her mother had brought from Freiburg. At a market she charmed an old farmer out of a large quantity of rancid pig fat that was left over from the previous year's pig killing that no one else wanted. All she needed to give in exchange was a small package of goat cheese and a smile.

The burning pig fat in the ceramic lamp bowl was much better for light – the light moved more and had a redder tone. But she still had no idea as to what to paint.

The priest had been wrong – she had been inside the church once in her life. She did it on a dare from two boys her age when she had been small and in the village with her father who had gone into the tavern. The boys had promised that if she went into the church by herself they would let her play with them. Once inside she was stunned to see the pictures painted on the walls – the 'stations of the cross' her mother had explained when she had asked about it later. So much suffering! She had cried and finally had to run out the door. The boys who had dared her to go in were waiting outside and laughed when they saw her crying. They did not let her play with them. "You failed the test!" they shouted, and walked away.

Christina did not think that the suffering Christ or martyred saints were the right themes for her painting. But then what? There seemed to be no other choice but to sit and wait until the direction came.

She had sat up late into the night several times without results. Then one night when she had fallen asleep sitting on the ground leaning back against the wall she woke with a start – one of her goats, Elsbit, was standing in front of her, licking her face. All the rest were asleep.

"Of course!" she said to herself.

She reached for the orange powder she had scraped from rusted iron, poured a little in a small bowl, then mixed in some deer fat. Using her fingers she made a simple outline of the goat's head on the wall. Curving horns, head, neck. Then the body and legs. Even a little tail at the end.

"So the outline is the first step," she said to herself.

"Black, I need black!" she exclaimed out loud and reached for the bowl of carbon black scraped from their hearth upstairs. Mixed with the deer fat and smeared in the right places in the goat outline it brought the first goat to life.

It was a wonderful adventure. She would simply sit and wait and the figures would come to her. She developed a sense for the colors she needed even before she needed them and sought them wherever she could find them in plants or earth or the village. At first she had painted with her fingers but later she used brushes that she made herself from goat hair. Over time the whole wall – six paces long and a little higher than her head where it met the beamed wood floor of the rooms above – was covered with complex interwoven figures. She did not think about what she should paint and did not plan it at all. She would feel in the mood to paint, go down into the room, light the lamp for light, get her growing range of colors ready, and the pictures would just come to her, or changes to existing figures would suggest themselves. This was always at night while her brother slept or was away somewhere with his friends.

The pictures were different than what she had expected. There were trees, plants, animals, and people, some dressed in unusually colored clothes, all looking back at her from the wall, all with eyes, even the trees. Sometimes she could hear them thanking her for helping them to be seen, for her seeing them.

It took her a year to complete the whole wall. With that finished she felt she had learned to paint. She never showed the painted wall to anyone though she was sure that Patrick had looked at it some. She never painted any more after the first wall. But sometimes at night she would come in and sit with a light, just looking, trying to grasp that she had done it herself. Now she could look anyone in Hildegard's community in the eye when they asked her what she knew how to do. "I can paint walls with pictures of animals and plants and people," she would answer. Just like Beret could make and sing songs. This new accomplishment was a source of warmth in her body that buoyed her up when she was feeling discouraged.

Collecting the money she needed for her dowry had been much more difficult. Despite every effort and ruthless bartering at market days in Merzhausen where she went to get better prices, she had only 32 silver pfennig collected. She had set herself the goal of 100. She was convinced that that much money as a dowry and an ability to paint would be enough for admittance into the Rupertsberg community.

Birth

Christina spread the waxed cloth over the wool blankets already lying on the packed earth floor. She lifted Frieda's knees one by one and slid it under them. The head would come out soon now. Keeping a cleaner space here on the floor where the baby would land seemed the right thing to do.

"More wood on the fire," she whispered to Friedhelm. He had been so focused over the last half hour watching Frieda's struggle that he had let the hearth fire burn low. Christina had delivered babies in the dark before and several times animals which seemed to prefer the dark. In ways she liked it too as you were thrown back on only touch, sound, and your inner sense of what was happening and what was needed. But in difficult cases like Frieda's where the baby had to be turned and the mother and father had so much fear a little light was not so bad. Friedhelm put several more sticks on the fire. The light in the room blazed up showing everything in sharper outline.

Frieda was in the center of the small room on her hands and knees. Her beige night dress was folded up now so that her buttocks were bare. Where her skin was visible it glistened from the sweat of the labor that had been going on for three hours now. The square table and three wooden chairs that normally filled the space were stacked to one side. The walls of the hut were wooden logs laid on top of one another with clay between them to hold back the wind. There were no windows, only a wooden door. The fire was in a corner backed with flat stones against the logs. Above the fire was a hole in the wooden beam and floorboard ceiling where most of the smoke from the fire went up. In another corner was a crude ladder leading up through a hole in the ceiling. There was no other light in the room than the fire.

When Frieda was between contractions Christina thought about how she had come to be here. She had rehearsed it with them beforehand: as soon as the serious pains began Friedhelm had hurried to find her at her house being careful to not let anyone see him and not letting anyone else know of the impending birth. Luckily Patrick had not been at home. As far as Christina could tell no one had seen them as she and Friedhelm traveled separately around the village to the small forest hut. By the time they had both reached the hut Frieda's water had broken.

Christina took up a new position, also now on her knees, behind Frieda. She put her open palms on Frieda's buttocks giving Frieda something to push against and also to keep the body contact. Frieda was tired and desperate and began to push even when it made no sense from the rhythm. "Take your time, Frieda," Christina whispered. "The baby is doing fine; only push when it pushes too." Frieda relaxed a little and laughed through her tears, "It's so big!"

"I can feel the top of the head now," said Christina. "It won't be long."

When Frieda pushed the next time the head slid out with the face toward Christina. As the head cleared the opening a fountain of dark fluid sprayed out of the baby's pursed lips and onto Christina's chest, propelled by the pressure of the womb. Christina laughed.

"This one already wants to play!" she said.

She supported the head with one hand while she reached in with her fingers to help the shoulders turn. Within less than a minute she was holding the newborn baby in her arms, still connected by the cord to the mother.

"And by the way, it's a girl," she said.

Frieda collapsed onto the blankets on the floor then rolled over carefully onto her back sobbing with relief. She looked expectantly to Christina. Christina hesitated for a heartbeat – would that this could be her baby! – then lifted up the night dress and placed the newborn on Frieda's belly with its head between her swollen breasts.

Christina dried Frieda's vagina then applied a cream to slow the bleeding.

When it felt right she took the baby out from under the night dress and laid it again on Frieda's belly. She turned the baby on its side, tied the umbilical cord twice close to the baby's navel with two strips of goat gut, then took her knife from its pocket in her boot and cut the umbilical cord between the two tied points. She wiped the knife on a rag then put it back into its boot pocket. She took some wine from a small bottle she had also brought with her and poured a little of it over the knot at the baby's navel. The baby struggled for air, wheezed in its first breath, then let out a loud cry – it was angry at the sting of the wine. Frieda and Friedhelm were both concerned but Christina was smiling.

"What a wonderful strong voice she has!" Christina said.

Christina dried the belly button and smeared on a herb cream she had also brought with her. She listened carefully to the coughing and difficult breathing of the baby that followed its crying spell.

"She still has some liquid in her lungs. It doesn't sound so serious but someone should stay awake with her all night. If she has real difficulty breathing or stops breathing blow air into her mouth while you hold her nose closed then suspend her upside down holding her feet for a minute and try to help her get it out."

Frieda and Friedhelm looked frightened by these instructions. Both of them had been raised in families with no younger children and in the city with no animals under the roof. But Christina thought they would make it.

The afterbirth took a long time to come but finally did come. Christina cleaned Frieda's vagina again and put more salves on it, then a compress of rags. There was very little bleeding now; Frieda would do fine. Christina took the placenta, cleaned it with a rag, and examined it as carefully as she could in the dim light. It was perfect with no abnormalities – a good sign for the little one. She wrapped it in more waxed rags that she had brought with her especially for this purpose and put it into her carrying bag. Frieda and Friedhelm were so entranced with the baby they had not seemed to notice her taking it. Christina was happy to not have to discuss it with them.

Christina showed Frieda how to make a poultice to bind her genitals with rags and the herb salve she had brought. She gave Frieda another preparation to use in case there was more bleeding and warned her to take it easy until it healed.

"I think that's about all," she said. She washed her hands and arms in a bowl of water by the fire then gathered the waxed cloths, rags, and medicines she had brought with her into her leather carrying bag and tied it closed. She would clean the cloths and rags later.

She sat down again on the floor opposite them and waited until she had their full attention.

"Please remember what we agreed: you will tell everyone that asks – and I mean everyone with no exceptions – that you had the birth yourselves with no help and it went well. I was not here and you did not so much as discuss the birth with me. For that matter it would be best if you forgot completely that I exist. If someone notices your medicines and pressures you, hesitate and stall as long as you can then tell them that you got them from Elisabeth. But do this only if you are forced to give some explanation. Elisabeth has agreed to this and will support your story. If we are all careful we can get through this without any trouble, if you know what I mean."

Frieda and Friedhelm looked at each other then back at her then nodded seriously. They knew exactly the kind of trouble she meant. Christina stood up to go.

Friedhelm stood with her at the door. "Thank you so much. Without you I don't know what would have happened." He looked back into the room at Frieda still lying on the blankets on the floor with the baby at her breast. He took a deep breath then looked up into her face.

"I don't know how we can repay you. We are just poor simple people with nothing..." His voice trailed off. Frieda was watching the exchange with concern from her place on the floor.

"I'll be direct with you," said Christina. "I need money, real money, a coin if you have one. You know I would not ask if I did not really need it." She looked him straight in the face without wavering, her expression serious. He looked down toward the ground. They had never discussed the matter of payment. From his reaction Friedhelm's worst fear was realized. He looked around nervously; everywhere but into her face. His hands touched and began to struggle with one another.

"Friedhelm, give it to her," said Frieda quietly.

Friedhelm nodded deeply, sighed, nodded again. He still did not look into Christina's face. This was hard for him. Christina opened the door herself and stepped outside into the night with her bag on her shoulder to wait for him to get whatever it was that they were going to give her from their hiding place. After a minute he came outside and without speaking placed a coin in her waiting hand, then went back into the house closing and latching the door. She folded her hand over the cold metal, closed her eyes, and nodded her thanks to the night sky. By its size and weight it was a full pfennig. "One more!" she whispered and smiled to herself. She put the coin carefully into the inside pocket of her goatskin jacket and paused for a moment thinking where she should go next if not straight home. It had been a long day and she was tired. At the same time she was exhilarated by the successful birth and not ready to sleep. From the position of the full moon it was about midnight.

By taking a little-used trail and cutting through some sections of woods she could come to Elisabeth's place, which was on this side of the valley, without passing near to any other houses. The people in the houses closer to the village would be asleep but the dogs were often a problem when one traveled at night. She headed upward to get to the right trail finding more strength in her legs than she had expected. The full moon lit her way as it streamed through the holes in the forest canopy. Here on the slopes the trees were not as dense as in the lower valley or along the river plain.

Remembering the placenta she paused and stood for a moment. She turned to look back toward where she had just been. With the help of the moonlight she saw the smoke from the hearth fire at the hut rising past the tree tops only a few hundred paces from her and some distance below.

This would be a good place, she thought to herself.

She left the trail to the right and pushed through some bushes to enter a clearing in the forest – a small meadow circled by larger maple trees with a small elderberry tree on the upper side, standing by itself in the moonlight. She walked slowly to the base of the elderberry tree and set her bag down on the ground beside her. She bowed her head for a moment and asked permission from the tree and the place for what she was about to do. She went down on her knees then began to move the surface leaves and grass clumps carefully to the right side. The earth here was soft so she was able to make the shallow hole using her naked hands. She put the moist humus that she removed carefully in a pile to the left side. When the hole was ready she took the placenta out of her carrying bag and out of its wrappings. She held it in her hands feeling the cool slick aliveness of it. It glistened in the moonlight. She raised it up for a moment and dipped it in a bow in the direction of the shining moon high in the south. She held it against her left cheek. Water came into her eyes. She closed her eyes and nodded to herself. The moment passed. She opened her eyes, looked at the placenta in her hands one last time then placed it carefully in the bottom of the hole. She slowly covered the placenta with the earth she had removed, then replaced the leaves and grass that had been there.

"Now the child will have a special connection with this place and with this tree. They will always be here for her when she needs them," she recited quietly in a ritual way out loud.

Just as Elisabeth had done this for her now she had done this for the new little one. She thought of her mother and it made her sad as it always did. She stood up, struggling with the temptation to lie in the grass and be comforted by the tree. "Thanks anyway," she whispered out loud to the tree, "but I have things to do." She bowed to the tree, to the circle of trees, to the moon, and lastly to the earth itself. She picked up her carrying bag and headed back through the undergrowth to the trail.

As she walked again up the trail toward the ridge she caught herself thinking that she must remember to tell the girl when she became old enough about the place where her placenta had been buried, although perhaps the girl would have found it herself as Christina had found her place.

But I will not be here to tell her – I will be gone, she realized. The thought made her sad and yet excited. She decided to tell Elisabeth about the place she had buried the placenta in case Elisabeth was still around when the girl was old enough to understand it.

* * *

"How nice to have you visit me, Christina!" Elisabeth greeted Christina cheerfully before Christina had even seen her.

"I have been expecting you. Did Frieda have her baby?"

Christina found Elisabeth sitting outside on the ground leaning against the trunk of the large birch tree in the moonlight. Christina put her bag down and sat on her knees in front of Elisabeth. The patchy bark of the birch tree was white and luminous in the moonlight, like a frame around Elisabeth's head. Elisabeth took Christina's hands in hers. They were quiet for a minute.

"Yes, she did – it went well. I had to turn it at the beginning like you have taught me. You were probably right that that was what had happened to her earlier babies. Then the rest was pretty simple. The baby has some liquid in its chest but I told them to watch it carefully and I think it will be okay."

"Good. I am glad to hear this news. Frieda was so afraid of the birth after her other two times. It was good that you were able to be there."

Elisabeth paused and then continued in a different tone. "Did anyone see you?"

"No, I think no one saw me. And I think Frieda and Friedhelm will not tell. If anyone asks them about the medicines they will say that they got them from you like we agreed. That could get you in some trouble perhaps but hopefully not too much."

"Oh no one really cares about a half-blind old woman in the woods as long as she goes to church sometimes, smiles at everyone she meets and sells beans on summer market days. I mix up a few medicines now and then but nothing that other people don't know about. That is the story anyway and so far it works," Elisabeth answered ruefully.

"It's you I am worried about," Elisabeth continued, leaning forward and grasping Christina's hands more tightly. "You live with your brother which is good in a way but I don't trust him at all, especially when he gets drunk which is as much of the time as he can manage. Who knows what he might say to people about you? You don't ever go to church; people tell me you look away if you meet the priest on the street; you dress strangely in these sewn animal skins; and most of all you are much too pretty for people to ignore especially since you spit on all the boys! Take the advice I have given you: go to church once in awhile, smile at the priest, get yourself some nice wool clothes like everyone else, wink at the boys, get fat, grow some hair on your face! Girl, you are headed for trouble. I just feel it! Watch out. Best would be to follow your plan and get out of here as soon as you can."

Christina was thoughtful. There was nothing here that she had not heard before from Elisabeth.

"Oh Elisabeth, I know you are worried about me but I am as I am. I can't go to church or smile at Father Gruber the way you do – I just can't. Just to walk by the church makes me want to scream – all their damned rules and big Father God – I just don't buy it. They think our work helping women have babies is interfering with God's judgment on who should live and who should die! And the boys! They are all so terrible drinking and fighting all the time and just wanting to get into the hay with me. You can't trust them!"

Christina said nothing more. She was thinking now about something else.

Elisabeth sighed.

"Okay, I know you can't change. And I know you do what you have to do. Just be careful, Christina, please be careful. Not just for your own sake but for the people that count on you. You have more skill than anyone I ever taught. And I feel like you will do something important in your life, more than just helping people like you do now, though I do not know what."

Thinking about the people who counted on her Christina thought about the placenta she had planted in the earth for the new baby.

"Elisabeth, I buried the placenta from the child born this night in a fairy circle about twenty paces across, with an elderberry at the north side, thirty paces south of the main trail about three hundred paces above their house. Can you remember all that? When she is old enough can you make sure that she has found the place and if she has not tell her where it is and what she should do there?"

Elisabeth was quiet.

"Why don't you tell Frieda? She's the girl's mother after all. Right?" said Elisabeth ironically after awhile.

"Yes, of course," answered Christina. "But I wanted to tell the girl myself somehow. And if I can't do it then I wanted you to."

Elisabeth was quiet again for some moments.

"Christina, you know that it's not your baby; you are just the helper for it to come into this world. That is a lot but it is not the same as being the mother. I understand your not wanting to tell Frieda – she is a stranger to our ways. But I will almost certainly be dead before the girl is old enough. I tell you what: I promise to pass this information on to Frieda before I die so she can show her own daughter the place. That would certainly be the best. Maybe being a mother and living in these woods will grow her enough so that she can understand it better than she does now. Will that be okay?"

"I hope so," answered Christina. There was silence between them.

"I need to go now," Christina continued abruptly, not looking Elisabeth in the face. She was hurt by Elisabeth's exposing her secret wish to be a mother to the newly born girl.

They leaned together where they were sitting and embraced for a moment. Christina stood up and shouldered her carrying bag.

Elisabeth continued to sit at the base of the tree looking up in the direction of the moon.

"Goodbye, Christina," said Elisabeth, still looking at the moon.

"Goodbye, Elisabeth," responded Christina. She turned and walked away.

Christina traveled slowly along the moon-lit path on her way back home.

She stopped to watch a fox that was coming along the trail toward her still some distance ahead. She had noticed him in the moonlight before he had seen her which gave her as always a special thrill. He saw her then and stood for a moment looking at her. She slowed her breathing and reached out with her senses to meet him.

Hello, Fox, she said inside her head. She had not seen this particular fox before; it was nervous but very interested.

The wolves up higher in the mountains to the east began to sing to the moon and the fox disappeared into the underbrush. Christina continued walking but more slowly now. In the pleasure of meeting the fox she had forgotten her anger and irritation over Elisabeth's lecture. Elisabeth meant well – she just did not understand.

Christina walked on, enjoying the night forest.

The wolves had gone silent some time ago.

She was on the ridge trail now not far from her house.

The first Saturday of each month was the market day and so it had been yesterday. After such a day there was often a party in the evening afterward at the village tavern since people from other villages often spent the night before beginning the walk home the next day. This meant that Patrick would not be home when she got there. If there was anything happening at the tavern he was sure to be there in the hope of getting free drinks from someone.

She slowed her pace as she approached her house.

There was some animal on the path ahead of her: It was one of her goats! She came up to it and it came to her. It nuzzled its head into her belly, confused to be outside at night, easy prey for wolves. How could this be? She was certain she had put the goats into their room and fastened the door latch before she had left to help Frieda.

As she came into the clearing before the house she whistled loudly in a rising tone. In a few moments all of the goats had come to her. She counted one through ten.

A thief would have carried at least one off, she thought to herself. Something else has happened here.

She led the goats through the wide door into their stall. After the goats were all in she closed the door, fastened it behind her and climbed the steps up into the house, her anger building step by step: it must have been Patrick! He went into the goat stall for something and then did not remember to close it. Typical. But there was a growing uneasiness in her belly. Coming into the common room she grimaced – the hearth fire had gone out and was cold. Patrick had again forgotten to keep the fire going so they could have a ready fire in the house. Or maybe he had not been here since she had been so that it was her fault. In the end it made no real difference – she would have to make a fire. She put her shoulder bag on the table then groped there for the candle in its holder. Christina sat and worked with the flint, steel, and shaved wood she took from a box on a shelf until the candle blazed.

Looking around she saw the room was in much more disarray than usual. She carried the candle to her brother's room. Even before she went in she could feel that there was no one there. Looking around she saw no evidence of the confusion of the common room – everything here was in its normal state of disorder. Her brother's bed was empty. She went over and put her hand under the feather comforter. It was cold there – he had not been here at all this night.

She went to her own room. The candlelight showed her even more confusion and riot than there had been in the common room. All of her things were thrown around haphazardly, piled on top of one another, or lying discarded on the floor. Every box and drawer had been opened and emptied. The bed itself had been torn apart. Someone had been looking for something. Suddenly several things snapped together in her head like the parts of a puzzle: the open goat stall, the wild search here in the house.

Holding her hand around the flame to keep it lit she went unsteadily out the house door and down the steps to the stall. She opened the door there. The goats were pleased to see her; they crowded up to her as she came in. But she paid no attention to them. She held the candle high with her eyes fixed on a spot in the back wall where an oak beam angled up from the ground level as a frame for the stone structure of the house. Here was where her painting had its right edge and where she had fashioned her hiding place for her dowry when she had remade the wall. It was just as she had feared. In the place where a large oval river stone had been – painted to be a great horned owl, with big yellow eyes, sitting on the angled oak beam like it was a tree branch – was now an empty blackness. The oval stone lay on the ground, owl-face down. She reached her free hand into the opening and felt around to see if there was something left there – but it was hopeless she knew. The leather purse was gone. Patrick had found her money – all of it outside of the single pfennig she had in the pocket of her jacket – and taken it with him to the tavern.

Christina slumped to the ground. She sat the candle holder on the packed earth floor without noticing that she did so, then rolled over and lay on her right side, crying softly. Her body curled around the painted owl-stone that she found there, turning it over and pressing the owl face against her, cradling the cold stone against her breasts with her folded arms.

"Oh, Owl, what shall we do?" she said.

The goats were startled by the weeping and drew back. After some minutes they came closer again. One licked her face. Then as her crying quieted they lay down one by one around her, their bodies touching hers, helping as best they could.

The gray light of first dawn was coming through the still open stall door when she awoke. The candle had long since burned out. She sat up and looked around at the goats. All ten were there. That was good. They were all okay. She looked down at her body and then at her hands. In the dark she had not noticed but now she saw there was dried blood on her goatskin skirt and on her hands. That would not do. She stood shakily and went over to the stone trough that was inside by the door where the goats had their inside water. Using the cloth that hung there she did the best she could to get the blood off her hands. It must be from the placenta she thought to herself as she had washed after the birth. The blood came off her hands but the skirt was hard to clean as the blood had been dry so long. She did not have another skirt so she would just have to clean this one. She untied the straps that held it around her waist, stepped out of the skirt and proceeded to scrub it in the cold water. The stains were stubborn and progress was slow. A goat bleated, then another. They were hungry, not having anything to eat since early the previous evening. "Yes, in a minute," she answered impatiently.

The blood was not all gone but it would have to do. She stepped into the skirt and tied it again around her.

What to do next? she asked herself.

She looked around the room. Her eyes found the round stone with the painted owl lying face up now on the floor. She let out a sharp cry. It was not a dream; it was not a dream at all. It had really happened. Her money, everything she had counted on, was gone, stolen by Patrick.

She stood still for a moment.

After feeling around again in the hole in the wall to make sure there was really nothing there, she picked up the painted oval stone and put it back as it had been, the owl sitting in his tree. She looked into his face, opened her eyes to his wide oval eyes in the dim light. She opened her mouth slightly, breathed more deeply, breathed more slowly.

Suddenly she knew the answer: she must go – now – immediately – leave this place. There was no point in waiting now. There was danger in waiting; she could feel it in her blood, in her bones, all through her body.

She turned and knelt on her knees on the straw-covered earth. She looked into the eyes of the goats that gathered in a half-circle around her.

"Friends," she said to them, touching each one on the head, one by one, "I must leave you now. Do not wait for me, as I will not be returning. Take care of yourselves and of each other. I wish I could take you with me but I cannot. Goodbye."

She stood, turned and walked decisively out of the stall, along the house wall and up the steps into the house. Her bag was still sitting where she had left it. She dumped the contents out on the table – her baby delivery things. She would not need them anymore. She put them on a shelf in the wall then gathered up the things she had always planned to take with her in her journey to Rupertsberg: the best of her paint brushes, several packages of the dyes she used to make her paints, all the dried meat and goat cheese they had plus a bag of walnuts. She added some useful herbs in small leather bags she might be able to trade. She closed and tied the bag. She looked at her hat on its hook by the door. It is my traveling hat, she realized. She put it on.

She walked out the door and started down the steps, leaving the door open. Then stopped and went back and closed the door. Let Patrick look for her, wait for her, whatever. He would gradually figure out that she was gone. She did not want to see him now. She was afraid she would kill him if they met and that would not really help anything. After all Patrick was just Patrick. There did not seem to be anything she could do about it.

She didn't need to tell Elisabeth she was going. Elisabeth would know it anyway, did already know it. She could feel Elisabeth with her right now, urging her on, concerned as ever but happy that she was going.

Her plan was to pass the village using the valley trail then head directly west for the Rhine where she hoped to find a boat to take her down the river or at least across. If there was no boat she would just start walking the river bank north. The only money she had was the single silver pfennig in her jacket pocket. She hoped she would be able to hold onto that but would use it if she needed it for the right boat passage for the whole river distance.

She sighed as she walked down the path. This was not how she had planned this journey at all. But perhaps there was a chance for her in Hildegard's community even without a dowry. The goats followed her of course. She stopped and spoke sharply to them. "Stay here! It's better for you here. You cannot come with me." At last they understood and began to wander off in various directions looking for food. She walked on more quickly now. She hoped that she would not meet anyone from the village.

But in a few minutes she saw three men coming up the trail from the road heading toward the point where it intercepted the ridge trail, already quite close to where she was. Ulrich was one of them. The other was a boy named Josef. The third, better dressed with a three-cornered black hat and black jacket and pants, was the tall man she had seen talking to Father Gruber in the village on the day she had met Beret. They had already seen her so there was no point in trying to hide or run away.

Instead of continuing their walking they stopped at the intersection of the paths and waited there. Clearly they had some business with her. Christina had no idea what this business could be but walked on resolutely in any case. Ulrich said something she could not hear to the taller man, who nodded his head in a way that Christina did not like. The boy Josef looked frightened.

As she approached them the men barred her path. Instead of asking them to move she put her head down and began to circle around them.

"Are you Christina Knecht, daughter of Bernd and Hilda Knecht?" said the tall man in a strange official-sounding tone.

Christina stopped and looked at him, then at the other men.

"You know perfectly well who I am, and if you do not, Ulrich or Josef here can tell you. And now may I please pass?"

"Take her," said the tall man. Ulrich and Josef moved unsteadily forward, each taking hold with both hands of one of her arms above the elbow. Christina was so surprised she did nothing to resist.

"You are under arrest," said the tall man in the same strange official-sounding tone, then turned and began to move off down the path toward the village.

"Under arrest for what?" she asked, not moving.

"If she speaks again, knock her out and carry her," answered the tall man to the two men without turning his head.

"I demand to know why I am being arrested!" shouted Christina, resisting the efforts of Ulrich and Josef to move her down the path.

The tall man stopped, turned, and nodded to Ulrich as if it was some kind of agreed on signal.

Christina looked into Ulrich's face. It was a face she knew: the blue eyes, the bushy eyebrows, the pocked red nose, the surprisingly soft mouth in the short gray beard. He had a look of fear and excitement on his face. He took his right hand off her arm and reached under his coat for something. Suddenly Christina felt a sharp pain in the back of her head and lost consciousness.

Witches Prison Freiburg

Christina had been dreaming again. Or not a dream exactly but a vivid memory of her early childhood. It was spring and her mother had taken Christina and Patrick on a picnic higher along the ridge trail towards the Belchen peak that they could see sometimes in the distance. They had found a small clearing on the ridge crest where they could spread what they had brought on a flat stone in the warm sun. Before eating their mother insisted that they sing a song that she had learned as a child from her mother, that she wanted to teach them in her attempt to be a good mother. And so they sang the song. At first it was awkward and uneven. But after some rounds of repetition she and Patrick had gotten into the rhythm of it and joined in with more and more energy. They had danced it together, hand in hand, in a circle.

Ring around a rosie,
a pocket full of posies.
Ashes,
ashes,
we all fall down!

And at the end, they all fell down, laughing.

She opened her eyes, but it made no difference in terms of being able to see. It was so dark here in the dungeon most of the time, including in this moment, that she could see absolutely nothing.

She was not certain how long she had been there. The only thing she was sure of was that she had been fed twenty-seven times. At least she had a clear head for numbers.

"The next time will be twenty-eight," she repeated over and over until she was sure that she would not forget it.

Assuming that she was being fed once a day then she had been here four weeks.

The heavy door to her cell was not so well fitted around the top and left side so that a little light came through, a kind of flickering, when someone was outside with a torch. There was always the same sequence when someone brought her food. She could hear the clang and creak of the upper door opening, the sixteen footsteps descending, something heavy – probably a bucket – being set on the floor, then a whack of some kind of wooden stick or serving spoon against her door as a signal. She would take her wooden bowl then, lift the leather flap that covered the rectangular opening, and hold the bowl out through the opening. Food was then dropped or poured into the

144

bowl – usually it was a vegetable soup with a piece of bread in it. Then the wooden stick or whatever it was would be banged against her door again and she would know that that was all. So she would draw the bowl back into her cell carefully so as not to spill anything. The leather flap closed by itself when she let go of it. She ate with her fingers and drank the liquid directly from the bowl. Talking with the person who brought her food was not allowed. She had discovered this after trying not once but twice to ask a question: "What is this place?" The answer was not silence but the clanging of the stick and walking away with her receiving nothing to eat. It had made an impression and she sought no more for answers. Except for the first time, when the full bowl had been passed in to her, the ritual had always gone in this way.

She had been surprised that they were feeding her so well. Christina was used to eating relatively little. It was not a lot that they gave her but it was more than she had imagined people got in such a place. The soup was of various vegetables dried and saved from last summer, so they were tough and chewy, plus some winter cabbage, but that was what everyone ate. Every few days there was a flavor of meat in the soup – sometimes chicken, sometimes beef, sometimes deer or rabbit. And the bread pieces in the soup were not the rock hard old bread of the poor people but bread you could actually chew and swallow.

Perhaps she had lost some weight but she was not overly hungry and did not think that starvation was in the plan. That was a relief at least. And not only were they feeding her but they had left her in her own clothes.

They had found and taken the knife that she always carried in her right boot in the pocket she had made for it there. They had also found the pfennig in the pocket in her jacket. They had been thorough. That was not surprising. But what could they possibly have in mind? Her boots, her skirt, her jacket, her under-things, even the felt hat she had made and worn when she was captured were all here with her. It was a great blessing. Although it was not really cold in the cell it was damp and cool. The skins of her clothing kept her warm better than anything outside of a regular feather bed would. Nor had her hair been cut.

Christina had seen condemned women being taken by wagon through Freiburg once when she was there with her father on a business trip when she was eleven. They wore black dresses and had their hair cut short. When she asked him why the women in the wagon looked like that he had said that was how they always did it so that people could see the guilty ones and remember themselves to stay on the right side of the authorities. This had made a deep impression on her.

"What have these women done?" she had asked her father.

"Who knows?" he had answered then looked at her sharply. "Forget about it," he had advised, and turned and walked on.

There were other mysteries to her imprisonment. The cell she was in was much larger and better out-fitted than anything she would have imagined. The ceiling was high enough that she could actually stand up and in the center she could not reach high enough to touch the roof of the vault which curved up from the pillars in the four corners. The room was large – five paces by five paces. In a corner on the left end of the wall opposite the door was a hole in the floor by one of the pillars with crossed iron bars in it which served as a toilet. It smelled of course but it astounded her that there was some attempt to deal with the prisoners' waste products. The floor was not rough as she would have expected but properly flattened and smoothed floor stones fitted together in a geometric pattern she could trace with her fingers, centered in a circle with four quadrants. Finally there was a pile of straw in the corner to the right of the door. It had not been changed since she was there but it had been clearly fresh-laid for her. There was no cloth sack to hold it together or even less a wooden frame around it. But it was an almost proper bed. After puzzling over it for a long time she had finally simply accepted that it was all as it was and it did not matter if she did not understand it.

What made it all bearable was what she had discovered early on: she was not alone in the cell. There were others with her supporting her and comforting her. Most of all Elisabeth was with her. She could talk to Elisabeth in an almost normal way. Christina did not speak out loud, as that did not seem right. And in case someone was listening she did not want anyone to think that she was crazy. But she would ask inside and often Elisabeth would answer. Sometimes others were there. Some she did not know. They had nothing to say. But they had come as if they wanted to see her or meet her. Her mother and father were several times with her. They were more relaxed now. Unlike Elisabeth they did not talk much but she could feel their presence like a warmth. Once she heard her mother say, "We are sorry we did not do better by you. We had many problems and did the best we could. But never think we did not love you. We did love you and we love you now and want to help you." This made her feel better and gave her courage to face the unknown that was yet to come.

A couple of times she had felt that Patrick was there too. But he was always very sad, said nothing in answer to her questions and then looked away. "I am sorry Patrick that it did not work out between us," she heard herself say to him. Then she realized that it was true. She was truly sorry.

Christina's Dream

Christina lay on her back in the center of her cell with her eyes closed but completely awake. Her thoughts quieted and she became aware of her body: her slow breath coming in and going out at its own rhythm, her arms at her sides with palms opened upward, her legs slightly apart and relaxed.

She noticed tightness in her face especially on the left side, where it often was and let go of whatever she had been carrying there, breathing it out, just as Elisabeth had taught her as preparation for supporting a birth. But no one is being born around here now, she thought to herself, amused at the idea of a birth in a dungeon.

She was completely at ease. Whatever had been, whatever might come in the future, in this moment she was at peace. She smiled again to herself at how strange that was, given the situation.

Resting in this peace she was surprised to notice a growing warmth underneath her. It felt very nice compared to the cold damp she was used to in her prison cell. As she welcomed the warmth it grew stronger and spread up into her body. What is this magic? she asked herself.

Then she noticed that her eyelids were becoming less dark, first red and then orange, as if there was light shining on them. She opened her eyes and was blinded by intense light. She closed her eyes but she could feel the light from above now on her skin – the unmistakable rays of the sun.

Christina sat up and carefully opened her eyes a small amount to see if there was anything to see. In front of her were large square white stones, fitted together in a line. Other than that there was nothing except flat earth ground around her and the powerful sunlight flooding it all.

She squinted looking down and saw her legs stretched out before her, white on her thighs and tanned and sunburned on her calves and feet with scratches and scars from days spent wandering in the woods and fields. She spread her knees and crossed her ankles to sit more comfortably then stretched her arms out in front of her and looked at them and her hands – tanned and sunburned and white, scratches and scars. She was grateful for them, she realized, for all they had made possible for her. Thank you! Looking down, she was naked. But that seemed quite natural. The chestnut brown tangle of curly hair below her belly was familiar like an old friend. Nothing to hide or be ashamed of. And then she noticed her breasts. The left one as always a little bigger than the right with the nipple pointing upwards instead of outwards. Why had she ever been ashamed of them? she asked herself. They were wonderful just as they were. She reached up and cupped one hand under each breast, enjoying the sensation of it. She closed her eyes.

The warmth in her body was still there. As she felt it more clearly it grew powerful and began to move. Up from the stone beneath her, into her lower belly, then rising in a column spiraling around her spine, spreading to touch her heart and breasts and hands, up through her throat, up to her eyes, swirling through her head, then streaming back down through her and back into the stone. A river of warmth. The more attention she gave it the stronger it became. After a while it began to calm itself and soften. She still felt the warmth but more as a gentle glow rising and falling throughout her body. She did not want to let it go. She wanted to stay like this for as long as she could.

But as the warmth calmed she had the sense that she was no longer alone. She carefully opened her eyes and peered through the glare of the brilliant sunlight. A strange looking man stood only six paces in front of her. He was wearing beige colored short pants and a beige colored shirt with short sleeves. His bare arms and lower legs were white blotched by tan and sunburn like Christina's. He had light brown curly hair that was sticking out in all directions and yellow boots with laces in the front. He stood facing Christina with his arms held away from his sides at an angle. His hands were slowly opening and closing as if seeking to take hold of something. His eyes were wide open and he seemed to be looking for something as his head moved slowly from left to right and back again. But Christina could tell that he for some reason could not see her.

Perhaps he is blind, Christina thought to herself. She stood up and slowly approached him. Even when she stood only an arm's length in front of him he gave no sign that he saw her.

"Hello?" she said out loud. But there was no response of any kind.

Perhaps he is also deaf, she thought to herself.

It was a kind of puzzle. He was looking for something, that much was clear, but could neither see nor hear what was right in front of him. Obviously he needed help.

Christina was feeling playful. She stepped forward, slid her arms left and right under his arms, placed her hands against his back and pulled her body against his in a hug. It felt very nice for her. But he did not respond in any way. It was like hugging a statue.

Christina released her arms and stepped back. She looked again into his face: the blank staring light blue eyes, the brown stubble of beard, the moist lips, his furrowed brow. He needs something more, she thought to herself.

She reached up and put her hands on the sides of his head, bent it to his left, then brought up her face to his and kissed him on the mouth. At first gently but since he did not respond with more force. Then there was a response – he opened his mouth slightly as if preparing to say something. She took the opportunity to slide her tongue into his mouth searching and finding his tongue. That was it! Something happened! She stepped back away from him.

His body began to shake. Christina put her hands on his shoulders and stood looking into his face. And he saw her! His eyes found hers, he breathed more heavily and quickly and his body began to shake even more. He looked as if he was about to cry. Then he suddenly looked away up to the sky. And when he looked back down from the sky in some moments he was again blind to her. There had been just that one moment of seeing and now nothing.

Christina sighed, released her hold on his shoulders and looked at him trying to understand what was happening. He is looking for something but he is not looking for me, she said to herself with a trace of disappointment. She looked back now at the stone where she had been sitting when she experienced the warmth. Seeing it from a distance she noticed it was different from the other stones. It had a yellow tone. Or was it pink? Or even green? It was shifting colors as she watched. It was worth a try – perhaps that is what he was looking for.

She took his hands in hers and stepped backward testing to see if he would move when she pulled him. At first it did not work but she persisted with steady pressure and finally he took one awkward step, then another, following her lead. In this way she led him the few steps until he was standing just over the stone. But he did not look down. He did not feel it's warmth.

Still holding his hands in hers she pulled him down to the ground onto his knees. Then she pressed his hands to the special stone with her hands on top on his holding them down. His face became anguished and distorted by some strong emotion. He began to cry, trying to hold it back at first and then loudly. Christina released her pressure on his hands. He had found it now, she was sure. He had found what he was looking for. He fell forward onto the ground, pressing his chest against the stone, spreading his arms and digging into the dirt with his hands at either side.

Christina stepped back a few paces and sat down to watch. After a while he became quiet and fell sleep with his arms and legs drawn up to his chest.

Looking at him now Christina saw him no more as a grown man but as a small boy curled up on the stone asleep. He is looking for his mother, she thought to herself. And as she realized this she could also see that his mother was there very close to him, hidden under the stone on which he lay. Will he find his mother? she asked herself. It was not clear that he would. But in the end it was his business. She had done her part.

Christina was tired but satisfied. She lay back down herself on her back on the smooth stones. She relaxed her mind and body. She slept.

The Trial

The time came when Christina sensed that something was going to happen. She tried to prepare herself as best she could. Although she had no water – the only water she got each day was the liquid in the soup – she rubbed her arms and face with the fur from her skirt trying to get as clean as possible. She had no comb or brush but did what she could running her fingers through her hair. It was long and matted and hard to work with but she was finally satisfied with how it lay under her hands. She felt like she was preparing for a play like the traveling mummers performed when they came to the village sometimes. She was waiting off stage for her moment to come to stand before the audience and say her lines. Who was the audience? What were her lines? She had no idea.

"You will do fine," answered Elisabeth, without actually answering the questions. "I am proud of you. You are doing so well with all of this." Christina felt better with this reassurance from Elisabeth even though she did not understand it.

Could you do something and not know what you were doing? she asked herself. Maybe that is what we are doing all the time, she thought. Then we just have to trust what comes to us to do or to say even when we don't understand it.

Spontaneously she picked up the felt hat she had been using all this time as a pillow between her head and the straw, stood up from where she had been sitting, and moved to stand in the place she knew to be the center of the room. She turned to face where she knew the door to be. She opened the hat, placed it on her head and adjusted it carefully with the narrowest part of the brim forward. Her arms hung loose at her sides with the palms of her hands open forward. She moved her arms slowly upward until her palms touched above her head. She pressed her palms together then brought them down together until they were in front of her heart as if in prayer. She bowed her head and kissed her joined fingertips. She raised her head and said out loud into the darkness, "I am ready." Her eyes were wet but she felt calm. She took a deep breath then let it out slowly. Her arms lowered themselves until they hung loose and relaxed again at her sides.

The door at the top of the stairs outside her cell creaked open. There were at least three people instead of the normal single person. They marched rhythmically down the steps then stood outside the door. She could see dim light fluttering around the door frame.

With no words being spoken a chain squeaked and rattled then fell away with a loud clank. The door was pushed open. The glare of the torch being held high by the man in the center was more than her eyes could bear and she had to close them. If the men were surprised to see her standing there ready to go they did not indicate it. After only a moment the man in the middle spoke.

"Take her," he said. It was the same man who had arrested her she realized. He seemed to have a pretty limited vocabulary. As she had no interest in being knocked out again she moved along obediently when the two men came into the cell and took her by the arms. These were other men than the ones she knew from the village who had been there at her arrest. They were both short and smelled of old leather. Their grips on her arms were not painful but very secure. It was difficult for Christina and the two men to get through the low cell door while they held on to her but they seemed determined to do it in this strange way and in the end managed. The narrow stairs were even more difficult. One went first, holding on to Christina's left arm, then Christina, then the second short man holding the other arm, then the tall man behind holding the torch for them to see the steps.

At the top of these steps Christina saw that the upper door led into a dark corridor with many small doors to the left and right. Each small door had a rectangular opening covered by a leather flap a third of the way up from the floor just as her cell had. Were there others in these cells? As they moved through the corridor the only sounds were their own footsteps, their own breathing, and the torch sizzling as it burned. At the end of the corridor was another large door standing open. They passed through it into a large room lit by small windows up high on one wall. The tall man put the torch out by sticking it into a small pot on the ground, then placed it in a holder next to others, pushed the door closed behind them and fixed it with a large noisy chain. Next they climbed a wide stone staircase where Christina and the two men holding her arms could walk abreast with the tall man following. At the top of this staircase another door and a small window waited.

And then they were outside. Christina squeezed her eyes shut against the blinding light then squinted them open in her eagerness to see. The simplest outlines and objects – the ground, the edges of buildings, the men beside her – shone with their own inner radiance and brilliant colors. Even the smelly city air tasted sweet and wonderful to Christina. She had gotten used to the dark and to the dank air in the room under the earth, she realized. One could get used to almost anything it seemed.

She could hear the noises of the city now – people talking, carts creaking, animals – but still at a distance. They were not on a city street. It seemed more like a courtyard. Their small procession entered another building. The door was opened for them by a watchman or guard who had seen them coming, apparently, as the door opened when they came to it without their having to say or do anything. Down another corridor. Through another door. There was a wide place in the corridor with a dozen or so plain wooden chairs lined up along the wall.

"Sit," said the tall man. With one man on each side Christina sat down. Christina's eyes were still not adjusted to the brightness but she could see more easily here in the corridor where the light came only from some small windows high up. Out of the corners of her eyes she could see the tall man fidgeting with his shirt and coat – adjusting them and brushing away real or imaginary flecks. He is afraid, she thought to herself. She was on the point of asking him about it but bit her tongue at the last minute. It wouldn't help anything to have him angry with her now. She stole a glance at the face of the man on her left, then of the man on her right, peeking out from under the brim of her hat. They looked straight ahead. But she could see at the corners of their mouths that they did notice her looking at them. They also noticed that the tall man was afraid and now knew that she saw it too. All three took secret pleasure in it.

Across from them was a door. Through the door they could hear the muffled voices of an argument or at least a discussion going on. The door was beautiful dark wood carved and set in square patterns with care as to the direction of the grain. At the top it was arched to a peak to match the vaulted curves of the ceiling high above them. The door handle was dark brass shaped like a ram's horn that curved up to the point. As Christina was admiring the craft of it the point dipped down; someone was opening the door from the other side. The door opened smoothly and silently. The voices in the room were suddenly silent. A thin older man in brown clothes with a white bow at his neck and silver hair stood to the side of the door bowing slightly in their direction.

The tall man seemed more nervous now than before. He motioned with one hand for Christina and the men to stand. He motioned for them to precede him into the room. Slowly the three stood and walked into the room. Christina was surprised to hear sharply in-drawn breaths and gasps. Now at last she understood: the tall man had left her with her clothes and hat for just this moment. He had wanted to make this impression of something wild and strange coming into this room confronting these people. Now she realized as well why she had been fed and not subjected to the torture that was common: it was all so that she would make the strongest possible impression in this moment. The man was using her.

The area into which they came was a part of the larger room sectioned off with a dark wood railing. There were two wooden benches one behind the other in the small area. The tall man motioned for Christina and the men to take the forward bench and to sit down there which they did. He himself opened a small gate hidden in the dark wood and stepped into the middle of the room.

Christina kept her head down covered by the brim of the hat but she looked up for a moment to sweep the room with her eyes. Sitting now head down and eyes closed she looked over the room which she held like a picture in her mind. The wall opposite where she sat was the most impressive – a whole row of arched windows. Each window was filled with colored glass in intricate patterns. She had not had time or the ability given the brightness of the sunlight on the other side to tell what the pictures in the windows were. But she had noticed a few things: crossed swords here, a lion there, a flower. She wished she had time to look at them more closely. The colors on the glass with the sun coming from behind were quite beautiful and the themes were not so far from the themes of her painting. But she doubted she would get the chance to get to know them better.

And now she was sure of where she was. With a room so grand as this they had to be in Freiburg.

"What in heaven's name have we here, Schlingermann? Is it a person or is it an animal?" The voice was loud and commanding without being rough or abrasive. Even though she was looking down when he spoke Christina was certain that it belonged to the richly dressed personage she had also noticed. He sat behind a long table at the center of a podium on the side of the room flanked by a dozen drabber others. The man had a red cap and a short red cape around his shoulders. He was either tall or was sitting on a higher chair. As soon as he had spoken others in the room began to murmur and whisper among themselves in outrage at the appearance of the prisoner.

"With all apologies, your Excellency, I think that it is imperative that the court see with its own eyes what we are dealing with in our work to eradicate the poison that infects our land. Therefore I took the liberty of bringing before you this woman who was caught exactly so dressed as she attempted to flee after committing the heinous crime of which she is accused."

This all came from the man who had arrested her whom she now knew as Schlingermann. His voice was also clear and commanding, educated and absent the rough accents and dialect of the country people she was used to. Her parents had come from the city after all so she had heard proper language in the home when she was small even if she did not use it very much. If you say something here you need to say it slowly and carefully in city language. She could do that. And the man in the red hat was "your Excellency," so her trial must be something special. It pleased her and scared her at the same time.

There were some subdued discussions; questions and answers between his Excellency and the men around him.

"All right," said his Excellency, "but do not think this is a precedent. I have checked and the proceedings are binding regardless of how the accused is dressed. In the future you are strongly advised to discuss such irregularities in advance. Do you understand me?"

"Yes your Excellency".

"Alright then, let's get on with it. Who is this person and of what is she accused?" said his Excellency.

A chair scraped the floor as it was being pushed back from the table.

A new voice spoke: "The accused is Christina Knecht, daughter of Bernd and Hilda Knecht, of jurisdiction Merzhausen, in the administrative area Freiburg. The crime of which she is accused..." here the voice faltered, coughed, then started again less strongly. "The crime of which she is accused is the theft of the soul of a newborn baby and the sale of that soul to Satan."

Again the room was filled with voices, louder than before, exclaiming over the accusation.

"Quiet!" called out his Excellency. The room grew quiet. He continued, "Schlingermann, we did discuss this unusual accusation before the proceedings and I agreed to allow it based on your insistence. But I warn you I am expecting real proof and not the vague second-hand gossip you and your people have been bringing to our courts lately. Although there is no precedent that I know of for this specific charge we can go forward as we discussed under the category of 'sins against God' with some confidence that we are not overstepping the legal boundaries. Please proceed with your case."

Christina had sensed the men on each side stiffen as they heard and understood the accusation. They had shifted away from her as far as they could without drawing attention to it. Their grips on her arms also loosened perceptively. With inner effort she attempted to confront the accusation: stealing the soul of a newborn baby and selling it to Satan. What could they mean by that? It was like a riddle.

"I call Father Malthus Gruber to the witness stand!" declared Schlingermann with a note of relief in his voice. Clearly he had not been certain he would get this far.

Gruber came from the back of the room where he must have been sitting the whole time though Christina had not seen him. She raised her head slightly to watch him as he made his way to a witness box not so different from the area where she was sitting but over under the windows. He had on his priest vestments. His thin hair was flat on his head and his beard was trimmed short. He did not look afraid. He stood and rested his hands on the railing of the box for support.

"Father Gruber, what can you tell us that is relevant to the case before us?" asked Schlingermann smoothly.

Father Gruber cleared his throat and began to speak. Christina focused herself and tried to follow what he was saying.

"If the court will pardon me, I would like to start by saying something about the family of the accused, as I am convinced it has relevance." He paused and looked to Schlingermann and then to his Excellency. They did not interrupt him so he continued.

"It was 18 years ago that the Knecht family first moved into the village parish. I had just been assigned to my post as village priest. They were my first new people and I took it very seriously as my responsibility to bring them into the fold as best I could. But it was not to be. They had come from Freiburg to 'live out on the land' as the woman expressed it. They professed to be Christians but even at that early stage there were warning signals that in my youthful innocence I did not see. If I had, perhaps I could have done something earlier to avoid this tragedy." Gruber showed some emotion at this point. He took a large handkerchief out of his pocket and blew his nose.

"Please continue, Father Gruber," interjected Schlingermann.

"After living for awhile at the village inn the couple found and purchased for cash a tract of land on a wild ridge south of the village. This place was notable for large boulders, rough weather, dangerous wild animals, and dense forest. Nowhere in it was there a place where you could farm or even have proper animals. No one could figure out what they wanted up there. There was no house only an abandoned hunter's hut on the land. They spent years constructing a kind of country house where they lived. At first they lived in a crude shelter they had constructed – not even a hut, really. Or so I have been told."

"And what did you find remarkable about this?" prompted Schlingermann.

"That they had no use for the Christian society of the village!" responded Gruber, with some emotion, helped by the question to come to his point. "They were never in the church, never in the village on festival days, never seeking advice or counsel from me or others in the village. That was how the parents were and so of course that was how the children grew up." For the first time he looked over at Christina. She had the hat brim down so she could not see his looking at her but she could feel it.

He continued his story. "Soon after their house building was underway their children were born: the twins Christina and her brother Patrick. They were baptized after birth but it was a sorry and unhappy ceremony. No one other than the parents, the children, and I were present as they had no friends in the village and apparently no relatives anywhere who considered the occasion important enough to make the journey. The weather was terrible – a spring storm with rain and lightning. The children howled the whole time. I do not remember a drearier christening in all my years as a priest."

"Schlingermann," came the voice of his Excellency, "I fail to see the relevance in this history. May I remind you we do not have unlimited time. So the girl comes from a family that kept to itself and the weather was bad when they were christened. Can you help me understand what that has to do with the business before this court?"

"Of course your Excellency," countered Schlingermann. "Father Gruber, could you move ahead to the events concerning the girl's mother, Hilda Knecht?"

"It will be three years ago this fall. One day Hilda Knecht came into the village by herself. She was in a dreadful condition with her hair awry and clothes dirty and in disarray. Her eyes were unnaturally wide. She seemed to be frightened of something and was asking people in the village as she met them on the street to help her although she could not explain what kind of help she wanted. By chance someone fetched me. I brought her back to my house, gave her some warm brew to drink and tried to help her compose herself. At first all I could gather was that she had encountered something in the forest that had frightened her. But her manner and way of speaking were so unusual and disconnected that I frankly feared for her sanity. I inquired about her husband and she was coherent enough to tell me he was away on a business trip. I pressed her to tell me what she had met in the forest, thinking perhaps it was a dangerous animal that the village hunters should deal with. She assured me that it was not an animal. It was, she confided in me after some hesitation, a spirit in the forest that had spoken to her."

There were again gasps and muttering in the room.

"Did she tell you what the spirit had wanted from her?" asked Schlingermann. He already knows the answer, Christina thought to herself.

"Yes," continued Gruber hesitantly, "she said the spirit wanted her daughter Christina, that the spirit had some work for Christina to do, and that the mother should give the daughter over."

The room exploded in exclamations and conversation.

"Quiet!" called out his Excellency. The sounds grew quieter. "I said quiet!" he repeated. The room was silent. "And how do we know that these were not just the ravings of a deranged woman?" he continued, looking from Schlingermann to Gruber and back.

Gruber provided his answer. "While she was still with me that day I tried to explain to her how important it was that she resist the power of this spirit, that the spirit was probably the devil himself, or at least one of his servants. That she should have nothing more to do with such things, that her soul and the souls of those in her family, especially of her daughter, were at stake. And she seemed to hear me. This explanation seemed to paradoxically give her some peace. She grew quieter and then slept. I went out to attend to an urgent errand, expecting she would still be there when I returned. But when I got back she was gone."

"And what steps did you then take?" asked Schlingermann.

"Well, I filed an official report, of course, and requested a summons for questioning through the normal church channels. It was clear we had to dig deeper into what was going on with her. The family itself was in dire spiritual danger and the community as well through them. So I filed my report and with it a request for a summons for questioning for Hilda Knecht."

"And did you get the summons?"

"It came back to me approved two months later. It is all so painfully slow, as we have discussed." He said this last to Schlingermann then cleared his throat as if he had said something inappropriate. "But as you know, by that point it was irrelevant."

"And why was it irrelevant?" prompted Schlingermann.

"Two weeks after my meeting with her Hilda Knecht took her own life. She was found by her children hanging from a tree in the forest near their house. It was all quite a shock."

Christina struggled to not to cry out. It had been truly terrible finding her mother there in the forest. It was time to eat the midday meal and she and Patrick had been hungry. Their mother had gone into the forest that morning but was not yet back. So at lunchtime they went to look for her. And they had found her. Christina breathed more deeply. It was a long, long time ago, she said to herself. It was a long, long time ago, she repeated and felt somewhat better. She had always suspected that the church had had something to do with her mother's suicide.

"And what then became of the children?" asked Schlingermann.

"Technically they still had a father so there were no grounds for the church to step in. In fact the father disappeared immediately after the burial. He deserted the family entirely. The twins were fourteen so they were no longer legally children. Without some further grounds there was really nothing we could do."

"Are you saying that you just left the children there on their own in this desolate place prey to whatever dark forces were at work?" asked Schlingermann with a tone of disbelief.

"Well, I tried to find some family in the village to take them in but there was absolutely no interest. No interest at all. I visited them a month after their mother's death to try to convince them to move into the village, but they refused. The truth is that we ignored them; we pretended as if they were not there. In my naivete I thought the danger was over – the mother had given herself to the spirit in place of her daughter. But I see now how wrong I was. I pray to God every night that He forgive my dereliction of duty in this matter. If I could have foreseen where it would all lead..." Gruber's voice trailed off.

"Thank you," said Schlingermann. "That will be all."

Father Gruber looked around the room, surprised that his ordeal was over. He nodded to himself and walked out of the witness box through the small gate to the back of the room where he took his seat.

"I call Friedhelm Kranz to the witness stand," said Schlingermann.

Christina was surprised. She had really thought that Frieda and Friedhelm would keep her help with the birth secret as they had promised. You just never know about people, she said to herself.

Friedhelm, like Father Gruber, had been sitting in the back. He got up and made his way to the witness box. Christina raised her head a little to look at him as he took his place. He was dressed as best he could but in his country clothes he still looked out of place. It was clear in the way he walked that he was afraid. Unlike Gruber he took no advantage of the box railing to steady himself but stood upright swaying slightly looking around for some indication of what he should do.

"Mr. Kranz, how long have you known the accused, Christina Knecht?" began Schlingermann.

Friedhelm looked at Christina, realized she was looking back at him, and looked back to Schlingermann. "About four months." He spoke in the country people's dialect but apparently the court was used to this.

"And how did you come into her acquaintance?" continued Schlingermann.

"My wife – that's Frieda – she was pregnant. We had some problems twice before when she tried to have babies. So we decided to see if we could get some help with this one. We had heard from the people in the village that the old woman Elisabeth could help or at least give advice. We are not from this area; we only recently moved here from the south. So we talked to Elisabeth. She said she could not help. But she told us to talk to Christina. That's how we met Christina." He was clearly relieved to have gotten so much out, even though it could be used against him.

"You are aware that it is specifically prohibited by law to interfere with God's judgment of who shall live and die in childbirth, are you not? You were planning to break the law, with Christina as an accomplice, or perhaps as the perpetrator. Do I understand that right?" Schlingermann's voice was colder now and accusing.

"Yes," answered Friedhelm quietly, "we knew it was wrong, but we so wanted a baby. We were desperate you see..." his voice trailed off.

"It is perhaps a distraction from our direction today, Schlingermann, but what about this woman he refers to as Elisabeth? She sounds like a ringleader of this dirty business of interfering with births. Has she been apprehended? Questioned? This is just the kind of thing we need to be pursuing." His Excellency seemed genuinely interested in the point.

"Based on the facts in this case," answered Schlingermann, "we did summon and question the woman Elisabeth Weide. Unfortunately we were not able to obtain any useful information as she died unexpectedly in the questioning."

"Sloppy methods! Sloppy methods!" berated his Excellency. "One more time I am reminded of how often incompetence and excessive zeal lets these criminals slip right through our fingers. We will talk later about this in private, Schlingermann. I am not pleased, I tell you. Quite the contrary. All right, get on with it."

So Elisabeth is dead now, said Christina to herself. Elisabeth had not expected to live much longer. And at least she had been spared the humiliation of a public execution. They had killed Elisabeth because ... because she tried to help babies come into the world in a good way ... because she would not betray the names of other women like Christina that did this work with her. Christina felt new emotions growing in her belly, flowing into her chest. Her breathing deepened and slowed. Her jaws clamped closed. For the first time she reached out with her hands and took hold of the railing in front of her for support. The men holding her shifted their grips to allow it.

Are you here, Elisabeth? Christina asked with her inner voice. There was no answer. Christina seemed to be on her own.

"Tell us briefly about the night of the birth, Mr. Kranz," said Schlingermann, bringing them back to the thread of the story.

"I had gone and fetched Christina when the birth pains began to get strong just as we had agreed. Christina came and helped with things and after a few hours the baby was born."

"And was the baby alive or dead?" asked Schlingermann.

"It was born alive but it had some choking. Christina told us to take care of it if it had trouble breathing but we didn't really understand what we were supposed to do. Then she left." Friedhelm looked down at the floor as if there was more to say but he did not want to say it.

"Was there something unusual that you noticed about Christina's behavior after the birth?" asked Schlingermann.

"I think she did not want us to see it. She turned away from us when she did it. But she took the afterbirth from Frieda, cleaned it, looked at it, then she wrapped it and put it in her bag. She took it with her." He looked at Christina.

Again there was a burst of conversation in the room. Some asked what he was talking about; others provided conjectural answers. From the drift of the questions and answers she could overhear Christina noticed how little these men really knew about the process of birth. So Friedhelm had seen her take the placenta. Maybe it would have been better to talk to them about it. It was in any case too late now.

"Quiet!" called his Excellency. "Continue."

"Please tell us what happened after she left, Mr. Kranz," said Schlingermann.

"The baby was okay for a while. Frieda slept. Then the baby started choking something serious. I woke Frieda. We both tried to do what we could but it was no use. Nothing we tried worked. After a while the baby stopped breathing. It was dead." Friedhelm looked down at the floor again. The room was quiet.

So that was it, thought Christina. The baby had died. And they were somehow going to blame her. Without her it wouldn't even have been born alive! And how could she know how incompetent they were? She had not killed the child – they had killed it, by their

162

incompetence! The anger that had been in her belly and chest returned.

"And what did you do then?"

"We were in such a state we did not know what to do. Frieda was so distraught from the baby dying and weak from the birth. I left Frieda there and carried the baby wrapped in a blanket into the village. It was the middle of the night. I didn't know where to go so I went to the priest's house. He was there. He took the baby's body from me and tried to help me get myself together. He asked me what had happened and I told him." With this last sentence, Friedhelm looked around the room, then at Christina. "I told him what happened," he repeated.

"Thank you, Mr. Kranz," said Schlingermann. "You may leave the witness box now."

Friedhelm made his way unsteadily out of the box, crossed the room, and returned to his place in the back right corner.

"If the court allows it, I myself am in the unusual position to personally fill in important details of the events of this terrible night." He turned and looked to his Excellency for a sign of agreement.

"The court allows the prosecutor to himself provide testimony. It is unusual but legal. Proceed," said his Excellency flatly.

"By chance I was in the village on this night staying there as a part of one of my regular tours of duty in the area. When Father Gruber heard from Mr. Kranz what had happened to the child he sent his housekeeper for me as it sounded as if it could be in my area of responsibility. I came within a few minutes. We then sent his housekeeper to fetch the village constable since there was a death involved. The housekeeper returned and told us the constable would be delayed due to urgent business but would come as soon as he could. When he did finally arrive he explained that he was so long in coming because he had been called shortly before to the scene of another death. A man on his way home from the tavern in the village had been attacked that night, robbed and killed by persons unknown. A couple in a house at the edge of the village had heard the noises of the attack and came out to help but they arrived too late. The perpetrators fled. The victim died from knife wounds within a few minutes of being found.

"Why do I recite this sad story of the robbery and death here, your Excellency?" Schlingermann paused for effect.

"Because the robbery and death of this man were not simply by chance on the same night as the death of the baby. The man who was robbed and killed was none other than Patrick Knecht, the brother of the accused! And the money that was stolen from him –

apparently a large sum – had been given to him on this very same evening by his sister, Christina Knecht, according to the statements of those who had been in the tavern with him."

Christina slumped forward. If it had not been for the men holding her up she would have fallen forward off the bench. Her hands slipped from the railing and found each other in her lap, then pulled up together against her chest. Patrick was dead. But the church had not killed him – the money itself had killed him. And the money came ... from her. She could see him in her imagination in the tavern, buying drinks for everyone, paying off debts real or imagined, smiling through it all and bragging that he had gotten the money from her. Why? To prove to them and almost to himself that she had loved him and did not despise him. Better any lie than that painful truth.

So, Christina thought to herself, all the people that meant anything to me are dead or have left me: my mother, my father, my brother, Elisabeth, and even the Kranz baby. They might as well get on with it.

She felt calmer and relieved by this clarity. Her anger was gone. She sat up straight on the bench and paid no attention at all to what Schlingermann was saying now.

She took off her hat with her right hand and extended it in the direction of the man sitting to her left who was still holding her upper left arm loosely in his right.

"Could you hold this for me for a moment, please?" she whispered.

Moved by some force he would have found it hard to explain the man nodded to her, reached out and took her hat. He let go of her arm and sat there holding her hat on his lap in his two hands looking straight ahead.

Distantly she noticed that Schlingermann had stopped his ranting. All eyes were on her in this moment. It was time for her to speak her lines. She looked into the face of the man on her right. He looked back into her face. She flicked her eyes down to indicate his left hand encircling her upper right arm, and then back into his face. His mouth began to tremble as if he might say something but he did not. She flicked her eyes again down to his hand on her arm then back to his face. She cocked her head to the side in a questioning look with a half smile. He slowly took his hand off her arm and brought his hands together in his lap. He looked down at his hands.

Christina stood up. She rested her hands on the railing of the box for support as she had seen Father Gruber do. She looked around the room in a relaxed but serious way. It was nice to be able to see

164

who was here. The ceiling of the room, which she had not been able to see before because of the brim of her hat, was soft sky blue. There were painted clouds floating across it and small golden angels helped support it at the four corners.

Schlingermann had been perplexed as to how to respond but now came to his senses and barked out commands. First to Christina. "The accused is ordered to sit down!" he shouted. "You there, and you, make her sit down!" he called out to the men on either side of her when she made no move to comply. They sat as if frozen both now looking down into their laps.

"Really, Schlingermann," intoned his Excellency, "I think you are overreacting. She has been sitting for a long time and maybe she just wanted to stand up. Maybe she has something to say to us?" It was clearly an invitation. His Excellency was enjoying Schlingermann's panic.

"Please, your Excellency," Schlingermann began. "She is dangerous, probably in ways we do not even suspect, we cannot allow her to stand here and ..."

"Come, come, Schlingermann," interrupted his Excellency. "As you say she may be dangerous. But we are dangerous too, or have you forgotten? So we do not need to be afraid. And there are no babies here for her to steal their souls. Am I right?" He looked to the left and right in the room to his entourage and the local functionaries that were present as if looking for babies. A few of the men responded with modest laughter.

Christina remained silent throughout this exchange. Her dark brown hair hung down in long waves from her head onto her shoulders and back. Her face was relaxed and peaceful. It would be best, she thought, if he actually invited me to speak. So she waited. Schlingermann stood petrified. Only his head moved as he looked back and forth from His Excellency to Christina. He was unable to take in what was happening or to decide what he should do about it.

"Do you have something to say, my dear?" asked His Excellency.

"Yes, your Excellency," she replied. "I have a question I would like to ask you."

"Well ask it then. I would be very interested to hear what you might have for a question," he responded.

"Your Excellency..." began Schlingermann, urgently.

"Schlingermann, I am warning you to keep silent!" responded his Excellency forcefully before Schlingermann could get his sentence out. "I am in charge of this court and not you. And if you interrupt one more time I will have you thrown out. Do you understand me?"

Schlingermann nodded bleakly.

"I do believe we are now ready for your question," prompted his Excellency.

Christina paused, took a breath, and spoke her question: "Why are you so afraid of women?"

Listening to the echo of it in her mind she was pleased with it and the way she had said it. Perhaps the accents were not all exactly right but it was city talk. No one could question that.

There were exclamations, a few muted denials and much muttering in the room. These sounds died down. All eyes turned to his Excellency to see what he would say.

"You ask a surprisingly simple question, my dear. If you had not neglected your religious education you could answer it yourself. As every child learns from the teachings of our holy scriptures sin itself came into God's perfect world through the woman. It was she that Satan turned to for an ally against God and not to Adam. It was because of a woman that we were thrown out of the garden, that we must sweat to earn our living, and – relevant for your case – that women must suffer the pain and risks of child-birth for new individuals to come into this world. This was God's judgment on women for their rebellion against him. And it is not recorded in the scriptures that Eve repented of her transgressions or ended her alliance with Satan. She continues to be his chief ally in his struggle against God. Some women are more involved on the side of Satan than others, of course. You, for example, seem to be in the thick of the fighting. But you should give up your rebellion, repent of your sins against God and throw yourself on the mercy of our Lord and Savior Jesus Christ. He can purify your soul and grant you peace."

He really believes it! thought Christina to herself.

It was his truth. There was nothing she could do about it. Thousands of babies were dying needlessly because the mothers received no help in the births. Thousands of women were being tortured and killed because they rejected the teachings of the church and sought to live in the old ways close to nature. And it was all happening in blind service to this man's insane truth. No one said anything more. They were all looking at her.

"Thank you," she said simply and sat down.

She took her hat from the man sitting next to her and put it back on her head, adjusting it carefully so that the right part of the brim faced forward. She felt dizzy and reached out for support to the two men beside her. Improbably her hands found their hands. She tightened her grip and they tightened theirs. She abruptly fainted.

Goodbye

She awoke in a dungeon cell she decided was one of those in the corridor she had walked past on her way to her trial. It was noisier here and there was more often light around the edges of the door and through the feeding slot than there had been in her earlier cell. The room was also smaller. It was not high enough for her to stand up anywhere in it and was only about three paces by three paces square. There was no hole for her waste products.

Food was delivered less regularly and when it did come it was of a lower quality. Under normal circumstances she would have rejected it as rotten and spoiled. She had decided to try to keep herself as fit as she could so she ate what was offered despite the difficulty of getting it down.

She developed some exercises to keep her body working. The one she did the most was what she called swimming. She would lie on her back in the center of the room with her arms and legs extended and raised. Then she would go through the motions of swimming as if she were in water. For her legs she used a frog-like stroke that was strenuous but felt good when she could keep it up for a while. Frogs did not use their front legs to swim so she had had to improvise a symmetric circular motion with her hands and arms. Sometimes after doing this she would shift into an agreeable state of awareness in which she was not swimming but was flying through the night sky looking down at the mountains, forests, rivers and towns that the moonlight showed her far below.

She still had her old handmade clothes. In all the confusion they had probably forgotten to give the order to have the people in the prison give her the right clothes.

No one had told her what was going to happen to her. She had fainted at the trial and not come back to full consciousness until she was here in this cell. But it was so obvious what came next that she would have felt foolish asking someone about it.

She was sad sometimes. Once or twice she cried. Worst was that Elisabeth and the others were no longer with her. She pondered what this abandonment could mean. Had she failed her responsibility? She had done exactly what came to her exactly as it had come. No more and no less. What else could anyone ask of her? Finally she decided that she had done the right thing: asked the right question, just as she had needed to. But now that her fate was sealed it must be that Elisabeth and the others had more pressing business some-where else with someone else.

The day finally came. It surprised her even though she had been expecting it. A man opened her cell, crawled halfway in, took her arm and dragged her out. When he had her outside he was surprised by her clothes and hair and shouted something to someone at the other end of the corridor. Another man standing there was also per-plexed. They spoke for a moment. One man walked quickly away and through the door at the end. In some minutes a middle-aged woman came back down the stairs with him. She was carrying a black dress, a pair of shears, and a reed basket.

"Off with those things," she commanded as she came up to Christina.

Christina untied her skirt and dropped it to the ground. Then she took off her jacket and shirt. The woman pulled the black dress over Christina's head, working her arms through the holes. It was some-what short and the woman looked with disapproval at the length of the calf exposed at the bottom. But it would have to do.

She waved Christina to turn around. The woman reached up and took handfuls of Christina's hair, cut each handful as close to the head as she could, and dropped the cut hair into her basket. Finally it was done. The woman picked up Christina's clothes and her bas-ket and walked quickly away.

While Christina had been changing and having her hair cut the same man who had pulled her out had taken four other women out of four other cells along the corridor. The women were all in worse shape than Christina. Three had difficulty to stand. Their bodies where you could see them showed bruises and burns. Unlike Christina they already wore the black prison dresses and had had their hair cut.

Another man began to tie the women together with a long rope. At each one he knotted the rope in a way to bind their hands to-gether behind their backs. Christina was the last in line.

As the man stepped toward Christina to tie her hands she tried to see into his face, to make some contact with him. And then he did look into her face for a moment. But it was a terrible look; not the human contact that Christina had unconsciously hoped for. Instead the man's face was flat and dead, his eyes dull gray without light or emotion. For him, she realized, she was not a person but something dirty that needed to be disposed of.

He was behind her now. He brought her arms and hands to-gether, then held them with one hand and looped the rope around her joined wrists, pulling it tight.

Christina felt a cramp in her belly, moving upward through her chest. Her legs felt suddenly weak. She struggled to stay standing. She slumped forward.

He looped the rope again and pulled it tighter.

The cramp moved up into her throat. Her jaws tensed against that which was building up in her, seeking its way out, looking for escape. Her eyes watered and her face ached with the pain of holding it back. And then she could not hold it back. She screamed with all of her force, her body shaking, the sound echoing down the corridor, stretching forward.

The man moved around in front of her, holding her slumping body up with his left hand grasping her right upper arm. He slapped her hard across the face with his right hand.

Her screaming stopped.

Her breath was slower now. The cramps in her belly and chest were still there but not so strong as before. She was able to stand without help. The man turned and walked away.

An order was given. The women who had been lying down were forced to stand. Then they all made their way up the steps into the blinding light, one man leading and one following behind.

A wagon waited there for them, hitched to a donkey with a man holding the lead. The wagon was flat with two large wooden wheels. It had posts around the edges that were tied together with ropes to make a cage with an open top. There was an opening in the ropes at the back. The men took the women one by one and lifted them into the wagon, leaving them connected by the rope. Then they looped ropes across the opening in the back to close it off.

The order to move out was given and the wagon began to roll. One man led the donkey and two men walked alongside. They crossed a courtyard and came to a gate that opened when they reached it. They rolled out onto the busy street. The wagon jerked as it rolled due to the unevenness of the wheels and the cobble stones of the street. Christina looked around at the people. Her eyes were not so blinded by the light; the day was dark and overcast. There were so many people and they were all so focused on the group of women that Christina decided they must have been waiting.

Several people pointed to her and spoke to their neighbors. Christina could not hear what they were saying. But mostly the people in the street grew quiet when the wagon passed after making way for it and standing to the sides.

The other women seemed very far away as if they did not notice what was happening. They did not look at the people or the town around them.

Christina, however, forced herself to be interested in the people, the buildings, the smells, the sounds, the goods piled in front of the shops. She tried to notice all of it; to drink it in like nourishment.

This is being alive, she said to herself.

It was not long before they came to the large cobbled square on the north side of the cathedral. At one end of it was a raised area built up of square stones roughly set with sand between them. There were five iron poles sticking up from the ground arranged in a circle in the middle of the raised area. There were heaps of wood branches and sticks arranged around the circle of poles and between them.

The wagon stopped. The men opened the back and helped Christina and the one woman who was also standing to step out. The three other women were sitting slumped barely conscious. The men lifted the women out of the wagon and laid them on the ground. The other woman standing and Christina were adjacent in the rope line.

Christina noticed that the woman standing by her seemed to have been revived somewhat by the wagon ride and was looking around at the scene.

"Hi," she said. "My name is Christina. What's yours?"

The woman was startled to hear her speak and at first did not answer. The men were untying the women lying on the ground then carrying them one at a time and binding them to the upright poles one woman per pole.

"Angelika," said the woman at last. "My name is Angelika."

"Pleased to meet you, Angelika," said Christina. She looked with a critical eye upwards to the dark sky.

"What do you think?" she asked. "Will it rain and we will get to die another day?"

Angelika stared at her in disbelief. It was a kind of joke she finally realized.

"No, I don't think it will rain. Today is our day to die."

She was not smiling but she was getting into the spirit of the thing, thought Christina.

"Well good," said Christina. "I can't stand the thought of being stuck back in that dirty hole in the ground where they were keeping me."

"I know just what you mean," answered Angelika.

Angelika was next. The two men came to her and untied her hands. They took hold of her arms.

"Goodbye, Angelika," said Christina.

"Goodbye, Christina," replied Angelika.

Standing alone Christina noticed it was quiet in the square. She looked around at the crowd circling the raised area but did not see anyone she knew. When she made eye contact people looked away and made the sign of the cross.

Then it was her turn to be untied from the rope, escorted to the pole waiting for her and tied there.

The men rearranged the firewood closer around the women and stacked it higher from a supply that was off to one side.

A man in a uniform came out, unrolled a paper and began to read in a loud voice.

Christina was not looking at him or listening to him. She was looking up. She had noticed a group of cliff swallows swooping through the air above the square catching insects.

Or maybe they are just flying for the fun of it, she thought to herself.

Cliff swallows were her favorite kind of bird: so sleek and fast and graceful and full of joy. Probably they nested in the facade of the cathedral. They were very flexible about where they lived. She was still watching them when the flames began.

All of this here is at an end, she said to herself.

I will fly away with the swallows.

And so she did.

Gargoyles

Christina had never before noticed the gargoyles high on the Freiburg cathedral's facade. She had seen gargoyles on other buildings though and knew that they were there to channel rain water from the roof away from the outer walls. The ones she saw now up close were wonderful. Each was different. Some were realistic but many were very exotic. They reminded her of some of the creatures that she had painted on her wall.

The gargoyle she was sitting next to was made to look like a cow. Christina reached out and scratched its head between its ears. It seemed to like that. What did the cow do up here all day, especially when there was no rain water to collect and spout out of her mouth over the edge? Does she get bored up here? "Do you get bored sometimes?" she asked the cow. It did not answer.

Or does she watch the things going on down below? Christina asked herself. Many things happened down there below. That is where the people had their market days, their festivals and...their ... – she struggled to find the word – executions.

"Christina?" said Elisabeth. "How are you doing?"

Christina turned. There sitting to her left on the edge of the roof on the other side of the cow was Elisabeth. Of course it was Elisabeth. Who else would be there with her, she thought to herself.

"I came up here with the swallows and am just getting used to being so high above the ground. It's a little scary but exciting. There was some terrible smelling smoke earlier but now the air is clearer and I am doing better.

"Did you also fly up with the swallows?" Christina asked.

"Yes, I also came with the swallows," answered Elisabeth.

As if in response several swallows swooped down, circled them, then flew further up into the air.

Christina looked down into the cathedral square. She vaguely remembered that earlier there had been a mass of people assembled there. Now there were very few. Four men had taken water from the fountain and were using it with buckets, brooms and shovels to clean around places where it looked like there had been fires. They collected the wet ashes and put them into a wagon hitched to horses. She watched for a while. Finally they appeared satisfied that they had collected all they needed to collect and walked away behind the wagon with one man leading the two horses.

The sun, moving toward the western horizon, peeked out from under the layer of clouds that covered most of the sky. The sun's rays lightened the roof of the cathedral and Christina could feel their warmth on her face. She closed her eyes, turned to face them more directly and relaxed into enjoying the setting sun.

Then the clouds shifted and the sun was no longer there. She opened her eyes and looked out at the city and at the mountains in the distance. There was a cool damp wind now.

Turning to her left she saw that Elisabeth was still sitting there with her.

"Thank you," said Christina. "I had thought we were no longer together."

"Yes, we are still together, you and I," answered Elisabeth.

The sky continued to darken. The cold wind grew stronger.

"I am afraid," said Christina.

"Shall we go somewhere else, then, where it is warmer and there is more light?" asked Elisabeth.

"Please! That would be very nice!" answered Christina and smiled.

They sat together on a large stone at the side of the trail near the top of the ridge near Christina's house. The sun was shining again though low in the western sky over the Vosges mountains. The Rhine valley stretched below them. From where they sat there were no towns or houses to be seen.

"How did you know?" asked Christina. "This is my special secret place to come when I need help! I never showed it to anyone."

"I just asked for us to be in a good place together," answered Elisabeth. "And this is what appeared.

"You have been through a lot lately. You need all the support you can get. This place has been important to you for a long time. And so it is today. Being here may help you open to what has happened and help you get through it in a good way."

"What has happened to me? I feel different but I don't know why."

"What do you remember? Do you remember being in the Witches Prison in Freiburg?"

Christina's spirit body began to shake. She closed her eyes and shook her head back and forth. "No, I don't remember that!" she said with some force.

Elisabeth got up from the stone she had been sitting on and sat on the ground. She opened her arms. "Come here Christina." Christina opened her eyes then moved unsteadily off the stone onto the ground and lay on her back across Elisabeth's lap. Elisabeth put her left hand under Christina's head. With her other hand she brushed the hair from Christina's face. Christina closed her eyes. Elisabeth closed her eyes and raised her head.

Christina began to cry, pulling her arms up to her chest with her hands against her chin. "No! No! No!" she called out. Her crying became louder. Time passed. She grew quiet.

"Yes, I remember the prison now," she said without opening her eyes or moving from Elisabeth's lap. "It was terrible. And then the trial. And you were dead they said and Patrick too. And they talked about our finding mama when she had hanged herself. There were two men there who helped me. Then I was put back into the prison."

"You did very well, Christina. You did all that was needed to be done. We are all very proud of you. Thank you from all of us."

Christina cried again now, though softly. Time passed.

"And do you remember how it was that you flew away with the swallows?" asked Elisabeth.

Christina moved out of Elisabeth's lap and sat up on the ground, very straight, with her eyes still closed but facing the setting sun. "Yes, I remember now. They took us all – Angelika and I and the others – to the square by the cathedral. The sky was full of dark clouds. There were lots of people there watching. The men tied us to iron poles with wood around us. They lit the wood and it burned. And so I flew up with the swallows." She opened her eyes and turned to look at Elisabeth. "Did you see it too?" she asked.

"Yes, I saw it too," answered Elisabeth.

Christina nodded to herself. She turned back to face the setting sun but with her eyes open. "So it really did happen. They burned us because they were so afraid of us."

"Yes, that is what happened," confirmed Elisabeth.

"Are we so dangerous, that they should have so much fear?"

"I do not know if we are dangerous. But we women give life. Without us there is no human life in this world. Perhaps that is what is so frightening for them: a power they think they do not have themselves but desperately need. And so they try to control us. And when they cannot control us they become afraid and seek to destroy us because in their confusion they think we have caused their fear."

Christina nodded again to herself. Her breathing grew deeper and slower. Her spirit body relaxed.

"But they cannot destroy us, right? They put me in prison and burned my body but somehow here I still am talking with you. We are not so easy to get rid of!" She smiled to herself.

"Right, we are not so easy to destroy," responded Elisabeth. "We are life itself. And we know it. These men who do so much damage are also life itself but they do not yet know it."

"Is there any hope, then, for this world when there is so much fear between men and women?" Christina asked.

"Yes, there is hope," answered Elisabeth. "But the change to find something new takes time, a long time. There are many who are working to make that change. Women and some men as well. Perhaps there will be more in the future. We will see.

"Christina, you need to look to yourself. What do you need now? What road will you take?"

"I do not want to take any of the roads that I know about. I want there to be new roads, new ways for us, for me. "

"I can understand that. So you want to make new ways, new roads, new paths? That lead somewhere else than to the suffering that there is here in this place and time."

"Yes, that is what I want."

"And are there other things that you want?" asked Elisabeth.

Christina was quiet for some moments. She closed her eyes, dropped her head to her chest and began to cry. Then she finished crying and sat up straight again. She opened her eyes.

"I want to have my own child," she said with conviction. "And I want to be able to protect that child against the insanity of this world. Is that possible?"

"It is a clear wish. But once a being comes into this world there are limits to what we can do to protect it. In the end it must always find its own way. But we can help for sure. You understand that?"

"Yes, I understand."

"Is there more that you want?"

"Where is Patrick?"

"I tried to help him after he was killed even though I was still in a body. Doing that is not easy but is sometimes possible. But it was of no use. I could not help him. His way forward was already determined."

"And what way forward is that?" asked Christina.

"He wanted to be with you – he really cares for you, you know. But he had made some bad choices and then died in a violent way. So he will have a very difficult time. Then when that difficult time comes he will either learn from it and grow or fail to learn and move even deeper into suffering."

Christina understood. She nodded to herself. She considered her choices in this moment.

"Can I be with him, then, in whatever comes next, but be his sister instead of trying like I have been doing to be his mother? Would that be possible?"

"If you follow him where he is going you can possibly support him in other ways than you have tried so far. But you need to realize that being there where he will be will mean more risk for you and for your child. You would have to accept that risk if you choose to go forward with him."

Christina was thoughtful.

"What do you think I should choose?" she asked Elisabeth.

"Well, that is hard to answer."

"I see that you are here with me, dear Elisabeth, but thinking about it, your teaching me, your being my friend, cost you your life. Am I right? So the choice you took is clear."

Elisabeth smiled. "You are smart, Christina. You are understanding a lot of things very quickly. And you are right, there was a lot of risk in my choosing this last life. But the choice was for me not difficult to make. Without my work, without teaching and supporting you and the others, I would not have found life worth living. It has been the story I have been living for a very long time. I love my work, regardless of the risks or the results. It is why I exist."

"Then my choice now is clear. I will be wherever Patrick is so that I can support him. Perhaps not as you have supported me, but in whatever ways I can. But I will not try to be his mother!" Christina laughed a small laugh at the humor of it.

"Okay, then it sounds like you have enough. Are you ready?"

"Yes," replied Christina. "I am ready."

"Then take my hand." Elisabeth extended her right hand and Christina took it in her left. "Close your eyes and see before you the life you have imagined, that you have chosen. Stay with that vision as long as you can."

The setting sun slid decisively into the horizon. The red and orange glow under the clouds filled the world.

Martyna

Martyna's spirit sat on the ground leaning her back on the iron post to which Christina's body had been tied for burning. Around her was the open cathedral square empty now in the dark late evening. In the buildings at the edge of the square there were a few lighted windows flickering through the darkness and torches at some of the doorways. The only sounds were of people sitting outside at tables in front of some of the buildings talking indistinctly. She noticed them especially when the people laughed: loud rough drunken laughter.

In her mind it was not clear how long she had been sitting there leaning against the iron post. An hour, a day, a year, a lifetime, a thousand years? Yes, she said to herself, all of that. I am here through all of it. I have been here through all of it.

She had witnessed the various lives as they flowed past her: Alya and Karu in Malta, Niwana and Timo in Africa, and now Christina and Patrick here in this place and time. She had also witnessed the transitions after those lives that linked to the next.

As all these scenes had unfolded she had gradually found answers to many of the questions she had had about herself as Martyna and Martyna's world: she understood now the many causes of the difficult relationship she had had to her brother Alex in her life as Martyna, she knew now why for her the struggle against Nazi oppression was the path that she had to take regardless of the risks and most of all she knew why having a child and protecting it as well as all the other children she could help was so at the center of her life.

But in the midst of all of that understanding one question had not been answered: Why do we do these terrible things to each other? Behaving like this makes no sense. It brings only suffering, sooner or later, for all of us. Yet we continue!

Why? she asked herself.

"Why?" she closed her eyes and asked the dark night sky out loud.

"Yes, that is a very important question," said Lela. "Why indeed is there so much that leads to such suffering?"

Martyna opened her eyes. There was more light now. Lela was sitting at her left side. The cathedral square scene, the buildings across the square with their flickering lights, the indistinct voices and the iron post that had been at her back were no longer there.

There were only the two of them sitting by each other on a hillside on the grass in the late afternoon sun. A river valley lay before them, winding its way between soft rounded green hills. There were trees and spring flowers and a few butterflies visiting the flowers.

Despite the change of surroundings Martyna stayed focused on her question. Regardless of how she struggled, Martyna had no answer. She sat silent.

"And so now do you understand enough to choose your way forward from your life as Martyna?" Lela asked. "If I remember right that is why we are here, why we started on this journey of remembering."

Martyna ignored Lela's question and stayed with the question of "why?" She pondered what she felt like she understood and what she knew she did not understand. And then it became clear to her what she wanted. In her lives men were the source of the suffering. Men are what she needed to understand.

"I need to know what it is like to be a man in this crazy world of ours. I need to understand why the men do the things they do. That is what I do not yet understand," she said to Lela.

"So you want to be a man in a next life?" asked Lela.

"No, I am not ready for that! That would be too much for me. What I want is to *understand* what it has meant to be a man in this world. And then perhaps understand why in all these lives my brother has been my destruction even when he may not have intended to be.

"Thinking about it now, I realize I never understood Alex, even when we were children. Then it got worse as we got older. And it has been like that for a long time, across many lives."

"So you think it would be helpful to understand at least your brother Alex better?" asked Lela. "That is certainly a more realistic goal than to understand all the men who have been your brothers. Or to understand all men."

"Would that be possible," asked Martyna, "to just learn more about Alex's life, his inner secret life that I never knew about? And the times in his life like during the war that he later never talked about, that he refused to talk about?"

"Yes," answered Lela, "that would be possible."

"But how can we do that? Can I 'remember' his life like I did mine?"

"The truth is that what you call 'lives' – all that happens and has happened – do not belong to you or to him or to me or anyone or even our so-called souls. It is all there available to experience for anyone who has the capacity for it, the relationship to it and the openness for it.

"So, Martyna, do I understand that you want to experience your brother Alex's life, as he experienced it, in order to better understand him?"

"Yes, that is what I want. And I know that he experienced some very terrible things. But perhaps those are exactly the things that I need to understand. So I am ready."

"Okay," said Lela. "First quiet your mind. You have been very caught up in the drama of Christina's life and death and transition. But now you need to relax and let all of that fade away. Then notice yourself as Martyna and as much as you can let all of that fade away as well. Become as empty and relaxed as you can. Then think only about Alex and the important choices he made in his life that you never knew about. See him in your mind."

"Okay," answered Martyna.

Lela watched while Martyna closed her eyes, slowed her breathing and relaxed. And then the time was right.

Lela reached out and took Martyna's hand.

Leipzig, Germany

April 16, 1940 C.E.

Elephants

The blonde-haired little girl in the yellow knitted sweater stopped walking.

"Oh, Grandfather, look what that man is doing!" she called out, pulling on the hand of the gray-bearded man walking beside her and pointing with her other arm. The man stopped, looked where she was pointing, smiled and spoke to her in a loud voice so that the person on the other side of the two high metal zoo fences and deep moat could hear him.

"First, that is a boy, not a man. And second, he isn't doing anything – the elephants are doing it and he is just cleaning up after them!" The man laughed.

"What elephants?" asked the little girl, since there were no elephants to be seen. Then she noticed a deer standing by the fence in an enclosure up ahead.

"Look, a deer!" she called out and raced forward. The old man stood there still looking into the compound. The boy stopped working, looked up, made eye contact with him, smiled and bowed slightly. The old man smiled back, responded with a nod of his head, touching the brim of his battered black felt hat with the index finger of his right hand. He turned then and walked off with an unsteady gait to catch up with the little girl.

Zoo visitors often made jokes about Alex's work in the elephant compound. He smiled when they did no matter how coarse the humor. He was happy with his job; it was, quite simply, the best part of his life. It took three hours each day: scooping up the mounds of droppings with his shovel; putting them with the soiled straw into the hand wagon; pushing the wagon then dumping its contents in the compost pile behind the wall by the greenhouse; then washing down the concrete throughout the elephant house and outside area with the water hose, flushing the urine and other dirt down the drains. After waiting to let the cement dry he put out fresh straw. He brought the vegetables and thicker grasses from the zoo animal kitchen in a wheelbarrow and put them into the feeding troughs with the vegetables – carrots, potatoes and cabbage mostly – on top. After nine months with this job he knew which elephants preferred which kinds of food and would sometimes feed it to them by hand when it was available. On Sunday afternoons he checked their feet, cleaning out anything caught in their foot pads. It had taken awhile before the animals had trusted him enough to raise each foot to him when he prompted them with the hooked stick. But now they did. On Saturday and Tuesday afternoons at 3 PM he would give all the elephants who wanted it a spray bath. This was even posted on the schedule by the main entrance – along with the lion and tiger feeding times – for the visitors to come and watch. Sometimes the younger male, Ganesha, would trumpet in mock irritation when Alex sprayed him, suck up some water in his trunk from the wading pool and spray Alex back. The visitors loved this play. Alex did too.

The elephant house and its six Indian elephants were a main attraction in the zoo. The compound had been built in 1926 in a grand style with a turreted house and open compound surrounded by a moat and iron walls. Two of the females, Lashi and Minnie, had been born in the zoo. For Alex they were all his friends.

When he had first taken over the job the previous summer Mr. Engelmann, the large animal director, had often come and watched him. Taking care of the elephants was dangerous work. In theory he could have herded the elephants into the elephant house and closed the big doors while he was cleaning outside then done the reverse as he cleaned the house. That is what had been intended when the elephant house had been built following the pattern of the tigers and lions that had previously been the zoo's mainstays. But it simply did not work. Getting the elephants to go where they were supposed to go on a schedule was beyond the capability of anyone in the zoo staff and appeared in practice to be significantly more dangerous than just letting the animals be where they wanted to be and working around them.

The man previously doing this job had quit after an elephant had stepped on his foot breaking several bones. After that incident it had proven impossible to find someone to do the work. Alex, who visited the zoo as often as he could and for whom the elephants were the best thing in the zoo, had noticed the animals were not being looked after properly and had simply volunteered. Mr. Engelmann was more than satisfied by Alex's work.

"Who would have thought that a schoolboy could do such a wonderful job with the elephants!" he would exclaim sometimes to no one in particular.

The part about the schoolboy bothered Alex – it was true but somehow awkward. The part about the wonderful job he did filled him with pride. For Mr. Engelmann to say such a thing really counted. As a young boy he had known Mr. Pinkert the zoo founder, although at that time Mr. Pinkert was old and not active in running the zoo. Now Mr. Engelmann was older himself, almost 50. He had lost his left leg below the knee to a tiger when he was in his thirties.

"A terrible tragedy," he reported that people had said then. Now, with most men with two good legs off fighting in the war and perhaps more to be called up if it continued very long it had been a blessing in disguise for a man like Engelmann who had no interest at all in killing people. He had been a soldier in the World War but had been assigned to taking care of horses and was not himself in combat. "One was enough for me, thank you," he would say when people talked about the new war.

Mr. Engelmann had told Alex that some of the people in the city government had said it made no sense to keep a zoo operating during a war – it required men who could otherwise be soldiers or could work in the war factories and then there was the considerable amount of food for the animals. But Engelmann was of a different opinion and so far those of his persuasion had won the discussion. "What about the children? What will they do if there is no zoo? And what will we do with the animals if not keep them here? Shall this crazy war destroy everything?"

Such comments were considerably over the edge of what one was allowed to say, Alex knew, but Engelmann was single and said whatever he thought without worrying too much about it. And it was true, there were still children in the city and they did come to the zoo.

Alex received good money for the job, five Reichsmarks a week. Free entry to the zoo was also counted as part of his pay. For his three hours a day after school and on weekends, seven days a week, he felt lucky to get any kind of work at all. That he got real money was a miracle. He was always paid by Mr. Engelmann directly, in cash, since he was underage and couldn't be on the regular payroll, or so said Mr. Engelmann.

Alex's income made a real difference in the family. With beer at 35 pennies a flask and bread at 20 pennies a loaf, his money could buy a lot. His father worked in a local leather goods factory. There had been no work for his parents back in Lodz, in Poland, so it had seemed like a good idea to come to Germany with his wife and the twins.

Mr. Bernstein, who owned the factory, had given his father a job and had provided a place for the family to live in the upper floors of his own house, which was across the street from the factory, at a very reasonable rent. For a while it had not been so bad. But with time the leather factory got fewer and fewer orders instead of a growing number. It was crazy really, since with the build-up of the military and now the war there was a huge demand for all kinds of leather articles. But the defense orders went to other businesses.

Alex's father Maximilian had fewer and fewer hours of work per week and he was paid by the hours he worked, not a weekly wage. There had been weeks when Alex's five Reichsmarks was more than his father made. On the other hand the Bernstein family had so many concerns they seemed not to notice if Alex's family had paid the rent or not and had let them get behind. No one could figure out how the Bernsteins had held on as long as they had. Almost all other Jewish businesses had been closed in 1938 after Crystal Night if not earlier and the families emigrated or were taken into custody and shipped off to places unknown. Maybe it made some difference to the authorities that Mrs. Bernstein was German and not Jewish and came from a well-known family in the town, though the rumor was that the family had cut off all contact with her when she had married a Jew. Or that their oldest son was a soldier in the Army, had volunteered even. But no one was sure.

Alex's mother had tried to find other kinds of work but always came back to helping out some hours a week at a clothes cleaning and tailor business run by another Polish family in a better quarter of the city. They too however had less work for her as the German people in the city were pressured to stop patronizing any except German-owned businesses. The Polish and other immigrant families did their own wash and tailor work.

In addition to the money he made it was good for Alex to get out of the house and off the street in the afternoons. It was boring sitting around the house arguing with his twin sister or doing nothing. But in the last year it had been harder and harder to find a place outside during the afternoon hours that was not dangerous. On the street he could get into difficulties without warning from passing teenage boys or young men. Sometimes it was more serious – questions came from the police or men in dark suits and overcoats who spoke in harsh voices: "Your papers!"

Luckily he had papers. He would pull his identification card out of the small folding leather wallet he always carried in his back pants pocket and hand it to them carefully while standing at stiff attention, his head high, which seemed to appease them. He was careful to give his pass to them with his picture and the typed information facing up: Name, Alexander Poloski; Address, Rosentalgasse 8, Leipzig; Date of birth, May 12, 1925; Place of birth: Lodz, Poland; Nationality, Polish; Residence code, B3; Profession, Student. He was not sure what residence code B3 meant. But so far it had always satisfied the men who had stopped him.

He was finished with his work for the day. It was spring and the weather was looking better than it had. Sunshine was coming down from between the high clouds. There was a cool wind from the west. The elephants had finished eating and had come out into the compound. It was a Tuesday and the spray bath show had gone especially well. Alex took a last look around. Nothing was amiss; everything was perfect for the moment.

He closed and locked the access gate behind him and pushed the cart to its place behind the elephant house. He stepped out of his green zoo worker overalls then hung them on a hook in a wooden locker that stood there. He took his brown corduroy jacket from another hook and put it on. He put on his cap.

He was planning to go to the zoo garden restaurant. Sometimes the people there kept food that had not been eaten by visitors for him on a plate on a shelf. His normal rhythm then was to stay in the back employee-break part of the restaurant, whether he had anything to eat or not, until it was late enough that people were going home from work. He liked to mix in with the hurrying people on the street. He walked like them with his head bent forward and his hands in his pockets, finished with a tough workday and eager to be home. It was safer than going through the streets alone.

But Mr. Engelmann was standing waiting for him as he turned to leave the enclosed part of the compound, between where the elephants were and the public area. Alex opened the gate with the key he carried, closed it behind him and then locked it carefully. He turned to face Mr. Engelmann. Alex could see it was something serious. Some animal has died, thought Alex, or they are going to close the zoo after all. Mr. Engelmann was dressed in his zoo overalls and green jacket with green worker's cap. His gray hair sprayed in every direction from under the cap. It was Tuesday so he had three days of new beard on this face. Alex could tell what day of the week it was by the length of Mr. Engelmann's beard.

"Alex, I can't make it work anymore," said Mr. Engelmann.

"What do you mean? What can't you make work?"

"Your coming here, your taking care of the elephants, all of it," replied Mr. Engelmann. "This was the last day, the last time. I am sorry. I did what I could but it was not enough."

Alex finally understood. "So, I have no more job, is that what you mean?"

"Yes, that's right. And there is more: you can't come into the zoo anymore. We made an exception because we knew how much you loved to visit the animals and then because you worked here; Hans at the gate looked the other way. But people have noticed and Hans is in trouble about it. He has a family, after all, not like me, so he has to be careful."

"But I'm not Jewish!" Alex declared.

"Alex, you know that's not the point; all public facilities in Leipzig have been closed to non-Germans, to non-Aryans, for years. And the zoo is a public facility."

"Here. It's your full week's pay even though it's just Tuesday." Engelmann held out his hand. In it was a five Reichsmarks piece.

Alex looked at the coin for a moment: it was new, the silver still shining, eagle side up. He held out his hand. Engelmann dropped the coin into it.

"Thanks," said Alex softly and put the coin in his jacket pocket.

"You know this is nothing personal, Alex, not at all personal. And I know we will never find anyone to take care of the elephants as well as you have done."

"Who will take care of them then?" asked Alex.

"I actually don't know. I will do it myself until we find someone."

There was silence for a moment between them.

"Do you want to say goodbye?" asked Engelmann. He means to the elephants, thought Alex to himself after a moment of confusion.

"No, it's okay as it is. They know I'm leaving." He looked over to the elephants. It was true, he realized: they all knew it already. Three stood watching. Not staring but watching all the same.

"No, it's fine. And thanks for all you have done for me. Good luck to you here with the animals and the zoo and everything."

"Thanks, Alex. I am glad you can see that it is not personal, that I had no other choice. And when this whole madness is over please do come back. As long as I am here there will be a place for you. I am sure that the elephants would also be glad to see you."

Mr. Engelmann held out his right hand, palm up. Alex stared at the hand. He was again not clear what was expected.

"Your key," prompted Mr. Engelmann.

Of course, thought Alex to himself. Without a word he took the key to the elephant compound out of his pants pocket, along with the little chain he had found for it and placed it in Mr. Engelmann's hand.

Through the Park

Alex went out into the public area. He turned and walked down the pathway heading away from the restaurant and the zoo exit. He was burning with shame. He could not imagine leaving through the normal entrance where the other workers would see him or much less going to the restaurant. They would all know what had happened. He headed for the back wall where the zoo bordered on the Rosental park. Once there he looked around to make sure no one saw him, as this route was forbidden, then went through a break in a hedge and along a narrow path. He used a low-hanging oak limb to raise himself then climb over the zoo wall that was not as high here. On the other side he was hidden by the bushes and small trees along the stream that flowed as a part of the park. He moved to the bottom of the bank, crossed the stream, and then followed it along until he was almost to the park entry on Zöllner Street. Once near the arched park entrance he looked around to make sure he would not be seen; the park was another public facility from which he as a non-German was barred. He saw no one except two old women on a bench talking and a young woman pushing a baby buggy. He walked nonchalantly through the park gate and was on the street. This route was tricky but he used it from time to time when he was late or when he felt some premonition that there might be trouble waiting for him on the main streets. He came to the corner of the street where he lived. He made the turn.

"We saw you come out of the park, you stinking ball of shit!"

Alex whirled to see what he had not expected: Jan, George and Franz were closing in on him fast. Normally he would have heard their running footsteps but he had been preoccupied. The boy's faces were red with the exertion of running and with the excitement they felt.

For them it is like hunting an animal, thought Alex to himself. They were all three his age and dressed almost as poorly as he was, though Jan sported an almost new black leather jacket that he had probably stolen from somewhere and their brown shoes from a Hitler Youth handout were significantly better than Alex's broken-down black ones. They wore versions of the same gray-brown cloth workman's cap that Alex had. Normally Alex would have run, especially since they were already winded. But today he was not in the mood to run. This surprised them and it surprised Alex too. They stopped about six feet in front of him, catching their breath. He stood opposite them, facing them. His head was higher than he usually held it.

"Be careful not to get too close," said George to Jan, extending a mock restraining arm in front of him. "You know he's covered with elephant shit. You don't want to get that all over you, do you?"

"There's no danger of that," added Franz. "He doesn't roll in the shit, he eats it! That's what these Poles live on, you know, big heaps of animal shit. You only have to worry that he doesn't throw up on you!" He laughed. The other two did not laugh although they did smile. They were looking at Alex trying to understand what had changed. Alex stood with his hands relaxed at his sides waiting to see what would come next. The joke was old and worn out.

They really have no imagination at all, thought Alex to himself.

"You haven't paid your rent yet this week," said Jan in an attempt at a grown-up tone. "And for late rent we have to charge interest, you know."

"Right! Interest!" chimed in George, like it was something novel and important.

Alex took a deep breath. He paused. "I lost my job. I've got no more money. I can't pay you rent anymore. It's over. It's really over." He said it all in a rush, in a low voice, looking down at the ground as he spoke.

He had had to tell someone and he definitely needed an excuse as to why he could not pay the "rent" they demanded of him. In a perverted way they were his only human friends. Most of the other kids in this area had been Jewish. He had been friends with some of them early on; he had even learned enough Yiddish to get by as they grew up together. But the Jews were almost all gone now and the few left kept very much to themselves. There had been some other Polish kids in his school earlier but they were also gone as there was no more work for their families here. The only kids left that were his own age were the lower class Germans who lived or hung out in this area. Like Jan, whose parents were out-of-work alcoholics who spent the day yelling at each other as to whose fault it was that they did not have enough money to buy the next bottle of gin. George and Franz both lived with their grandparents, as their fathers were off in the war somewhere and their mothers had disappeared. A couple of the German boys his age at the vocational school where he went for training had been friendly at first when he had started there but for the last several months – since Germany had invaded Poland in September of the previous year – they all ignored him, even when he spoke directly to them about anything but school work.

Jan thought over what Alex had said. He scratched his chin, looked up to the sky, then looked back at Alex with a grin. "Then why were you sneaking through the park?"

"I was just over there to see the elephants," said Alex but he had never been able to tell a good lie.

"It's not true!" shouted Jan. Then "Grab him!" to George and Franz who both lunged forward.

Alex suddenly realized his situation: in the distraction of being fired he had left the money Engelmann had given him in his jacket pocket where he as a rule carried only small change. He had forgotten to put the five Reichsmark piece in the hiding place in the sole of his right shoe. In the whole time he had been working in the zoo no one outside his family (and Mr. Engelmann of course) had ever known how much he really made. Jan had eventually believed that Alex made 50 pennies a week since that was the maximum amount they had found in his jacket pocket. And from that they had calculated that he owed them 25 pennies each week for the privilege of living in their neighborhood.

The action was fast and brutal, but took some new twists. As usual George and Franz sought to each grab one of his arms and wrestle him to the ground so Jan could search his pockets. Franz managed to get Alex's left arm, but Alex reacted by hitting him directly in the face with a strong right. Franz let go to tend to his nose. George, who was larger and stronger than Alex, took Alex's right arm and bent it behind Alex's back in a wrestling hold, driving Alex down to his knees. Franz recovered enough to take Alex's left arm again and help push him face down on the grass. Then they rolled him over on his back, each one of them holding down one of Alex's arms. This was the moment for Jan to step in. He began searching Alex's pockets. Alex tried to twist away from him as Jan's hand went into his right front jacket pocket. He heard and felt the pocket fabric rip away from his jacket.

"Wow, what do we have here! Five Reichsmarks!" exclaimed Jan. He held the large coin up high to admire it and show it off to the others.

George and Franz let go immediately and stood up themselves in awe of what they had found. Alex lay on his back on the ground, half on the sidewalk and half on the grass, looking up at them.

"I think that will even cover your interest," said Jan, looking down with a smile at Alex. "And here is your change," he said, tossing two smaller coins – a five penny piece and a ten penny piece that had also been in the pocket – onto Alex's belly.

The three marched off together discussing the possibilities of what they could do with their new-found wealth. Franz was holding a handkerchief he had borrowed from George to his bleeding nose.

The woman that had been at the park entry earlier was coming back now and pushed her baby carriage past him. She had to curve around to avoid him, going partly onto the grass. Alex was still on his back, looking up at the sky, noticing the clouds. She did not look at him or make any comment; she stared straight ahead gripping the carriage handle tightly with both hands. Alex was shaken by it. It felt like he had stepped or been pushed over a threshold into a new un-known realm, invisible to others, excluded from life.

Martyna and Maciej

Alex walked slowly down the street toward his house. His jacket pocket was torn almost off, his upper lip was sore and his right hand felt like there were broken bones from when he had smashed his fist into Franz's face. He had never fought back so hard before. But there had never been so much at stake. And he had never before felt so desperate and trapped.

Number 8 Rosentalgasse was a grand house made of light colored stone three and a half stories high. The house door was as always locked. Alex took the key from under the mat and used it to open the door then put the key back where it had been. He made his way quietly up the stairs to the third floor where his family lived in an apartment that made up the right half of that level. He was home an hour earlier than usual. He looked forward to being there by himself before the others in the family arrived. His whole world had cracked and broken today; he was struggling to hold himself together.

On the third floor landing he let himself into the apartment using the key that was hidden on top of a wall light fixture and closed the door behind him. As he expected it was silent and empty. His father and mother had work today and Martyna was probably off with her friends somewhere. She was of an age where she should have been in school, at least in the mornings, like he was. But she had had so many arguments with the teachers in the nurse training school where she had studied that the point came in which they threw her out. This was exactly what she had wanted. Now she was a free woman able to run with her older friends. And to get into trouble! thought Alex to himself. He disapproved of Martyna's friends. They were always talking about politics in such a wild way. He could not understand why their parents did not step in and stop it somehow. They only chided Martyna when she said something completely outrageous: "It's dangerous to say things like that!"

Alex lay on his bed in his room. He had been home for twenty minutes but had not changed his clothes; he was still dressed as he had been in school in the morning and then at the zoo and in the fight. At least he did not appear to be bleeding anywhere. His mother would be angry with him if she found him lying on his bed in the clothes he wore to work at the zoo, even though he wore overalls. It was a recurring theme between them. She could not understand how the smell of the elephants – on his clothes, in his bed, on his hands – was a comfort and support for Alex. When he could not smell the elephants he was not fully himself. So he would have to get up and change and wash himself Alex thought.

Before he could get up, however, he heard an unusual sound. It was otherwise quiet in his room, as it was in the back of the house away from street noises. The sound came from above him, clearly from above him. That was strange, as there was nothing above him but the attic space between the ceiling in their apartment and the roof. It was little more than a crawl space, really, though you could stand up in the middle. When he had been small he and Martyna had played there sometimes. There was a folding ladder in their storage closet next to his room that came down from the ceiling and led up to the attic. It had been awhile since he had been up there. It was crowded with stored things – some from his family and some things from the Bernstein's that they had probably forgotten about, as they had been in this house for generations and had only converted it to apartments shortly before Alex's family had moved here.

Now that he listened he could hear it more clearly: it was a rhythmic sound of something scraping or bending. It seemed to be growing louder. It definitely wasn't just a rat crawling around looking for something to eat. He really needed to find out what it was.

He got up and stepped through the hall to the storage closet. The door was closed. He opened it quietly and immediately two things became clear. First, the ladder to the attic was down. There was very little light in the storage room, only from the open door, as the room had no windows, but it was enough to see the ladder. The second thing was that he knew now what the sounds were. Two people were making love up in the attic. With the door open and a clear path through the hole in the ceiling where the ladder went there was no mistaking it: a man and a woman. He could hear their breathing and the sounds they were making. He could not think what to do. Go up the ladder and interrupt them? Go away and leave them their privacy? The sounds of the couple grew more intense. They both peaked together in orgasm, muting their sounds but still unmistakable. The woman's voice was clear to Alex now as she said something he could not quite make out – it was Martyna!

He charged up the ladder making a lot of noise in the process as the ladder swayed and creaked. There was light coming through the dirty dormer window in the attic. The two were lying together on an uncovered mattress on the floor, propped up on their elbows looking at him in surprise. It was Martyna and her friend Maciej, both completely naked.

"Martyna," he shouted at his sister, "what do you think you are doing!"

"I would think it was completely obvious what I am doing," she answered, then smiled at Maciej and lay back on the mattress, relieved that it had been only Alex coming up the ladder and not someone else.

"Hello Alex," said Maciej.

It enraged Alex that they didn't grope for their clothes or cover themselves with a blanket or something.

"What the hell are you doing here?" he asked Maciej, now in a hoarse whisper, as a whole other aspect of the situation dawned on him. "The police are looking for you. There are pictures of you plastered all over the city. 'Dangerous Provocateur' they say. If they find you here we are all done for."

"You are right about that, Alex. I am truly sorry to put you all in danger. I did not want to put even myself in danger. But I got a little too excited in a Polish community meeting last week and said some things that are true but not allowed to be said. Unfortunately it appears there are some Poles not to be trusted. So now the so-called authorities of our city are looking for me along with all the many others who 'threaten the public order'. It was not my idea to come here; Martyna thought of it and – to my surprise – your parents agreed. I cannot stay here long; sooner or later they will hear of my interest in Martyna and come for a visit. We are looking now for a place for me to go to next."

"You will get us all killed!" exclaimed Alex in his hoarse whisper.

"Well at least some of us will have a nice time waiting for the Gestapo to come for us," said Martyna. She reached over and stroked Maciej's beard. Maciej looked back at her and smiled.

"You are both impossible," hissed Alex. "At least be quiet up here. How do you think I found you anyway? The whole house was shaking!"

He was exaggerating of course but he could not think of anything else to say. There was nothing for it; they were crazy. He went back down the ladder, left the storage closet, closed the door, went back to his bedroom, closed his door, and lay on his bed. At least it was quiet now.

Many thoughts and emotions surged through him. He felt the same confused rage at Martyna that he always felt when she flaunted her relationships at him. Why does she do that? he asked himself. She was so beautiful and so sensuous and always laughing and ready to have a good time. So of course all the boys were crazy for her. Whereas Alex on the other hand ... he tried to see himself as he looked to other people, as if looking in an inner mirror. The image was always blurred and gray. Who was he anyway? Why was he so sad and afraid? Why didn't people like him? Martyna teased him that Alex seemed to prefer the company of animals to that of people. And it was so. He felt his face redden in the half-dark room as he thought again of Martyna and Maciej making love in the attic. Would he ever have the chance to find out what that was like, to make love with someone, with someone who wanted you, and wanted to be with you and live with you, and have babies and the whole thing? It did not seem very likely. Although fully clothed and lying on top of the bed, he drifted into a dream-filled half-sleep.

Mura

"Hello?" called his mother from the hall. She was home, of course, before he could get his clothes changed. He sat up on the bed.

"Is anybody here?" she repeated. The door to his room opened and she looked in. Immediately a look of disapproval came over her face as she saw his clothes. She still had her gray overcoat on, with her gray work dress under it. Her dark hair was drawn up tight and bound at the back of her head. Her forehead was wrinkled above her dark eyes.

"Alex, how many times do I have to tell you ..." she started. Then she stopped, came into the room and sat on the bed next to him.

"What is it? What has happened?" she asked in a frightened voice.

She reached her hand up to touch his face. He shrugged away from the touch, turned his body to look out the window and crossed his arms over his chest. But he could not bring himself to say anything.

"He came home and found me with my 'friend'," said Martyna, leaning against the door frame, her red bathrobe tied around her. "For some reason it seemed to bother him. Just because he has no fun he doesn't want anyone else to either," she added, in her characteristically sarcastic way.

"That's not it!" said Alex, more loudly than he had intended. "Or at least that's not all of it."

"Then what is going on?" asked his mother.

Alex turned on the bed to face her. There was real concern in her eyes. She really does care what happens to me, he said to himself. Tears filled his eyes. He uncrossed his arms and put both hands to his face, leaning forward.

"I lost my job!" he sobbed, "and then Jan and his thugs took the money Mr. Engelmann gave me for this week, all five Reichsmarks!"

So, there; it was out. He put his hands down and looked at his mother. She was no longer looking at him. She was looking down toward the floor of the room. Then she glanced up to the ceiling. She brought her left hand up to cover her mouth and then put it down. She stood up and said simply and without emotion, looking in the direction of the window, "Well, I'm sure we'll get by somehow."

She took off her overcoat, folded it over her arm and walked out of the room. She put the coat away, then went into the kitchen and, from the sound of it, was already starting to set the table for the

197

evening meal even though she had not changed from her work dress and it was much too early.

Martyna was looking at him with an angry expression. She had her mother's dark hair and eyes.

"So, you just let that punk Jan have our money, huh? What is wrong with you?" Her voice was rising in volume. "Don't you want to live? Don't you want us to live? Because that's what it's all about now, you know, about who lives and who dies! We can't just sit around like brave little sheep waiting for the slaughter; we have to do something, and do it now. Why can't you see it! God, you are hopeless!"

She turned and walked away, leaving his door wide open.

Alex got up and closed the door to his room then lay back down on his bed. His eyes wandered to the nail in the wall near where his head was. It seemed strange that there was no key hanging there. It felt like a bad dream in which everything that was precious to him had been lost. He closed his eyes and tried to sleep.

Maximilian

The family sat in the kitchen at their usual places around the small square table. Alex sat opposite his father. His mother, to her husband's right, sat opposite Martyna. Each had a plain white porcelain dinner plate, a knife, a fork and a glass. No one had spoken since they had sat down. Alex, while he was still lying on his bed, had heard his mother explaining to his father what had happened. He could not make out the exact words, as she spoke quietly, but he could tell what she was talking about just the same. As far as he could hear his father had said nothing in response.

On the table were a pitcher of water, a half a loaf of rye bread on a cutting board with a bread knife beside it, a medium sized sausage on a small plate, an open jar of mustard and a bowl of boiled pota-toes. A large flask of beer stood by his father's glass. Normally they just started eating without saying anything. Now they all sat there not looking at each other as if waiting for some signal.

Alex looked at his mother. He wondered if she regretted having pressured his father to leave Poland and start a "new life" here in Germany twelve years before. Both had come from the same small farm village fifteen miles west of Lodz. Maximilian had had a difficult time growing up, the fourth of six children, and the third son, in a large family. There would be no inheritance for him and he had found no trade so he had had to labor on the family farm for no wages and often not even thanks for his work. He and Mura had met when they were children. Her situation in her family was very much like his. They talked of running away together to a city somewhere and making a real life for themselves, far from the dirt and drudgery of the country farm life. After Mura became pregnant they felt they needed to get away even more desperately. They went to Lodz and got married then lived for a time with her older sister's family while the twins were born and for the time following. But there was not enough space and no matter how hard he looked Maximilian could find no work for an unskilled and uneducated farm boy. When they got word that someone was there looking for people ready to come to Germany to help build up a new leather goods factory – offering a good wage and a place to live – it sounded like a dream come true. When they had realized on arriving how much less his wage brought him in Leipzig compared to what it would have meant in Lodz they were disappointed but accepted it. They had fantasized that Maximilian would soon become a manager in Bernstein's factory and they would live the good easy life of city people.

His mother looked at his father for awhile as if prodding him to say something. Although she was only 32 she looked old, with her hair drawn back tight on her head and her face stressed.

When her husband ignored her look she turned to Alex and said what she felt was important to say.

"Alex, we don't blame you that you lost the job. It was a miracle really that you found it and held onto it so long."

His father looked at him now but struggled to say anything. His brown hair had hints of gray, his face was too wrinkled for his age and there were dark circles under his brown eyes.

"It's okay, Alex," he said at last.

He sat back in his chair relieved that he had gotten that much out. He opened the beer flask and poured himself a half a glass of beer, then took a small drink from it. He took the bread knife and cut the loaf into five thick pieces. Martyna reached out and took two and put them on her plate.

"Hey!" said Alex before he could think. Martyna grimaced and rolled her eyes upward, making motions with her eyebrows.

"Oh, right," said Alex quietly, ashamed of how soon he had forgotten about Maciej.

His father took the sausage and cut it with his own knife into five pieces. Martyna again took two and put them on her plate.

Each one got some of the potatoes.

They ate their food in silence, not looking at each other. When they were done Martyna got up with her still half-filled plate, walked out of the room into the hall, then to the storage room where she opened the door, went in, then closed the door behind her. Alex could hear the creak of the ladder as she went up to Maciej.

His mother and father went about what they did as if Alex were invisible: his mother stood washing the dishes in the sink, drying them and putting them away; his father sat at the table taking small sips from what was left of his beer and looking off into space. Alex still sat at his place at the table watching his parents.

They are zombies, thought Alex to himself, completely lost in their thoughts.

If he came or went, they would neither notice nor care. He went into his room, closed the door and lay down again on his bed. He still had his work clothes on but his mother had not seemed to notice. There was light outside but his window faced northeast so he could not see the sun that was setting. A medium-sized gray-brown bird landed on his windowsill. Alex did not know what kind of bird it was. It looked in at him. It turned its head to the left, then to the right. It pecked on the glass once and flew away.

School

It was only 9:30 AM but Alex was ready for the school day to be over. The first hour – from 7:30 to 8:30 – had not been so bad. Mr. Drechsler had been lecturing for the last week about the various kinds of metals that one could work with and the qualities that they had – what each type of metal was good for and what not. The focus today was on types of alloy steel. Alex found it interesting how even small quantities of other materials, mixed in with the iron, then processed hot enough and in the right way to make steel, could give so many different results. In this subject like all of his subjects he was a careful and attentive student. That was the reason he was here, because his carefully written application, with recommendations from three of his teachers, had been accepted and his grades in his earlier school had been good enough. Thankfully this school was free. He even got his books free. After only seven months in his first year he had learned a lot. At the end of his next school year, after only two years of study, he would get a certificate as a qualified apprentice metalworker. From there his future was bright, as there was lots of demand for metalworkers. All he had to do was to stay with it long enough to get his certificate.

The second class hour had been more difficult. It was practical application and training in the back half of the large work room. The class of 32 was organized into 8 work groups of four boys each. Each work group had an assigned metal lathe machine. They took turns in each group taking a short piece of rod made of soft steel and making one end of it into a cone-shape using a specific angle of 35 degrees from the center line. In theory it was simple. But for practice they left off the cooling oil that would have normally been flowing over the steel as it was being cut. If you were not very careful the thin steel near the end would burn and twist as it got overheated when it was thinning to a point or if you moved the cutting tool against it too fast. The other boys in his team had gone first as usual and had done passable jobs. The sound of all the machines going was deafening. They all had to wear eye protection but for some reason it was not allowed to cover your ears. Alex had found it hard to concentrate. His hands had been shaking. It was impossible for him to get the sharpened steel point to look reasonable. Finally time had run out. He had doused his pitiful attempt in oil, dried it, hung up his work apron on the hook along the wall alongside the aprons from the others and returned with his piece of metal to sit at his place at one of the tables where they had their lessons.

Each boy sat with the result of his work on the table before him. Their teacher would go through the class now, one at a time, examining and measuring their results, giving out praise and judgment, and making suggestions for improvement. Alex's jaw tightened at the thought of what was to come for him.

The door to the classroom opened. A city police officer came into the room. He was a sergeant if Alex was right about the gold pattern on his upper left arm. He was unusually tall and fat – a really big man, probably in his 60's. He walked with a limp, dragging his left leg behind him a bit. "Heil Hitler!" he greeted their teacher, saluting and clicking his heels. "Heil Hitler," returned Mr. Drechsler, raising his arm but without clicking his heels. Mr. Drechsler stood waiting to see what the man wanted. Instead of saying anything the policeman peered out over the class, scanning the faces. Apparently he couldn't find what he was looking for.

"Is the student Alexander Poloski in this class?" asked the policeman, turning back to Mr. Drechsler.

"Yes, he is," answered Mr. Drechsler, but continued looking at the policeman instead of saying anything more. Several students shifted uneasily in their seats. Alex, who was in the back row, was surprised to see that not one of his fellow students looked at him although they all knew his name.

"Well, which one is he?" said the policeman in an impatient tone.

"What do you want with him?" asked Mr. Drechsler in a quiet voice. Every student in the room froze in position. No one breathed.

The policeman's face worked in a strange way as if he were having trouble swallowing something. Finally he spat it out, rough and loud.

"That is of no concern to you! Enough now, point him out to me!"

Alex saw Mr. Drechsler's face tighten. He was struggling too now, searching for his answer. This is stupid and dangerous, thought Alex to himself, and nothing good can come of it. Alex stood up.

"I am Alexander Poloski," he said in a calm clear voice, surprising himself.

The policeman who had been staring at Mr. Drechsler huffed in an animal-like way and then turned to face Alex. He raised his left arm high with his hand bent down and his index finger pointed at a place on the floor beside him.

"Come here!" he commanded, jabbing the finger downward.

Alex looked down at his things on the table in front of him – the sheet of paper and the pencil he had been using to take notes, the bent and twisted steel point he had been working on – and at his school bag on the floor next to his chair. He was sure he would not be needing these things any more so he left them all where they stood. And if he did return, they would be here waiting for him. He took his newly repaired jacket off the chair back and slipped it on. His mother had sewed the pocket back on this morning while he got ready for school. He moved from his seat, walked along between the tables and approached the place the policeman had indicated. Alex had not looked at them directly but he knew every student in the room and Mr. Drechsler as well were watching him now.

When Alex was within reach the policeman grabbed him by the upper right arm and shook him.

"Enough of this insolence! You are coming with me and coming now."

Alex did not resist or show any emotion on his face. The policeman pulled Alex out through the open door and into the hall. He slammed the door behind them.

I thought my arms were supposed to be in the back, Alex thought incongruously as the man put handcuffs on him immediately after they came into the hall outside his classroom, with his hands in front of him. But he said nothing.

A black Mercedes city car was waiting for them outside the school, parked right at the steps where it was not allowed to park. They got in the back seat after the driver had stepped out of the car and opened the door for them. He closed it behind them. Now Alex understood: only with his hands in front of him could he sit comfortably in the car.

The back and side windows were smoked glass so it was not so easy to see out. The car had a powerful engine and soft seats. Alex had never ridden in such a car before. He found he liked it despite the strange situation. All the people he had ever seen picked up by the police had been taken in windowless vans, thrown in the back like parcels to be delivered.

They drove deeper into the city center. Finally they drove through an iron gate that had opened by itself as they approached and into a parking area behind a large office building with bars on the windows. The door was opened again by the driver and Alex and his escort walked up the steps. After a buzzing sound the main door opened and they walked into the building. The policeman spoke through a grilled window on the right.

"Prisoner Alexander Poloski."

"103" was the answer he got.

They went up a stair and down a hall. They stood before a num-
bered door: 103. The officer knocked and when someone from inside answered they went in.

And now here we are, thought Alex to himself.

Interrogation

"Heil Hitler!" said the policeman that had brought Alex in, dragging his left leg up next to his right one, clicking his heels awkwardly and shoving his right arm out high and straight.

The three men who had been sitting around the rectangular table in the medium-sized room stood up, turned to face him, saluted and answered "Heil Hitler." One was slower and less polished in his salute. Alex knew him: it was Officer Schmitt, who was responsible for the police beat in Alex's neighborhood. He was an old man, probably over 70. Alex had always liked him. The other two men did not wear uniforms but were dressed and carried themselves in such a way that they did not need to. Alex could actually smell it: Gestapo. Maybe they all wear a special cologne so they can recognize one another even in the dark, thought Alex to himself. He was afraid, of course, but this thought helped him.

The room had no windows but there was a large light fixture hanging from the high ceiling making it well-lit. The walls were light green. There were no pictures on the walls. The floor was gray linoleum with a pattern to make it look like marble.

"Here is the prisoner Alexander Poloski," declared the officer that had brought him.

"Take the handcuffs off him, then leave," said one of the men Alex did not know.

"Yes sir!" answered the policeman smartly. He pulled a key from his pocket, unlocked the handcuffs, took them off Alex's wrists and hung them on a clip he had on his belt. He stood then at attention and the whole Heil Hitler ritual was repeated so he could leave the room.

"Sit down, Alex," said the man who had ordered the handcuffs to be removed, indicating a fourth chair at the table, opposite where he was, as he sat down himself. Alex decided he would call him The Boss. He was thin with delicate features, blue eyes and short blonde hair. His tone was decisive but not unfriendly. The Boss also nodded at Officer Schmitt, who then took a seat at the end of the table to the right of the chair that was designated for Alex. Schmitt looked down at his police uniform; he seemed to be examining it for lint.

Alex sat down. He sat straight with his hands on his knees not touching the table or the back of the chair. The third man, middle-sized with brown slicked down hair and a dark suit and tie like The

Boss, remained standing looking at him sternly with his arms folded on his chest.

"Would you like something to drink?" asked the Boss. "Water, for example?" he said to Alex, indicating a pitcher of water and three glasses that stood on a file cabinet in the corner of the room.

"No thanks," answered Alex.

It was not clear what would happen next. Alex waited.

"Hello Alex," said Officer Schmitt, speaking for the first time.

He was trying to sound friendly, Alex realized, but was very unsure of himself. Alex nodded to him and then looked back to the man across from him. There was no point in asking questions; he would find out what they wanted soon enough.

"As you wish," said The Boss and straightened himself in his chair, leaning slightly forward, looking at Alex intently.

"Alex, we are going to ask you some questions and I want to make sure you understand how important it is that you give us complete and truthful answers. Do you understand me?"

"Yes sir," answered Alex quietly.

"Where were you at 4:45 PM yesterday afternoon?"

Alex's brain raced with alternative explanations of what this could be about. Nothing he could figure out in the few seconds he had to think made sense. He decided to answer as exactly and truthfully as he could. He calculated the time. He had finished his work at the elephant compound at his usual time, 4:30, but then gone home instead of to the zoo restaurant, so...

"I was walking down the street where I live, Rosentalgasse."

"Good, good," said the man. "And what happened as you were walking down Rosentalgasse?"

Alex couldn't believe it. He was being asked about his run-in with Jan, George and Franz.

"I met some ... friends of mine."

"And what happened when you met?"

"We had a disagreement. There was a kind of fight."

"A kind of fight? What do you mean?" he asked as if he really wanted to know.

Alex looked down at the table. Instead of pressuring him the Boss turned to Officer Schmitt.

"Officer Schmitt, what are the exact accusations that have been made against Alex?"

Officer Schmitt pulled a folded paper out of his inner jacket pocket.

"Attack on a German citizen causing severe bodily injury and grave personal insult," he read in a formal tone.

"Yes, yes, we know that; but why did they fight?"

"The boy – his grandmother brought him into the station but the boy did all the talking – said that Alex owed them money that they were trying to collect and he refused to pay. Instead he attacked them," said Officer Schmitt.

"Is that the way it was, Alex?" asked the Boss.

Alex paused to consider for a moment. "Yes, that is what happened," he said, with resignation in his voice.

The man across from Alex nodded slightly to himself, leaned back in his chair and addressed himself to Officer Schmitt and the other man.

"Well, it is all pretty simple, apparently. Alex does not deny the charge so there is no reason to go through the effort of an official hearing. Officer Schmitt, thank you for coming in. You may go now."

Schmitt hurried to stand up. The Boss also stood up. "Heil Hitler" all around and Schmitt left the room. The man who had stood the whole time closed the door behind Schmitt.

Alex stayed seated. The Boss sat back down across from him.

"I am actually sorry to hear this about you, Alex," he said. "I have had the chance to ask about your background and I am told you are an excellent student with lots of promise – conscientious in your work and never before in trouble. The Fatherland needs more young Poles like you to help in the great work of building the new society. We Germans cannot do it alone. But now with this one stupid mistake you have lost it all – your place in the school, your future, your freedom." He paused to judge the effect of his words. Alex was looking down at the table.

"I will put in a good word for you, I promise you that. Your cooperation in this interview has been commendable. You will get off rather lightly, probably not more than a year in prison." Again he stopped to judge the effects of his words. Alex continued to gaze down at the table. Alex began to get a sense of where this was going.

"You may take Alex to the holding cell now," said the Boss to the other man and stood up. Alex stood up to go, turned and waited to follow the other man.

"But wait, I just thought of something," said the Boss. "Sit back down for a moment, Alex," he said in a friendly way. Alex sat back down. This time the Boss did not sit down but continued to stand.

"There just might be another way out of this for you, Alex," he said.

Alex looked up at him. "Like what?" he asked with as much calculated sarcasm in his voice as he dared. The two men looked at each other. The Boss looked back at Alex.

"As you know the last few months have not been especially easy ones for German-Polish relations. After we were forced to take action last September to protect the German citizens who were being persecuted in parts of what at that time was called Poland, many of your people could not understand the bigger picture, the scale and the vision of the project we have underway. Some Poles have even gone so far as to say that instead of joining together with the Germans to build the new society they should actively resist. I think you are able to understand how short-sighted and useless that would be. Am I right, Alex?" He paused.

Alex looked up from the table. "Yes, I understand," he said. The Boss nodded. He walked to a corner of the room where the file cabinet stood. He took a gray folder off the top of the file cabinet and then took a stack of pages out of it.

"I am glad you understand," said The Boss, "and that you know there is a much better future in working with us than in being against us." He stood across the table from Alex; he pushed the chair where he had been sitting earlier up under the table.

"We have a delicate situation here in Leipzig. Unfortunately there are some misguided people, Poles among them, who not only refuse to take their allotted place in the new structure but are actively advocating resistance and sabotage. I wish there was some way we could reason with these people and help them understand their mistakes but our attempts in that direction have not been successful. What we are now forced to do is to bring these people into protective custody, to protect both them and society in general from their dangerous and diseased thoughts before thoughts become deeds. But some of them have not proven so easy to find. We are certain they are still in the city or in the area. Any help you could give us in finding them would be very much appreciated. I can even go so far as to say that this regrettable incident yesterday might just ... disappear, get lost in the paper shuffle, if you know what I mean."

"I can't help you. I don't know where any of the people you are looking for are," said Alex.

"Are you certain you are so well informed as to who we are looking for?" said The Boss and smiled. "Would that all of the Poles in our town were so careful to keep up with the bulletins!

"Just to make sure, I have some pages here with the pictures of some of the people we are looking for. I will show you each of the pictures and you will tell me if you know anything, anything at all, about them. Do you understand, Alex?"

"Yes, sir," responded Alex.

Instead of saying anything further the Boss simply placed a letter-sized page containing a large format picture and the name of the person on the table in front of Alex. After about 10 seconds with no reaction from Alex he placed the next one on top of the stack. The Boss had been right: some of the people's pictures had not been posted anywhere that Alex had seen. He pretended to look into the faces and to read the names but all of his concentration was going into preparing him for what was to come.

And then it came. He had been counting as a way of distracting himself. The fourteenth page, with Maciej Machik's picture and name, lay before him. Despite all his preparation Alex could not help himself. Something in his body betrayed him. He did not know what it had been – tightened lips, intake of breath, arms pulling together – in the end it did not matter. The Boss picked up the stack of pictures, straightened them with the other pictures he had not yet shown and walked over to the filing cabinet. He put the stack of pictures back into the folder. He walked back to the table, pulled out his chair and sat down in it. He looked across at Alex, who was peering down at the table. He leaned forward.

"Where is he?" asked The Boss. His voice was not loud and not directly threatening. But it drilled like a piece of iron into Alex's belly. What could he do now? Now that they knew he knew something about Maciej they would be at the apartment in minutes, just on the chance that Maciej was there, no matter what more happened. And his whole family would be publicly executed to show others what it cost to hide someone they wanted, not to speak of what they would do to Maciej.

Alex looked up. The face he saw was not young, probably forty or so. The man was totally concentrated.

"I can't tell you," said Alex.

"But you do know?" asked the Boss.

"Yes, I know."

"Then why can't you tell us?"

"Because he and his friends have threatened that if we tell they will kill me and my whole family," answered Alex.

He had tried to make it sound convincing without overdoing it. Amazingly, from the look on The Boss's face, The Boss believed it. It fit in with how he would do things. It fit in with the kind of boy that he thought Alex was, that would betray Maciej out of a sense of duty or fear unless there was a powerful reason not to. It seemed to almost relieve him; finally he heard something about these people that he could understand. He leaned back in his chair and shook his head back and forth then looked up at the ceiling smiling to himself at Alex's predicament.

"Well, Alex, you seem to be in a difficult situation. If you do tell they will kill you and your family and if you don't tell we will have to deal with you all in a similarly consequent way. How shall we find our way out of this dilemma?"

"I don't know," said Alex and looked down at the table.

Alex lifted his hands to his face and began to cry. He squeezed his eyes shut, trying not to see. He thought about his mother, his father, about Martyna. In his mind's eye he saw them all dead, naked and covered with blood, in a pile with other bodies. It was real! His nightmare was real and it had all happened because of him just as in his nightmare! His neck and throat were tight with the tension of holding back the wailing that rose up in him from his belly and chest.

It is too terrible to bear, he thought to himself. I will explode.

"There, there, Alex, no need to take it all so seriously. I am sure we can find a way out of this for you."

The Boss motioned to the man standing who at first did not understand. The man finally understood. Alex suddenly had a large white handkerchief in his hands. He looked up at the standing man in surprise. The man for the first time was looking away. Alex blew his nose. He looked across the table to The Boss. Alex no longer felt a need to cry. He folded the handkerchief and sat it on the edge of the table. The standing man did not pick it up.

""What kind of way out?" he asked.

"If you tell us all you know and we are actually able to take Machik into custody I promise you we will protect you and your family from the retaliation of his associates. We will make sure you will be out of their reach."

"You mean, kill us, is that it?"

"No, no, Alex! I mean you will all be in a safe place where they cannot find you. None of you will be harmed."

Alex thought about it for a moment. "Okay," he said. Alex nodded. "Okay," he said again. Alex took a deep breath.

"He is in the attic above the storage room in our apartment."

"Are there others hiding there with him?"

"No."

"Do you know where any of the others are hiding?"

"No."

"Is Machik armed?"

"I don't know. I don't think so."

The Boss nodded to the man standing there and then made a motion with his hand when the man hesitated to leave, waving him away. The man went immediately to the door and through it; closing it behind him.

No time for Hitler salutes now, thought Alex to himself. There is work to do.

The Boss relaxed. He leaned back in the chair.

"I want to thank you Alex for helping out is this situation. It restores my faith in human nature when people like you do the right thing in the end even when it is difficult. My job is not an easy one as I'm sure you understand."

Alex did not know what to say. He nodded.

The Boss got up and walked to the filing cabinet. Alex watched him without turning his head. The Boss opened the top drawer of the cabinet and took out a sheet of paper which he placed on top of the folder of pictures. He took a fountain pen out of the drawer, opened it and proceeded to write several sentences on the paper, pausing once to look over at Alex, then put the pen down. He took a stamp and stamp pad out of the drawer and carefully stamped the page. He picked up the pen again and initialed the stamp, then closed the pen and put it back in the cabinet. He took a drying roller out of the cabinet drawer and carefully rolled it over the page. When he was satisfied that it was dry he folded it twice and walked to the door. He pushed a button next to the switch for the light then turned and stood looking at Alex. Alex could feel him looking but did not turn around.

"Stand up, Alex," The Boss said.

Alex pushed back the chair and stood up. He turned around. They looked at one another.

In half a minute a policeman came into the room without knocking.

"Heil Hitler!" The policeman and the Boss saluted each other.

"Take Mr. Poloski to the building command office. Give them this order. They will know what to do."

"Yes, sir," answered the policeman. He took the paper and placed it in his breast pocket. He took the handcuffs that hung at his belt and closed them on Alex's wrists with Alex's hands behind him. He held Alex's upper right arm firmly in his left hand.

"Good luck to you, Alex," said the Boss and nodded to the man that he could now leave.

"Heil Hitler!" the two saluted. Alex and the policeman left the room.

Arrival

The railroad car rolled to a slow stop.

Alex extricated himself from under the man who was lying across his legs and stood up. They had been underway for two days. During most of the journey from Leipzig they had not been actually moving but rather parked somewhere waiting for some other train or trains to pass. Once, from the sound of it and the motion of the car, they had been separated from the train they had first been a part of and connected to another one.

There were about eighty men of various ages, backgrounds, and conditions in the freight car.

"This is not crowded," said a man in Polish as someone had complained at the beginning of the trip. "Believe me, you don't want to know what crowded means."

No one had said they did want to know.

There had been nothing additional to eat after the piece of bread and half sausage they had each been given at the start of the trip but there had been some water late at the end of the first day and this morning as well. Alex had managed to get some for himself both times, drinking out of the metal bucket that was passed around after having been handed in through a small door at one end while they were stopped. He had kept some of his bread and half his sausage hidden away in his inner jacket pocket. His stomach was burning with hunger but it seemed far away and not so important. There was a small iron-framed hole in the floor at one end of the car where one could take care of one's business but the car still reeked of urine and excrement.

When the train had been moving it had been hard to talk due to the roar of the wheels on the rails. When the train had been stopped it had usually been quiet in the car among the men but now and then there had been a conversation or even several at one time. The languages were mixed but mostly Polish and accented German. Twice someone had tried to start up a conversation with Alex. "Where are you from?" was the first question. "Where do you think we are going?" was the next question a day later. Alex had just turned away without answering, even when both times the questions were repeated in German and Polish.

There is no point in it, he had thought to himself.

Less than a minute after they had stopped the door to the car rolled open.

"Out, out, out!" a voice commanded in an urgent tone.

The men stood up as best they could and moved toward the door. The first few jumped smartly out of the car and moved over to the other side of the train platform where soldiers were directing them to stand. The ones who followed were slower. There were more shouted orders. Alex's turn came and he stepped down out of the car. At least a dozen soldiers were standing along the far edge of the platform, all armed with rifles at the ready as well as handguns in their holsters. Several dogs of various breeds were also part of the group awaiting them. It was not a train station but the end of a siding. Alex could see now that there were four cars with a locomotive at the far end which had backed down the siding. All four cars had been full of prisoners and all were being unloaded at the same time. From the height of the sun it was late afternoon. The sun was in what must be the west, streaming through the upper branches of a line of large maple trees with new green leaves appearing on the lower branches. The air was wonderful after two days in the railroad car. He turned his face toward the light with his eyes closed against the unaccustomed glare.

Something smashed into his right shoulder. He staggered, lost his balance and fell.

"I said move it, you lazy animal!" shouted the man who had hit him and kicked Alex in his side.

Alex rolled over and got up as quickly as he could. He hobbled to find a place in the lines that were forming there, standing up straight and acting as if nothing had happened when he got there. Alex could see the man who had hit and kicked him now. The man was not dressed in the same uniform as the military guards but was in striped prisoner's clothes. Instead of a gun he carried a short black stick, larger at its end, which he was using to prod or beat the arrivals. Some of his blows seemed to be designed to get them out of the car and into ranks as quickly as possible. But much of what Alex saw seemed to be simply sadistic cruelty. The man wore an armband: "Kapo" was written on it.

The formations were separate for each of the cars. The men stood close together and were yelled at and prodded until they understood that they needed to stand in rows and columns, with ten men in each row. All the commands were in German and many of the arrivals appeared not to understand what was being ordered. For his car it was seven rows of ten men each plus a short row of six. Two of the soldiers moved methodically along the lines of standing men checking for things the men were carrying in bags or cases or in their pockets. Anything they found that was interesting to them they put in a small wagon that one of them pulled. Resistance to this process or hesitation to give up something they found interesting was met with immediate blows and curses. Alex held his arms out from his sides ready to be searched when they passed him but they walked by without even looking at him.

While this process was going on the man with the stick had looked around in the car in a careful way then stood waiting looking down the platform in the direction of the other cars. Alex saw there was something going on by the first two cars although there was only limited searching of the prisoners. The Kapos there had taken two men out of each group and ordered them to get back into the cars. The men dropped bodies one by one out of the car doors. A heap of bodies grew in front of each of the cars. Eventually the two pairs of men went back to their places in the lineups. The prisoners from the first two cars looked thinner and frailer than those in his car, even at this distance. They were all dressed in gray uniforms with vertical stripes in a darker gray and most of their heads were shaved. Those in the other two cars were dressed in civilian clothes as he was and had normal hair and occasional beards.

"Count verification!" shouted someone from the far end of the platform. "Wagon one!"

"Wagon one reporting! 68 living and 8 dead, sir!"

There was a pause.

"Wagon two!"

"Wagon two reporting! 75 living, 6 dead, sir!"

Another short pause.

"Wagon three!"

"Wagon three reporting! 81 living, no dead, sir!"

"Wagon four!"

"Wagon four reporting! 76 living, no dead, sir!" shouted the man who had organized their exit from the railroad car.

"All counts correct! Permission to move out!" shouted the voice from the far end of the platform.

"Move out!" shouted their Kapo to the men and gestured with his stick as to the direction they needed to go along the wide brick-cobbled road.

The military men and their dogs took up places to the left and right of the columns and they all began to trot quickly along the road, one guard in each group pulling the wagon full of things that had been confiscated. The guards prodded or threatened anyone they judged to be falling behind.

A large flat-bed wagon came into view heading back to where the marching men had come from. It had four rubber truck tires attached to a large wooden frame about 10 feet long and six feet wide. The two front tires could be turned to steer by the movement of a tongue that stuck out in front and was guided by two men, one on each side of it. The whole thing was pulled by four pairs of prisoners in gray striped uniforms on each side wearing leather harnesses with a wooden crosspiece like what a pair of horses would wear to pull a coach. The flat wooden bed of the vehicle was empty. There were also two military guards and a dog trotting along beside the wagon and a man with a Kapo armband trotting in the lead. The wagon and its human horses passed close to Alex as he was in the leftmost file of his group. He risked looking at them as they passed. The men pulling the wagon were staring straight ahead. From what Alex could see not one of them so much glanced at the new arrivals. It reminded him of the woman who had pushed her baby carriage past him only a few days before as he lay on the ground after the fight.

After a short time they came to a white two story building with a watch tower on top of it. The building was set in a wall with a large iron grill-work gate in the middle of a passageway at ground level. In the center of the gate toward the top were the words in German, worked into the metal of the gate: "ARBEIT MACHT FREI": ("Work makes (you) Free"). The gate opened from an electrical actuator after some shouted exchange and the men marched inside.

"Halt!" came the order from their Kapo after they were only about 100 paces inside the camp. "No talking! No sitting down! Remain at attention! Stay in formation!"

The groups from the other three cars came in behind them and stood apart from them.

Alex had a chance to look around. They found themselves to one side of a very large flat area, like a parade ground, at least a quarter of a mile across. To the right was a large U-shaped building with people coming in and going out. To their left were rows of single-story barrack-like buildings stretching into the distance along both sides of a wide tree-lined street. The parts of the area that he could see were encircled by a high concrete wall with barbed wire on the top, an open strip inside the wall perhaps 20 feet wide, then a second inner fence made up of iron posts and more barbed wire. Finally there was an inner ditch filled with water. At the corners of the outer walls and mid-way down the longer sides were watch tower buildings. In the tower closest to him, on his right, he could see a man in the room at the top of the tower with a mounted gun pointed down into the area. There were words written in large letters on the sloped roof of the U-shaped building that were visible throughout the entire area. Alex translated the German: Obedience, Honesty, Cleanliness, Sobriety, Diligence, Order, Dedication, Truthfulness, love of the Fatherland.

So, it isn't so different from the primary school in Leipzig, he thought to himself. I should fit right in.

The guards and dogs that had been with them left. Only the Kapos remained, standing by each of the four groups. Prisoners and guards came and went across the large open area, all ignoring them.

After half an hour six armed men in black SS uniforms came out of the U-shaped building and walked to the groups. They were young and muscular and made jokes among themselves. They merged the four groups and organized 15 rows of 20 men and marched them closer to the main building where they were ordered to wait.

Alex had noticed that another group in prison clothes had filed out of the same building, though from a different door, and stood in formation waiting for whatever would come next. Some men came and ordered them to march off, which they did, down the broad tree-lined street between the long lines of barracks.

People walk in, people walk out. Not as bad as it could be, thought Alex to himself.

Just as the first row from his group was going in, Alex smelled something unusual in the wind that was coming from behind them. He turned to his left and saw a column of black smoke rising from somewhere at the other end of the compound, or perhaps just outside it. His eyes met the eyes of the man who was next to him. He was an older man, probably in his 50s, well-dressed with a short carefully trimmed beard and glasses. His eyes twitched in the direction of the rising column of black smoke and he nodded slightly to Alex, as if to agree with what he had somehow understood was Alex's conclusion: the dead from the train were being "processed" as well.

After another ten minutes they came for another row. Alex's row would be next.

For the first time since the interrogation Alex asked himself the question, What do I want? Do I want to live or do I want to die?

If he wanted to die, it looked like he was in the right place. He was sure they would oblige him. But how could one live in such a place? He realized that that is what he wanted – to live. At first he did not know why. It surprised him. But the last words Martyna had said to him still stung his ears: "We can't just sit around like brave little sheep waiting for the slaughter; we have to do something, and do it now. Why can't you see it! God, you are hopeless!"

They were all themselves dead now – Martyna, his mother, his father, Maciej, or in the process of dying, he was sure. The promise of the Gestapo interrogator that they would be safe had been a cruel farce. If Alex, who had turned them in, who had betrayed them all, was sent here, he could all-too-easily imagine what their fate had been.

He would do it for Martyna, he decided: he would live, he would survive, he would not just be a brave little sacrificial animal any more, accepting slaughter. He owed it to her somehow. He would live as tribute to her. He would finally "do something." He was not sure what it might be but he was sure that dead he would not be able to contribute anything.

He noticed the bulge of his remaining bread and sausage in his inner jacket pocket against his left breast. He glanced around cautiously – no one seemed to be noticing him. He reached up with his right hand, picked it out of his pocket, and brought the sausage up to his mouth and into it. He swallowed it after only a few studied slow bites to make it into smaller pieces. The bread was easier: he held it in his mouth and crushed it until it broke up and then swallowed it. The feeling in his stomach changed immediately. It still burned but with a different sensation.

Who knows what happens to us in this building now? he said to himself. At least it will not be so easy for them to take my food away.

It was time for his row. They walked single file into the building and stood in a queue before a desk. There was a soldier sitting at the desk and three others standing nearby. Alex was the second in the line.

The well-dressed man with the beard that had been walking beside him from the train was just ahead of him now in line. After providing his name and nationality (Polish), he was asked what he had for a profession.

"Politician" he said, after a pause.

That generated great amusement among the soldiers doing the processing. One struck the man unexpectedly in the belly with the but of his rifle. The man crumpled to the ground. The soldier raised him up by his collar and put his face into the man's face.

"That is what we do with politicians! Now, don't you want to find a new profession?"

All of the soldiers laughed. The man behind the counter asked the question again as if nothing had happened.

"Profession?"

The man gasped something that could not be understood.

"Okay, salesman," said the man behind the desk and wrote that down.

"What is your crime?" he asked next.

The man struggled back to awareness. He could stand on his own feet now. The soldiers watched him intently with smiles on their faces.

The man answered in a hoarse voice: "I am not guilty of any crime. I have been unjustly arrested. I am a duly elected representative in the government. I demand ..." was as far as he got.

The soldier that had hit him before hit him again in the belly with the butt of his rifle. The man crumpled to the ground.

"Clearly a case of a-social refusal to work, to find an honest profession," the soldier behind the desk said in a resigned way and wrote something in his book. He took a black triangle out of a pile he had, wrote a number on a small square of paper and pushed both the triangle and paper to the edge of the table. But the man had passed out. The soldiers ordered two of the men in line to drag him to a corner where they left him for the moment. It was Alex's turn. Alex stood at attention, his arms straight at his sides, his head facing forward without actually looking at anyone.

"Name?"

"Alexander Poloski," said Alex, as smartly as he could.

The man looked through the typed list he had until he found the entry and made a mark beside it.

"Nationality?"

"Polish."

"Right," said the man, comparing what Alex had said to the entry in the list.

"Profession?"

"Metal machinist!" shot back Alex as briskly as he could. He continued to look off into space. The man at the desk paused and looked up. The soldiers were still there but looked bored. One had organized a wet cloth and had ordered another prisoner to use it to revive the unconscious politician by covering the man's face.

"It says here 'Student'," said the man, as a question.

"Yes, sir! Student of metalworking with machinery, sir!"

"Okay, okay, no need to shout." He appeared to have written it down.

"And what is your crime?" he asked. This question had given Alex the most trouble since he had no idea what they had in the list.

"I am Polish, sir!" responded Alex.

"No, no, I did not ask your nationality, I want to know your crime so I can assign your color," said the man.

"That is my crime, sir: I am Polish," responded Alex smartly staring off into space.

One soldier began to laugh, then another one.

"Finally we have someone today who really understands the situation!" the first soldier said. There was laughing all around.

"Okay, okay, this is taking too long," said the man behind the desk. He wrote down a number on a small piece of paper and shoved it along with a red triangle of cloth across the desk to Alex.

"This is your number and this is your chevron. When you get your uniform sew the chevron on your sleeve, write a P in the middle of it, and write your number above it. The other prisoners will show you how. Forget your name; it is of no use to you here."

Alex walked on down the hall to the next stop. He took off all of his clothes, emptying his pockets and placing everything on a board that was there for that purpose, then stood naked before another man at a desk. No one had said to do it, it was just what the ones ahead of him in the previous line had done. He still had the two coins. They lay there on the board: a five penny coin and a ten penny coin. The man who sat behind the desk was not a soldier but apparently a prisoner, as he was dressed in prisoner's clothes. He wrote down a list of the items Alex had provided as he put most of them in a paper box with a lid and Alex's number on the side. The boxes and numbers had been prepared in advance.

He pushed Alex's belt and worn shoes in Alex's direction. "You can keep these," he said.

He made an entry in another list then turned the page around.

"Sign here," said the man.

Alex signed. The man made another entry in another list, then wrote something on an index card, stamped it with a stamp he had, then initialed the stamp. The man picked up the two coins. He put them into a box behind him on another small table.

"Here is your account number and opening balance," said the man, handing Alex the piece of paper that was card stock, not just writing paper. On it was Alex's number, 16891, the date, April 29, 1940, and an entry of 0,15 under the column "balance."

"Take care of this paper. You need to have it to deposit more money into your account or to take money out," the man said.

Alex had many questions but decided it made no sense to ask now.

"Thank you sir!" he said smartly in formal German. For the first time the man looked up into Alex's face. For the first time since his interrogation Alex looked back into another human face, into another human's eyes, that were really looking into his. He struggled not to cry out. He bit his lip.

"You are very welcome," said the man softly in Polish and tipped his head to the right as a signal for Alex to move on.

Arrivals Block

It is probably about 5:00 AM, thought Alex to himself as he woke.

He opened his eyes and looked up. The lights in the barracks were not yet turned on but since the outside compound lights were never turned off and the curtains were not large enough to cover the windows there was enough light for him to see the slats of the bed above his. The beds in the Arrivals Block were wooden and built four high. He was in the bottom level since that was the least-desirable and he had made no special attempt to affect the assignment of his bed.

If he was right about the time, in a few minutes the block leader would storm into the room pounding boards together and yelling that it was time to get up. Then they would jump out of bed and go through the frantic morning process of using the toilets, cleaning themselves, cleaning their part of the block, cleaning the windows, polishing the floor, making their beds, and drinking the grain-based "coffee" they got for breakfast. He was glad to have a few minutes to himself to reflect on the events of the two weeks since his arrival at the camp.

His processing the first day had been easier than he had imagined and much less painful than it had been for some of the others in his group. For some of them the situation continued to be difficult. Simple things seemed to be beyond their capability to learn – like how to make their beds in the morning to the exact specifications that had been given: using long boards to straighten and flatten the straw-filled mattress, getting the blanket tucked over the mattress with square corners and a flat surface, getting the pillow lined up exactly. If this was not done precisely right and it was discovered in an inspection the penalty could be 25 blows at the punishment block, with the special whip they used, or even being hanged by your hands from one of the trees along the main street. Such a penalty for such an offense was beyond some prisoner's comprehension.

In the first week there had been a "grace period" since they were all learning under the instruction of two older and more experienced prisoners that had been assigned to teach them. But now it was serious. Some of them were paying a piece of their bread to others to make their beds for them.

How will they survive here if they can't even make their own beds? he had asked himself. And he knew the answer: they would not survive.

The arrivals block contained only the people from cars three and four from the train he had been in, plus the others who had arrived after them. The fate of those in cars one and two was not known to him.

The two more experienced prisoners assigned to them took some care to educate them as well concerning the camp rules and organization. This took place in one of the Education blocks. The "Block Leader" of their block, a German political prisoner named Reissner, also took time to instruct them. He talked mostly about camp punishments – what they were and how to avoid them. He didn't yell at them and Alex had never seen him hit anyone, though Alex was sure he was capable of it if the situation required something like that. Reissner understood some Polish, but he always spoke to them in German, which they needed to learn if they did not already know it he had explained. Once it was clear to the others in the Block that Alex understood German as well as Polish he found himself in demand as a simultaneous translator. He saw that the Block leader had no problem with this – in fact was pleased with it, so Alex settled into the role.

That Alex was so young was not unusual. There were others in the block and in the camp even younger than he was. One young Polish boy recently arrived admitted to being only 11. They were all just prisoners and the same was expected from all of them: unquestioning obedience to the slightest whims of the Kapos and SS guards and meek acceptance of everything that occurred regardless of how monstrous. So Reissner had explained it to them. Break either of these rules and you would be "noticed."

Each morning and evening they participated in the Roll Call in the large assembly area in the compound in front of the "Industrial Building", which he now knew was the official name of the U-shaped building where he had been processed at his arrival. At seven each morning and at sundown each evening they all had to be there, standing in carefully organized rank and file organized by barracks block. Enough guards loitered around to make sure they took it seriously. Sometimes it took awhile for the SS officer responsible for the roll call to show up. When he did arrive a long process of counting out and checking the number of men in each block began. If there was any discrepancy with the records – whether due to miscounting or one or more prisoners being missing, one never knew at first – the entire prisoner population had to stand there at attention until the source of the problem was discovered and corrected.

Even the dead from the night or the day had to be carried to the roll call area so that they could be counted. Every morning it seemed there were some who had died in the night. And every evening there were dead counted in some of the blocks.

After roll call the bodies were loaded onto the Moor Express and hauled to the Crematorium located at one corner of the complex for cremation. The Moor Express was the official name of the wagon bed pulled by men that Alex had seen on his arrival at the camp. The whole camp area had been a marsh before the camp was built, so they were on a moor. And everyone going anywhere had to move at a run. Therefore Express. Pulling the Moor Express was a work detail like any other.

There was a hospital block that regularly contributed to the count of dead. Sometimes the men there were counted in the Hospital Block, and the count relayed to the roll call by the block leader, especially when there was some infectious disease in the camp, which people said was often. Reissner had explained this to them in response to a question. At other times, like now, the Hospital patients also had to stand in the roll call formation.

After morning roll call the work details were organized and moved out as soon as they were in formation and counted. Each work detail operated under the control of a work detail leader, or Kapo as they were called. They might have assistants to help them if the group was large. For the first two weeks Alex and those who had arrived with him were assigned to an "Arrivals Work Detail" so they could learn the process and be organized in their training. Reissner told them that this was a pretty short time for Arrivals to learn the ropes, but there was for some reason a push to hurry up the whole process.

Some of the work details seemed to be very stable in terms of who was in them. They formed up and counted off quickly then moved out smartly, singing from a selection of approved songs. Some of these details went to specific barracks inside the camp which were actually small workshops organized by outside firms or as part of the SS factory support operations. Most marched out of the compound gates headed for other workplaces within the larger complex or even to factories or workplaces in the area.

Other work details were quite the reverse. They formed up more slowly, despite curses and prodding from the Kapos, and were almost never initially at full strength. Any failing manpower was then organized from a list they had of people not assigned to any work detail.

After their first two weeks in the camp they were told they were no longer in the Arrivals work detail. It would be decided later what block they would move to, except for a few of them who had already been assigned to specific work details and moved to other blocks. In the meantime Alex continued to sleep in the Arrivals barracks, which was becoming very full. Some prisoners were being forced to sleep two to a bed.

There were always prisoners left over on the roll call grounds that had not been assigned to any work detail. At first Alex and the others from his arrival group who were not assigned anywhere thought that these were lucky not to be chosen. But those not in a work detail had to simply stand around outside, regardless of the weather; it was forbidden to enter the barracks or to sit or lie down on the ground. That was bad enough, but the real problem was that the guards on duty took it as their responsibility to "exercise" the prisoners. This could take many bizarre and tortuous forms. Duck waddling, hopping in place, and running quickly back and forth were favorite methods of exhausting the idle prisoners. When a prisoner was judged to be too slow, or worse yet stopped or fell down, he would be cursed and kicked until he got up and continued. Or until he was dead. Alex had felt a deep fear as he had seen this happening around him. How long could he survive in such a place?

The terrific noise of two large bed-making boards being slapped together made Alex jump.

"Out of your beds, you lazy dogs!" shouted their block leader.

He's not really such a bad one, thought Alex to himself and got out of his bed.

Plantation II Work Detail

Roll call that morning went quickly. The weather was clear and cool but not cold. The rising sun cast an orange light over everything as it climbed above the horizon. The officer in charge had arrived on time and all block counts were correct.

The bulk of the work details had been called up, counted, and marched off. Alex still stood with the remnants of his Arrivals block.

"Plantation II Outdoor Work Detail – Form Up!" came the shouted command, amplified by the public address system that filled the entire area with reverberating sound. A number of prisoners came trotting from where they had been standing with their block groups and took places in the formation. Other prisoners came more slowly. It was a large work detail with over one hundred prisoners. Many of them looked frail even by the standards of the camp. Soldiers hurried stragglers along with commands and jabs. Although no one more was coming there was no count shouted out.

"The following prisoners are hereby assigned to the work detail Plantation II Outdoor," shouted out a voice, then proceeded to call out numbers.

As each prisoner's number was called that prisoner trotted in the direction of the work detail formation and took his place in a row there.

And suddenly there it was, ringing out in the cool morning air: "16891!"

Alex trotted toward the formation. Once there he took his place in a row being formed. He stood at attention with the others.

Twelve new members had been assigned to the work detail. When the count was checked and accepted the group trotted in formation toward the main gate.

At a command from the Kapo they began to sing a German folk song about a soldier who goes off to war and his girl friend that is left behind. They sang it loudly and with a rhythm and tempo that matched their jogging. It was one of the songs that Alex and his fellow arrivals had been taught the first week.

They came to the main gate and were challenged. Their Kapo responded with the detail name and count. The gate opened and they were outside the inner camp. They turned right and continued running and singing. It was his first time outside the main compound since his arrival. Alex saw now that there was really a complex of camp areas and buildings with roads and paths connecting them and various walls and barbed wire fences separating them. As they trotted Alex began to notice how weak some of the others in the work detail really were. They struggled to keep pace and only mouthed the words to the song.

After about fifteen minutes they were ordered to halt. Some of the work detail members in the front rows trotted off on command to a large shed next to some greenhouse buildings, opened the shed and came out pushing wheel barrows loaded with garden tools, mostly hoes and shovels. Balanced on one of the wheel barrows was a large folded tarp.

Maybe it won't be so bad working outside on a day like today, said Alex to himself. Just seeing the well-tended fields and the stands of forest in the distance lifted his spirits.

After the gardening tools had been distributed, apparently with no other plan than that each tool needed to be carried by someone, they were ordered back into formation. Again they trotted singing the same song along a path between two fields. There were pansies growing in neat rows along the path here: yellow, white, blue, purple. The fields on both sides had been turned and were waiting for spring planting or appeared to have been recently planted. In a couple of fields green shoots were peeking up through the earth in long very straight rows. Other work details were arriving now at the greenhouses they were passing. The men were going into the greenhouses or beginning work in the small gardens that surrounded the greenhouses. In contrast to Alex's group there were no soldiers with these groups nor did there seem to be any orders given.

After some minutes they came to the end of the road they had been on. It branched here to the left and right and was only gravel and dirt from this point. A large square expanse of land that had been cleared of bushes and small trees lay in front of them, about five hundred yards on each side. The detail stopped. A ten by forty yard part of the larger area had been sectioned off with a yellow ribbon tied to sticks, at a height above the ground of about a foot.

The ten wheelbarrows were parked in a line outside the ribbon. The black tarp was unfolded and laid out on the ground on the other side of the road. All of the prisoners were ordered to move into the ribboned-off area.

The Kapo in charge made a crude show of the meaning of the ribbon for the newcomers.

"Attention!" he shouted, to make sure all the prisoners were looking at him.

First he stood inside the ribbon and made the motions of digging energetically, nodding and smiling. Then he stepped outside the ribbon with exaggerated care. He raised his bare right hand to the side of his head, with his fingers making the form of a gun.

"Bang!" he shouted, then rolled his head to the left with his mouth open and tongue out as if he had been shot. Then he laughed.

The two assistant Kapos chose five men each, ordered each of the men to take a wheelbarrow and ran with them off down the road in the direction they had come.

The four armed SS guards that had accompanied them from the camp sat down together outside the ribbon, opened a backpack they had brought, spread a blanket on the ground, sat down on it and proceeded to have a breakfast of bread and sausage and beer.

The lead Kapo with two prisoners he had selected laid out string lines held up by sticks driven into the earth. The lines were placed two feet apart and parallel to the road, each line ten yards long. There were sixteen of these lines. This took some time as the distance between the lines had to be exact and it seemed to be important that the lines were straight and parallel to the road.

The earth had been cleared and turned over some time before – during the previous fall probably – but was already full of shoots of grass and other growing things. It had been a semi-swamp before it had been drained and put to this new purpose, one could see that here and there in the puddles of standing water and short stands of reeds.

The first group of five men with five wheelbarrows returned at a run. The wheelbarrows were full of seed potatoes – small and already sprouted. At an order from the man who had accompanied them the men dumped the seedling potatoes in a pile just inside the ribbon zone then parked the wheelbarrows in a row just outside the ribbon.

"Today we plant potatoes!" shouted the lead Kapo, as if it was wonderful news they would all be overjoyed to hear.

He looked around at the group, a large smile on his face. "And to make it more fun we will do it in teams!"

Alex noticed the expressions of his fellow prisoners. They looked as if they expected anything but fun.

The other five wheelbarrows arrived, fully loaded with what looked like compost fertilizer. The men pushing them dumped this also just inside the ribbon line. Instead of joining the others they raced back down the road, their wheelbarrows bouncing, their assistant Kapo urging them on.

The lead Kapo went through the process of organizing the prisoners into eight teams of twelve men each. He gave the teams numbers: "You are team number 1," etc. In each team he choose a "Team

Captain". Alex was in team number 4 with a tall older German as team captain.

With the team captains gathered close to him the Kapo explained how the game would work. The other prisoners listened as well. Each team had responsibility for two rows, the Kapo explained The goal was to finish the ten yard long stretch by the 11:00 AM break for lunch, and to at least be ahead of the other teams. Within each row, the earth had to be completely cleaned of any plant material there, or any stones. He repeated again the word "completely". Anything they found that was not earth had to be carried and placed in a pile just outside the ribbon at a designated place. At the same time the earth had to be turned and the compost fertilizer thoroughly mixed in. Then the earth needed to be formed into a ridge mound running along the line, six inches higher than the ground level between the rows. Once this was all ready the seed potatoes were to be planted at a depth of two inches in a zigzag pattern along the top of the ridge with ten inch intervals. Any failure to meet the standards and the responsible team would be "penalized." As if it were an afterthought, he added that anyone stopping working without an order or lying down or sitting down would be "personally penalized."

The eight teams with their allocated hoes and shovels lined up each at the west end of their two rows. The Kapo nodded to the SS guards who were now standing watching with mild interest, their breakfast finished. One guard drew his handgun and fired a shot into the air.

With an energy that surprised Alex all the teams began immediately to clear the earth in their rows of any plant material, beginning at the starting point. There was not enough room for all the men to work together at one place, so the team captains devised various strategies – most commonly four men worked at a line moving forward, but at two points, one ahead of the other. Two men with hoes turned the earth over and two men used their hands to find and pull out whatever was not earth.

Alex only watched at this point as he had not been assigned to one of the four person groups in his team. He noticed the first strange things: the working prisoners pulled up grass and roots, some with tools but mostly with bare hands, and always stooping over, as it was not allowed to sit on the ground to work. This was not easy to do under normal circumstances, but for some of the prisoners it was hard for them to keep their balance. As soon as they had a handful they stood up and raced back to the "debris deposit point" and dropped it there. It was not allowed to accumulate more, or to use a wheelbarrow. At first this distance was relatively short – about five yards. But as the work progressed it would be further and further. Efficiency in the planting did not seem to be the goal.

"You get compost," ordered his captain and handed him a shovel, taking the hoe he had held from him and giving it to another man who was assigned to clearing the grass out. Alex followed the other compost haulers back to the compost pile where each took a shovel full of compost and raced back. When he got back to his team they were not yet ready for the compost – a section about a yard long was still being cleared of roots and stems and small stones. Alex stood waiting, his shovel full of compost at the ready.

There was considerable noise as the men worked. But a sharp sound and a loud groan behind him caught his attention and Alex turned. A man still holding on to a shovel was lying on the ground, curled up. One of the assistant Kapos was standing beside him kicking him repeatedly in the back.

"What is it?" asked the head Kapo approaching.

"This man spilled some of the compost!" was the answer.

"Sloppy swine!" yelled the head Kapo and joined in the kicking.

The men around continued working; except for Alex no one stopped or even looked in the direction. Alex stood transfixed.

"Now! Now! Put the compost in now!" he heard the voice of his team leader as if from far away. The team leader grabbed Alex's arm. "What is wrong with you? Do it now!"

Alex dumped the shovel of compost onto the area of cleared and turned earth.

"Now get more, hurry," said the team leader.

Alex turned and ran back to the compost pile. As he passed where the man had fallen the main Kapo was bending down examining the still body. The head hung at a strange angle, the mouth and eyes open, the side of the head covered with mud where the Kapos had stomped with their boots.

Standing up, the main Kapo gestured to two prisoners nearby, pointed to the body lying on the ground, then to the area where the tarp lay unfolded outside the work area. Without hesitation the two men lifted the body – one holding the body by the upper arms the other the legs – carried it and deposited it on the tarp, then returned to their work. The arm chevron of the dead man was a red triangle with a yellow triangle behind it – a Jewish political prisoner. The shovel the man had been using was picked up by the man's team captain and given to another man.

Two teams were so far along that they were putting in potatoes. A man assigned to fetch potatoes racing back and forth between the seedling potato pile and his team's rows was signaled to stop by the head Kapo.

"They are so precious and delicate!" the head Kapo exclaimed, examining what the man was carrying. The Kapo used his left hand to take one of the two potatoes out of the man's hands.

"Just one at a time!" He pressed his lips together, shook his head back and forth, then wagged his right index finger in the man's face.

"Promise you won't do it again?" the Kapo said.

"I promise!" said the man, panic stricken. The Kapo motioned him to continue with his work, which he did. The Kapo walked back to the potato pile and dropped the seedling potato onto the pile. He watched the ongoing work for some minutes.

"Stop! Inspection!" he called out. All the men stopped what they were doing and stepped back out of the rows they had been working in. Every team had managed to clear and compost at least a couple of yards along their rows.

The head Kapo took a hoe from a man and turned over the ground a bit in the first row, then the second, and so on, examining the earth carefully. Three times he found pieces of grass or root in the first couple of feet of rows. Each time he shook his head in disappointment and disbelief.

"Alright, teams 2, 4 and 7 over here!" he shouted. "The rest of you back to work." Alex and the others whose areas had not passed inspection were lined up in rows off to one side. The other teams continued their work.

"Hops in double-time," called out the main Kapo. Immediately the men began to do an exercise that Alex had learned his first week: hopping up to stand with feet apart and arms raised and together overhead, then feet together with arms at the sides.

"Count!" ordered the Kapo. The men began to count on the feet-together beat.

"One and two and three..."

Alex was in good shape compared to many of the others. He could keep up with the count. But some found it difficult. The assistant Kapos jabbed with their sticks at men who fell behind the group rhythm. At the count of seventy a man collapsed.

"Get up, you lazy dog!" an assistant Kapo cursed, prodding the man with the stick he carried. And the man did get up and somehow got back into the rhythm.

The assistant Kapo called out "Congratulations!" and made a small bow in the man's direction.

At the count of ninety a second man collapsed, tried to get up, but could not. He rolled over onto his back, his eyes opened, his mouth wide breathing hard, his arms at his sides, his hands open. The Kapos did not kick him or pay any special attention to him.

"Stop!" called out the main Kapo when the count reached one hundred. "All of you get back to work except this lazy one on the ground who wants to sleep."

The men rushed to get back to work; the other teams had gained real ground while they had been getting their punishment.

"Officer, can you help me here?" called out the main Kapo looking over toward the guards. "This man here would like to go to sleep, but with all this noise it is not so easy. Can you help him get to sleep?"

"Of course," answered an SS guard. "We are always ready to help."

He stepped into the ribboned area, walked to where the man was lying, pulled his handgun and pointed it down at the man's face. The man closed his eyes and brought his hands together at his chest. The guard fired a single shot into the center of the man's forehead, then replaced his handgun in its holster and walked back to where the other guards were watching.

Alex was at this moment on his way to get compost. The main Kapo motioned to him and another man who had also been going for compost, then pointed to the body on the ground. Alex and the other man lay down their shovels and hurried over. The other man moved to the legs, so Alex moved to take the arms. They both took hold and lifted. The body was remarkably light. The head hung down loosely. Open eyes, open mouth, black hair and dark skin, the small dark hole in the forehead, the back of the skull open and broken. They laid the body on the tarp next to the other one and moved quickly back to retrieve their shovels and continue their work.

The morning passed.

A loudspeaker blared a distinctive tone sequence in the distance.

"Form up!" shouted the main Kapo. All work stopped immediately. The men brought their tools to the edge of the ribbon area and laid them on the ground in neat rows then joined the ranks. There were eight bodies on the tarp. At a command two men folded one side of the tarp over them. The ranks were ready. An assistant counted the men, counted the dead and called out the count. He checked it against a number on a piece of paper he had in his pocket.

"Count correct!" he called out.

"Move out!" shouted the Kapo.

The men began to move forward. The Kapo began singing a sentimental song about bravery in battle and loyalty between comrades.

The prisoners picked it up quickly and sang as they trotted along. Lunch soup was waiting for them and probably bread.

Alex trotted with them but he could not sing. His whole system was in shock. He had not yet learned the tricks of not seeing, of not feeling, of not thinking. He stumbled slightly but caught himself and did not fall.

So this is what hell is like, he thought to himself.

Life In Hell

Alex woke with a start. He had had another nightmare. The boy sleeping in the bed beside him did not wake up this time at least.

In his nightmare he had been running through the backstreets of Leipzig near where he had lived being chased by Jan and the other boys. But then this changed and he was being pursued by large dog-like creatures that yowled and barked on his trail. To hide from them he dodged down a dark alley that led to a dead end. The creatures did not notice his turning down the alley and raced past. Their barking grew dim in the distance. He sat down on the cold stones to catch his breath. As his eyes grew accustomed to the dark he could see what lay around him: heaps of tangled naked bodies – men, women, children – thrown together. They were motionless. But then a slender arm began to move near him. A hand reached out toward him as if to ask for help. A soft voice called his name. It was at this point that he woke up shaking, trying not to scream.

Around him now he could hear the sounds of the men sleeping – their breathing, snoring, coughing. How many would die tomorrow? And which ones? Would it be his turn?

He looked now at the young boy sleeping next to him. The boy had arrived three days before in one of the endless series of trains from Poland. His crime? He had been a student in a prestigious private gymnasium in Lodz – that appeared to be enough. He was 12 years old. It was crowded in the bunk together but not so bad as it was for the grown men who shared bunks, or the many who slept on the floor with no straw. Alex turned his back to the boy and tried to sleep.

Crash! The slap of boards resounded through the block. Alex jumped up and raced toward the washroom to get a place on the toilet to shit. With so many men in the block it was chaos now to get everything done in the morning.

And then it all began again from the beginning – cleaning and polishing the windows and floor in the block, making beds, scrambling to get some of the grain coffee that served as breakfast, forming up for the Roll Call count, joining up in the Plantation II Work Detail, the road to the fields, the crazy work pace and crazy games of the Kapos and guards, the dying. The brutality had gotten worse even in just the two weeks he had been a part of the detail. The guards were shooting people who took a moment to lean on their shovels and the Kapo and his assistants were beating to death anyone who failed in the smallest way to meet their "standards" or just at random. The wheelbarrows were no longer enough to carry the dead. The Moor Express now arrived at the end of the day wherever they were working. The dead were loaded onto it and taken back for Roll Call. The assistant Kapos counted the dead and made notes as to the prisoner numbers as they were loaded onto the bed of the human truck.

Alex was growing weaker. The strenuous work, continual stress and lack of nourishment were combining to wear him down physically and emotionally. The days merged together into a blurred struggle to simply put one foot in front of another. And for what?

It seemed to Alex that the German guards and Kapo had only one goal – to destroy as many of the prisoners as possible and as painfully as possible. It was only a matter of time before the last one of them would be dead. But as each one died two new arrivals took his place. An endless expanding cycle of meaningless maddening humiliation and destruction.

On the evening of the first day of his third week on the Plantation work detail his Block Leader Reissner came to him after the evening soup and asked to speak to him privately. They went outside and stood by themselves.

"This is your lucky day, Alex," he said quietly.

"What?" asked Alex. Reissner's voice came from far away. Alex struggled to understand what he had said. Reissner looked around as if to make sure no one else could hear.

"You are finished now with that damned plantation death squad. Tomorrow morning at roll call when the Praezifix Work Detail is called Praezifix is where you go and not to Plantation Outdoor. Do you understand? And do not talk to anyone about this beforehand or afterward, okay? Just do it."

"Yes sir, I understand," said Alex. He felt a strange emotion swelling up in the middle of his chest. Alex closed his eyes. He breathed more deeply. It was hope. He opened his eyes. Reissner was still standing there, looking at him. Maybe it was not another dream.

"Thanks, really thanks for this," he managed to get out. Reissner seemed to be waiting to make sure that Alex had understood.

"That metalworker profession thing you got into your records when you arrived was the trick. If we had known about that earlier we could have had you out of here and into Praezifix straightaway."

Alex nodded, but his head was suddenly functioning again.

Who did Reissner mean by 'we'? he asked himself.

"And another thing," Reissner added. "When you come back at the end of the day tomorrow come here first to get your things then you go quick as you can to Block 12 where the other Praezifix people live. Got that? Block 12. Steiner is Block Leader there. He's expecting you."

Alex nodded again. "Praezifix, Block 12, Steiner," he said carefully.

Reissner went back into the barracks.

"Praezifix, Block 12, Steiner," Alex repeated to himself, afraid the words would slip away. After a few moments he followed Reissner back into the block building.

Praezifix

It had all happened just as Reissner had described.

And now Alex was standing here outside a white two story building in the early morning spring sunshine.

He looked around. They had trotted and sang after forming up and leaving Roll Call for only ten minutes and were still inside the camp complex. But it felt like another world. There was a sign – Praezifix – above the entry. Medium-sized birch trees in two rows paralleled the longer part of the building with a few chairs and a small table as if for breaks beneath them. A small river meandered past at the end of the row of trees.

Further along under the line of birch trees were two SS guards sitting on chairs opposite each other at a small round table. They were smoking cigarettes and playing cards. They had ignored the arrival of the prisoners.

Connected to the left of the main building was a long solidly built one story windowless structure of raw concrete with heavy double doors set deep in concrete every five yards or so. The doors were all open and sounds of metal-working began to fill the early morning air.

"Wait here. Maloff needs to check you out," Steiner had said when the work detail arrived at the building.

Then Steiner himself had gone into the two story building as had a couple of the other prisoners. The remaining prisoners out of the group of twenty had gone into the one story building through the various doors.

Alex waited.

A short somewhat fat middle-aged man with white hair, thick glasses and a white goatee came out of the building and looked around. He was wearing regular workman's pants and a shirt. He did not appear to be a prisoner.

"Are you Alex?" he asked, not finding anyone else.

"Yes sir," Alex answered.

The man pursed his lips and shook his head back and forth. "But you are just a boy! Can you really do metalwork? What we do here is not so simple you know!"

"I honestly don't know what kind of work you do here but I can try," answered Alex.

"A good answer," said Maloff. "Follow me." He went down the steps and into the first of the open doors of the lower building. Alex followed him.

The noise inside the room was deafening. There were four identical lathes, each painted light green, clearly worn but clean and well-kept, all in action at the same time turning cylindrical pieces of metal. At each lathe was an intently working prisoner wearing a leather work apron and eye protection goggles. Boxes of materials stood around. The room smelled of engine oil and cooling oil and hot metal. The floor was smooth concrete painted gray.

Alex stopped, startled by what he had noticed.

"What is it?" asked Maloff above the roar, noticing the surprise on Alex's face.

"I am surprised by the machines you are using – the lathes," shouted Alex, straining his voice to be heard above the din.

"Yes, you are right. It is unusual. But these are all we can get and they were not so expensive when we started this up. The really good metal-working machines are all needed in the main war factories like BMW in Allach for the other airplane engine parts. What we do here is simpler but still requires skill. But these lathes are fine for us."

Alex nodded. The lathes were exactly the make and model he had been using in school in Leipzig only a few weeks before.

"Heinz, stop for awhile," said Maloff to one of the men working. "We have someone here who would like to work with us and needs to show us what he can do." The man leaned back, turned off the lathe, removed a small piece he had been working on from the lathe jaws, laid it aside and stood up.

"I'll take my break now, then," he said. He took off his leather work apron and goggles and handed them to Alex, then picked up a paper sack that was sitting on the shelf of a nearby cabinet and walked outside.

Maloff looked through a stack of paper sheets on a small table in the room. He took out a sheet, looked at it, then handed it to Alex.

"Here is the specification for the machine bolts to hold the motor head to the block for the new KFZ 4 aircraft motor they are building now at BMW. Here are your raw materials." He indicated shelves to the side laden with neatly organized and labeled steel rod stock. "And here are your lathe, screw dies and measuring tools," indicating the place Heinz had vacated.

"I will be back in thirty minutes. Ask the others questions if you need to," he said and walked out of the bunker.

Alex put on the apron, read carefully through the specification sheet, located the right rod stock, put on the goggles and set to work. His lips moved silently in prayers of gratitude to Mr. Drechsler back at the school; if there was one thing he knew how to do, it was how to make a bolt.

In thirty minutes Maloff came back. Heinz was with him. Alex was so intent on his work that he did not notice. Maloff had to shout.

"Alex, I am back. How is it coming?" he said, leaning over to examine the bolt in the jaws of the machine.

Alex stopped working and turned the machine off. When it stopped rotating he released the pressure on the lathe jaws and took the bolt out, holding it with pliers. He dipped it in cooling oil, then wiped it clean. Maloff took it from him in his hand and held it up looking at it critically. He reached over and picked up a pair of calipers and measured the bolt's dimensions. He tested the threads in a nut that he selected from a box. The nut went on and came off smoothly.

"Not bad," he said at last.

"I think it is my best one so far," said Alex. It was quieter now in the room. The other three men had also shut their machines off and stood watching. Maloff peered at Alex with a puzzled look.

Alex looked over to a nearby shelf. Maloff's eyes followed his gaze. A row of four shining new steel bolts lay on a piece of cloth. Maloff's face broke into a broad smile. He placed the bolt in his hand carefully next to the others then turned.

"Welcome to Praezifix," he said and reached out his hand. They shook hands.

"Now you need to meet Kramer," Maloff continued, wiping his hands on his work coat. "He will explain how we do things around here. Follow me."

Alex followed Maloff out of the bunker into the sunlight then into the two story building and up the stairs to a large office area on the second floor. There were shelves against the wall holding binders and stacks of paper, all neatly labeled. There were two writing desks against one wall and a large square table in the middle of the room with chairs. Several technical drawings of bolts and fastening assemblies lay on the table. There was also a daily newspaper from Munich lying on the table, Alex noticed. There was one person in the room who was working at one of the writing desks with his back to them as they entered the room. He was dressed in a normal prisoner's uniform.

"What is it?" the sitting man asked as they came into the room without turning around or stopping his writing.

"We have a new member of our work detail, Kramer. His name is Alex. I think you already have his paperwork. I told him you would explain everything he needs to know."

Kramer stopped his work and rotated his wooden swivel chair to face them. "Hello Alex," he said. Kramer was thin with delicate features and hands. Alex remembered him as one of the prisoners who had come with them from the camp that morning.

Maloff took off the work coat he had been wearing, hung it up by the door and cleaned his hands again on a towel that hung on a hook. He took a black gentleman's day coat off a clothes hanger that hung nearby and began to put it on.

"I have to get going now. I have a meeting with Mr. Pruddle in town at 9:00. Are the accounts from last month ready to show him?"

Kramer stood up, took a small binder from a shelf and handed it to Maloff.

"And don't forget, that special order for Ludwigsburg has to go out today!"

"I had it sent to the train station last night. They should be loading it on the train about ... now," he answered, looking up at the clock on the wall.

"Good, good," murmured Maloff. He put his hat on and went out the door and down the stairs without saying anything more, the binder under his arm.

"Sit down, Alex," said Kramer, indicating a chair by the table. "I don't have much time but at least we can make a start. You are Polish, right? Where are you from?"

Alex sat down. "Leipzig," he answered. Kramer sat down across a corner of the table from him.

"Ah, Leipzig!" he exclaimed. "Wonderful town, wonderful people. I always managed to enjoy myself there." Kramer looked up at the ceiling, distracted by his thoughts.

Alex just waited.

After awhile Kramer looked back at Alex.

"What do you want to know?" he asked.

Alex searched through the many questions in his head. He found one.

"What is this place?" he asked. Kramer wrinkled his brow.

"I am afraid you will have to be more specific – my time is limited. Do you mean what is this world, with all its wonders and mysteries? Do you mean what is Germany, struggling now to fulfill its dark dream of victory over its own ghosts? Do you mean Concentration Camp Dachau, this bold experiment exploring the outer limits of gruesome inhumanity? Or do you mean this small shimmer of civilization, this island of reason and balance we have created here in the midst of awesome chaos – that is, Praezifix?"

Kramer had used his hands and arms while he talked, sketching each of the options in the air.

"I mean Praezifix, sir," answered Alex softly.

Kramer sighed. Despite his protest that he had little time it appeared he was disappointed at being asked such a narrow and specific question. It seemed he had been ready to answer any one of the broader questions or maybe all of them together.

"Well, for prisoners like me – and now you – and the others who have found this place, Praezifix is a lifeboat in a rough sea filled with drowning souls. It is not the only lifeboat in Dachau – there are several – but it is one of the most stable."

"I don't understand," said Alex simply.

"Where were you before you came here?" asked Kramer.

"I was in Arrivals Block for awhile, then two weeks in Plantation II Outdoors."

"Ah, yes. Perhaps you notice some differences in how the prisoners were treated in the Plantation work detail and how things are here?" Kramer swept his hand around to indicate their surroundings.

"Yes, I have."

"Do you understand why the differences exist?"

"No."

"Let me explain." Kramer sat up straighter in his chair and took a moment to collect his thoughts.

"We are in the midst of an experiment by the National Socialists, an experiment directed personally by Himmler himself, to determine if forced labor – that is, slaves; that is, people like us – can be used for skilled industrial production. It is already well-proven that forced labor can be used for all manner of unskilled labor – like the agricultural work in Plantation and the building of bunkers. The Egyptians were the first masters of this strategy and every major civilization since their time has followed their model. Ask any American Negro, for example; he will be able to tell you how it works simply by reciting the history of his people in the New World prior to the American Civil War.

"But now we are in the industrial age. What is the best way to 'organize the workers'? I was a communist earlier in my life so this question has occupied me a long time. The capitalist and communist systems seem to offer the only two modern models, but as we have seen they are both deeply flawed in practice.

"Do you know how old Concentration Camp Dachau is, Alex?" Kramer seemed to change the direction of his explanation.

"No."

"It was organized in 1933 by Himmler when he was still police chief of Munich to hold people rounded up because they opposed the National Socialist rise to power. In 1933 more than 4,000 were kept here. Many were later released, but it was the beginning of something important. From 1934 through 1937 about 2,000 per year were brought here. Their main work was to build the camp you see here now but they also started the agricultural work and the first simple industrial workshops to make parts for the factories in this area."

"So they built this building and the bunker?" asked Alex.

"No, these were already here – this is an old ammunition storage bunker from the time of the World War when troops were stationed here. Where was I?"

"The main work was to build the camp you see here..." repeated Alex.

"Yes, of course. Then in 1938 as a part of the Crystal Night pogrom of the Jews more than 18,000 of them were brought here. They also worked to build the camp and the complex, and in the fields and workshops."

"But there are only around 10,000 prisoners in the camp now – that is clear from the block counts. Where did they all go?"

"Many died from the conditions here but most were eventually shipped away to other camps, other places."

"I still do not understand," said Alex.

"Sorry. I will try to be clearer: it is here that the Nazi's are conducting their experiment to determine if forced labor can be used for really skilled work – for example, fine-tolerance metalwork. We are a part of that experiment, and a very successful part if I do say so myself."

Kramer looked at Alex, who seemed as puzzled as ever.

"Maybe I can explain it another way. In Allach only a few miles from here BMW is building airplane engines. And these engines need screws. Pruddle used to have a company here in Dachau to make screws and bolts for BMW but when the military buildup came he lost most of his best workers to the army. What was he to do? He could get the orders from BMW – they trusted him – but where could he get skilled workers?" Kramer paused as if he expected an answer.

Alex thought for a moment. "From the prisoners in the camp?" he answered.

"Yes, Alex, that is it! The SS is a business and is organized as a business to make money for the state and at the same time to solve the problem of labor for the industrialists. Every day you or I are here at Praezifix the SS is paid a wage. It is much less than what you or I would cost Praezifix as independent workers – but it is many times what it costs the SS to keep and feed us. So everyone wins – the war production continues even though the men are all off fighting, the prices of finished war goods are kept low and dangerous elements like us are kept from doing any damage. A perfect solution! From the National Socialist point of view anyway. For Pruddle there was the added advantage that he got in early in the game and leased these two buildings right inside the camp at very good terms. That makes his fixed costs low, plus keeps his transport costs down since he also uses prisoners from the camp for most of his transport."

"How do you know all this?" Alex asked.

"Why, because I am the accountant for Praezifix, of course!" answered Kramer as if it were obvious. "That's my skill. That's why I am still alive, after two years in this hell." Kramer looked down at the floor, then out the window.

Alex was trying to take it in.

"So what about the others in the camp who have no skills?"

The question revived Kramer.

"Those fall into three groups. In the first group are those who are physically able to do unskilled work and do not belong to an identified 'enemy race'. For them there is plenty of work still – like agriculture and construction. The second group are those who have no useful skills and belong to the defined enemy classes, who are publicly held responsible for whatever evils have befallen the Germans over the last hundred years – that is, the Jews, the homosexuals, the Gypsies. The Nazi's are not yet clear about what will happen to them but it does not look good. For now they are being collected in camps. The third category are 'special cases' like the many Polish Priests coming into the camp now. They have no technical skills but at the same time cannot be simply killed due to political sensitivity. And they can't be turned loose because the Polish Priests are openly resisting the German destruction of Polish society that is going on in the occupied areas. It is also not clear how that will develop.

"Oh, I really have other things to do now," said Kramer looking up at the clock.

"But what do I need to do?" asked Alex.

"Three things: stay out of trouble with the guards and Kapos, don't get sick and do a good job at your work – do the best job you can do."

"And that way I can make it through the war?" asked Alex.

"Alex, I wish I could promise you that but I cannot. None of us know what tomorrow will bring. And lately as the Germans are having so much success I have stopped expecting that this will all change when the war is over. If the Germans win the war this will be life as people like you and I will come to know it. There will be thousands of work camps like this all over Europe not just the hundreds there are now."

"So, what you are saying is that we are not just helping the Germans build airplane engines to put in airplanes to bomb and kill people, we are helping them to perfect a new way to organize workers that they will use to dominate and enslave the world? Do I understand that right?"

"Yes, Alex, that is right. It is wonderful that you understand this all so well. It is too much for most people. It took me a year and much study to understand this," responded Kramer thoughtfully after a pause.

"I won't do it," said Alex. "I won't be a part of it."

"Alex, if that is how you really feel we can arrange for you to be assigned to another work detail and living block. But it is a tricky process to make a change. One never knows how it will come out. Maybe you should think about it first. Take a few days."

"Okay," said Alex after a few moments reflection.

"And look at it another way: if the Germans do not find a way to organize slaves for skilled work, the whole of non-Aryan Europe will be condemned to some version of the Plantation work detail. Is that what you want?"

"Why are you telling me all this? It makes being here even worse!" Alex protested.

Kramer sighed. He leaned back in his chair and folded his arms across his chest.

"I am sorry, Alex, I honestly did not want to make it harder for you. But not many people understand these things and I don't want them to be forgotten. You are young and strong. Maybe you will survive. Many of us will not. Maybe you can tell the story some day."

Kramer stood up and walked out of the office leaving Alex sitting where he was at the table.

During the following weeks Alex was afraid that he would wake up and discover that it had all been a dream. Or that during the work detail formations some SS man would come up behind him, grab him by the neck, yell at him and drag him back from the Praezifix Work Detail formation to Plantation Outdoor. But neither of these things happened. Gradually he began to accept his good fortune. He had af-

ter all promised he would survive and Praezifix seemed to offer better survival chances than any other alternative in sight.

The work was not difficult. Alex had quickly understood what
was expected of him and in just a few weeks was turning out good
quality production in above average volumes. "Slow down, Alex," the
others had said to him. "You'll make the rest of us look bad." And so
he had slowed down.

Praezifix Transport Detail

"We have a problem, and unless we do something I am afraid it is going to get worse," said Kramer and looked at the others around the table: Maloff, Steiner, Schwarz and Alex. Alex understood why the others were there. Kramer essentially ran Praezifix on a day-to-day basis as well as being the accountant. Maloff was their connection to the owner and their production manager. Steiner was the Kapo leader of the Praezifix work group as well as being Block Leader in their barracks block. Schwarz was their "Block oldest" and so involved in any serious issues. Alex was there because Kramer had asked him and the others had not objected. But he knew nothing about the reason for the meeting – it could be any one of several things.

It was the middle of the afternoon and already half-dark outside the windows of the second floor Praezifix main office. The sky was thickly overcast and there was snow falling. It was four days before Christmas, 1940. The winter was proving to be a hard one. Deep snows had fallen twice already and the prisoners were as always required to clear the whole inner area of the camp immediately after it fell – or even while it was still falling. All by hand with shovels and wheelbarrows.

There was the scabies epidemic in the camp. A thousand affected prisoners had been quarantined, jammed into barrack 9 that had been set aside for the purpose. So far though the Praezifix people had not been affected and they were continuing to be careful about keeping themselves and their block clean.

Production had been going well with no reports of quality problems as far as Alex had heard. And he would have heard about it if there had been quality problems. Maloff had made him into "Assistant Quality Control Manager" after his first two months. Alex knew how to make quality fasteners and to spot problems in the work of others. That was something that Maloff valued as did his boss. It was what the company was all about. When there were quality problems with their products on the assembly line there was hell to pay – cash penalties in fact – it was all in the contracts.

"Our problem is transport," said Kramer, ending Alex's inner speculations.

"The SS requires us to use the Moor Express for all of our transport of materials from the train station to here as well as of our products back to the train station or direct to the factories in the area when there is no convenient train running. They absolutely refuse to budge on this no matter how much pressure we apply at which level. Of course we pay them every time the Moor Express moves something for us. But I don't think money is the issue. Given our profit margins we could afford a truck even if we had to buy it ourselves. But they say that would set a bad example for the other factory groups and is at odds with how they want things to be here – that we are self-sufficient. It is a disadvantage we have being here inside the camp complex.

"And the Moor Express has become increasingly unreliable. We have no control over which prisoners they assign to it. Often they are not fit enough even when they start. But after a few hours pulling that monster through the snow and sludge, poorly clothed, with broken shoes or even wooden clogs they simply break down. And that is when there is no cargo. Load a half a ton of steel rod on it and the situation is even worse. Often the whole thing just stops. The Transport Kapo and guards can scream and hit as much as they want – that is simply the end of the line for some of those prisoners. So they have to get more prisoners and that takes time. In the mean-time pickups and deliveries don't get made. Our customers don't want to hear any of this of course. For them it is our problem for us to solve. But so far I have not been able to find a way to improve the situation. Do any of you have any ideas?"

No one said anything.

"The problem is the poor state of the prisoners they use plus the lack of protection from the weather especially in a winter like this one. The Moor Express was developed for normal transport inside the camp and as a way to further demoralize and break down pris-oners and not as reliable all-year heavy transport," continued Kramer.

This was true, Alex realized. Most of the men he had noticed as-signed to the Moor Express were Jews who had been in the camp system for some time – not fit enough for the demanding work by it-self much less the abuse from the Kapos and guards.

"So we need to get different, healthier prisoners, outfit them bet-ter against the weather and find Kapos and guards that are not so savage," said Alex, almost to himself but out loud.

"Right, Alex," said Kramer after a pause. "That is the solution. But where will we get healthy prisoners?"

Everyone looked at everyone else for a few more moments.

"We could ask the priests," said Alex quietly. No one else said anything. They looked at Alex with surprise but interest.

The priests in the camp had been the subject of a lot of rumors recently. Only a few days before the camp commandant had given the order that all the priests, or actually all clergy, since there were a few German protestant ministers as well, would be combined together in one block, Block 26, effective immediately. People said that as soon as they had moved in they had cleared out Room 1 of their barracks and made it into a chapel. There were about 900 of them, all but a handful arrived this year from Poland, so this meant they were now more cramped than they would have been. But apparently having a chapel was important to them. They had let everyone know that Christmas Mass would be celebrated and had invited everyone who was interested and who was not in quarantine. But it was not clear yet what the SS would allow.

"Why would the priests want to pull the Moor Express?" asked Schwarz. "They get mistreated by the guards quite a bit as it is. There have been priests in the Transport Detail in the past and I don't remember any of them mentioning that they enjoyed it."

"I don't know why they would do it. The idea just came to me," answered Alex.

"Well, we can't lose anything by asking," said Kramer. "And since you are Polish and we are not maybe you should be the one to ask. Tomorrow is Sunday. You can walk down there in the morning break and see if you can get a conversation about it started."

The next morning Alex walked down the main street to Block 26. There was a crudely made metal cross above the main entry door. Alex walked in.

"I need to talk to the Block Leader," he said in Polish to the first man he met. "You mean Father Vincent. He's over there at that table," the man answered pointing after looking Alex up and down. "The one with the priest's hat."

And it was true; the men were all dressed in normal prison clothes but one had on a black priest's hat like they wore in Poland. He was in conversation with four other men sitting around one of the tables normally used for meals.

Alex walked over to the table and stood there waiting for a break in the conversation. When it came he spoke as clearly as he could. "Father Vincent, it is very important that I speak to you privately."

Father Vincent looked up. "Important for whom?" he asked.

"Important for you and your priests," answered Alex without hesitation.

Father Vincent turned to those at the table with him. "Brothers, I must ask you to give me and ..." He looked up at Alex.

"Alex Poloski," said Alex.

"and Mr. Poloski a few minutes of privacy. When he and I are through we need to decide that issue we were discussing."

The men got up and walked to a table at the other end of the room where they sat down and continued talking.

"Sit down, Alex" said Father Vincent. Alex sat down. "Now tell me what is so important."

Alex thought about where to begin, about how to begin.

"Why do you think they moved you all into one block?" It was a question that had haunted Alex in the days since he had heard of the move.

Father Vincent seemed to be put off balance for a moment that Alex had started with a question. "Tell me first what you think their reason is."

"I think they are trying to reduce the influence that the priests scattered around in barrack blocks were having on the other prisoners. They want to isolate you so you will not give the other prisoners hope," said Alex.

Father Vincent scratched his chin and considered. He looked at Alex. "I am afraid you are right. If you must know there has been some pressure put on the SS, on the German government, from the Vatican to give us better treatment, as well of course better treatment for all the prisoners. Our situation is not unknown – some letters got smuggled out as I think everybody knows, the SS made such a big stink about it when they intercepted one. But this idea of putting us all together in one block came from the SS, not from us. It has its advantages, of course. But we are more cut off now, that is true."

"Is that all you wanted to talk to me about, Alex?" he asked.

"No, Father, there is more. I have noticed that fewer and fewer priests are being called up for the death details where the conditions are very bad."

"Do you think so? I had noticed it too but I have had so many other things to think about recently – just getting vestments together for the Mass has been a big challenge. But how would you know about this? Where are you here in the camp anyway; what do you do here? I don't remember seeing you before."

"I am with the Praezifix Work Detail. I have been there since the summer. We are the ones who make the most use of the Moor Express, which I am sure you do know about."

"Of course I know about it. A truly dreadful device. But I don't see the connection between Praezifix, the Moor Express, and how we priests make out here in the camp. Is there a connection?" Father Vincent seemed interested.

"Have you noticed that in the last week no priests have been called up for the Praezifix Transport Detail – for the Moor Express? No priests at all – and before it was a usual thing."

"I had not noticed. But how is it that you have noticed?"

"I check every load of material that comes in to Praezifix and every load of finished product that goes out – that is part of my job. And it all arrives or leaves via the Moor Express. So the Kapo and guards that work the Transport Detail and I are on pretty good terms. I sometimes have something for them – chocolate for the Kapo or something they want – I have connections. I complained to them a few days ago about the poor health of the prisoners they were using to pull the Express. I admit I even asked them why they had no priests since the priests had always been in better shape than the average prisoner they had. They told me – in strict confidence, of course – that they had been told not to order up any more priests for the Moor Express detail. That it was no longer allowed."

"And what was the reason for this unexpected mercy from the SS?" interjected Father Vincent.

"That is exactly what I asked the Kapo when I had him alone. I acted angry that the priests were being let off so easy. To my surprise he laughed, then admitted that the whole thing had been cooked up by the camp commander – they were to go easy on the priests, no more Moor Express details, etc., separate them into their own barracks block – and all to create as much distance and resentment as possible in the other prisoners' attitudes towards the priests."

Father Vincent was thoughtful. He looked up and noticed the men he had been talking with were waiting for him at the other table. They seemed to have finished their conversation.

"Thank you, Alex, that is quite a bit. I will have to think about it. I can't see what we can do exactly to counter this move by the SS. They are cunning, I give them that." He stood up.

Alex did not stand up. "I think there is a way that together we could organize things to defeat this plan of the SS," he said.

Father Vincent sat back down. "What way do you mean?" he asked.

"With pressure from Praezifix where I work we could force the SS to reverse their policy – instead of not using priests they could change to using priests exclusively. You are, if I may say it, the healthiest group in the camp." Alex stopped for a moment.

"But how would it work?" asked Father Vincent.

Alex leaned forward. Suddenly it became clear to him. Up to this point he had been feeling his way.

"Each morning you priests could choose 18 from among you that are the fittest and most ready to pull the Moor Express for that day. The next day a new group, and so on. You yourselves would control completely who goes into the Praezifix Transport Detail."

"And why would we agree to do such a thing?" asked Father Vincent.

"I can think of three reasons," answered Alex. "First, because in doing this you will be saving the lives of hundreds of prisoners who would die this winter pulling the Moor Express. Second, because you will show the whole camp, SS as well as prisoners, a model of courage and inspiration that they will not soon forget. And third, because if you are a critical operating part of one of the SS's most profitable businesses – Praezifix – the SS will be just that much less likely to ship you all out on a train together one day to disappear – they will be getting paid good money for the work you are doing, many times over what it costs them to feed you."

"But how will we survive in this cold?"

"I promise you we will do everything we can to make sure you will have adequate boots and jackets. Yes, I am sure we can do it. If necessary Praezifix can pay for them."

"This is really a lot to think about. I need to talk to some others about it and pray as well. Can I wait to tell you of our decision until after Christmas?"

"Sure, take what time you need," answered Alex. "I'll come back by after Christmas."

They both stood up.

"Alex, can I ask you a question?"

"Certainly."

"Why are you doing this?"

"It's my job, Father. I work for Praezifix and we need more reliable transport."

"You wouldn't be just a little interested in saving a bunch of naive priests from stumbling over their own self-involvement, would you?"

"Oh, no Father. I wouldn't presume such a thing," answered Alex.

"Well, thanks for your ... help ... in any case," said Father Vincent.

Allach

"Alex, we got a call from Grossmann at BMW yesterday afternoon while you were out," Kramer said as soon as Alex entered the office.

"The new bolts for the KFZ-6 wing brackets are not long enough. It was a mistake in the specifications. They have a crisis: a batch of ten finished engines have to go out today but they have no way to securely mount the engines to the wing brackets. Maloff has put together a box of possible replacement bolts. But we need somebody to go down there and deal with it face-to-face. Grossmann is panicked. What do you think?"

"I'll go," answered Alex. "The Express should be here in a few minutes anyway to pick up the other BMW deliveries for today."

"And I have another note here as well. Yesterday we didn't pick up the bodies at the Allach camp."

"But we didn't have any deliveries for BMW yesterday," protested Alex. "And the deal with the SS is that we bring bodies back from Allach to the crematorium only when we have to make deliveries for BMW."

"Yes, I know the deal. But after this latest round of Allied bombing they have stepped up the pressure to finish the bunkers for the production facilities. And more pressure means more dead."

"Okay, after BMW we pick up bodies at Allach," said Alex. "And if we do that then I want to try out what we planned, with the priests I mean. The priests have been ready the last two times but I was not."

Kramer rotated back to his desk, took a key that hung from a cord around his neck then unlocked and opened a large file drawer.

"How much do you think you need?" he asked without looking up.

"Twenty Reichsmarks in five Reichsmark pieces. That should do it."

"Okay," said Kramer. "We can afford that."

He took some coins out of a box in the drawer, laid them on the desk, then made notes on a sheet of paper and put it in the drawer.

"What else have you got in there – something special, maybe?" Alex asked.

"How would this be?" asked Kramer, reaching in then holding up a cellophane wrapped package of black silk stockings. The printing on the package was in French.

"That will do just fine," answered Alex smiling. He took the four five Reichsmark pieces. He held them in his hand for a moment, just looking at them then dropped them in his pants pocket. He unbuttoned his shirt and stuck the stockings in, then buttoned it back.

"Good luck," said Kramer.

Alex nodded, walked out of the office, down the stairs and outside to wait. The sun was shining. The air was cool and clear. It was the 6th of April, 1943, a Tuesday. Alex looked down at the neatly labeled boxes waiting on the pallet at the bottom of the steps. He pulled out the sheaf of papers in his other pocket and checked the list one more time against the labels on the boxes. It was all there.

In a few weeks, if he lived so long, Alex would have the third anniversary of his arrival in the camp. A year before the prisoners had been convinced that the war would soon be over with the Americans coming on so strong and the Eastern front against the Russians. But despite the situation the Nazi government seemed more determined than ever. Crazy, really.

The previous October all the Jews still in Dachau had been shipped out. To Auschwitz, Kramer said. They would have had to stop using Jews for the Express in any case.

And here came the Transport Detail now, rumbling along the road at a good pace. The wagon made a sweeping turn and came to a halt in position to load the heavy boxes.

Alex knew most of the priests in the detail. He nodded to a couple of them when they made eye contact but said nothing. He raised his eyebrows in a question to Father Hubertus. The middle-aged priest rolled his eyes to the left and his head back slightly to indicate the small backpack he was carrying. Alex gave him a nod.

The negotiations between Praezifix management and the SS over "the Transport Reliability Improvement Proposal" had not been easy. In the end Praezifix got the boots and coats by paying more for transport in the winter months. The rank and file SS liked the idea of having the priests to abuse. The attempt to influence the choice of Kapo or guards had failed completely. But the priests had accepted this in the end.

Two other men came out of the bunker and helped Alex lift the six boxes of finished parts and the blue box of replacement bolts onto the bed of the truck. Together they took the leather straps rolled up on the sides and stretched them across to secure the boxes.

"I come with you today," he said to the Kapo who was standing waiting.

"Why not, it is a beautiful day for a walk," answered the Kapo, smiling.

"Don't you all think so?" he asked the prisoners harnessed to the wagon. He waved the stick he was carrying as if directing a choir.

"It is a beautiful day for a walk," they answered in sing-song unison, following the movements of the stick.

"Then let's walk!" he shouted lightheartedly and set out in the lead back down the street, beginning the first line of a song, waving his stick until they had begun to sing it with him.

Alex went to the rear of the wagon and pushed to help get it moving. With the light load, the many men, and the cobbled street it rolled along easily. Alex trotted behind it.

There were only two guards assigned to the detail. Earlier in the war one would have had more but the Germans were now desperate for soldiers. And apparently the SS did not expect the priests in the detail to give them much trouble. Both guards trotted behind the wagon, one on each side of Alex. One of the guards was known to Alex. He was German and young, probably about 18. He was not particularly smart but seemed capable of doing whatever the Kapo told him to. The other guard was new for Alex. He was even younger, probably 16. Alex tried to make eye contact with him to have some kind of connection. But it did not work. The boy was in another world. His eyes were red and swollen.

He has been crying, Alex thought to himself.

The Kapo and the two men at the front who steered knew the way to Allach: back into the main compound, then out the south gate.

"Praezifix Transport Detail, 20 prisoners, two guards, Delivery for Allach," shouted the Kapo.

And then they were out in the world, the camp left behind. The few cars and trucks on the road treated them as they would a farm tractor – following behind when there was no other possibility, then passing when there was room. The prisoners were a well-established part of Dachau and had been for almost a decade. The town had not been methodically bombed but here and there were damaged buildings. A team of prisoners that Alex recognized as coming from Dachau, complete with Kapo and guards, were repairing a section of road. They passed the group without comment from either side.

Now they were traveling between the open fields along the road to Allach. The whole distance was about ten miles. Soon they could see the large rectangular factory buildings ahead of them. Since January a line of dirt hills had grown up near the factory buildings: prisoners were working to excavate the earth then construct an enormous bunker complex where the BMW production could continue underground safe from the increasingly frequent bombing. Parts of it were already completed. Since January it had become officially "Work Camp Allach" and not just a group of work details from Dachau. The two thousand prisoners who had been going there every day from Dachau got their own extensive camp. With additional arrivals of prisoners from Russia and France there were now said to be 5,000 working on the Allach bunkers and in the factories. The camp had everything that Dachau had with the exception of a crematorium for the dead. Instead the SS had enlarged the Dachau crematorium.

And now they were through the guard check point and at the BMW receiving gate. Grossmann was waiting for them – probably he had talked by phone to Kramer and knew they were coming. He was a thin dark-haired Bavarian, always wearing workman's clothes despite his responsible position. And always worried about something.

"Where have you been?" Grossmann scolded. "This is an emergency!"

"Of course, Mr. Grossmann," Alex began. "We came as quickly as we could. We are hoping that other bolts we had in reserve will solve the problem. There was not time to make new ones and we were not sure what the corrected specification would be in any case. The possible replacement bolts are in this box here." Alex indicated the blue wooden box as he loosened the holding straps on the load.

"You two, bring the box!" Grossmann ordered two prisoners standing waiting. They took the box between them by the rope handles at its ends.

"Come with me," said Grossmann to Alex. Other prisoners unloaded the other boxes.

"And what exactly are we supposed to do now?" the transport Kapo asked Alex.

"Wait, just wait," said Alex and followed Grossmann into the building.

It was quite a distance through the labyrinth of the factory. Finally they came to the area where finished engines were prepared for shipping. It was a high and long underground room with a vaulted concrete ceiling and lit by large hanging light fixtures. A railway siding ran the length of the room, disappearing into a dark tunnel. Two flatbed freight cars stood empty on the siding. On the concrete platform next to them were ten finished airplane engines on wooden pallets. There were two lift cranes mounted in the concrete between the platform and train cars. Wooden crates made to fit over the engines in transport stood to one side. There were several workmen standing around.

"They are beautiful," said Alex upon seeing the engines in the glare of the overhead lamps in the bunker. He had never seen the finished engines before.

"Yes, they are beautiful," answered Grossmann. "But unless we can get these wing brackets mounted they are useless. Here is the problem."

He went to the closest engine and bent down. Along each side of the engine block were a series of three threaded holes, each about 3/4 of an inch across. He lifted up an angled piece of steel a little longer than the block itself and laid it over the line of holes until the holes matched up. "Schultz, come here," he said. One of the workmen came over.

There was a cardboard box sitting on the pallet to one side of the engine block. In it were 6 large bolts. "Show Alex," he said simply.

Schultz picked up one of the bolts and placed it alongside the hole were it was intended to go. The problem was immediately clear to Alex – the bolt was too short. The mounting brace was so thick that the bolt would only have about a quarter of an inch of hold in the engine block itself. That was too little; the engine would simply fall off the plane after a few hundred hours of operation. And if they tightened the bolts too much the threads in the block would strip.

Alex pushed the bracket aside, pulled a small folding metal rule from a pants pocket and inserted it in the hole in the block to measure the depth. He checked all six holes in the block. They were all deep enough. Then he measured the thickness of the mounting brace at a place where a hole went through it.

"It is much thicker than in the specification we have. How did that happen?" he looked up at Grossmann.

"The braces are made by another group. There had been some problems with strength so they made them much thicker. I knew from the first it was stupid – much too much weight for an airplane part. Then trying to mount them yesterday we noticed the old bolts were too short to provide a stable connection."

"Bring me the box," ordered Alex. The two prisoners who had carried the box brought it over and set it on the concrete floor by the pallet.

Alex opened it. There were 60 bolts in groups of six, each group wrapped in heavy paper.

"These should work," he said, unwrapping a group and selecting a bolt then inspecting it carefully. "Put two lock washers by each one and weld the heads to the brace so the vibration won't loosen them," he said to Schultz.

Schultz nodded. Alex took five more bolts out of the box and laid all six on the pallet. Schultz went to the side of the area and came back with tools and a box of washers. Another workman came bringing a spot welding system set up as a trolley with two tanks. The man helped Schultz align the brackets, then put in and tighten the bolts with the washers.

"I think that will work," said Alex as the men completed bolting on the two braces for the first engine.

"I think you are right," said Grossmann.

Alex went around to each of the pallets, laying out six bolts each. He took the short bolts that had been there and put them into the blue box.

"Is there anything else?" he asked.

"No," said Grossmann.

"Then could somebody get me and the old bolts back to the receiving gate? I really have to get going."

"I'll take you myself," he said. "Schultz, you know what to do?" he asked.

Schultz nodded without looking up, busy putting in bolts on the second block. Another workman was firing up the welding rig to weld the bolt heads on the first block.

Grossmann started off back through the labyrinth. Alex and the two prisoners carrying the box followed him.

The Moor Express, the priests, the two guards and the Kapo were still waiting at the gate. Alex had the men put the box on the wagon then strap it on.

Once they were ready the order was given and they moved out past the checkpoint, through the gate of the factory area and back onto the road but this time with no singing. They started back the way they had come. Within a half a mile they branched off on a side road and in another half mile they came to the outer wall of the Allach camp.

After passing the checkpoint at the gate they drove in. The open area of the camp was smaller than the Dachau camp. The buildings were of poorer quality but larger and closer to together. There were a few work details being trotted around by Kapos and guards but the camp seemed mostly deserted. The prisoners were all at work building bunkers or doing other work in the factories.

The Kapo knew where to go: down one long street between the wall and buildings to the last building on the right. The building had big double doors large enough to drive a truck in which were closed. There was a strong unpleasant smell in the air. The Kapo had them stop outside the building.

"Okay, you get your break now," he said to the priests. They uncoupled themselves from the harnesses and stood off to one side in a group, not sitting down.

The older guard took out a cigarette and lit it. He offered one to the younger guard but got no response. He shrugged and leaned back against the bed of the transport smoking.

"You two, get the tarps out," ordered the Kapo to two of the priests. There was a storage area at the rear of the wagon under the bed level. The priests pulled two large folded black tarps out and laid them on the ground. They took the blue box off the bed of the transport and put it into the storage area where the tarps had been. They opened one of the tarps and with the help of other prisoners spread it across the open bed of the transport.

The Kapo walked around the area trying to find someone in charge but there was no one there.

"Hello?" he shouted. "Is there anyone here?"

An SS sergeant came around the corner of the building. "So, you are finally here! Yesterday you didn't come at all and today you are late!"

"Yes, we are late but we are here. We can start loading now. Where is your loading detail?" asked the Kapo.

"They will be here in a minute. The gate let us know you were here. They were tending to some other business. But they will be here soon."

"How many do you have for us?" asked the Kapo.

"We have a hundred but I know you cannot take them all. I have called for a truck from Kaufering to get the others. You can take forty, right?" answered the sergeant.

"Right. Forty," answered the Kapo.

"Here is the transport order," said the sergeant handing the Kapo a piece of paper. The Kapo took it, looked at it briefly then folded it and put it in his pocket.

"Okay. I have to check on some other work. I'll be back," said the sergeant and walked hurriedly away.

Alex walked over to the Kapo. "Sir, if you want I can oversee the loading – I know how it goes. With so many it will take awhile I am sure. I wanted to tell you that I found out from Grossmann that they got some new girls in last week at the bordello here, straight from Paris they say. I know how much you enjoy a good time."

The Kapo seemed interested. "Yes," he said. "That would be fun. But I have no money with me and even if I did my name will not be on the approved list for this camp."

"Well, if you give them these," Alex said, slipping two of the five Reichsmark pieces into the Kapo's hand, "you don't need to have your name on the list and you can even get a half hour instead of the normal fifteen minutes."

"Aha, very interesting! But you know I am in the end just a prisoner – I cannot go romping around the camp by myself."

"Right, you need a guard to organize you!" said Alex.

Both of them looked over at the smoking guard.

"Snyder, come over here!" called out the Kapo, motioning with his arm.

Snyder walked over.

In the meantime the loading detail from the Allach camp had arrived and were standing doing nothing waiting for someone to give them an order. There was no Kapo with them and no guards.

"Alex wants to give us a present – a visit to the new French girls in the bordello here!"

"Why would he want to do that?" asked Snyder, looking suspiciously at Alex. The Kapo looked at Alex. "Yes, why?" he asked.

"As a part of the Praezifix Transport Quality Improvement Plan of course! Haven't you been briefed on it?" They shook their heads.

"We are doing everything we can to make sure that those involved in the Praezifix Transport Detail are fully supporting and cooperating in our mission for on-time delivery. People like yourselves, of course – guards and Kapos. Here, does money lie?" he asked. He reached out and took Snyder's hand and placed two five Reichsmark pieces in it."

The two men looked at each other.

"What about private Braun?" asked Snyder, nodding his head in the direction of the younger guard who was standing alone near the transport.

"At least one guard has to stay with the transport; that's the rule," said Alex.

"Okay, it looks good to me," said Snyder and walked back over to Braun. "The Kapo and I have business in the camp. Your duty is to watch the prisoners until we get back. Okay?"

Alex could not detect any response from Braun. There was something not right with him. But Snyder came hurrying back anyway.

"Which way to the fun?" he asked the Kapo. The Kapo looked at Alex.

"All the way down this street, then a right for two barrack rows, then ask someone. It is there somewhere."

Snyder and the Kapo took off running down the street.

Alex turned and nodded to the priests. Father Hubertus took his back pack off and opened it. The other priests gathered around him.

Alex walked to the group of ten prisoners waiting to do the loading. They were a pitiful bunch: bone thin, stooped, dirty, bruised.

"Do any of you understand German?" he asked, in German. No sign of recognition.

"Does anyone understand Polish?" he asked, in Polish. One man raised his hand. "A little" he answered in Polish, with a heavy Russian accent.

Alex walked up to the man. "I will explain to you what we are going to do then you explain it to the others, okay?" The man nodded.

Alex explained what was going to happen, then walked away from the men, walked away from the priests, walked away from the transport. Braun, he noticed, was sitting on the ground now, his face in his hands, crying.

Alex stood with his back to the scene facing down the long, mostly deserted camp street. Behind him he heard the large doors creak open. The smell changed from unpleasant to overpowering. He could hear the sounds of the men moving now and the voices of the priests. Perhaps it would work. He turned around.

Eight of the loading detail prisoners were working in pairs going into the building and bringing out bodies one body at a time. There were male dead as well as some female. The bodies were all naked as the uniforms had been stripped off to be reused for other prisoners.

As each body was brought out of the building it was laid on the ground in front of one of four kneeling priests. Each of the four priests had a white cloth around his neck as a vestment, a small cross in one hand and a vial of oil in the other.

As a body was laid on the ground before him the priest spoke a prayer asking God to pardon the sins and faults of the person, sprinkled oil on the forehead then nodded to the two prisoners standing by. They picked up the body and laid it onto the truck bed then went back into the building to bring out another body. Two prisoners from the Allach detail were standing on the truck bed taking the bodies and laying them together in rows.

It is just as Father Vincent envisioned it, thought Alex.

Every effort by the priests to perform last rites for the dead from Allach when they were brought to the crematorium had been strictly refused by the SS. So they had turned to this.

"What the hell is going on here?" asked a voice behind Alex. He turned to find the perplexed Allach SS sergeant standing before him.

"A new procedure," said Alex. "Weren't you informed?" he asked.

"But this is crazy – these are just dead bodies, not people – it makes no sense. Where is your Kapo?"

"He has gone to take care of other business in the camp," said Alex. "And what harm does it do if these priests want to help their fellows? There is no damage being done. What do you think?"

"This is crazy. You have to stop."

"Sergeant, do you have a girl friend?" asked Alex.

"What are you asking? What business is that of yours?"

Alex opened a couple of buttons, reached inside his shirt and brought out the package of stockings. He showed it to the sergeant.

"Because we have a problem. A shipment of these was delivered to us by mistake instead of the machine tools we had ordered. But we have no girl friends so we have no one we can give them to. Maybe you can help us?"

The sergeant's eyes gleamed. His irritation with the priests and what they were doing was forgotten.

"Okay," he said. He took the package, put it in his shirt as Alex had done and walked off.

"You better get this business done quickly; the truck from Kaufering should arrive soon for the other bodies and I don't think you want to try to explain all of this to the Kapo that runs that detail," he said loudly over his shoulder as he walked away.

Alex turned and was surprised to see that it was in fact all done now. Forty bodies lay stacked on the truck bed. As he watched some of the priests put the second tarp over them, then tightened the ropes across it to hold it all down.

The four priests were still standing in their make-shift vestments. Hubertus opened his back pack.

"We too," said the one man who had spoken Polish indicating himself and the others. They all knelt in front of the priests and themselves received the prayer for forgiveness, kissed the cross, were touched with the oil.

"Come, we have to get this thing out of the way," ordered Alex as soon as that was done. Since the Kapo and other guard were not there they could not go very far. Without putting on the harnesses they pushed the transport into the corner of the compound wall. There was a guard tower there but there did not appear to be any-body in it.

They sat on the ground, then, hidden from the view down the long road by the transport itself.

"Kneel!" came a command. They all looked up, startled. They had forgotten about Braun. He was standing with his rifle at the ready pointed at them. His helmet was off.

"Now, against the wall; I mean it!" shouted Braun.

"Is this really necessary?" asked Alex in as calm a voice as he could. Braun turned to point the rifle at him.

"No, not you – you are not one of them!" he said to Alex. "You, get over there," he indicated and pointed with the gun toward the back of the wagon.

Father Hubertus stood and took a step toward the boy, reaching out a hand.

Braun fired a shot into the ground. "I mean it! Kneel on the ground, facing the wall!" He brought the next round into the firing chamber.

Father Hubertus knelt on the ground facing the wall.

"Now you others, in a line with him!" commanded the boy.

The other priests did as they were told.

"Now pray!" ordered Braun. They raised their hands to their chests, palms together, and began to pray.

"It is a nice game, but this is far enough now; the Kapo and Snyder will be back any minute – you don't want them to see this, do you?" said Alex, approaching Braun.

"It is not a game!" Braun shouted.

"Then what is it?" asked Alex quietly.

Braun's body shuddered.

"In the bombs five days ago my whole family in Munich was killed – my sister, my younger brothers, my mother, my grandparents. My father was already dead on the front. There is no one left. No one!"

He turned from Alex and indicated the line of kneeling priests with his rifle. "It was them and their hatred of Germans that started this war – we were just defending ourselves. And now it is their turn to understand hatred."

In two steps he was behind Father Hubertus and fired close range into the back of the kneeling priest's neck. Father Hubertus's body slammed forward against the wall and slumped to the ground. Braun brought another round into the firing chamber.

He moved to the next priest.

"What was your sister's name?" shouted Alex.

Braun stopped at the incongruity of the question. "Susanna," he said, and bit his lip.

"Ask Susanna about what you are doing, ask her if this is what she wants!" pleaded Alex.

"That is crazy," said Braun. "She is dead!"

"Ask her, just ask her! Ask Susanna!" pleaded Alex. "Would she thank you for this or would she want you to stop?"

Braun closed his eyes and raised his face to the sky. He began to cry. He dropped the rifle onto the ground and wrapped his arms around himself. Alex came to him and put his arms around him lowering him slowly to the ground. The priests stood up. Some looked to Father Hubertus.

"What in God's name is going on here?" roared their Kapo, trying to take in the scene. The other guard trotted up.

"There was an accident with Braun's gun. He was just playing around. Father Hubertus was killed. Braun feels bad about it now," Alex explained.

"Well, regardless of what happened, we are damned late. Let's get this thing rolling," said the Kapo. "Put the priests body on the truck, on the outside, under the straps. We need him in the count or we'll be in trouble when we get back to the camp."

"God, what a big pile!" he said, taking in the size of the load for the first time. "How will we make it when we are a man short?"

"I can take Father Hubertus's place," said Alex. The priests and Alex put on the harnesses.

Snyder gave Braun, who was still lying on the ground, a kick; "Game playing is over, time to get rolling," he ordered. Braun got up. Snyder handed him his rifle and his helmet. Braun put on his helmet and took his rifle.

"Move out!" ordered the Kapo. He waved his stick in the air in a big curve.

"Altogether now," he shouted and began to sing a song. The priests joined in. The wagon moved out, at first slowly, then picking up speed.

The ten men of the loading detail watched it disappear in the distance through the camp gate.

Babies

When Alex had first heard about it he had thought it was a joke: there were babies in the camp! Hungarian Jews evacuated west to Dachau as they were moved away from the advancing Russian troops had included women, some of whom had been pregnant. Earlier the SS had always forced abortions when the women were in the first months of pregnancy – how could a woman with a baby work? But now some kind of line had been crossed as the end of the war approached. The babies were allowed to be born.

It was Sunday morning and Alex had some free time. He put four pieces of cured ham and a tin of crackers into his pockets and walked down the main camp street to the block where the women were living. Entry cost him a piece of the ham with a guard there. And then he was inside.

It was true. The women had outfitted one end of one of the block rooms as a nursery. There were little beds for the babies and next to them beds for the women. On one side was a small table with a red and white checkered tablecloth and a large cream-colored bowl. In the bowl were things people had brought for the women and the babies.

It was like another world here hidden inside the one he knew so well. There was a different quality to the light and a different smell. He stood there taking it all in. The room was not crowded. There were five baby beds and five women. The women, all in prison uniforms and with closely shaven hair, had been sitting talking together on chairs around the table holding their babies when Alex had come in. One of the babies began to cry. The woman holding the baby opened her shirt and gave it her breast continuing to talk in Hungarian.

Alex just watched as if he were in a dream. The women stopped talking and looked at him.

He took the remaining pieces of ham and the tin of crackers that he had brought and put them in the bowl with the piece of prison bread and the can of condensed milk that were already there. The women saw what he had brought and smiled. They said thank you in Hungarian.

Alex said "this is for you and the babies" in Yiddish.

They were delighted that he spoke some Yiddish.

"Where are you from?" one asked. She was a thin young-looking woman whose black hair was beginning now to grow back. Alex did not answer.

"Good luck to you all and God be with you," he said to them again in Yiddish and walked out of the block.

He could finally believe it: the war would soon be over.

For the next several Sundays Alex spent as much time as he could with the women and the babies. It was like food for his spirit after a long deep hunger.

He got to know the woman who had asked him where he was from. Her name was Ruth. She was 19 years old. Alex had little experience getting to know young women and the situation was especially challenging. He had made several mistakes. The first one was the biggest.

"Do you know where her father is, if he is okay?" asked Alex when Ruth had told him Sophie's name and had even given him Sophie to hold for a minute.

Ruth's expression froze and her eyes lost their focus.

"Oh, I am sorry!" responded Alex quickly. "It's none of my business; I shouldn't have asked."

The concern in his voice seemed to bring her back. She looked into his face.

"It's okay" she answered. She seemed to consider something for a moment.

"Would you really like to know something about Sophie's father?" she asked. "Really?"

He did not need to think about it. "Yes, I would really like to know," he answered decisively.

She nodded to herself. "Well, the truth is I don't know who Sophie's father is. He could be any one of a large number of men. At the camp where we were before I came here I was one of the girls that they organized into a bordello for the camp guards and prisoners. It was not so nice as you can imagine. But that is probably why I am still alive. Maybe even why I was sent here instead of to ... another place." She paused to consider the effect of her words on Alex.

Alex looked down at Sophie who was lying in his lap playing with the carved wooden horse that Alex had brought for her. He looked up at Ruth.

"Sophie is a beautiful child," he said softly. "And she is lucky to have you for her mother."

As he handed Sophie back to Ruth a strange thing happened. Somehow in the process Ruth had her head on his shoulder and her arms around Sophie who was still in his lap. Alex had his arms around Ruth's upper body. It felt very nice. He noticed that it was quiet in the room. He looked around. The other women were looking at them with soft expressions. One was crying.

Liberation

Even with all the excitement of the liberation of the camp Alex's main thoughts were about the Hungarian women and the five babies. What would happen to them now? He walked down the main camp street. It was bustling with activity. He breathed in the air of freedom. It was hard to believe the war was finally over. He came to the "Mother's Barrack". All five of the women were sitting outside in a line of chairs with each holding her baby and smiling at the people streaming by. A female American photographer took some pictures. An American soldier with her tried to talk to the women in stilted German but it was no use. The women just laughed and shook their heads at the incomprehensible questions.

"Hello Alex," said Ruth, in German. She had seen him coming he realized. What was there to say?

"Hello Ruth," replied Alex in Yiddish. "How is Sophie with all of this?"

"She was a little unsure at first but now it is fine. She likes it when she gets so much attention."

Alex nodded to the other women. They nodded back to him smiling like school girls then went back to talking among themselves in Hungarian. He sat down on an empty chair next to Ruth.

"So, ...what will you do now?" asked Alex. Ruth took a deep breath and let out a sigh.

"I am not sure. If I understand right the Americans are offering to send us all back to Hungary to the villages where we came from. But that feels wrong for me, for us."

She looked down at Sophie who was trying to get her shirt open to nurse. She opened her blouse and Sophie began to nurse. Ruth looked up at Alex then down to the ground.

"All of my family are dead. Instead of following the deportation orders we tried to escape but were captured by soldiers. Everyone in the group trying to escape except me was executed as an example to the others in our village. I was put into a camp. No, I won't go back. There is no reason to go back."

Alex listened but said nothing.

Ruth looked up to the sky.

"Of course there is the talk of going to Palestine like there has always been. It sounds like some people will really do it now after all that has happened. But that will be just another fight and no place for a baby."

She paused. "I really don't know what I should do."

She looked up at Alex again. "Do you have family somewhere?" They had never talked about his family or his past.

Alex hesitated. "No," he said after a pause. "I don't have any family ... not anymore." He looked away.

"So we have something in common, you and I," said Ruth.

Alex turned back to her. His face brightened.

"But I do have a job, I have work waiting for me. At least there is a good chance I have a job."

"That is wonderful!" she said and smiled. Sophie was finished nursing for the moment. She turned from the breast and looked up at Alex.

Elephants Again

Alex had been at the zoo for three months. It was late summer. While he was at work he simply did what was to be done which was a lot more than it had been before.

His work for this day, a Wednesday, was almost over. He did the buffaloes and deer in the mornings and saved the elephants for the afternoons. He worked 9 hours a day for six days of the week – Tuesday through Sunday. His pay was better now. He was thankful to have a job he liked when so many in Leipzig were out of work and even homeless.

He finished the final inspection round in the elephant compound, put the wagon away in its place, stepped out of the inner compound and closed and locked the gate behind him. He walked the few steps to the outer gate, opened it, stepped through, then closed and locked it behind him. He looked at the key in his hand. It was the same key he had had as a boy – large and strong and slightly rusted. Mr. Engelmann had saved it for him. The little chain was still on it. He put it in his pocket.

As Alex turned to walk along the path toward the zoo exit he noticed a young woman coming down the path toward him. He had seen her sitting on a bench earlier and now she had gotten up as he had come out of the compound. She was looking at him.

Her face was somehow familiar to him. He felt panic in his body.

"Hello Alex," she said.

Alex stopped in his tracks. It was Martyna! He could not speak.

She came closer to him. She smiled. She cocked her head to one side with a questioning look. "Don't you remember me?"

"Yes, I remember you," was all he could say.

She came up to him, opened her arms and embraced him with her head on his right shoulder.

"I missed you," she said, holding him gently.

Alex's body was tense and stiff. His arms were still at his sides.

"You are alive," he said, softly.

Then taking her hands in his he held her at arm's length looking at her up and down as if to make sure it was really her. Taller, fuller-figured, new hair, older face, but it was definitely her. She wore a yellow summer dress with short sleeves and a v neck. Her breasts were fuller now and she was thicker around the waist.

He took her back into his arms, holding her close this time, his right cheek on her right cheek. The last time he had seen her she had been taller than he was. Now he seemed to be a little bit taller.

"I missed you too," he said, his eyes closed.

After a few moments they stood again looking at each other, hands in hands. Alex had no idea what might happen next but Martyna, as always, seemed to have a plan.

"Come," she said, "there are some other people that would like to see you too."

She released her right hand from his left, turned, and began walking up the path with his right hand in her left. He followed her but his steps were uncertain. He had to concentrate on each movement. It was as if he were in a dream.

"Who...?" he managed to ask.

"You will see," she said.

There was a curve in the stone path, the same familiar trees he saw every day, then another curve and they came to the restaurant. To one side was the covered terrace with tables and chairs. There were people sitting at a round table, all well-dressed like Martyna was. There were two older people – a man and a woman – and a young man with a smartly shaped beard and a child sitting on his lap. On the table were glasses, a pitcher of water and plates. There were no other customers on the terrace.

"Well finally!" exclaimed the woman at the table pushing her chair back with a loud scraping noise and standing up. "We were about to come find you two." It was his mother.

"You know how it is with Alex and his elephants," said Martyna. "He worries over them more than most mothers do their children. I thought he would never get finished."

"Well, it is wonderful that you are here now," said his mother.

She came out from behind the table and walked to him. She extended her hands to him and took his hands in hers.

"Hello, Alex, it is wonderful to see you again after so long." Her eyes were damp but she did not cry.

"Hello, Mama."

His father stood up now scraping the chair out from the table. Then the younger man set the child on the ground, pushed his chair out and stood up himself.

His mother embraced him. Then she held him out from her, looking at him with a big smile on her face. She looked down at his body.

"What have you been eating? You look a bit thin if I do say so."

Now it was his father's turn.

"Hello, Alex. It is good to see you," he said and stuck out his hand to shake. Alex looked at the hand then took it and did his best to shake it.

"Hello, Papa."

Martyna led the young man over to Alex.

"Guess who this is?" she asked in a teasing voice.

Alex looked down at the ground and shook his head back and forth. It was all too much for him.

"It's Maciej of course!" exclaimed Martyna with a satisfied smile.

Maciej stepped forward and held out his hand. Alex did not respond so he took his hand back.

"Hello, Alex," he said with gentleness in his voice. Alex looked up into Maciej's face. Maciej looked serious and concerned.

"Shall we sit back down now?" asked his Mother speaking to all of them.

"One more, Mother," said Martyna. She took the little girl by the hand and presented her to Alex.

"Beatrix, this is your uncle Alex you have heard about." The girl looked to be about five years old. She was pretty with hair in cascading brown ringlets that matched the color of Maciej's beard, a fancy pink dress with flourishes all around it and black pumps over white socks.

"Hello, Uncle Alex," she said quietly.

"What is your name?" asked Alex. He really could not keep this all in his head.

The girl looked up to her mother for a moment then looked back to Alex.

"Beatrix," she said.

"I am very pleased to meet you, Beatrix," said Alex. He looked to Martyna, then to Maciej, then back to Martyna.

"I need to sit down," said Alex. He noticed he was having trouble standing. He did not feel at all well. Martyna and Maciej helped him to a seat. He sat down.

"Just as I said," noted his Mother. "Catching up on family things when we have been so long separated is nothing to be done standing up."

"Alex, can we get you something to drink?" asked his Mother.

"Water would be good," Alex managed to say.

Martyna sitting to his left poured him a glass of water from the pitcher that was already on the table using a glass that was waiting near where they had sat him down. She passed him the glass. He took it, drank a small amount from it, set it down on the table and then looked around at the ring of faces. It must be a dream, he said to himself. A dream to torment him. Something in his look must have prompted Martyna.

"I'll go first," she said. "The rest of you know the story but it is new for Alex."

Alex fixed his eyes on her in desperation. Perhaps it was a dream but it was a good dream. He prayed that it would last a little longer. Martyna had apparently expected some kind of additional response from him but when it did not come she started her story anyway.

"Alex, the morning the police came to take Maciej I was with my friends at a meeting to organize Polish resistance in Leipzig. Maciej would have been there but his face was too well known so I went as a representative. When I got back to the house it was clear that something had happened as the front door was broken down. Luckily I had looked before I went up the path. When I saw how it was I just kept walking. At first I had no idea of what to do but I found places to stay for the first few weeks passed from friend to friend. A person in the administration office let us in the resistance know that my name was not on any of the arrest lists so they were not looking for me very hard. But the conditions were so delicate that I was still concerned. And there did not seem to be any official record of what had happened to the rest of you except Maciej so I feared the worst. Then I realized I was pregnant. Only 15 and pregnant! Not what I had planned, but I decided for the sake of the child to give up the resistance work and focus on just my own survival and the survival of the child."

She looked over at Beatrix who had become bored with the adult conversation and was feeding pigeons with bread crumbs left over from their sandwiches on the far edge of the terrace.

"There was a well-to-do German Doctor Warner here that lived in a suburb. He and his wife had five small children, had been looking for a nanny and were secretly very much against what the Nazis were doing. I had met him when he did some of the training in the nursing school where I went before. They took me in and we all made it through the war one day at a time, Beatrix's birth and all of it. Doctor Warner was responsible for one of the city's hospitals where wounded soldiers were treated, then later those injured in the bombing. Some of the bombing raids were bad but their house where I lived with Beatrix in an attic room was never hit. They had a small back garden with high walls where we could be outside with the other children or just us. I did not leave the house or grounds for five years. When the war was over I started looking for the rest of you."

Martyna's eyes passed around the circle: Maciej, her father, her mother, and Alex.

"I had let absolutely no one know where I was during the time I was in hiding since there was no telling what might happen." She seemed to be finished. She looked at Alex again as if expecting some response. He felt numb and had nothing to say.

"And then she found us," continued their mother. "But I suppose I need to let you know what happened to us after that day when we were separated." She looked at Alex.

"Well, it was somewhat confused. Clearly they were looking for Maciej but they took us in as well. Both your father and I were there in the apartment when they came. We had no work that day. We expected something serious. The penalty for hiding someone they were looking for was execution as an example to the public. But the next day they handed your father and me deportation papers directing us – with Martyna's name there as well – to return to Poland. We couldn't believe it. We thought at first it was a trick. I asked the man who had given us the papers why we were being deported and why we did not get something more serious – I was very stupid in those days. And he answered me: he said that the situation was very different when somebody freely turned in a fugitive and cooperated with the authorities. He himself, he said, would have been happy to let us stay in Leipzig as we had demonstrated that we were good citizens. But the official order was to ship us back to Poland. And so that is what they did. They gave us travel papers and three train tickets on a train the next day back to Lodz – for us and Martyna. And they told us we had to be on that train – staying was not an option. We tried to find out what had happened to you and Martyna, to try to take you with us, but there was no trace at all. We could get no answers at all. And so we got on the train ... without you." She stopped at this point and remembered the moment. No one said anything.

"It was me, I turned Maciej in to the Police," said Alex, in a quiet voice.

"We know, son," said his father. "It took us some time to patch it all together but in the end it was the only thing that made sense. We were insane to leave you in that school with all the pressures they put on you."

"And you were so angry when you found me and Maciej together;" added Martyna. "You were convinced we were all crazy."

Alex lifted his head and looked at Maciej.

"I betrayed you to the gestapo," he said simply to make sure none of them misunderstood what had happened.

"I thought something like that had happened from the beginning," said Maciej.

"It was clear from the moment they came into the building that they knew not only that I was there but exactly where I was hiding. Martyna or your parents would have died before they would have betrayed me. The only other person that knew was you."

"But they had you, then," responded Alex.. "You were one of the main ones they wanted. How is it that you are here? I know what they do with the ones they are afraid of."

"I was held with a group of people that they had rounded up in suppressing the resistance in Leipzig at that time. For a week we were in a political jail expecting every hour to be dragged out and publicly executed. But instead we were taken together to be loaded on a special train that was headed for God knows where. We did not think we would enjoy the journey much less the destination so we attacked the German guards as they were transferring us out of a bus at the Leipzig train station. Most of us were captured and some were killed but I escaped. As a young boy I had played there by the train station and in the warehouses of that quarter and knew my way much better than the police and army searching for me. A sympathetic German friend I was able to contact stuck me in his car trunk, talked his way past the checkpoints and got me out of the city in the first few hours. From there I traveled eventually back to Lodz where I joined the resistance and met up with your parents. Of Martyna, regardless of how I searched or who I asked, there was no trace."

"But she found us easily enough after the war as we had been living in the house with my sister and her husband the whole time in Lodz," interjected his mother.

"Then we were all together except for you," said Martyna. The group was quiet, looking at him. He looked away. Beatrix was now sitting on a bench at the edge of the terrace with a pigeon on each shoulder in the middle of a sea of pigeons. She had a piece of bread in the pocket of her dress. She would break off a very small piece of it, then hold the piece out letting the pigeons compete as to who got it. Alex looked back to the circle of waiting faces. It must be his turn.

"I was in a place called Dachau..." he said, to begin. But then he could not continue. He closed his eyes.

"We know," said his mother softly.

Alex was startled. He opened his eyes and looked at her. "How do you know?" he asked.

The others looked at each other. His mother took the lead.

274

"About two months after the war was over two priests returned to Lodz after four years in a German prison camp they said was named Dachau. They were not in good condition but they were alive. The community organized a homecoming celebration for them which we attended. We talked with them since we had also been in Germany and had some dealings with the authorities. In the course of the conversation they mentioned that there had been a Polish man in Dachau who was named Alex Poloski. After some questions and answers it was clear that it was you."

Alex said nothing. His secret was out now; there was nothing for it.

His mother continued, speaking slowly and with emphasis, leaning forward.

"They said that you had been a great help to them there and a great help to many others. They said that without you many more would probably have died, that they might have died."

"They said that?" asked Alex, incredulous.

"Yes, they said that."

Alex looked again upward, as if avoiding the group and speaking to someone else.

"But I did many more things in Dachau, some of them...I helped the Germans with the war!"

His body began to shake with emotion. He began to cry, looking down and bringing his hands up to his face.

"But otherwise you could not have been there to help, right?" said his mother.

She said it again to make sure he had heard it.

"If you had not been in Dachau, if you had not done those other things, then you couldn't have helped the people that you helped, am I right? So we decided to find you. The priests said they were certain you had survived as you were there during the quarantine after the liberation. So we began to search for you. It was only a matter of time before we thought of the zoo."

Alex stopped crying. His breathing became deeper and more rapid. He slipped to one side coming off the chair. Martyna moved off her chair beside him and caught his body cushioning him as he slid to lie on his right side on the ground, her left hand under his head and her right hand on his side. Alex opened his mouth wide as if he was going to throw up. At first no sound came out. He breathed faster now and even deeper. A rasping came up from his belly. It grew louder and became a scream but unlike a scream from a person. It lasted a long time. Then he took another deep in-breath and gave out another long tortured scream. And then another. Martyna knelt by him on the ground with her hands still on him supporting him.

Maciej stood up and went to intercept a group of concerned zoo visitors.

"He is having a seizure, that is all. It happens sometimes and he just has to go through it."

"Should we fetch a doctor?" offered one of the visitors.

"No, thank you, that will not be necessary. We are his family. We will take care of it."

The people in the group exchanged looks between themselves, shook their heads, and walked away.

The people working in the restaurant stood watching and talking quietly among themselves. Mr. Engelmann came trotting up, as best he could with his replacement leg, then stopped when he saw the scene. He took off his cap and stood holding it in his two hands.

Alex's body took a long deep breath, stiffened, held itself rigid. An enormous scream poured out of him. Before it ended an elephant from the nearby compound trumpeted in response, then another elephant trumpeted, then both again. Alex's body was now limp and relaxed; his breathing was normal. His head was in Martyna's lap. After awhile he opened his eyes and looked up at her.

Beatrix was back from pigeon feeding, having run out of bread. She stood next to her father with her hand in his.

"Papa, is Uncle Alex sick?" she asked.

"He has been sick but I think he is getting better now," answered Maciej.

Alex did feel better. Martyna helped him to sit again at his place at the table. It was later in the afternoon now. The sun was shining from under some clouds in the west, coming now through the line of birch trees that lined the path.

His father organized bean coffee for all of them except Beatrix, who received an ice cream. It was a wonderful treat that the restaurant had real coffee instead of the fake grain-based coffee that had been all one could get during the war.

Alex looked at the full coffee cup before him. He closed his eyes and took in its smell. He looked at the others drinking their coffee. He took the warm cup in both his hands and drank. It was with milk and no sugar, just as he liked it. It tasted very good to him.

No one said anything. Maciej wiped dripping ice cream from Beatrix's chin.

"How is it here at the zoo for you now?" asked his mother after awhile.

Alex hesitated. He looked around at the surroundings again as if to remind himself where he was.

"It's quite fine, actually. I have a proper job now. Not just elephants; I take care of the buffaloes and deer as well." He paused to take in their reactions.

What could he tell them about the zoo? he wondered.

Then he remembered the plans the zoo organization had been making. They all looked interested.

"The big news is that we are going to make everything new now; we want to have a new kind of zoo."

He was surprised by his use of "we" in the sentence. But it sounded right. And he had actually been involved in the planning for the big animals which was the most important part of it so it was true.

"The main idea is to get rid of cages and to let the animals roam as freely as we can manage more like it is when they are in nature. We will need a lot more space, of course, but the city has said we can have whatever land we need from Rosental park next door. That part of the park is not used by people much anyway. Right now we are looking for donations to help plan and build it all. I was pessimistic when I first heard about it. But when I looked at the plans for the new elephant area I was really impressed. It will be a whole new world for them."

He looked around at his family. Could they understand his enthusiasm?

"This is wonderful news, Alex," said his father in a loud voice. "I propose a toast: to Alex and his new zoo!"

He raised his coffee cup and reached across to meet the cup that Maciej had raised. Then to his own amazement Alex raised his cup and toasted around. Beatrix raised her ice cream glass, still with some strawberry ice cream left in it, and toasted around joyfully as well, lying on the large round table to stretch to the others.

"To Uncle Alex's Zoo!" she said as she clinked her glass against Alex's coffee cup, smiling broadly.

"To the Zoo!" responded Alex happily and laughed.

"Alex?" came a female voice from nearby. All turned to look at the young woman standing on the path next to the restaurant terrace. She was thin with black hair under a flowered scarf, wore a simple dark blue dress and was pushing a baby buggy.

"I came to meet you instead of waiting at home; the day is so beautiful," she said, in German but with a strong accent.

Alex stood up. His eyes met the eyes of the woman. They both smiled. Alex turned to his parents, to his sister, to Maciej, to Beatrix.

"And now I have some people that I would like you all to meet!" he exclaimed, and opened his arms.

Gaienhofen

April 29, 2015 C.E.

Down by the Water

Martyna awakened as her hand slipped out of Lela's. They were on the bench by the lake shore again. It was late afternoon. Scattered clouds, sunlight, light breeze. A bearded male jogger in blue spandex and matching sport shoes trotted past from right to left huffing and puffing with exertion. He did not look at them.

Martyna felt wonderfully refreshed.

She looked over at Lela. Lela looked different now. She was wearing a dark red hoodie with a faded Wonder Woman movie promo picture stenciled on the front. Old blue jeans. Worn white tennis shoes. Dark wraparound sunglasses. Her hair was in dreadlocks with yellow beaded ends.

Martyna laughed.

"What you laughen at?" said Lela with an accent. "Just look at yourself!"

Martyna looked down. She had on a worn men's gray overall at least one size too large for her over a blue long-sleeved shirt. Red bandanna around her neck. Worn black workman's boots. Her body was young and felt delicious. She wanted to dance.

"Do you remember that outfit of yours?" asked Lela in her normal voice.

"It's familiar but I am not quite sure."

"It is what you were wearing to the demonstration when you were fourteen and Maciej first saw you. He fell immediately and hopelessly in love."

"But he always said it was the cap that did it!" protested Martyna. Then felt on top of her head and there it was: the torn and faded miner's cap on her head at just that perfect angle. She took the hat off. Looked at it. Looked at the backs of her hands – the young smooth skin. Wiggled her fingers. Laughed. Then put the cap back on.

"What is happening now?" she asked after some time had passed.

"Nothing in particular is happening. We are just relaxing into who we are," answered Lela. "Opening into all these possible selves we have been and that we might become."

"I need to decide now, right? I need to decide what I want next."

"Yes, you need to decide," said Lela. She took off her sunglasses and put them into the belly pocket of the hoodie. She waited, looking at Martyna.

"Sitting here after having remembered so much of Alex's life I re-alize how much I have missed being with Maciej and Alex. It is al-most as if my life without them was not really living," said Martyna.

"From remembering our lives I know now how much we have been through together. And we have made some real progress com-pared with where we started. But maybe there can be more?" She looked at Lela.

"What do you mean, 'more'?" asked Lela. "More of what?"

"More of doing things in the world. More of helping people who are going through difficult things like we have been through. There seems to be a lot of that needed right now."

"Yes, there is a lot of need for that."

"So there you have it: *I want to be with whoever Alex and Maciej have become and together with them find new ways to help those who need help.* That's it. That's what I really want. Is that enough?"

"Yes, that is enough."

"So what do we do now?"

"The situation is not simple. I first need to explain some things to you.

"When Alex and Maciej died their soul wishes – their deep desire for the future – after seeing so much suffering in the world and hav-ing experiences of it themselves was the same as yours: to be to-gether and together to find new ways of relieving suffering and of helping people find happiness."

"So they are somewhere doing that right now?"

"Yes, they are doing that right now. Although they have not yet met each other in their current lives my sense is that they will meet soon and from that meeting will come new possibilities."

"But they died 20 years ago. Can I join them somehow?"

"That is the interesting part of this situation between the three of you. Their desires were for the two of them to meet again but like you they also wanted for you to be with them."

"But I couldn't, right, because I was still alive, so I – or at least my soul – couldn't start a new life with them."

"You might think so, but when old connections are so deep and new visions are so strong as between the three of you new possibili-ties appear."

"What new possibilities?"

"Do you remember how you felt in the months after they died? What did you want?"

Martyna had never told anyone before. "Actually I did not want to live any more without them. I was ready to follow them into death even without knowing what that might mean."

"But you did not die, did you?"

"No. I felt it was my responsibility to stay and keep the family together. And I couldn't imagine suicide. I was healthy and could not think of another way to die. So I stayed when they left. It was painful. Often I cried alone at night."

"And then you left everything there in Lodz and moved here to the Bodensee, right? Moved here with Agnes and lived a very quiet life here for the last 20 years. Right?"

"Well, yes. Why are you asking? You know all of this."

"I am asking because I want you to think about what you actually were doing when you moved to the Bodensee."

"What do you mean?"

"Did you ever wonder why after you moved here you rarely traveled anywhere? And why you never started any new projects? And why you made so few new friends? And why you spent your days dozing looking out at the lake when before you had always been very active?"

"Well, yes, I did wonder. But I decided that I was old, that all that was just a part of being old."

"Are you ready to hear that that is not what it was, that it was something quite different from 'being old'?"

"What do you mean? I am confused."

"Okay. I will tell you. When Maciej and Alex suddenly died, instead of dying yourself your soul as you call it incarnated in the same place as they had, even though you Martyna were still alive. This created the possibility that new versions of all three of you might be able to eventually meet and fulfill your visions as to what good you could do together in the world."

"But is that possible?"

"Challenging. Unusual. Not recommended. But possible."

Martyna was stunned.

"So some version of me has been out there somewhere while Martyna still lived?"

"Not a version of Martyna but an incarnation of what you call Martyna's soul. Someone who also carries your story forward. In this case a female person. And yes, she was born 19 years ago. She has been through some difficult times. But my sense is that she may meet up soon with the incarnations related to Maciej and Alex. They will all three recognize each other and then perhaps accomplish some important things together."

"Wow!" said Martyna, "that is a lot to take in." She thought about it for a while. Looked concerned.

"So I slowed down my life here ... so that my soul could have the energy to start a new life?"

"Something like that," replied Lela.

"But wouldn't it have been a lot simpler if I had just died around the same time as they did? Then we could have avoided this situation with one soul and two lives at the same time."

"You are right. It would have been simpler. But you have forgotten something Alya had once promised. It was not yet fulfilled."

"And what was that?"

"The promise to me to find the Mother that Alya had hidden."

Martyna was stunned. "You mean the statue has not been found?"

"The statue has been found. A young archaeologist found it in 1839. The Mother statue is safe and well-cared for now. It has a place of honor in the archaeology museum in Valletta."

"So was that a version of me, of my soul, in 1839, that found it?" asked Martyna.

"It might have been but there are other ways it could have happened," answered Lela. "Do you remember Christina's dream in the dungeon just before her trial?"

"No, I don't," replied Martyna. "And anyway that was in the early 1600s if I understood it right and you say the statue was found two hundred years later. So helping find the statue can't be something that Christina did."

"Don't be so sure. Time is much more flexible than most people think especially when we are talking about dreams. In the end there is always the mystery. Maybe best to leave it at that," responded Lela.

"But why 1839?" asked Martyna.

"The answer is complicated," responded Lela. "But to put it simply that is when the anti-slavery movement was gathering strength, when women were fighting to be more included in politics, when old empires were breaking apart and new directions in society – especially relationships between men and women – were being explored. Some men were appearing who understood what had been lost and were ready to cooperate with women to find a better way forward. So it was time for the Mother to reappear in a more public way to continue her work to bring things into balance. The point is that the Mother statue was found and returned to a place of honor."

"Then I don't understand why I couldn't have just died in 1995? The statue had been found. Alya's promise to you had been kept."

"Alya or Niwana or Christina or Martyna – whoever was carrying this particular story at particular points in time – had kept half of the promise. You all had kept the outer form of the promise: to hide and then enable the finding of the statue."

"There was more? I don't remember anything else that was promised."

"I understand. The *inner* part of the promise – which was the most important part but which I could not explain then to Alya – was about hiding then finding the Mother in another way."

"And what way was that?"

Lela leaned forward. "To find the Mother *in yourself*, to realize that you are her, you are exactly her and no less. That you are the Mother and therefore the source of everything in this world." Lela paused then continued.

"So the secret part of the promise was to find the hidden Mother-of-us-all in yourselves where it had always been but hidden. And then to live your lives expressing that."

"And we really did that? We became the Mother? I don't understand what you mean but I do admit I always felt great satisfaction when a birth, especially a difficult birth, was successful. Was that part of it?"

"Yes, for you that has been a part of it. And that is what your dream and so much of what happened was about: to challenge you all to your limits, to be the resistance against which you could push in birthing your true selves. Nothing more and nothing less than that. It took time but you and your other selves stayed with it. Congratulations!" Lela smiled then leaned back on the bench and looked out at the lake.

"But what about the men?" asked Martyna. "Don't they have something they need to do to change? Otherwise the old problems will just continue."

"Of course," answered Lela, turning back to look at Martyna. "Becoming the Mother is not at all about being a woman or a man. It is about seeing everyone as a part of you that needs to be respected and supported, especially when that is difficult. That is what the men must learn. That is what we must all learn."

"What do you mean 'supported'? If someone is harming me or others I don't think I want to help them do that!" responded Martyna emphatically.

"For sure you are right," answered Lela. "To truly support someone you help them to understand what they are doing or not doing that causes suffering for themselves and others. And you help them step out of that pattern. You help them leave it behind. That is supporting someone in the most important way."

Martyna nodded to herself. She leaned back and looked out at the lake. She thought about how it had been to meet Alex at the zoo after the war. She remembered how loving and careful he was with Ruth and Sophie. And he had stayed that way throughout the rest of his life. Not just with them, but with many others, including Martyna. He had for sure changed. Tears came into Martyna's eyes and she cried softly for awhile. There is hope, she thought to herself. There really is hope.

They were quiet. The blue spandex jogger trotted back in the other direction huffing and puffing. It was growing late in the day. The sun was moving toward the western horizon.

"So what will it be like for me when I really let go of being Martyna?" she asked. "I am feeling afraid again."

"It is a paradox," answered Lela. "You could as well ask what it feels like to be a cloud when that cloud has disappeared. There is no cloud there to feel what it is like. But everything that made up the cloud is still there somewhere, though in a different form. So something is felt. Just like your physical body returns to its elements – earth to earth, dust to dust, ashes to ashes and so forth – your subtle parts separate and become available to form something else. For example the good qualities that you have developed recently become available for others. And your intention for what comes next in the story helps to shape and birth new life. That is an important part of what you give forward."

"What are you talking about? What good qualities have I developed recently?"

"Since you have been living with Agnes in Gaienhofen you have learned a lot about how to get along well with others. About how to live happily with others. Am I right?"

"Well, yes, you may be right. I even get along with my daughter now. She visited me for a week last summer and we had a great time; we didn't fight even once! And I had never thought we could make it that far." Martyna laughed.

"Well, those qualities that you developed may be exactly what your next self needs," clarified Lela.

"But what about this other person that my so-called soul formed when Alex and Maciej died? What will it be like for this person when I – Martyna – really die, when I let go of what my life has been?"

"That is up to her," replied Lela. "But in the best case she will feel a burst of new energy with new confidence in herself and in others. In the worst case it could be confusing for her. There is always her choice as to how she responds to what comes. It is not up to us."

"I understand," said Martyna. And in that moment she did feel like she understood. It all made enough sense to her that she could trust it. Finally really trust it. She would die but from that something else could be born.

Moments went by.

"So what now?" asked Martyna eventually.

"Are you ready?" asked Lela.

"Yes, I am ready," answered Martyna. They looked at each other.

"Then take my hand."

Martyna reached out with her left hand to take Lela's offered right.

They both closed their eyes and bowed their heads.

"Your name is Naravna," said Lela. "You are 19 years old. And you live in a city named Mariupol."

Scene Index

Gratitude

Birthing this book has been a long, often challenging process. My deep gratitude to all those along the way who encouraged and supported me in that journey. And to all those before me who have shared their journeys and insights in such a brave and inspiring way. They paved the path.

Special thanks also go to those who took the time to read the evolving manuscript and provide feedback suggesting improvements. This is your book as well. In alphabetical order Alexandre Komorowski, Andreas Demmel, Jeanne Wandel, Lara Sloan, Leslie Barnett, Petra Sloan, Ruby Webber, Sariya Sloan, Steffi Grömmer, and Yamuna Kerstin Becker.

Notes, References and Resources

There was a considerable amount of research done during this book's development. In addition to studying various books and publications this included time spent "on location" at the Leipzig zoo, the Dachau concentration camp near Munich, several field trips to Malta and trips to Freiburg and Horben in the German Black Forest. My intention in doing research has been that there would be nothing in the book that contradicted a documented (or archaeologically reconstructed) account of the historical period and specific locations described.

For the Malta material about the introduction of Patriarchy there around 2600 B.C.E. I relied in part on the details provided in the break-through book by Gerda Lerner, "The Creation of Patriarchy" which in turn relied on translated clay tablets of laws and court cases from the ancient middle east that document the precise process that was used to subjugate women.

The term "Gender Reconciliation" in the sub-title is a reference to the work of Cynthia Brix and William Keepin through their Satyana Institute and Gender Equity and Reconciliation International (GERI) organizations. Since 1992 they have developed, delivered and taught an approach to gender reconciliation evolved from the Truth and Reconciliation process in South Africa initiated by Archbishop Desmond Tutu after the ending of apartheid. GERI-trained facilitators use an intensive multi-day group process for persons of various genders together in which – through a secure container, clear boundaries and mutual respect – individuals share their stories of pain, shame, and insights around gender and listen deeply to the stories of the others. Out of this deep sharing in a safe space there can arise a powerful experience of loving community that has a lasting healing effect on those participating. One perspective on this book is that it is an attempt at just such a sharing in a trans-personal and public context.

I plan to collect the results of my research – notes, references, and resources – and share them for those who may be interested. The information will be available on the book website at www.rafop.com.

Related Books from
Stream of Experience Productions

Healing Our Deepest Wounds: The Holotropic Paradigm Shift by Dr. Stanislav Grof (SOEP, 2012, ISBN: 978-0-9826077-2-5)

Dr. Grof's consciousness research has shown that the deepest roots of trauma often lie in experiences from birth or in events from human history that have not yet been resolved and are still active in the collective unconscious. This unresolved personal or collective history then expresses through an individual or group that has some connection to the earlier events. Traditional therapeutic approaches which focus only on events in the personal biography or tranquilizing medications do not access or heal these deeper wounds in the human psyche. From a more general perspective, Dr. Grof examines the broad problems of violence and greed in society and finds that the widespread fear and aggression between individuals and groups may also originate in large part from the unconscious acting-out of unresolved historical traumas from the collective unconscious. The message of Dr. Grof and this book is, however, a hopeful one: there are approaches to therapy which utilize a specific non-ordinary state of consciousness which enables individuals, with support, to access and heal these deeper levels of trauma from the personal and collective unconscious. He has named this state of consciousness Holotropic, a composite word which means "oriented toward wholeness" or "moving in the direction of wholeness" (from the Greek holos = whole and trepo, trepein = moving toward or in the direction of something). Dr. Grof describes various approaches to achieving this Holotropic state and using it for healing with his focus on a form of breathwork which he developed with his partner Christina and psychedelic therapy, which he pioneered in the 1950s and which is now experiencing a renaissance of clinical research for treatment of addictions and PTSD.

Returning to Membership in Earth Community: Systemic Constellations with Nature compiled and edited by Francesca Mason Boring and Kenneth Edwin Sloan (SOEP, 2013, ISBN: 978-0-9826077-5-6) with contributions from 14 constellation facilitators from 5 countries who are working in a wide variety of ways to heal the split between humans and nature.

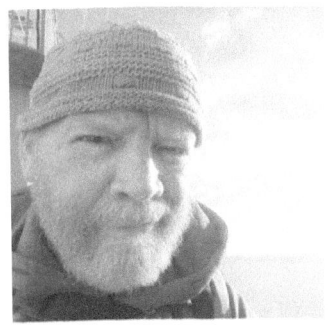

Kenneth Edwin Sloan was born in 1946 in Decatur, Texas, USA. After attending the Massachusetts Institute of Technology and spending two years in the US Army he began a career in computer software that eventually led to engagements as a consultant in organizational development for multinational companies. Since 1995 he lives in the Black Forest of Germany where he and his partner operate a small retreat center.

www.ingramcontent.com/pod-product-compliance
Lightning Source LLC
Chambersburg PA
CBHW020542020726
47494CB00006B/1879